Beer Mats &
Budgie Smugglers

A tale of blood and beer

By

Wyndham James

Other Books By Wyndham James

Fiction

By Any Means

Non-Fiction

Find Your Freedom

Contribution To (Non Fiction)

How To Live An FGL (F*cking Glorious Life)

BLUE CABIN PUBLISHING

This paperback edition first produced by
Blue Cabin Publishing 2025

Paperback ISBN: 978-1-0684802-2-5
Audiobook ISBN: 978-1-0684802-3-2

Dedication

This is dedicated to all the beautiful, weird and wonderful artists who create from their souls and whose fear prevents them from letting their creations go. It is my heartfelt belief that the world needs your human creativity more than it ever has before. So, create, release it into the wild, create some more and let the critics wallow in their own fear!

Prologue

The light flickered as the last of the hooded figures took their seats, the candles' red wax dripping like tears—tears of blood. A low resonant chant filled the room as the shadows skittered around the walls. Heavy drapes hung over the doors and windows, ensuring the congregated group of men remained safely ensconced in the chamber. The room was dark, even with the light provided by the candles scattered around the room; the heavy dark wooden table seemed to absorb what little illumination there was. At the head of the table a figure sat, cowl obscuring the face, hands tucked into the wide sleeves of the cassock-like robe. On the table directly in front of them was an ancient-looking wooden box, ornate carvings etched into the lid. Delicate wisps of ethereal smoke wafted hypnotically from a small aperture in the top, pooling momentarily as they reached the ceiling before dissipating towards the edges of the room. A crash of thunder and the sound of rain pelting against glass filled the space. It was time.

"Gentlemen, I now bring this first meeting of the Secret Society of Hopmen to order," the figure at the head of the table declared, the sound of thunder crackling over his words. Slowly, he raised his hands to the cowl shrouding his head and started to lower the hood.

"Er…sorry, excuse me?"

Five shrouded heads turned towards the man whose tentatively spoken words had interrupted the ceremony.

"I'm really sorry Jeff, but what with Steve's sinuses," the speaking cowl gestured with his thumb to the hooded figure to his right, the unmistakable snuffle, pop, whistle and squeak of blocked sinuses emitting from the shadow of his neighbour's hood. "And with the bloody thunder and rain, I can't make out a single word you're saying. I really don't mean to be difficult, but you know that since the explosion, my hearing's going. I don't care what you do. You can either shout, or turn the thunder down, but if you want me to hear what you're saying, you'll have to do something."

After a brief moment of stunned silence, a frustrated Jeff replied, "Well, that's just great, isn't it?"

"What?" shouted Terry.

"Well, I can't keep shouting, Terry. I've got a sore throat," Jeff replied, irritably.

"You could turn the thunder down," Steve, with the bad sinuses, ventured through the pops, whistles and snuffles.

Jeff peered around the table as one by one each of the assembled men tentatively started lowering their hoods.

"Fine," Jeff huffed, as he eventually lifted the lid on the box in front of him.

A large plume of smoke billowed out enveloping the two men either side of him, drawing choking coughs. After a moment or two, during which another two chandelier rattling claps of thunder had shaken the room, Jeff finally retrieved a plastic remote control from the box. Raising his hand above his head he angled the remote towards the corner of the room. Instantly the sounds of thunder and rain disappeared with a whirr as a CD player spun to a stop.

"I don't get you lot, I really don't," Jeff said, pointing around the circle, his voice raised. "There are certain protocols for secret organisations. I know. I've done the research."

There was an uncomfortable pause from the assembled men, as they all tried to avoid Jeff's gaze sweeping from one to the next, like a prison searchlight, relentlessly hunting down the escapee missing from roll call. Each of them embarrassed both at and for Jeff. Eventually, a somewhat theatrical clearing of a throat drew everyone's attention.

"While we're on the subject," one of the figures added, "is there any way we could get rid of the smoke? It really gets in my eyes, and it must be playing havoc with your throat, Jeff."

Jeff stared to his left.

"Fine, Derek, fine. I suppose while I'm at it you want me to get rid of the candles and the drapes as well, do you?"

The men stared at the tabletop again, it suddenly being imperative to ascertain the age of the tree that gave its life for their society's meeting table.

"Well, it is a beautiful day outside," Steve offered. "And a bit of fresh air wouldn't go amiss with my sinuses." He reached back and lifted a corner of a drape. A lancing flash of light pierced the gloom, blinding everyone within. "And frankly, Jeff," he added, covering his eyes against the sudden brightness, "you have the nicest beer garden of any of us, and that beer is incredible. Seems a shame not to take advantage of it…"

Five men, some slightly balding, all sporting various levels of middle-age spread, looked enthusiastically towards Jeff, who remained sat with his arms crossed, sulking. After a few minutes of uncomfortable drawn-out silence, only interrupted by a few additional coughs for emphasis, Jeff finally shrugged off his recalcitrance.

"It's actually the best beer garden in the whole of the county. And possibly the best beer in the world, but before we all rush outside," the other members of the society paused in their haste to escape the room, frozen like naughty school boys having been told by the teacher that the bell is for their benefit not the children's, "we do have some serious business to attend to," Jeff said ominously.

One by one the men nodded their heads in appeasement, then, shrugging themselves out of their robes they all rushed towards the patio doors leading to the beer garden.

Alone in the room, Jeff sighed. It was a shame, he thought, that more people didn't understand the importance of symbolism and ceremony. Secret societies were supposed to be wreathed in strange initiations, spankings and the acceptance of Beelzebub or something, although to be honest he wasn't entirely certain about the last bit.

He rose from his chair and went to the CD player. With another whirr the disc slid out and Jeff returned it to its case. The Weather's Greatest Hits had been an inspired purchase he had thought at the time, what with British weather being so unpredictable; it was always good to know you had some hefty thunder in your pocket if you needed it. He reached to the second CD player and pressed a button. The chanting stopped and the room was silent, the only sounds now coming from the garden. Jeff looked around the room at the piles of robes and the candles. Maybe the others were right, he thought. Too much unnecessary ceremony. But he was right too. He would agree to drop the theatrics but they had to act. No longer would they be helpless at the hands of a faceless behemoth. Jeff had a plan. Not necessarily an easy plan to sell to the rest of the Secret Society of Hopmen, but a plan that might just work.

Finally, having blown out all the candles, Jeff pushed open the heavy door to his dining room and headed through to the bar to organise drinks for the S.S.o.H.

Chapter 1

Dominic checked his watch. It was 7.40pm—Beth was late. For the 20th time in the last ten minutes he checked his phone. The lock screen was void of any notifications but still he unlocked it. With no little red circle showing on his WhatsApp icon he knew there were no new messages but dabbing his thumb to the screen he opened it anyway. "Be there in 10mins," showed as the last communication from Beth sent at 7.17pm. Even though the only people who ever sent him text messages were his mother and his employer, he thumbed the app open. The most recent message thread was indeed from his mother and had been sent earlier that afternoon. "DON'T FORGET I'M AWAY FOR THE WEEK FROM MONDAY LUNCHTIME. I'LL EMAIL MY ITINERARY AND AS ALWAYS MY WILL IS HELD BY JOHNSON AND OLANDER…… CAN YOU LICK UP MILK….?" His response showed beneath. "I'm not a cat but I'll give it a go." Deliberately misunderstanding his mother's texts or taking auto-corrects as if they were intended was one of life's small pleasures for Dominic. "I NEVER SAID YOU WERE A CAT…… GIVE WHAT A GO……?"

"Excuse me sir, can I get you a drink while you wait?"

Dominic looked up at the smiling waitress. "I'm actually waiting for someone."

"No problem at all, sir. But can I get you something while you wait?" she repeated, feeling as if Dominic hadn't entirely understood the question.

I want a beer. I want a beer. I want a beer. Dominic became aware of part of his brain pushing him to slake his thirst and slay his nerves. A momentary flashback to some of his previous dates helped make up his mind.

"Just some tap water is fine, thank you."

"Of course." The waitress smiled and headed towards the bar. There was a chime from Dominic's phone. He opened it eagerly, only to be met with immediate disappointment. The message was from his friend Gareth and predictably taking the piss. "Been stood up yet?" He ignored it. A moment later the waitress returned with a bottle of water and poured him a glass before setting the bottle down and heading off towards a bald man in the corner of the restaurant performing the globally recognised mime for 'can I have the bill please?'

He was just thinking that perhaps he should have a quick shot of something to calm his nerves amidst the prospect of having been stood up when he saw Beth across the restaurant talking to the floor manager. He smiled as the woman pointed across to where Dominic was sitting and waved as Beth smiled back.

Almost leaping from his seat, he immediately realised he'd gone too early as Beth wove her way through the restaurant's clientele. Watching her navigate a path through the room gave Dominic time for a small pep talk. "Come on Dominic, stay cool. This is going to be fine."

"I'm so sorry I'm late," Beth said as she arrived at the table and offered her cheek to Dominic.

"Don't worry," he said, momentarily suppressing the panic of not knowing whether Beth was going for one peck, two pecks, three or, heaven forbid, four. He silently congratulated himself having correctly plumped for two, as Beth shrugged off her coat and handed it to the waitress, thanking her as she sat.

"Welcome to Andriana's. Can I get you something to drink while you check out the menu?" the waitress asked.

"Ooh, that would be lovely," Beth replied. "I'll have a gin and tonic please."

"Of course. We have an extensive range of artisanal gins from around the world." The waitress signalled to the drinks menu on the table. It was practically as thick as a novel. Beth screwed her face up.

"Is this one of those places that has 150 gins each with their own specific mixer?" she asked. The waitress smiled.

"Something like that."

"Dominic, what do you think?" Beth asked.

"All I know about gin is that I quite like it," he replied. "So, I will follow your lead."

Picking up the menu Beth allowed it to drop open. Circling her hand above the page a few times she randomly jabbed her finger at a gin.

"That one please."

"Very good. And you sir?"

Copying Beth's approach Dominic pointed to a gin on the opposite page to the one Beth had selected.

"Both excellent choices," the waitress said, managing not to sound sarcastic. "I'll give you a few minutes," she said, indicating the food menus before leaving to make their drinks.

"Is that how you always pick your drinks?" Dominic asked, pouring Beth a glass of water.

"Only when there's a 100-page drinks menu. That's far too much choice and I don't know enough about gin not to end up with a random choice anyway."

They made small talk until the waitress returned with their drinks and took their food order. Beth picked up the wine menu.

"Do you mind if I choose?" she asked.

"Not at all," Dominic replied. "My knowledge of wine is equal to my knowledge of gin."

He watched as Beth ran her finger down the pages of the list before saying something Dominic was fairly sure was Italian. Once the waitress had gone Dominic reached for his glass.

"Well, cheers." Dominic raised his gin and tonic and chinked Beth's glass.

"Cheers."

"And can I say, without meaning to sound too needy, thanks for coming. You've allowed me a big two fingers up to Gareth."

"Oh really? What did the crazy Cornishman have to say?"

"He sent me a text just before you arrived asking whether you'd stood me up."

"Oh no, and I was ten minutes late. I'm so sorry. My taxi driver didn't have the faintest idea where he was going." They each sipped their drinks in silence and for all her apparent confidence Dominic realised she was also nervous. "Anyway, I was waiting long enough for you to ask me out, why would I stand you up?" She smiled as she took another sip of her drink, looking at Dominic over the rim of her glass. He smiled back, between them an ocean of eddying possibilities.

Don't say anything stupid, Dominic's brain let him know somewhat unhelpfully.

"Well, I'm very glad to have corrected that particular omission. And may I say you look absolutely stunning."

"Oh this tatty old thing?" Beth said looking down at her LBD, which even to Dominic's limited knowledge of women's fashion was clearly not a 'tatty old thing'. "I just threw it on before I came out."

"Yeah, me too." Dominic looked down at his obviously specially and pristinely pressed shirt.

They looked up at each other and their pitiful attempts to make light of their efforts to impress and laughed just as their phones simultaneously announced they each had new messages. Beth reached for her phone.

"Do you mind if I…?"

"Of course not," Dominic replied. "Although, if that's your half hour into the date, 'Do you need rescuing?' text, I would point out you've technically only been here ten minutes so I hope the answer will be no. I'm not sure I could eat two starters and two mains."

Beth laughed.

"I imagine that's exactly what it is. I'm just not sure whether it's from my flatmate or my mother." She clicked the screen of her phone. "Ah, look at that, both of them." She texted a few lines to each and then put her phone in her bag. "You not checking yours?"

"No. It's either *my* mother or Gareth. If it's my mother it will be to remind me to buy milk and if it's Gareth, he'll just be taking the piss."

"Do you live with your mother?"

"I do," Dominic replied a little hesitantly. "Ever since my father died she's needed a little support." It wasn't a lie as such, but equally it wasn't the whole truth. "How about you?"

"No, but she's staying with me for a few days, or rather using my flat as a hotel, hence her interest in this evening." Beth's phone chirped again from the depths of her bag. A few seconds went by in which Beth was obviously trying not to think about the unread message on her phone. Dominic laughed.

"Please, just check your phone."

Beth shook her head but reached for her bag. "It's awful how dependent we are on these things now isn't it?"

"Well, I really only get messages from Mum or Gareth, possibly my sister."

Beth clamped a hand over her mouth to suppress a laugh and turned the phone to Dominic. On the screen was a woman who could only have been Beth's mother, a beaming smile and her two thumbs repeatedly going up and down in sync with her eyebrows as they appeared to bounce on her forehead. The resemblance was uncanny, even down to the cut and colour of their hair, and had Dominic not had the context of their previous conversation he would have been inclined to guess at sister.

"This is Pamela and I should never have taught her how to use Boomerang," Beth said, shaking her head but smiling affectionately.

"Wow, you and your mum look exactly the same," Dominic replied.

"Are you saying I look like a fifty-five-year-old woman?" Beth said in mock annoyance.

Immediately realising his mistake Dominic started backpedalling.

"Oh God no, I wasn't saying that at all. There's no way your mother looks in her 50s." Beth raised an eyebrow enjoying watching Dominic squirm. "That's not what I meant either. I'm just saying there is a clear familial similarity."

Beth's stern look softened to a smile.

"That's ok, my mum's a stone-cold fox."

Dominic drummed his fingers before reaching for his glass.

"I'm just going to have a sip of my delicious, if randomly selected gin and tonic because I have no idea what to say to that."

"Good decision," Beth said, smiling as Dominic took a long swallow from his glass. "And in the nick of time." She indicated to the waitress making her way to the table with their starters.

"Thank God for that."

"So, worst date story?" Beth asked.

They had just finished their mains and Dominic was taking a slow sip of his wine, mentally congratulating himself on not spilling any of his food so far. He looked at Beth.

"Really? You want to go down that route? And we were having so much fun. Why must we dredge that particular pond?"

"We don't have to," Beth replied a little reproachfully. "Not if you have something to hide." She sat back in her chair and innocently swirled her wine in its glass.

Dominic laughed. "Oh, very clever. Now if I don't tell you about my dates you'll think I was the reason they were crappy." He looked up, caught the eye of the waitress and signalled for another bottle of wine. "Alright, but you first."

"No, I asked. You first."

"Yeah, but you have to show willing."

Beth paused, thinking, a slight wrinkle appearing on her forehead.

"I'll go first if you want?" Dominic said.

"It's alright, I was just thinking of which date to start with."

The waitress returned with their wine and offered Dominic the chance to try it. Having no real idea why it was necessary he dutifully took a small sip and declared the wine to be lovely. Once the waitress had poured them both top-ups and left the table, Dominic turned back to Beth.

"So your dating history's that good huh? After you then, please." He gestured across the table as if giving Beth the floor and sat back.

"I once went on a date with a guy who, when he took his coat off, had egg and ketchup spilled down the front of his t-shirt—which had Thundercats on it by the way—and he then apologised because his mum hadn't done his washing."

"Oooohhhh. Not good. I'd just like to say that although I live with my mum, I do my own washing."

"Do you?"

"No, not really, but I wouldn't blame her if that happened to me." Beth laughed and Dominic smiled as her eyes seemed to sparkle.

"Your turn," she said.

"Ok, I once went on a date that lasted all of ten minutes because the woman I was on the date with wasn't able to order."

"What?" Beth asked, confusion on her face. "Was she mute?"

"No, she just turned out to be a massive racist and the waiter happened to be black."

"What?" Beth practically shouted.

"I know. I didn't understand what was going on at first so I asked the waiter if we could have a couple of minutes at which point she asked me if we could move to another section. When I asked why she made some heinously derogatory comment about the waiter."

"What did you do?"

"I told her she could move where she wanted but the poisonous atmosphere she created would follow her wherever she went. Then I picked up my coat, apologised to the waiter and left."

"That is unbelievable."

"I know. It kind of took the wind out of my online dating sails to be honest. So can you beat that?" Dominic asked. Beth blew out her cheeks.

"Well, I haven't had any quite like that but I've had some shockers."

"Please, do tell. Maybe you can lift the spirits a bit."

"Well the last date I had can best be summed up by the term 'dick pic'."

Dominic coughed into his wine glass causing Beth to laugh and similarly nearly choke on her wine.

Finally composing himself, he said. "I've heard of these obviously, and that's a real thing? Blokes sending you, presumably unsolicited, pictures of the old…" he indicated beneath the table in the general region of his crotch.

Beth nodded. "Yes, unsolicited." Dominic sensed annoyance at his glib comment and he held his hands up in apology. "And yes, it's a thing alright."

Dominic shook his head. "I'm fascinated by the thinking behind that. So what happens? You went out for a date and then later that evening or the following day he sends you a dick pic?"

"If only," Beth replied. "He sent me the pic mid-date while he had gone to the loo. He literally had been gone for less than a minute when he sends me the picture with a smiley emoji, an aubergine emoji and the three drops of water emoji followed by the crying with laughter emoji."

"Jesus Christ," Dominic replied. "What did you do?"

"Put my coat on, picked up my bag and left. What do you think I did?"

"And what did he do?" Dominic asked, feeling uncomfortable at his fellow man's behaviour.

"Oh you know, the usual. Pestered me via text for a few days. Telling me it was just 'bants'. Asking me where my sense of humour was before accusing me of being both frigid and a slut, finally plumping for lesbian to explain my rejection of his advances. A truly delightful guy."

"Bloody hell, men are complete pigs. I feel like I should apologise for all of them," Dominic said, shaking his head.

"Well, some of them give you guys bad press but I'm hopeful that not all of them are complete dickheads." She looked into Dominic's eyes and he was almost pushed backwards at the jolt of electricity.

"Any desserts for you guys?" the waitress asked, appearing silently and beaming at them.

"Ummmm," Dominic managed, trying to get a grip on all his faculties. "Would you like to share something?" he asked Beth.

"Sure, why not?"

"What a perfect end to a perfect meal," Beth said as Dominic split the last spoonful of ice cream in two and gently pushed her half closer to her.

"I couldn't agree more." They smiled at each other. Dominic raised his glass. "And here's to proving that first dates needn't be complete aberrations." They clinked glasses.

"That makes it sound like this is the end of the date."

For a split-second Dominic froze, thoughts tumbling through his mind. *What does that mean? Does that mean what I think it means? Or might it mean she just wants another drink? What do I do? I don't want to rush things but I definitely hope she means what I think she means. But what if I assume she means what I think she means but doesn't and means something I haven't even considered?*

To his credit he styled it out quite well.

"No, I just meant we've proven that first date dinners can end without calamity. There are a couple of good bars nearby if you fancy a post-dinner drink?" He took a gulp of wine.

Beth rolled the stem of her wine glass between her thumb and forefinger. "I guess we could go to a bar if you wanted to."

"Er." Dominic had no idea what the right thing to say was. Thankfully Beth saved him.

"We could go back to your place?" Beth said. Dominic froze, a wave of panic threatening to overwhelm him.

"Or we could go back to my place?" She looked up from her wine. "I make a fantastic mojito." She smiled at Dominic.

"That sounds like a great idea." He smiled back and signalled the waitress for the bill.

After a valiant effort and half an hour of trying to ignore it, Dominic's bladder finally won out. Peering through the darkness he looked at the clock on Beth's nightstand: 0358. His mouth was bone dry and he could feel the hangover beginning to pulse slightly behind his eyes. Next to him Beth was breathing softly, the duvet cinched around her waist, her bare back enticing him to gently run his hand across it. He resisted, smiling at the memories of a few hours ago.

Careful not to disturb Beth, he slowly slid out from under the duvet and tiptoed across the bedroom. With exaggerated care he turned the door handle and made his way towards the bathroom. Closing the bathroom door behind him he flicked on the light, immediately screwing his eyes shut as he was momentarily blinded. He lifted the seat and sat down, eliminating the potential of waking Beth as he did a passable impression of a racehorse relieving itself, as well as eliminating the potential for unwanted splash. He hadn't been in this sort of scenario too often but the embarrassment of the first time, before he had implemented the sit down wee protocol, stayed with him.

He sat there for a few minutes while nature took its course, replaying events of the previous evening. He smiled to himself thinking he was becoming some kind of grinning idiot. To say the previous evening couldn't have gone better would be an understatement, even before they headed to Beth's flat. The effortlessness of the whole evening was what struck him the most, they just sort of gelled. His eyes now fully acclimated to the light, he looked at himself in the mirror.

Almost whispering, he said to himself, "Well done mate, congratulations on not screwing this one up." Just as he was getting up, he heard the creak of a floorboard outside the bathroom and mentally tracked the movement to the kitchen. Gently lowering the toilet lid he clicked off the light and opened the door. The corridor ran down one side of the flat with the lounge, two bedrooms, the bathroom and the kitchen all coming off one side. As Dominic peered into the darkness, all night-vision destroyed by the bathroom light, he saw Beth's unmistakable silhouette at the sink in the kitchen. Moving soundlessly he tiptoed down the corridor, keeping to the edges to minimise any floorboard squeak. Beth stood with her back to him drinking deeply from a glass of water. Dominic stepped up behind her and gently reached around her, slipping his hands inside her towelling dressing gown and cupping her breasts.

"Good morning gorg..."

"Aaaaaahhhhhhhh. RAPE!"

Dominic took a step back, stunned at the screaming and the volume, his partially aroused morning glory wilting immediately. As he staggered backwards, Beth turned, the scream still pouring from her. His eyes widened as he realised it wasn't Beth but the woman from the picture Beth had shown him earlier the previous evening, her mother.

"RAPE!" she continued to shout but as she turned, the look of shock on her face changed to a look of anger and determination. Before Dominic could say another word, in one smooth movement Beth's mother balled her right fist, and pivoting from the hip, drove it into Dominic's face.

Caught completely off guard, Dominic took the full force of the blow to the nose, as Beth's mother drove the punch past the point of impact, sending him reeling into the kitchen table. Without a moment's hesitation Beth's mother closed the gap between them and slammed her knee into Dominic's testicles. Not knowing which part of his anatomy to cradle most, entirely off balance, naked and confused, Dominic fell to the floor in a heap.

Suddenly the lights flared and Beth was standing in the doorway. She quickly took in the scene. Her mother was advancing round the table, her right fist drawn back threateningly towards Dominic who was cowering on the floor, one hand trying to cover his nakedness while the other tried to protect his face as blood poured from his obviously broken nose down his chin and chest. As well as the broken nose there was a large gash across his cheek caused by the diamond and sapphire ring her mother wore. Given the circumstances, her question was entirely reasonable.

"What the hell's going on?"

As far as dramatic falls from heady highs went, this was a belter Dominic thought as he waited at the bus stop outside the A&E department. Even though his response to Beth's question had been the truth, the whole truth and nothing but the truth, it had still felt lacking.

While 'I thought it was you' accurately explained the circumstances that resulted in him lying naked on the kitchen floor, trying desperately to cover his genitals while stemming the blood flowing from his nose, having been punched in the face by her mother after he'd inadvertently groped the woman, somehow it just didn't seem enough.

Beth's mother had calmed down almost instantly once Beth had explained who Dominic was and within a few minutes was even smiling about the situation. Even Beth had been able to see the funny side of it. The only person who couldn't (and never would) was Dominic.

His apologies had been profuse, if garbled, so panicked was he at the implications of what he had done. He had even rejected the offer of calling an ambulance to get his nose sorted out. Of course Beth and her mother were not the kind of women to allow shock, embarrassment and bravado to get in the way of the right course of action, so having given Dominic some time to recover, clean up the blood and get dressed, they had taken him to hospital. He had suggested he just get a cab but Beth wasn't having any of it.

"Don't be silly," she said. "It's the least my mother can do having assaulted you."

"Technically, he assaulted me first, darling," her mother pointed out calmly, picking up her car keys from the hallway table and straightening the collar on her coat.

"Really, I think it would be best if I just get a cab," Dominic replied, desperately hoping for a portal to Hades to open beneath him.

"Now Dominic," Beth's mother said, a mischievous glint in her eye, "don't make me make you."

Dominic tapped his bank card on the bus's payment point and climbed the stairs to the upper deck. Sinking into the seat he rubbed his face. Pain flashed through his newly set nose and a slight whimper escaped his lips. With the pain subsiding to a general dull persistence he looked out the window. He didn't think he had ever had so many feelings at the same time. Shame, embarrassment, regret, dread, pain, confusion, a little anxiety, despair, you name it, he was probably feeling it. Of the catalogue of emotions he was going through though, one stood out clearly above the others: disappointment.

He couldn't believe that something that had been so perfect had been ruined by something so ridiculous. It was the shame he felt that meant he could never see Beth again, even if she wanted to see him, which he strongly doubted.

As the bus pulled up at the end of his road he shuffled down the stairs and stepped onto the pavement. He sighed deeply and headed towards his mother's house. Flashbacks from the previous evening exploded in his brain, everything perfect until about five minutes past four in the morning, then disaster. All he wanted to do now was fall into bed and pretend last night had never happened.

So much for racists and dick pics for worst dates ever, he thought as he put his key into the lock and pushed open the door.

Chapter 2

"I really don't want to go," Wilbur muttered petulantly, kicking absent-mindedly at his pristinely polished dress shoes. His wife tutted in response.

"You always say that. 'I don't want to go,'" she mimicked in a deep, stupid-sounding voice. Wilbur stared at her from beneath his long, wispy, white eyebrows, unmoved. "Tonight is a celebration and a huge honour. Lifetime achievement awards aren't given out for no reason, darling. Besides, you know Jeff won't accept non-attendance from any of you this evening." The last few words were slightly muffled as Mabel stared into the mirror and applied her deep ruby lipstick.

Behind her, Wilbur turned his hand towards himself and opened and closed it as if conducting a conversation with a glove puppet, only in this instance minus the puppet. He nodded his head from side to side in unison with his hand opening and closing and muttered his lips. He knew his wife was right but that didn't mean he had to like it.

"Er, this room comes with a mirror you know, you foolish old man."

Wilbur looked up to see his wife staring at him in feigned annoyance. He muttered an apology and reached for his bow tie. Getting to his foot, his hopped journey across the room to the mirror was accompanied by creaks and groans as his joints protested at the sudden increase in activity, his hip, knee and ankle suffering under his somewhat portly frame. He handed the tie to his wife and looked around the room.

"Where's my leg?"

"It's over there," his wife replied, pointing to his day leg leaning in the corner of the room by the nightstand.

"No, my dress leg."

"It's in the wardrobe with the rest of your things, now hold still." Mabel forced his head round to face the mirror as she twisted and looped the tie into a perfect bow. "Beautiful. Now hurry up hop-along, we're all meeting in the bar in 5 minutes." She slapped his bum affectionately and propelled him towards the wardrobe.

Wilbur opened the door and removed a sleek aluminium travel case. Taking it to the bed he clicked the locks and lifted the lid. The sound of a vacuum seal being broken and a faint whoosh accompanied the action. There, in an injection-moulded foam inner, sat his nickel-plated left lower leg prosthetic, complete with a pair of white gloves so as not to leave greasy fingerprints on the shiny surface when putting it on. Sitting on the side of the bed, he pulled up the left leg of his dress trousers and screwed the prosthetic into the plate he had affixed just below his knee. He twisted the limb until, with a satisfying click, it slotted into place.

"Come on then Lee Majors, let's not keep the public waiting. After all there's lots of champagne to be drunk, sycophantic praise to bask in and money to be raised."

Mabel smiled reassuringly and reached out her hand to her husband who sighed wearily.

"I bloody hate these events," he muttered as he took the proffered support and left the room.

Down in the hotel bar the guests had been arriving over the preceding hour and welcomed with a glass of bubbly and hors d'oeuvres. The reception at The Savoy had attracted the young and the beautiful, actors, singers, business leaders, politicians, even the Prime Minister was present. Anybody who was anybody and plenty of people who were nobodies were there. No one had wanted to miss the event of the year.

The atmosphere was building as more and more guests arrived and circled the room, striving for the best vantage point from which to have their photographs taken by the team of snappers, who in turn were waiting for the faux pas that would make the front pages and hopefully end someone's career.

In a small anteroom connected to the main ballroom, Wilbur and his colleagues could hear the excitement building, his own dread increasing in parallel. He hated these events. Around him stood his friends and colleagues, all nervously sipping their glasses of champagne, to a man wishing it was a tankard of ale. They had been separated from their wives who were mingling in the main bar prior to being directed to their places in the ballroom, and without Mabel's calming hand Wilbur's agitation was growing.

The only one of their number who seemed to be enjoying himself was their leader Jeff. He smiled broadly, joking loudly with a man Wilbur was vaguely aware of as being a famous television host or comedian or something similar, who was there in his official capacity as master of ceremonies.

Although they had started out with far nobler ambitions, it was impossible to deny the accolades and fame they now enjoyed were considered by some of the group, Jeff in particular, just deserts for years of hard work and sacrifice they had all put in. In honour of the evening, and a tasteless show of wealth Wilbur thought, Jeff had even had a diamond and ruby motif set into his eye patch. 'Bling', he had told Wilbur earlier, and apparently it was all the rage. Perhaps, Wilbur thought, if you were a twenty-year-old rapper or overpaid footballer, all lithe and oozing machismo, smelling of your own eau de toilette. He didn't think it was quite the same if you were a one-eyed seventy-year-old master brewer, all rheumatic and creaking, oozing deep heat and reeking of your own odour toilet. It rather spoiled the illusion of 'Bling'.

Wilbur looked around the room, taking in the men he had spent the majority of his life working and playing with. They had indeed made far greater successes of their lives than any of them could have reasonably hoped for and a lifetime achievement was, in all honesty, on the surface of things at least, well deserved. Almost single handed they had raised the profile of Real Ale from its humble and old-fashioned past to the rarefied air far beyond the level of other beverages. Even the rappers had deserted their previous allegiances to Cristal or Hennessey.

"High maintenance women walking 'round in a huff,

I don't need that in my life, all I need's my Nun's Chuff!"

The line made famous by Big Dig had undeniably catapulted Hopmen Breweries, and their limited edition ales, into the public consciousness and sales into the stratosphere. Their insistence on keeping certain beers strictly available for limited periods, never to be repeated, had ensured they could establish and maintain premium prices rivalling those of vintage wines and there were always plenty of people desperate to buy.

The Secret Society of Hopmen, in their public guise of Hopmen Breweries, had managed to achieve the ultimate. Alongside Aston Martin, Apple, Sunseeker and Patek Philippe, Hopmen Breweries was officially a 'cool brand'. A lifestyle brand, a must have for the go-getter. A measure of success as obligatory as the Lear Jet, the holiday homes and the wine cellars, cutting across all segments of society and establishing itself as one of the truly globalised super brands.

To get there however, they had all worked hard and suffered for their success. Wilbur ran through a mental checklist of the five other men he had been in business with for the best part of forty years. Six fundamentally able-bodied men, who had come together all those years ago, on a fateful summer's day when Jeff had invited them to his pub to listen to one man's idea of how to save their livelihoods and secure their futures. The six men who that day, long ago, had formed the Secret Society of Hopmen. In the intervening years they had all suffered physically and mentally. Success cost, of that Wilbur had personal experience. It was just a case of at what point did the price become too high.

He looked at his friends, the physical cost each had paid only too obvious: Jeff's eye patch, Steve's missing fingers, Terry's pinned jacket sleeve emphasising his loss of an arm, Derek's wheelchair, Martin's missing ear and Wilbur's false leg. Between the six of them they probably only totalled four complete human beings—a heavy price indeed. And the psychological cost, well that was another matter entirely.

He nodded to himself; oh yes, they had all paid for their success so maybe he should try to enjoy it. Mabel was right. They were raising money for a good cause—children with leukaemia—and it was only for one evening. He drained his champagne.

But that was the problem: it wasn't just for one evening. The guilt he felt bubbling inside him had been increasing year after year. He reached for another glass, drained it and replaced it with a full one. Was that four or five now? He couldn't remember, but drinking wasn't necessarily the best way to get through this. His general melancholy combined with guilt, all mixed with a large amount of alcohol, felt like a precipitous slide to one inevitable outcome. Loose lips and all that, and there was no way the other members of the Secret Society of Hopmen would stand for their particular ship being scuttled. After all, their guilt was shared—mutual responsibility and therefore accountability—and they had agreed long ago that one man's conscience could not be allowed to take the rest of them down. He finished his fifth or sixth champagne and was hit by a wave of nausea.

The maître d' walked into the holding room and waited while the six members of Hopmen Breweries and the famous television presenter finished their conversations.

"Gentlemen, the other guests are now seated and it is time for the guests of honour to be introduced," he smiled warmly at them.

The master of ceremonies clapped his hands together. "Marvellous," he bellowed. "Let me go on first then I can give you the proper build up." He flicked his hair away from his face excitedly, turned on his heels and, not waiting for a response, marched into the Lancaster ballroom.

The six men looked nervously at each other and waited as they were introduced with a potted history of their success. From their humble beginnings as publicans to a radical idea to take on the larger breweries, through to today where they enjoyed the status as the most successful, if judged by accolades and profit margin rather than size, brewery in the world. "Ladies and gentlemen, please put your hands together and give a warm Savoy welcome to a group of men affectionately dubbed by the Sun, in what can only be described as top class Sun punning as, 'The Happy Hoppers.'" He motioned to the side of the stage and clapped vigorously, encouraging the rest of the guests to follow. One by one, table by table, the guests stood, peering expectantly towards the doors through which the famous 'Happy Hoppers' would emerge. The scene was set for a Hollywood, John Woo-style slow motion walk to the stage. It called for chiselled jaws, dry ice and smoke machines, doves and huge fans, Aerosmith providing the power chords. It would have been majestic.

What actually happened was six OAPs slowly shuffled, limped and wheeled their way into the ballroom trying very hard to keep their teeth in, accompanied by Pink's 'Raise Your Glass.'

Each table sat twelve people and one seat on six lucky tables had been left free for one of the guests of honour. Wilbur forced a smile as he wearily took his seat between a heavily made-up young woman and a matronly-looking older lady who was looking disapprovingly at the younger woman. In front of him was a full glass of champagne. The glass swam in and out of focus for a while as Wilbur tried to reach it. Well, that confirmed it, he thought, he was pissed. He had to pull himself together. Come on, he told himself, you can do this. Engage in conversation. Focussing on that will make you keep it together. Besides, everyone here looks very interesting. I'm sure this evening will go swimmingly and we won't need to worry about guilt and such things. Pep talk over, he turned to the younger woman next to him who paused half way through saying something to her other neighbour.

"Oh, I'm sorry," said Wilbur, "I didn't mean to interrupt."

"Oh don't worry," the girl drawled in an unmistakably three-sheets-to-the-wind Newcastle accent. "We were just talking," she indicated to the gentleman to her left, a pale, excitable-looking man with beads of perspiration forming on his top lip, "about my time on Big Brother and that some people were shocked when I was the first person to openly have sex on the show but I say that if you want it, have it. God wouldn't let us get horny unless he wanted us to do something about it…"

Wilbur looked at her, his face blank, and lifted the glass to his lips. *Oh dear God please kill me now,* he thought, before draining the glass and remembering nothing thereafter.

Chapter 3

As Todd pulled out from the underground carpark beneath the Leverage building he finally let the elation of his close call show. Banging the steering wheel of his Aston Martin DB12 he let out a scream as he blasted through the traffic lights.

"Come on," he shouted, leaning hard on the horn. Accelerating aggressively, the traffic lights ahead turned to red. Slamming on the brakes, the nose of the DB12 dipped violently and came to a halt with three quarters of its bonnet over the line.

He let out a huge sigh and a massive grin spread across his face. That's how you do it, he thought. You make a decision and people bend to your will. Damn he was good—victory from the jaws of defeat. Looking around, he saw the faces of people going about the drudgery of their daily lives. He shook his head. These people would never know the feeling he was enjoying now: the feeling of being in control, the feeling of being the best at what you do, the feeling of invincibility.

A horn blast from behind dragged him from his reflections. Looking in the rear-view mirror he saw a middle-aged bald man shouting at him from behind the wheel of his Ford Fiesta. Todd didn't have to be an expert lip reader or a clairvoyant to realise that, far from angry, the other driver held the same opinion of Todd as Todd did himself. "You fucking rock!" was clearly the message.

He smirked to himself. Yes I do, he thought, waiting for the lights to go amber before flooring the accelerator, spinning the car's rear wheels, leaving the Fiesta driver cursing him at a red light.

As Todd laughed again and followed the road round to the left he failed to see the nondescript Bedford Rascal, rendered almost invisible by its courier livery and requisite dented panels, leap out from behind the Fiesta, run straight through the red light—eliciting angry horn blasts—and speed after Todd.

Inside the battered van, Hank swerved hard left to bring it back onto the correct side of the road. With the accelerator acting more like a volume control than a speed adjustor the van slowly accelerated in an attempt to catch up with the DB12, which was rapidly disappearing into the distance.

"I said get a van that looked shit but drove well." Hank looked across the cabin at his accomplice. "And would you take the balaclava off Razor? It's a little bloody conspicuous."

Razor turned his head towards Hank and growled. All Hank could see was two eyes—one bright blue, one disconcertingly milky—and a mouth full of small, almost childlike, pointy teeth.

Slowly turning back to the road, Razor pointed up ahead to a right hand turn which the car they were following had taken.

"I see it. Ok, get ready. And remember we just want the car ok? No departures from the plan and definitely no casualties. Get your game face on." Hank looked across at Razor's bared teeth and psychotic eyes, saliva dripping from his retracted lips, the fine veins in his one good eye seeming to throb, perfectly embodying his other nickname of Mad Dog. "Yeah, that about covers it."

They had followed the car from Mayfair, through London and out down the A3 into Surrey. Periodically Hank had flexed the rules of the Highway Code in order to keep within sight of the powerful GT, the panels of the small van now showing additional battle scars from walls and other vehicles. At one point, as they had driven down Knightsbridge, Hank had narrowly avoided hitting a line of Japanese tourists, too busy popping off camera flashes to notice the dark and battered Rascal as it weaved through the traffic. Thankfully, the DB12's driver had himself been failing to observe the Highway Code, by loudly talking into his mobile phone, and taken no notice of the reflection of the van veering wildly left to right and back again in his rear-view mirror.

A few moments ago they had taken an exit from the A3 and were now headed for Esher, home of stockbrokers, fund managers and footballers; massive houses and estates, the natural environment for the type of car they were following.

Up ahead the Aston had stopped at another set of traffic lights. Through the rear window Hank and Razor could see the driver distractedly reaching for the glove box. The two men looked briefly at each other before Razor swung open the passenger door and sprinted up to the Aston Martin. Hank reached for his own balaclava and slipped it over his head and pulled the two sets of replacement number plates from the ledge beneath the dashboard on the passenger side. Up ahead, Razor had yanked the driver's door open and brandishing a pistol he had seemingly conjured from thin air, had persuaded the driver to move to the passenger seat. Hank watched, nervously tapping the steering wheel. He watched as Razor smashed the butt of the pistol into the driver's face and pulled the door closed. That's enough Razor, Hank thought, knowing only too well his partner had a distinct tendency to use unnecessary levels of violence. Thankfully it appeared the pistol whipping had been sufficient to control the car's owner and Hank could see he was now cowering in the passenger seat. The attack had been so swift and brutal that at first glance no-one seemed to have noticed. Hank flashed his lights and the back end of the powerful car squatted down as Razor floored the accelerator. The DB12 spun its wheels and left the lights in a cloud of burning rubber, leaving Hank in the Rascal choking on the noxious smoke. As the lights turned red once more, Hank followed his colleague out of Esher heading for a small industrial estate nearby.

Razor had not held back from using the Aston's incredible power to put some distance between himself and Hank and it was with no slight concern at what he might find that Hank finally pulled in behind the car a few minutes later, inconspicuously tucked away behind a disused warehouse.

Jumping out, he ran over to the car in time to see Razor forcing the barrel of the gun into the car owner's mouth. Yanking hard on the driver's door, Hank just managed to reach the pistol and put his hand over Razor's. Hank would never be entirely certain whether Razor was messing about or not. That was the problem with Razor. He was entirely mental.

"What are you doing?" shouted Hank. "You know the protocol: no unnecessary violence. In what world does this constitute necessary violence?"

Hank looked across at their captive who, during the terror of his ordeal, had apparently lost control of some of his bodily functions.

Thankfully the interior was leather so the physical damage was limited; psychologically however, Todd appeared to have checked out.

"And you're cleaning that up," Hank indicated the unpleasant mess in the passenger seat. Razor growled menacingly at his captive, as if in some way he himself had nothing to do with the direction the situation had taken. "Now get him out the car. I'll get the tape."

Hank turned back to the Rascal and opened the side door. In the back of the van was all manner of nefarious paraphernalia the police would refer to as 'going equipped'. There were a couple of crow bars, two baseball bats (one of which was snapped in half), numerous rolls of elephant tape, a DeWalt tool box, a laptop and a plastic bag full of boiler suits. The rest of the floor of the van was covered eight inches deep in discarded fast food wrappers. Hank could hear the muffled protestations of the Aston's owner as Razor manhandled him from the car, the pistol still in his mouth, as he searched through the rubbish for the Stanley knife.

Pulling the door closed he turned back to the car to see Razor disappearing round a corner with his prisoner at arm's length. Bloody hell, he thought, I should have dealt with him and Razor could've got the tape. He hurried after his accomplice. Just as he turned the corner of the building, he heard a deafening CRACK. He was just in time to see Todd's head snap forward, following the Barry-Bonds-style swing of a piece of 2x4 Razor had picked up. He had hit Todd so hard that the wood had snapped.

"Fucking hell Razor, what did I just say to you?" Hank ran across to the unconscious figure and felt for a pulse. It was very weak. He gently lifted the man's head and could see thick dark blood starting to seep from the point of impact.

Hank stood up and started pacing around the man. This was bad. Their client wanted the car and wouldn't give a toss about what happened to the current owner. But there was a huge gulf between car theft and GBH or potentially murder. This wasn't supposed to turn into some Natural Born Killers crazyfest. First things first, they needed to sort the car out. The man they were doing this job for had clients who weren't to be messed with, which in turn made their employer a man not to be messed with. He turned to Razor.

"Go and sort the Aston out. We need plates changing and then you need to run the Gateway programme through the car's CPU. Give me a shout when you're done."

Razor looked down at the prone figure on the ground, growled then nodded curtly and wandered back to the cars.

Now that the car was being sorted, Hank didn't have the faintest idea what to do with its owner. Razor had clearly hit the man so hard the back of his skull had given way. Hank was no doctor but even with his limited knowledge he knew that claret of all kinds was intended for the inside. The dark stain on the ground was growing as Hank deliberated. The plan had been very simple. Razor would knock the guy out then they would drive here, change the identity of the car so it would pass a quick check, bind and gag the owner and leave him somewhere that he would be found in a few hours. By which time the car would have been safely delivered and they would be miles away enjoying a pint, or better still, breakfast the following day. Simple. But that lunatic Razor had fucked everything up. Hank didn't mind separating people from their belongings or even from their consciousness, depending on the job, but murdering people was a little beyond what he typically got involved in. Those were the kinds of jobs you walked away from or subcontracted out. Finally, he came to a decision, just as he heard the horn from the Aston sound. Razor grinned at him as he walked back to the van.

"All done?" Razor nodded and bared his teeth again. Hank shuddered involuntarily at his partner. He was glad they were on the same side. Hank looked over the car. The new plates had been taken from the van and stuck on top of the existing plate, some personalized nonsense T0DD5T3R. Razor was just disconnecting the laptop from the car's scart port. "Gateway loaded alright?" Razor nodded again and wrapped the long cable round the computer and tucked it under his arm. "And you cleaned the seats? Cos there's no way I'm driving this car if it's full of piss."

Razor indicated to his boiler suit, now screwed up in a stained ball, discarded in the hedge.

"You can't leave it there Razor." Hank said, attempting to hide his exasperation. "That's covered in your DNA and the police have crime scene investigators remember? If you leave that there it won't take them two minutes to be hammering down your door. So make sure you grab it before you leave." He briefly surveyed the scene. Satisfied, he turned back to Razor. "Ok, you take the van back to the lock up and I'll deliver the car. I'll meet you back at my place in a couple of hours alright?"

Razor dropped the bonnet on the DB12 and watched as Hank climbed in and pulled the door shut. The powerful engine roared into life and with a final nod between the two men, Razor watched as Hank turned the car around and headed for the exit road.

The sun had just set and Hank flipped on the halogen headlights. On any other day he would have been enjoying driving such a prestige car but today he had more on his mind. As he drove he constantly swept the roadsides for a phone box. There was no way he could let the car's legitimate owner die just for having the misfortune of owning the exact make, model and specification that someone in the Far East wanted. Finally, he saw a phone box outside a station and pulled over.

Three minutes later he was back behind the wheel of the car and was making his way to the drop-off destination. Assuming there was one available an ambulance crew would be making their way to the disused warehouse.

As the miles grew between Hank and the unconscious body, he started to relax. There was no way T0DD5T3R would be answering any police questions before Hank had a chance to conclude this piece of business, of that he was sure. And once he did come round it would be too late. No one had seen them on the industrial estate and no one had really seen him at all. The car's owner would probably be able to identify Razor in a lineup (a blind man would remember those insane eyes and creepy teeth), always assuming he didn't spend the rest of his life eating through a straw and repetitively nudging a pointer at a computer screen with his forehead. The plates on the van were fake and they would change the van for the next job. In short, Hank was confident that he was in the clear and hopefully the stupid bastard wouldn't die. He turned on the Bowers & Wilkins sound system and settled into the drive to the rendezvous.

Chapter 4

There was no gradual resurfacing from the coma-like sleep; no gentle awakening with the sun tenderly encouraging consciousness. This was what people referred to as 'a rude awakening.'

"'ERE, KNOB'EAD, GEDDUP!"

Dominic groaned as the words ricocheted clumsily through his eggshell-fragile skull.

"I said geddup."

The comfortable cocoon of safety he had fashioned his bed into during his unconsciousness was rudely ripped from him, revealing a very hairy and suitably leering Cornishman gurning down at him. In an attempt to protect his modesty, Dominic made a grab for the duvet that had been stripped from his prone figure.

"Come on, get yer arse out yer pit, we've got work to do."

Dominic peered out from beneath his crusted eyelids, attempting to ration the amount of daylight reaching his retinas, slowly acclimatising to the new day.

"How the hell did you get in here Gareth?" Dominic eventually growled. His voice, a good octave lower than usual, hinted at the excesses of the previous evening. Still lying horizontal, he pulled the duvet back over his head and whimpered quietly to himself.

"I broke in," Gareth replied. "Tha's just one of my skills: gainin' entry." He raised his eyebrows a couple of times in emphasis and wiggled his fingers. "Whether that's to a pissed mate's 'ouse or the affections of some bootiful maid, I am the master of access." Dominic could hear the grin on his friend's face. "Not really, yer mum let me in. Now geddup, I'll put the kettle on."

Dominic sighed heavily, nearly choking on the fetid atmosphere of stale alcohol his body was emitting and which his duvet was trapping and recirculating back to him.

"I 'ave to say," Gareth said after a few moments, "this being the first time I've been in yer bedroom, I'm more than a liddle surprised."

Slowly Dominic pulled the duvet away from his face and eyed Gareth warily.

"I mean, I know yer in yer thirties and still livin' at 'ome, but the wallpaper and duvet cover are unexpected. No wonder you bricked it when Beth suggested comin' back 'ere."

Dominic endured the lancing pain as he tentatively moved his eyes around his room. Repeatedly over the years he had regretted moving back in with his parents following his graduation, but at the time it had been necessary. A greater regret was that his parents had transformed his childhood bedroom into an almost entirely unused study/library the moment he had started his first term at university. The upshot of that being the only room available to him when he came home "for a couple of months" while he sorted his plans out, was that of his younger and more successful sister. Who, having been obsessed with *The Incredibles,* had refused any offers of redecorating from the age of eight through to her own departure for university. The resultant wallpaper and matching duvet had lasted surprisingly, and for Dominic, disappointingly well.

"I told you, this was my sister's room and my parents refused to redecorate when I moved back in," Dominic managed, swinging his legs to the edge of the bed. As he slowly sat up, a tsunami of nausea threatened to separate him from his stomach lining and redecorate the wall. "Ow!" he managed feebly. Gareth looked from Dominic to the walls and back again.

"Why don't *you* redecorate?" he asked, an expression on his face so open and honest it could only be disguising obvious mischief.

Eventually, following a brief struggle not to be sick, Dominic mustered his response.

"Shut up Gareth."

"Just a thought," Gareth said, raising his hands in a gesture of surrender as the openness on his face was replaced with a broad, knowing grin.

Dominic watched as the sixteen stone Gareth, his thicket of bedraggled hair practically touching the sides of the doorframe, headed out of his room. Bloody hell, he thought, I feel rough.

Fifteen minutes later, Dominic—now showered and dressed identically to Gareth in the company's black and red polo shirts, and feeling marginally more human, on the outside at least—walked into the kitchen.

"Good morning love," his mum said as Dominic pulled a chair out and Gareth slid a mug of strong black coffee across the table. "How's your nose?"

Dominic grunted in response.

"Patricia and I were just talkin' 'bout yer bedroom," Gareth said, an ever-increasing twinkle in his eye. "And we both agree you really should do somethin' about it. I mean, it just dun't feel right for a man of your age to be making do with *The Incredibles* all over the place."

Dominic flashed him a look that showed he was reaching the end of his patience with this particular line of piss taking.

"Oh he's always been one for putting off today anything that will keep for tomorrow," Patricia offered helpfully, seemingly oblivious to the true purpose of Gareth's line of conversation. "Even as a child there was a distinct difference between what he wanted and what he could be bothered to do." There was a slight but unmistakable air of sadness to the smile she offered Dominic as she placed a plate of toast in front of him. "I had rather hoped he would grow out of it by now though. I mean I just don't know where he gets it from Gareth. His sister is the complete opposite."

"Yeah, and look how well she's done for herself," Dominic added sarcastically, only too used to where this conversation would end up.

"Well, you say that but she's just been named New Young Business Woman of the Year and has been tipped by The Times' 'Entrepreneurs to Watch' section, as the woman most likely to change the landscape for women in big business." Almost from nowhere Dominic's mother produced a laminated article from The Times with his sister Lisa's face smiling out at him.

Dominic opened his mouth to speak before being cut off by his mother.

"And before you say anything, I know you were promoted to supervisor." She paused. "But it is only a supervisor for a *removals* company, which I can't imagine is overly taxing. I mean you're just picking things up and putting them down somewhere else. No offence Gareth."

Gareth waved a hand to dismiss the need for an apology and watched as Dominic focussed on his coffee, realising his humorously intentioned jibes had in fact rekindled an ongoing saga for his friend.

"How you doin' mate?" he asked eventually, as Patricia gently put the clipping away then collected cutlery and took it through to the dining room.

Dominic eyed the big Cornishman warily, alert to any potential traps looming in his seemingly genuine question. The man was something to behold. A little shy of six feet tall, Gareth weighed close to sixteen stone and was hairy. In fact that would be an understatement. Gareth was covered head to toe in hair. He wasn't quite as hairy as 'the Wolf Boy' the Discovery Channel seemed so keen on but he was pretty hairy; hairy to the point that most of his colleagues and friends called him Carpet.

"I've felt better thanks," Dominic replied, tentatively sipping at the steaming coffee, his lips pulling back from his teeth as the industrial-strength liquid seared its way down his throat. "How is it you look so good?" Dominic diverted the conversation without subtlety or apology. "Comparatively that is," Dominic corrected as he saw the smile return to Gareth's face.

"I'm more of a man aren't I?" He replied "And admittedly, I 'ave the smallest of advantages when it comes to body mass," Gareth said, patting his stomach lovingly. He was rewarded with a deep growl from somewhere that sounded disturbingly intestinal. "Be still my pretty—soon, soon."

"Why do I feel so shit? I only had a few beers." Dominic slid his chair across the floor to the countertop and pulled out a drawer. Sifting through a pile of takeaway menus, batteries and screwdrivers he finally found the Ibuprofen. Sliding the chair back to the table, a brain-puncturing screech of the chair legs on the floor threatening to rob him of consciousness again, he popped three tablets from the blister pack and washed them down with the tar-like coffee.

"Ah but they were that chemical lager rubbish weren't they with God-knows-what in 'em. Anything that dun't feature something recognisably organic, either animal or vegetable, floatin' in it should be banned," Gareth said, smiling.

Dominic coughed and heaved at the same time as he felt the tablets catch in his throat. A couple of further swigs of coffee and they cleared. A few deep breaths managed to calm the storm in his stomach.

"You and your bloody real ales. Strangely enough, a pint of Badgers Bollocks doesn't sound too appealing to me."

"No, according to my CAMRA guide Badgers Bollocks int out yet. It was Budgie Smugglers I was drinking last night. Bleddy bootiful and bleddy 'ard to find." He dropped his fists loudly on the table and smiled at Dominic. "And I got laid," Gareth beamed across the table.

"Budgie Smugglers? I have a *pair* of budgie smugglers but until you mentioned it, I would never have considered them something you could drink. Who was the lucky lady?"

"Oh, she weren't no lady, I can promise you that." Dominic shook his head at Gareth's raised eyebrow. "She wanted me to do things to 'er that even Ron Jeremy would have had second thoughts at. But I'm a trooper, see," he said, inspecting his nails. "So you just put yer 'ead down and geddon with it."

To say Gareth Rowe had no standards when it came to sexual conquest and experimentation would be unfair. He had very specific standards; they were just fairly simple to qualify for—they absolutely had to be both female and alive, no exceptions.

"Words fail me," Dominic eventually managed, having tried hard to think of anything Ron Jeremy (the porn star) would turn his nose up at, or down at depending on the situation and required orientation.

"Well, I agree it ain't nothin' compared to you and Beth. I mean, a ménage à trois with 'er and 'er mum, Christ, some bleddy maids. My 'eart swells wi' pride. It's gonna give you the status of legend when I tell the boys." Gareth grinned as Dominic's face, recently having regained its colour, drained to an ivory white again.

"Oh my God, I'd very nearly forgotten about that. What the hell am I going to do?" Dominic sat with his head in his hands, agonisingly reliving the horror of two nights ago.

Once he had got back home on the Sunday morning, he had literally mustered sufficient strength and concentration to make cheese on toast, deflect a few pointed questions from his mother regarding being out all night and the broken nose, stumble into the shower and then fall into bed. It was only the incessant ringing from his phone later that afternoon that had dragged him awake, and Gareth's insistence that resulted in him being down the Seven Bells for their regular Sunday catch-up and one too many beers. After the fourth pint he had finally told Gareth of his calamitous experience with Beth's mum under pain of death should he repeat it to anyone. Dominic looked up.

"And don't forget," he said pointing across at Gareth, "you are bound to secrecy until after you die. And even then you can only mention it if asked by God himself. And even then you won't need to mention it because he's omnipotent."

Gareth laughed. "Alright mate, yer secret's safe wi' me." He held his hand up over his heart in a solemn oath. "But you do realise that Beth will most likely tell Bridgette, and Bridgette will almost certainly organise a mail shot or hire a sky writer or somethin'? There's no way you're gonna protect a secret as juicy as this. Sorry mate, get used to it."

Dominic sighed heavily.

"Fuck." Not overly cerebral but it did seem to capture the mood.

"Language, Dominic," Patricia stated in the disapproving tone recognised around the world as she passed the kitchen doorway.

"What's the job today anyway?" Dominic finally managed after a few minutes silence.

Gareth checked his smart phone for the job details sent through by the office.

"This is one of O'Connell's jobs. We're movin' a young family, Caterham to Clapham Old Town."

"And who do we have the pleasure of working with on this job?" Dominic asked, draining the last of his coffee and rubbing his eyes, trying to rid himself of the last vestiges of sleep and annoyance. A wave of alcohol fumes washed back from the mug and brought on a fresh deluge of nausea.

"Looks like O'Connell's put The Premiums back together," Gareth said with the unmistakable sound of joy in his voice. "We've got Otter, The Fuzz, Weasel and Gravy," Gareth offered with a knowing smile. "Apparently they're going via the yard to pick up the van and will meet us at the address."

"Bloody hell, O'Connell must be short-handed. I hope we're up to date on our insurance," Dominic said, getting to his feet and collecting his keys and wallet from the countertop. The Premiums, as they had become known, had something of a reputation for speed over accuracy, resulting in an insurance claim by the client in two of every three removal jobs they worked on. Having worked for Swift & Smooth for nearly five years, Dominic had been promoted to supervisor and as such was team leader for the jobs he worked on, and therefore responsible for the performance of the team. It was no secret that Alfie O'Connell, Swift & Smooth's Operations Director, didn't like Dominic. The fact that Dominic had been given The Premiums as his team for the day was a sure sign that O'Connell was looking for an excuse to give Dominic a hard time.

Dominic followed Gareth out through the front door with a half-hearted goodbye to his mother. Climbing into the passenger seat of the branded Ford Fiesta Gareth had arrived in, Dominic tried to will his hangover away. Today was going to be a very long day.

At the Head Office of Swift & Smooth Removals & Storage, Alfie O'Connell checked the time on his PC and clicked open the desktop SMS programme the company had invested in. He selected Dominic Morgan as the recipient then clicked on the text box. O'Connell was quite a big man and had yet to fully appreciate the difference between a typewriter's action and that of a computer keyboard. With forefingers rigid as iron he pounded out his message to Dominic and clicked send.

"MAKE SURE YOU GET TO THE BARTON'S ON TIME!!!!! AND THIS TIME TRY NOT TO BREAK ANYTHING!!!!! THE COMPANY IS DISCUSSING THE POSSIBILITIES OF FINING TEAMS FOR BREAKAGES!!!!! AND PROMOTIONS CAN BE REVERSED!!!!"

He knew The Premiums wouldn't let him down and although the reputation of the firm took a hit every time a job didn't go smoothly, the fact Dominic would have to shoulder the blame would be worth it. Eventually he would demote Dominic, purely for his own amusement.

He clicked open another application. The company had also bought an internal instant messaging system. No one had understood why the company had felt the need to buy a system. At the time the managers had cited email overload and something about data protection and ISO 27001 and certifications none of the employees gave a toot from a monkey's trumpet about. But that was only part of the reason. The other reason the company had bought the system was so they could monitor it and, therefore, the productivity of its employees.

O'Connell scrolled through those users currently logged on and hovered over the accounts team. He was disappointed to see that Beth was not logged on and presumably therefore not in work. Ever since she had started at Swift & Smooth, O'Connell had developed a fixation with her, and although there was absolutely no evidence to back up his theory, O'Connell was convinced she liked him in return. The fact she kept their interactions completely professional and always in the company of another employee only served to convince O'Connell further of her hidden intentions. He put her refusal to acknowledge her feelings outwardly to him down to his marriage. Nice girls like Beth would never want to be a homewrecker, he thought. But if she understood that he didn't want anything serious and that it would just be a bit of fun, perhaps that might do it. They would both get what they wanted: she would get the chance to spend some quality naked time with him and he could finally end the frustration of not getting anywhere with her and eliminate the source of ridicule from his golfing buddies.

That was the kind of man Alfie O'Connell was: arrogant and sexist, blinkered to everything that didn't conform to his view of the world. When someone met him for the first time he presented a professional persona. He was well dressed, always in a suit and tie, and came across as friendly, charming even. It was only after you had met him a few times you realised that actually he was only friendly to the women and men he felt could be useful to him. With the women he had the habit of looking at them a little longer than was comfortable. Once you had known him a few weeks you realised he was selfish, petty and a bully. He seemed to suffer all the issues of small-man syndrome while having a six-foot-four frame.

He noticed the icons for Beth's team were vibrating slightly, indicating they were actively engaged in a conversation. He clicked on Bridgette's name and scrolled to the top of the conversation.

Mark: Is Beth in today?

Bridgette: No, she's got a week's holiday :(

Mark: She going away anywhere?

Bridgette: Dunno. Maybe we should ask Dominic ;)

Mark: Really? Why the wink?

Bridgette: They went out Saturday night but that's a secret so don't tell anyone.

Mark: You can trust me : } Do you reckon they did it?

Bridgette: : o (that's my version of blowjob not surprise) ha ha ha lol

Mark: Defo : o I know I would lol

Bridgette: Lol, not my cup of tea but each to their own :)

O'Connell could feel the anger building. That little bastard Morgan was moving in on his territory and didn't even have the courtesy to be open about it. Bastard! Well, O'Connell would see to it that Dominic Morgan's time at Swift & Smooth became the very definition of a shit job. He was even happier that he had saddled him with The Premiums now than when he had originally done so. From now on Dominic bloody Morgan would be doing all his jobs with the screw-ups of the business. He opened the job planner and started combing the coming weeks for the worst jobs he could find. He would ensure that Dominic continued having a shit time then either quit or eventually had so many disciplinary charges on his record that O'Connell could sack the little prick once and for all. Whichever way ultimately presented itself, he wouldn't be sniffing around Beth much longer.

Chapter 5

The sun streamed through the canopy of trees that lined the driveway, leaving dappled patches across the gravel and herbaceous borders. Wilbur and Mabel strolled down their drive and turned left. It was a five minute walk to the downs, where they spent about three quarters of an hour every day before turning for home. It had started when Wilbur had lost his leg as a method of exercise and physiotherapy to help him keep fit and mobile, and now it had become part of their routine.

It had been two days since the Savoy and Wilbur and Mabel still weren't exactly sure what the fallout was going to be. Wilbur had shown great foresight in recognising the dangers of drinking on a guilty conscience but insufficient willpower to do anything about it. The following morning, Mabel had filled him in on what he had done. That evening's thought about loose lips and sinking ships was apt if Wilbur considered himself and his wife ships.

He hadn't heard from any of the other members of SSoH since the event, which in itself wasn't unusual. He would have expected some kind of debrief following the awards though. And with the brewery working towards the launch of its latest limited edition ale in the next few weeks, he would have assumed there would have been more contact. Then again, over the last three launches he had begun to feel marginalised; his involvement less and less with each launch. Perhaps he hadn't hidden his discomfort as well as he thought he had.

As they turned onto the downs, Wilbur saw a glint away to his right from a dense thicket of gorse. Squinting into the distance he stopped and stared at it. After a few seconds, the glint disappeared and Wilbur felt the gentle tug of his wife pulling at his arm.

"Come on," she said smiling. "The daily constitutional will help ease your troubled mind."

Wilbur gave the gorse bushes a final look and followed his wife. Perhaps he was being paranoid. Ah, his mind prompted, but that doesn't mean they weren't out to get him. The real problem was the lack of contact with the rest of SSoH so he could gauge how much they had heard and what their feelings on it were. Wilbur had tried them all the previous day but none of them had taken his call. Finally he had even tried Jeff, knowing that if there was to be fallout it would come from him. No answer. It was only now, in his heightened state of stress, that he realised how scared of Jeff he was. Out of all of them, Jeff had changed the most over the years. He had got over that initial event the quickest and somehow persuaded the rest of them that it was ok and they should build on it. And build on it they had.

He was drawn from his thoughts to find his wife had stopped and was looking at him, a slightly lopsided smile on her lips. He looked around and realised they had arrived at the small clearing, shielded on one side by a massive oak. A crescent of rhododendrons looped around the tree leaving a small clearing completely secluded from the rest of the downs and any passing strollers.

"Well, that's half an hour since tea," Mabel said, tapping her elegant watch.

Wilbur looked down. Almost like clockwork he saw the front of his trousers start to move. Since discovering Viagra three years previously, Wilbur and Mabel's sex life had reached peaks otherwise only known to people half their age. Maybe that should be like cock-work, Wilbur thought. And with great libido comes great creativity. Like many other septuagenarians, the Forthrights enjoyed a nice cup of tea and a slice of cake mid-morning. In Wilbur's case, this was accompanied by a small blue pill. They now had the time delay down so perfectly that Wilbur was no longer certain his erection was brought on by the drug or the slightly mouldy smell of decomposing leaves. Pavlov would undoubtedly have had an opinion. Either way, a little alfresco disco had proved to be immensely exciting. At first there was something of a steep learning curve, with Wilbur discovering a healthy dislike for squirrels. During a post-coital snooze he had come around sharply to find a pair of furry paws pulling at his testicles, stretching his already half-mast scrotum to ridiculous, cartoon-like lengths. Rule number one: No sleeping afterwards.

After that unfortunate incident they had got into the swing of things and now their pre-lunch constitutional was as much a part of their routine as getting dressed in the morning. They were both much happier and felt much younger.

During his frequent afternoon internet trawls Wilbur had read the theory that men are in their most receptive state the moment immediately after ejaculation. Their minds momentarily blank allowed them to simplify and understand, to see past the complexities of ideas, problems and challenges and arrive at a central truth. "Orgasm Thinking" was unlikely to take off in management consultancy circles but there was undeniably something to the theory. Wilbur allowed his furrowed brow to relax and over the next twenty minutes finally reached a state of relaxation that allowed him the clarity to reach a decision.

As he and Mabel left the clearing half an hour later, he had a clear plan. Mabel wouldn't like it to begin with but they were partners and once he had outlined the danger he now realised he had put them in, she would understand. With a vigour and purpose he thought he had spent in the clearing, they headed home.

So focussed was he on his decision and the plans he needed to put in place, he failed to notice the glint in the gorse thicket as they left the downs and headed for home.

"Well?" Jeff demanded, not giving his colleague the time even to bring his wheelchair to a stop.

Derek tried to finely adjust the joystick to line up his wheelchair directly in front of Jeff, who sat in his big, comfy, reclining wingback. The over-sized off-road tires Derek had fitted for the day's job screeched on the parquet flooring as he made small adjustments left and right. Jeff couldn't help notice what appeared to be bits of gorse sticking out from the wheels.

"What are they, special disabled spokey-dokeys?" he asked unkindly.

Derek bristled with annoyance, his moustache twitching as he finally got his chair positioned as he wanted it.

"There's no need for that Jeff. After all, it wasn't my idea to spy on Wilbur, it was yours."

"You heard what he said the other night," Jeff replied, as if this completely explained why Derek had just spent the best part of two hours wedged in a gorse bush, being pecked at by starlings, spying on one of his oldest friends with a pair of high-resolution binoculars.

"Actually Jeff, none of us heard what he said, this is all just hearsay."

Jeff folded his arms and stared at the TV for a while. They were sitting in the front lounge of Jeff's country pile, although you could easily confuse it with the saloon bar of Jeff's pub. For some reason the man had a strong affinity with horse brasses and terrible paintings of fox hunting.

"Ok, but you did hear what that bimbo sat next to him said. I know you heard that because I was with you when she said it. Where would she have got something like that from if not from Wilbur?" Jeff left the question hanging as Derek desperately tried to find an alternative explanation. In the end he gave up. They all knew that Wilbur was always going to be the most likely to break. Seeing the resignation on Derek's face, Jeff softened slightly.

"So what did he get up to?"

Derek reached forward and rummaged through the basket he had attached to the front of his wheelchair. A big wicker affair, it wouldn't have looked out of place on the front of a 1920's butcher's boy's delivery bicycle. Eventually he pulled out a small A5 notebook and flipped through the pages.

Jeff watched impatiently as Derek went through the process of preparing to give his report. Each time he appeared about to start he shuffled in his seat to get comfortable or cleared his throat three or four times or patted his pockets, looking for what, Jeff had no idea. Eventually he was ready.

"Right." Derek peered through the half-moon glasses perched on the end of his nose. "I picked up the surveillance just as the target left the high street and embarked on his daily stroll around the downs. This was at 11.18am. He paused for a moment and seemed to be staring right at me. After a while he turned around and walked off with Mabel. Giving them a slight head start, I extricated myself from the gorse and followed across the downs. Approximately 15 minutes later at 11.33am, I had cause to notice the target and his wife secrete themselves in a little-known clearing. I proceeded towards them and briefly saw what they were doing." At this, Derek paused and cleared his throat. Continuing he said, "Approximately 31 minutes later at 11.54, they left the clearing…"

"Wait a minute," Jeff interrupted. "You can't just skip 30 minutes of the report. What were they doing?"

Derek looked uncomfortable. "I'd rather not say," he muttered.

"Oh for God's sake Derek." Jeff ran a hand over his face. "We're men in the waning years of our lives. Whatever it is, you can tell me."

Derek muttered into his basket, making an exaggerated show of looking for something else.

"Out loud!" Jeff added.

"I caught them *flagrante delicto*."

Jeff stared at Derek.

"It means…"

"I know what it means Derek. I'm just trying to get my head round it. So you saw them…" Derek nodded. "And he was..?" Derek nodded. "And she was..?" Another nod. "And together they were..?" Another nod from Derek. "And all of this outside on the downs?" A final nod from Derek. "Bloody hell!" said Jeff.

He was trying to think of the last time he had indulged his physical desires. It took him far longer than he was happy about. Jeff had never been the kind of man to accept others having more than him and the fact Wilbur had not only been running off at the mouth about their business, but was indecently exposing himself with his wife in the downs only added to his annoyance. He shook his head in an attempt to clear the image Derek had helped conjure.

"And afterwards?"

"As I was saying, at about 11.54 they left the clearing and walked home. I had secreted myself back in the gorse bush once I had successfully ascertained what they were doing in the clearing and then followed them all the way back to their house."

"And nothing looked out of the ordinary and he didn't look different, or was acting oddly at all?"

"You mean apart from a seventy-year-old man and woman indulging in dogging on the downs? He looked a bit sleepy but having seen what they were doing, I'm surprised he had enough blood left in his brain to remember the way home."

"Technically that doesn't sound like dogging," Jeff responded distractedly. He was thinking about what his next move should be. The bimbo had specifically mentioned a sensational diary and he needed to verify its existence and contents.

"What?" asked Derek.

"What?" Jeff asked, still thinking through the dilemma. "Oh the dogging. Technically dogging is where people partake in sexual relations in an outdoor environment where multiple participants are encouraged and the voyeuristic element is a key component of the whole experience. This just sounds like a bit of alfresco action."

Derek stared in surprise at Jeff. After a few moments of being ignored it became apparent that Derek had served his purpose and his audience with Jeff was over. Only too happy to get the hell out of there, Derek gently eased the joystick backwards in an attempt to quietly leave the room. He wanted to get home and get these ridiculous wheels off his chair, which now looked like the bastard offspring of a monster truck and a go-cart. Jeff looked at him as the oversized tires screeched on the floor as he manoeuvred his way into the corridor.

As Derek squealed his way down the corridor he thought back to his little problem. If there was a diary, what would it contain? Wilbur was hardly a pressed flowers kind of guy. What did you write in diaries other than important life events? And the events the SSoH had been involved in would certainly qualify as important. He needed to see that diary. He needed to understand the scale of any potential fallout should the diary be discovered. How much detail could it contain? Thinking back over the years and their meteoric rise, there had been far too many events that could and would vie for inclusion. Best-case scenario was the diary didn't exist and Wilbur had been more drunk than any of them had realised. Worst-case scenario was the diary contained minute detail of all their deals: dates, times, locations, cargoes, everything; in short, all the sordid secrets that had made the Secret Society of Hopmen successful. What was the saying the military used, Jeff thought: Plan for the worst and hope for the best. That was his only option. The timing was unfortunate considering the delicate state of their other piece of business, but this had to be dealt with now.

He needed to get hold of the diary, but there was only so much he could expect from any of the members of the SSoH at their age, and knocking on Wilbur's door and asking for the blasted thing seemed unlikely to yield the required results. This would have to be another job for their outsourced service provider. Jeff lifted himself from his recliner and groaned involuntarily as he straightened up. Walking through to his den at the back of the house, he flicked on the computer monitor and selected the email programme. He quickly opened a new email and typed in the address. In the subject bar he merely typed **Help Wanted** and clicked send. Once the email had been received at the other end, the recipient would place a call to Jeff's encrypted phone and his requirements would be discussed. Their contractor had never let them down before and his skills were extremely varied.

Chapter 6

Hank opened his eyes to complete darkness. He lay on his back, his eyes staring upwards, waiting for the slightest bit of light to allow his brain to build a picture of his surroundings. He turned his head towards where he knew the windows were, but perceived no evidence of their existence, not the faintest hint of a strip of light differentiating between the wall and the window. He turned his head to the right and where the door was. Again, there was no noticeable evidence of the entryway. Yawning, he rolled over and felt on the bedside table for the clock. Gently tapping the top the digital face glowed faintly orange, the time highlighted in black: 10:06am. Probably time to get up.

After the stress of the previous evening, Hank had decided a lie-in had been hard-earned. He had arrived at the drop-off point on time and had been only too pleased to hand over the Aston Martin to those who had hired him to obtain it. The breaking news that a banker had been carjacked and left for dead of no consequence to them. Within moments, the car had disappeared into the back of a trailer unit, where Hank could see two mechanics pop the bonnet and start dismantling the tracking system. Within twelve hours the car would be well into international waters and the banker would have to make an insurance claim, assuming he lived.

Arriving back at his flat a couple of hours later, he found Razor drinking beer and watching TV. They had shared the fee for the job equally and Hank had thrown Razor out. He was the last person Hank wanted to see at that point. Hank hadn't even bothered to eat dinner. He had merely stripped and got into his sensory-deprivation bedroom and slept completely uninterrupted for eleven hours.

He swung his legs out of the bed and sat there for a moment, allowing his internal gyroscope to acclimatise to the sudden onset of verticality. Flicking the light switch, a gentle glow emitted from the floor level up-lighters. Over the next minute, the level of light slowly increased, allowing his eyes to gradually come to terms with being awake. Once he was fully compos mentis, he got up and headed for the hallway and the kitchen.

His flat was modern and minimalist, in so far as he hadn't got round to buying very much stuff for it, rather than being a style choice. He really only used the flat for when he was working in London. The building he considered his home was more than two hundred and fifty miles away in Cornwall and looked and felt very different.

Hank took a few moments to prepare his stove-top coffee maker. He lit the gas beneath it and wandered through to the lounge. Slipping on a pair of shorts that were draped over the radiator, he clicked on the digital radio and booted up his laptop. As the processors whined up to speed, he dropped to the floor and forced out fifty fast press-ups, then fifty fast sit-ups. His brief workout complete, he turned to his laptop and clicked on his email. A few moments later, his inbox told him he had nine new messages. He skim read the subject bars:

Bowling tonight?
Ford for sale
Single and Horny
Happy ending
Grow bigger cock fast!!!!!
Usual time?
Cock too big? 30% off now
Home delivery
Help Wanted

The system he had implemented was very simple. With every new client he acquired, they agreed a simple short term or phrase. This unique phrase identified the client to Hank and when he received an email with the phrase in the subject bar he knew they wanted to speak.

He looked again at the subjects and automatically associated them with the appropriate client. Typical, he thought. Even with all his spam filters working overtime, he still received all the shit. Of the nine emails he had received, six of them were from legitimate clients. As for 'Single and Horny' he didn't know whether that was a statement, a question or a philosophical debate, and to receive an offer to downsize the old one-eyed trouser snake a mere forty minutes after an offer to grow it fast, made him glad he wasn't fickle and flighty of thought. He wondered which thirty per cent they offered to remove. Hopefully not the bottom third.

Bowling tonight? was from a man in his fifties who was having a boundary dispute with his neighbour and wanted Hank to "persuade" the neighbour of the veracity of his client's claim.

Ford for sale related to a young woman who had been married for all of six months before finding out her husband was cheating on her with her maid of honour. Hank's job was to kick seven shades out of the husband. His client was yet to make a decision on whether the maid of honour should suffer as well.

Happy ending was a guy who wanted to kill his boss. A little heavy for Hank personally but he could always act as the middle man—he did know Razor after all.

Usual time? was properly fucked up. Here was a white guy dating a black girl who wanted Hank to arrange for him to get jumped, preferably by some black guys so he could prove that he was just as much a victim of racism as his girlfriend. Hank had found that most of the people he encountered were pretty twisted.

Home delivery was the client he had acquired the Aston Martin for and who was now probably after another car. These weren't his usual type of clients, being professional crooks themselves, but you had to diversify when times were hard.

Help Wanted now these guys were repeat customers and their requests varied from the mundane and simply achieved, to the very peculiar and enormously expensive.

Hank was a crook, of that there could be no doubt, but he was a special kind of crook. Think the A-Team. If you had a plan, a disreputable mastermind piece of illegality but you lacked the necessary contacts, skills or commitment to perpetrate it yourself, then Hank was your man. If you had a plan to commit a crime, if no-one else could help and if you could find him, maybe you could hire Hank. He had to admit the last bit didn't quite scan as well as the original but it encompassed what he did quite well: criminal for hire.

Hank heard the coffee pot bubbling away and went to pour the first of his caffeine hits of the day. It had been shortly after being released from prison fifteen years ago, halfway through a thirty month sentence for burglary, that he had been struck by his thunderbolt of an idea.

There was never any danger of Hank going straight, but he had also vowed never to go back to prison, and he had big ambitions for his future. All he needed was a means through which to make lots of money (without doing an honest day's work) and not being sent back to prison. Hmmmm, how about alchemy?

The answer had come, as such answers often did, completely out of the blue while Hank was in line at the local post office.

All he had gone there for was six months car tax. Unfortunately, he had forgotten to get it in advance and as of midnight, his car was liable to be towed and crushed. This was back in the days before the government abolished the need for a physical tax disc and before the transaction could be completed online. It was get organised and send for it in the post or get yourself down to the Post Office. The other unfortunate element was that the day he went to the Post Office coincided with benefits payment day, and the post office was packed. With seven pensioners, five mothers with toddlers and a couple of wheelchairs in front of him, Hank sighed and settled in for an extended wait before he could step up to the only functioning window.

He was still trying to figure out what he was going to do with the rest of his life when he received a heavy shove in the small of his back. As he turned, ready to give the shover a mouthful, a large expanse of red and blue rushed past him. This expanse of primary colour was quickly followed by an expanse of black, an expanse of gold and red, and finally a smaller expanse of green. As Hank watched in amazement, it rapidly became apparent the small post office was currently under attack from the heroes of DC and Marvel. Spiderman, Batman, Iron Man and an almost sarcastically undersized Incredible Hulk were all trying to get to the front of the post office. What also became apparent, as Hank watched the farce begin to unfold, was that they hadn't thought this through very well.

As Spiderman rushed up to the counter, screaming for everyone to get down and stay quiet, Batman, Iron Man and the Hulk piled in after him. Unfortunately, due to the restricted confines of the post office coupled with the large number of people already there, by the time the 5'2" Hulk had rushed in with his huge green plastic hands professing, "Hulk Smash" over and over, they were practically backed up to the door.

"I said, everyone get down!" repeated Spiderman, his voice beginning to falter. "Batman, now."

Pressed up directly behind Spiderman's spandex clad buttocks, Batman was struggling with a bag slung over his shoulder. After a seemingly interminable fight with the duffle bag, he eventually managed to free what looked like a pump-action shotgun. At that point several things happened at once. Firstly, as Batman freed the barrel of the weapon, it flicked up and hit the back of Spiderman's head causing his mask to spin round. Stepping back and apologising profusely, Batman trod on Iron Man's foot who immediately fell backwards into the Hulk, who in turn fell and got wedged in the automatic door. Having seen Spiderman, one of their favourite characters, seemingly suffer an almost certainly fatal neck injury, half the kids in the building started screaming. The remaining kids, seeing two of their heroes rolling round on the floor desperately trying to get back to their feet, took this as the cue for a bundle and threw themselves at the celluloid-immortalised comic heroes, shouting and screaming in delight.

Hank watched all this unfold in the space of a few seconds. With two of their number down and covered in kids and one whose only means of seeing what was happening was unhelpfully now located at the back of their head, Batman was the last of their number left standing. As the Dark Knight stood there nervously shaking, constantly readjusting his aim at the slightest movement from the quivering, crying, screaming or laughing masses in the post office, Hank noticed the bright orange plug in the barrel of the pump action. In less time than it took for Batman to realise they were screwed, Hank realised that the Justice League were trying to rob a post office with a toy gun, plastic hulk hands and absolutely no idea what they were doing.

"Barry, what are we doing?" Batman asked, panic now evident, twitching the end of the toy gun around the room, finally resting on Hank, the only non-superhero still standing. The rest of the post office was chaos.

In response, Spiderman was wheeling around like a blind man, his spandex head emitting muffled obscenities as he bumped into things. Eventually, in a fit of frustration, Spidey pulled his mask off causing an ear-splitting increase in decibel level from the kids. What he saw did not improve his mood.

As the first cry for everyone to get down had been given by the at that point confident Spiderman, the queuing adults had hit the deck. Good start. However, since Spiderman's Exorcist impression, a portion of the kids had taken screaming to previously never before experienced levels, while the other kids were swarming over Batman's fallen comrades like they were an exciting, living bouncy castle. In addition, one of the pensioners was alternately driving his Cheetah, King of the Road mobility scooter into Iron Man's head then reversing three feet into the Incredible Hulk's testicles. The 'Eat My Tread' demand of the octogenarian's bumper sticker, something the smaller man's girlfriend would be able to comply with later should she wish.

As Hank stared at the now unmasked superhero, he was surprised to say the least. Clearly, following the complete and utter shambles that had just played out in front of him, he hadn't been expecting a hardened professional with scars, a sneer and a jaded outlook on life but he certainly hadn't been expecting an accountant.

Stripped of his disguise, Spiderman now looked like a normal Joe Shmoe. Admittedly one currently very scared at the prospect of spending time in prison having failed to rob a post office with his mates dressed as a superhero, but Joe Schmoe nonetheless. Less like being robbed by John Dillinger and more like Fathers for Justice after some spending money to keep up with the new man in their ex-wives' lives.

Hank looked directly at the heavily sweating accountant and was struck by his thunderbolt. Watching Spiderman usher Batman out of the post office, barely stopping to help Iron Man and The Hulk get to their feet, and then running off down the high street, Iron Man holding his head groaning, and the Hulk cradling his repeatedly run over testicles to the ever more distant threat of "Hulk Smash", Hank smiled.

He hadn't thought about that day for a long time. Who would have thought such success could have been sparked by a bunch of desperate idiots? He sipped from his mug and headed back to his laptop.

He had actually been quite surprised by the success of his venture. Over the last fifteen years he had also been surprised at the number of supposedly normal people who held dark desires close to their hearts. That said, these dark desires had made him a very wealthy man. He was now thirty-seven and figured he had another five years and then he was on easy street. Fewer than five years if **Help Wanted** continued to send jobs his way.

He noted the time the email had been sent. His client was probably after an update on the latest job he was working on for them. Primarily for this client he acquired things—weird things. Their latest order had taken even him by surprise and he had nearly declined the job. It had felt a little like coming home and being faced with a bush tucker trial of kangaroo anus and eyeball stew. Probably a bit much for most people, regardless of any previous penchant for foie gras or tripe. However, what price squeamishness? Hank had got over his uncertainty when they told him how much they would pay. There wasn't really room for judgements and squeamishness in his line of work. He picked up his phone and dialled.

Chapter 7

Dominic and Gareth pulled up behind the Swift & Smooth removal van outside the Barton's new-build three bed detached house in Caterham. The atmosphere had cleared during the drive and Dominic had regained his sense of humour a little, to the point where Gareth had raised the redecorating again.

"Even if you dun't want proper adult decorations and linen an' that, you could man it up a bit. Go with Batman or something like that. You know, something legitimised by serious cinema. I think Beth would really go for the evident complexity of character that duality demonstrates in a man. It's not weird and infantile at all."

"Shut up about the wallpaper alright. I'll get around to it," Dominic replied, thinking he really must get around to it and maybe buy a double bed as well. In fact, he probably ought to think about moving out but first things first, wallpaper. Although thinking about it, he might just buy a tin of paint and hide the offending wall hangings, that was probably easier. Anyway, as ever, all that could wait. "And I don't think Beth will be willing to give me the time of day let alone offer critique on my wallpaper. Not after what I did." He waited for the comment to come from Gareth, but true to his word the previous evening, currently the topic was off limits for jokes. Dominic wondered how long that would last.

As Gareth stopped the car, the doors on the van opened and out jumped the other four members of their team. Dominic swung open the passenger door of the Fiesta and climbed out. His hangover, having receded during the drive down, now occupied a small area behind his eyes, only periodically thrusting forward with a vengeful pitchfork of pain.

The six guys congregated between the two vehicles and Dominic surveyed the resources the company had left its reputation in the hands of. Otter, The Fuzz, Weasel and Gravy, as well as Gareth and Dominic. What a team, he thought.

Standing outside the Barton's house Dominic looked at his watch, five to nine, spot on. As they started walking up the drive, Dominic checked his phone. Beth hadn't called since her five attempts around

Sunday lunchtime and he didn't really know how to feel about it. He should really man up and call her back, it had after all been a misunderstanding. A massive one he thought and he couldn't imagine Beth was too happy he had accidentally groped her mother, even if he had had his arse kicked in response. A wave of embarrassment and shame crashed over him. He needed to make things right, but had no idea where to start. He was drawn back from his thoughts as the six of them walked up the short driveway, not quite long enough to accommodate the massive 4x4 parked on it, with The Fuzz and Gravy trading comments.

"You're such an idiot for being here. You don't even need to work," The Fuzz said, evidently continuing a conversation started inside the van.

"Ah, but what is need?" answered Gravy in an attempt at early morning philosophy.

"It's me *needing* to work in order to buy food."

"Oh in that case no I don't. I just get OrganoScran to drop a mixed box of free range delights round to my house every couple of days."

It was comments like that that really made The Fuzz want to punch Gravy. And it was the reaction to comments like that that really made making them enjoyable for Gravy. Gareth put his big arms around The Fuzz to restrain him.

The Fuzz and Gravy (aka Darren and Tristan) were complete opposites and spent every minute they were together needling each other, always seemingly on the edge of physical hostilities breaking out. The Fuzz was from very humble backgrounds, growing up on a council estate with his single mother and four siblings. He was small and wiry and had achieved his moniker through his numerous interactions with the local constabulary of wherever he was at any given time. Gravy on the other hand was a trustafarian. Coming from old money, he had received a very generous trust fund on his eighteenth birthday and embarked on a series of life decisions designed almost entirely to piss his parents off. Now in his mid-twenties, his latest wheeze when he wasn't taking ketamine, was to work (something he didn't need to do) as a removal man (something his parents would never have considered being a job and if they ever had needed one, would have had their butler organise it). The nickname Gravy came simply from the train he was riding.

"You're such a dick," The Fuzz muttered, struggling against the Cornishman's embrace.

"What the hell happened to your face?" asked Weasel, unnecessarily pointing directly at Dominic's swollen nose and blackened eyes. The rest of The Premiums stared at Dominic.

Weasel was exactly that—weasely. He was endowed with all the qualities, stereotypes and slanderous comments one would associate with the animal. Skulking and cunning were the traits of the animal and man alike. It didn't help that Weasel also had a very weaselly face. No one remembered who christened him as such but sometimes the obvious nickname is the one that sticks. None of the team knew what his real name was or anything about him outside of work. It wasn't that he was a bad guy, he just looked untrustworthy.

Dominic unconsciously raised a hand to his nose.

"Some bloke in the pub last night fell backwards and headbutted me," Dominic responded with the well-practised line he and Gareth had agreed upon in the pub the night before following Gareth asking the same question and Dominic being unable to lie his way out of it.

"Wow. That looks really painful!" Gravy said unnecessarily.

"Did you lamp him back?" asked The Fuzz, finally shrugging Gareth off now he had calmed down.

"No, it was an accident. He didn't mean it," replied Dominic, keen for the conversation to move on to more comfortable ground. "Anyway, what were you guys talking about as we arrived?" He aimed this at Gravy and The Fuzz, confident they wouldn't need further bidding to reignite their contradictory views of the world. Just as Gravy was about to launch into another provocative jibe at The Fuzz, Dominic's phone chirped loudly.

"Actually that can wait guys. I've just got a message from O'Connell."

"Tooooooooool!" the group sang in unison. Regardless of their intergroup issues, everyone was united in their dislike of O'Connell.

"Motion seconded?" Dominic asked, looking round the group.

Five arms rose instantly.

"Motion carried unanimously. O'Connell is indeed a tool. But that aside, he's proposing taking any breakages out of our pay so we really need to not fu— Good morning Mrs Barton." Dominic seamlessly slipped into polite professional mode as the front door opened and the very elegant and attractive Mrs Barton smiled at them. "We're Swift & Smooth," Dominic added redundantly. The massive lorry and a Fiesta parked outside the house with Swift & Smooth plastered across them made it unlikely they were trying to push Watchtower.

"Well of course you are dear. How smooth and how swift we will wait to see," she replied, a glint in her eye as she surveyed the group. "Please come in." She turned around and walked into the house passing heaps of boxes and bubblewrap.

As they walked through the house, Mrs Barton talked them through the contents of each room and their importance. None of The Premiums said a word except Dominic who dutifully managed to mutter a periodic "ok" or "of course."

Back in the lounge, having toured the whole house, Mrs Barton turned to face them. "Now, you boys can start downstairs while I have a quick bath. If you need anything just shout." As she left the room she raised a hand to Gareth's face and gently stroked his bearded cheek as she left.

Once she had gone, The Premiums looked at each other.

"I thought they were s'pposed to be fully packed." Gareth said.

"They were," Dominic replied. "But there's not a lot we can do about it now so I suggest we get cracking. Gravy and The Fuzz you guys better continue with the packing and the rest of us will start to shift stuff to the van."

"What about packing up her bedroom and clothes and things?" Weasel asked, weaselly raising an eyebrow.

"I've got that," volunteered Gareth, sprinting out of the room before anyone could contradict him. Weasel sulked. Gravy and The Fuzz bickered about the best ways to pack and Otter said nothing.

"Apparently he is," Dominic said. "Let's crack on and please, try not to break anything."

Intimately getting to know someone through the handling of their most personal objects and items isn't the usual manner of developing a close relationship. However, once you get to the point where you have sufficient belongings to furnish all the rooms in a flat or, heaven forbid, even a house, there are certain options which cease to be available to you. When all you had to worry about was the contents of your bedroom and perhaps a standing lamp in the lounge, you could call on friends or family with the promise of a takeaway and some cold beers as recompense for a day's hard labour. As those handling your things were known to you, it is a necessity to clean up the worst of the mess you have been living in and hide the nurse's outfit. Putting the lubricant and porno mags under your flatmate's bed is also a standard manoeuvre relying on you having outwitted them in the game of "last one out plants the porn."

When you are the sole occupant of a premises, things are different. When the call goes out for assistance you notice the phone goes strangely unanswered or emails unreturned; you know they have been opened because of the read receipt, therefore you are simply being ignored. Eventually those people who you thought would do you a favour come back to you but knowingly too close to the move date for you not to have arranged something else. Therefore you are plunged into the hands of the professional removal firm.

Those that choose to 'go pro' typically fall into two clearly defined categories, which invariably depends on how nice the stuff being moved is. Category one, or Concourse la Pit du Merde, is a built-up area full of burnt-out sofas and electrical equipment up on bricks. The concept of leaving the place clean is an alien one, although aspersions will be cast on the moral fortitude of the outgoing owners of the destination property by those incoming. The owners want to look as if they are concerned by what the removers are doing but know it's hardly worth the effort so are resigned to having their furniture delivered as kindling.

Category two, or Boulevard Magnifique, is a different story. Tree-lined with perpetual spring blossom is the way of this avenue. Time, effort and money have been invested in collecting just the right comfy chair, the ideal lamp, the perfect antimacassars. There is no way the wellbeing of these items will be left solely in the protective custody of someone earning marginally more than minimum wage, who fundamentally couldn't give a flying blue toss about the 18th century Italian marble splashback they have been asked to move. All they know is it's very bloody heavy and wet, which makes it slippery, which makes it a fair bet for an insurance claim. Constant supervision is needed by the customer. The slightest raised voice from somewhere in the house causing the mobilisation of a survey squad faster than the Red Cross manages at times of natural disasters.

Of the two types it was marginal which The Premiums preferred. Category one was less likely to result in an insurance claim against them, but you were more likely to encounter dirty underwear down the back of the bed or something mouldy behind the fridge. Category two made for less chance of revulsion and greater chance of lunch being provided. It also came with much greater levels of stress and far higher likelihood their lack of forward thinking when packing the van would result in a stomach-curdling crash as they braked for the first roundabout.

Mrs Barton was somewhere between the two. Her house and possessions were undoubtedly Boulevard Magnifique but her attitude more Concourse la Pit du Merde and the ambiguity was causing uncertainty in the simple minds of The Premiums. It hadn't had an auspicious start.

In Dominic's experience, the very worst sound he could hear when working in someone's house was laughter. Well actually it was the unmistakable WHOOMP as gas ignited accompanied by the smell of singed hair. However, immediately after this it was the sound of laughter. Not any kind of laughter though. A raucous laugh or an unselfconscious display of mirth was fine. However, the negative silence of two people desperately trying not to laugh, or if they must, at least laugh with the mute button on, could only be a bad thing.

It was this sound he heard, or rather didn't hear, as he made his way down the front path to the back of the van an hour or so later. Mrs Barton was still upstairs bathing or powdering as far as he could tell. Gareth was supposedly packing the remaining bits and pieces in her bedroom and Gravy and The Fuzz were doing likewise with the dining room. This left Otter and Weasel who had started moving the larger items of furniture out to the van. As Dominic rounded the end of the tail lift and looked inside, he saw Weasel crouched against the inside wall, tears rolling down his cheeks. Otter was standing sheepishly next to a flower patterned three-seat sofa they had manhandled into the van. In his hands he held one of the seat cushions and was looking at it with worrying intensity.

Dominic jumped up onto the tail lift and crossed to Otter. Grabbing the cushion, and with the contagious nature of trying to be quiet, he whispered, "What the hell are you doing?" However, in the time it took him to say it, he had a fair idea. As he turned the cushion over, he was met by the unmistakable sight and smell of a streak of some form of animal waste in what looked like the front quarter of a perfect size 12 footprint, right in the middle of the cushion. Looking down to the sofa he saw another footprint on one of the other cushions. "For God's sake Otter, what are you doing?"

Weasel, momentarily regaining control, had at least re-joined the audible register. He wiped the tears away on his shirt and sighed loudly in an attempt to clear the laughter from his system.

"Otter trod cat shit into the sofa," he managed before collapsing again into fits of negative registry laughter, the aural equivalent of dark matter.

"Thanks Weasel, I can see that. Go and see if there are any cleaning products in the kitchen."

Otter lowered his eyes to the floor of the van and shuffled past Dominic.

Bogdan Kowalski, the name by which Otter's parents referred to him, was of Polish descent and had been with the company for the last eight months. He was the powerhouse, along with Gareth, of the team. Standing six and a half feet tall with broad shoulders, he appeared to have been used as a muscle repository. It was as if a production line had over budgeted and merely thrown the leftovers at the final unit off the line. His huge biceps stretched the sleeves of his polo shirt and his width tended to block out the sun. His trapezius muscles angled up from his shoulders, seeming to join the base of his skull obscuring the presence of his neck. His closely shaven head and constant furrowed brow gave him an imposing look, but he was the epitome of a gentle giant.

Between his silent guffaws Weasel managed another contribution.

"And see if she has a sewing kit as well." This sent him back to his alternate reality where sound as we know it doesn't exist. Dominic looked at him quizzically as the huge form of Otter jumped from the tail-lift and disappeared into the house.

"Why would we need a sewing kit?" Dominic asked, already dreading the answer.

Weasel merely pointed to the left arm of the sofa. On the flat top surface of the armrest, right at the end, was a four inch tear. Dominic ran his finger over it before gingerly pushing through the edges of the gash. He turned to Weasel and raised his eyebrows questioningly. There was no cause for words in that instance, besides in the strange realm Weasel kept drifting in and out of their value was questionable. After a few moments to compose himself, Weasel finally filled Dominic in.

"As we were carrying it out of the front door, we got it stuck under the corner of the radiator. Neither of us had seen that was what was causing it to get stuck, so that muscle-bound freak flexed and just gave it a twist. Unfortunately it would appear sofas are softer than radiators." Weasel had got to his feet and was inspecting the damage with Dominic.

"Oh crap. How good at sewing are you?" Dominic asked Weasel.

"Why are you asking me? Are you saying I look like someone who has to mend their socks?" he responded antagonistically.

"No you bellend, it's just…" Dominic pulled his vibrating phone from his pocket and opened the text. "It's another message from O'Connell…"

"Tool!" said Gravy and The Fuzz who had lifted a large kitchen dresser onto the tail lift while Dominic and Weasel had been assessing the sofa.

"…apparently I need to go and do another quote so this needs to be fixed while I'm gone," Dominic concluded.

"Ooooh, what's gone wrong this time?" The Fuzz asked, rubbing his hands together, gleeful in the knowledge it wasn't him who had messed up.

"Otter trod cat shit into her sofa and ripped the armrest," Weasel helpfully brought them up to speed. "How good at sewing are you Gravy? You aristos never throw anything away do you? I bet the socks you're wearing were keeping the toes of your ancestors warm at Bosworth Field."

"And you think *I'm* a pikey," added The Fuzz, jabbing Gravy in the ribs with his elbow. "At least I can afford new socks when I need them."

"I can assure you The Fuzz, that I do not consider you a pikey." For some reason no one ever abbreviated The Fuzz to just Fuzz. "My parents were approached by a..." Gravy searched for the collective noun for Pikeys, "...a caravan of Pikeys offering to re-do their driveway and they were nothing like you. They all wore hats for a start. No, you're not a Pikey, you're a chav," Gravy explained matter-of-factly, waiting for the rise he knew was coming. The Fuzz riled visibly. Dominic intervened before matters came to blows.

"Interesting though your social differentiation is Gravy, it's more important we get this fixed." He pointed to the tear.

Otter returned with an armful of detergents and bleaches, sprays and mousse and dropped them on the sofa, marginally missing the rapidly drying cat excrement. He looked into the beaming faces of Weasel, Gravy and The Fuzz and the less welcoming annoyance of Dominic. The Fuzz clapped Otter on the back in a gesture of congratulations.

"So with that in mind, can anybody sew?"

The five of them looked at each other expectantly, but no-one offered themselves forward as being in possession of the mystical power of sewing.

"Oh wait a minute." The Fuzz darted forward to the sofa and with his back to the group busied himself for a few seconds and then stood back beaming triumphantly.

"Ta da. Good as new."

They all looked down at The Fuzz's handy work. Where the tear had been mere moments previously there was now nothing but uninterrupted floral pattern.

"You've just put the arm rest cover over it." Dominic stated, distinctly unimpressed.

"Ta da," repeated The Fuzz, spreading his arms and smiling broadly.

Dominic looked at his phone which had vibrated again signalling another message from O'Connell chasing a response to his message of a few minutes previous.

"Look, I have to go and do this other thing. Please, between you, clean up that cat shit and come up with a better solution than placing something over it for the armrest. I've to go and see some bloke called Forthright and give him a quote. I shouldn't be too long, he's only a few streets away." Dominic pushed the phone into his pocket and looked at two thirds of The Premiums. He wasn't convinced leaving them was a good idea but O'Connell seemed to be particularly narked today and was proving to be more of a tool than usual.

As he jumped down from the tail lift he saw an ominous shadow on the carpet immediately inside the front door of Mrs Barton's house. He looked back up at Otter.

"You did take your shoes off when you went back inside didn't you?"

If possible, Otter looked even more sheepish as Weasel dissolved into further fits of laughter. Dominic signalled to the mess in the house and went to get the keys to the Fiesta from Gareth.

According to O'Connell, this Forthright quote was urgent with a very short lead time until the actual removal and the customer was willing to pay for the inconvenience. Dominic was fairly certain the inconvenience would be his.

Chapter 8

"Have you heard back from 'The Groper' yet?"

Beth looked up from her book and gave her mum a warning stare. Beth had called Dominic a number of times the previous day to see how the hospital had been, and then when she heard nothing back had sent a couple of texts all to no response. Now it was Monday, she had heard nothing and Dominic would be at work with limited time to call her, if he felt so inclined.

"Don't call him that mother."

"And don't you call me mother. It makes me sound old. And I think if we've learnt anything from the last couple of days it's that I neither look nor feel old." Beth's mum had a wicked glint in her eye and a smile touched the edges of her lips. "Alright," she said in response to her daughter's look. "Have you heard from Dominic yet?"

With similar caution to that which Dominic had shown under interrogation by Gareth, she replied, "Not as yet, no."

The immediate aftermath of early Sunday morning had been interesting. Beth had been ripped from a very contented sleep by her mother's scream. She had run to the kitchen fearful for what she might find, never in a million years expecting to witness what she did. The sight of Dominic naked, sprawled on the floor and her mother advancing on him looking like she was intent on beating him to a pulp had been a first for her.

It had become clear immediately what had happened and but for the blood pouring from Dominic's face and the clear distress he was in from groping her mother, Beth would have laughed. Even her mother had seen the funny side while Dominic cleaned himself up and dressed. Dominic however, quite understandably, had failed to see the funny side, what with the broken nose and sore testicles. The drive to A&E had been uncomfortable to say the least. So much for what had been a perfect first date, she thought.

"Well, considering some of the introductions to your previous boyfriends, I'd say it went well. Top 25% easy," she said, a smirk touching her lips.

"He isn't my boyfriend. And even if he were, I don't imagine you punching him in the face and kneeing him in the balls would make that relationship viable in the long term."

"Nonsense. Any well-rounded man who respects women would be delighted to know that the mother of their significant other can take care of herself. And it doesn't hurt to let a man know you can kick his arse from time to time."

Beth considered this. "You really think Dominic is likely to view this in a positive light?" she asked, doubtfully.

"Oh no, men are idiots and egotists. I said a well-rounded man would be able to view this positively. I imagine your Dominic will be trying to find any excuse to explain away me beating him up. That and cradling his swollen testicles of course." Pamela broke into a broad grin as her daughter rolled her eyes at her.

"It's not funny Mum. I need to apologise for you assaulting him."

"You don't need to apologise for anything, ever!" She said a serious edge to her tone. "Besdies," she continued innocently, "He assaulted me first. I was merely following my training. I told you those self-defence classes would be useful. Sensei Steve will be delighted."

"He thought you were me," Beth replied defensively. "And if he had done what he did to you, to me, it wouldn't have been assault."

"Actually, he *was* very gentle for a sexual predator." Pamela's smile was broader than ever. "Is he that gentle in his normal love-making or is that just with me?" she asked, teasingly.

"Please, stop now. I am not having this conversation with you." Beth pressed the screen on her phone and held it to her ear. After a few rings it diverted to voicemail. "Hey Dominic, it's Beth. Please give me a call back when you get this. It would be good to talk."

"Not ready to talk to you yet?"

"He's at work. I just want to explain, that's all."

"Darling, there is nothing to explain," Pamela said, her joke attitude softening. "It was obviously an unfortunate misunderstanding for all concerned. I'm sure the mutual embarrassment felt by everyone will cancel each other out and we can all move on."

"You don't seem very embarrassed."

"Well no, that's true, I'm not. But from my perspective I thought I was being attacked so I think I actually went lightly on him."

Beth tapped Dominic's name and held the phone to her ear again.

Pamela reached across, taking the phone and disconnecting the call. "Look, at the moment he is probably in a state of shock. It isn't every day you grope your girlfriend's mother and then have your arse handed to you by a woman in her mid-fifties. On top of that he will clearly be having to explain the broken nose, black eyes and gash on his cheek in a way that is a million miles away from the truth. As a man he's almost certainly struggling with whatever lie he has concocted on the one hand, and coming to terms with truth on the other. Give him some time to figure out what's happened and I'm sure he'll come round." Beth looked at her, doubt writ large across her face again. "If he's well-rounded," Pamela added.

Beth wasn't so sure and glanced at her phone again.

"Come on, you can't sit around here staring at a phone that isn't ringing. You've called him what, six, seven times now?" Beth nodded. "Right, then you have absolved yourself of any responsibility you might feel. A real man would realise you are worth a small beating. If he can't see that or his ego gets in the way you are better off shot of him. You've got the week off and I go home tomorrow. Let's go shopping. Is Naomi around?" she asked, referring to Beth's housemate who spent the majority of her time at her boyfriend's house.

"No, she's at Joel's I think."

"Right, then I'll buy you lunch and you can tell me everything that happened in the lead up to 4am yesterday morning." Pamela's eyes shone with mischief.

After a few moments and another look at her phone, Beth looked at her mother.

"You're right. It's up to Dominic now." They stood up and took their coats from the hooks in the corner of the kitchen then headed through the flat to the front door. "Lunch though is not going to be cheap and we will not be talking about the lead up to 4am, as nice as it was," Beth said, smiling.

"Fair enough. And don't worry, I know there are dangers lurking around every corner in London, but I'll protect you." Pamela raised her large and rather beautiful sapphire and diamond ring to her lips and kissed it as Beth pulled the door shut.

Chapter 9

Dominic found the address of the Forthrights easily enough via a near miss with a wheelchair user as he turned into the driveway. Experience is one of those things that comes with time and merely by looking at the outside of the imposing home he was about to quote on, Dominic knew this would be a million miles away from Concourse la Pit du Merde. Homes like this one just didn't do IKEA.

After a few moments, the door was opened by an elderly man with thick white hair. Half-moon glasses perched on his nose allowing his eyebrows unfettered access to the world around them; the long wispy hairs appearing to reach out at Dominic. Pleasantries were exchanged and Dominic was ushered quickly into the house.

Once inside, Mr Forthright visibly relaxed.

"Sorry for the rushed welcome," he said distractedly. "Need to keep the drafts out. Can't abide the cold you see. It gets into my bones and ruins my day."

Dominic nodded, looking out the window at the beautiful warm sunny day outside and waved off the apology as unnecessary. Evidently old people couldn't control their own body temperature. No biggie.

"Thanks for the speed of your attendance as well," Wilbur continued, agitation evident in his voice and mannerisms. "My wife and I appreciate we have set some very tight timelines on this."

They were still stood in the reception area immediately inside the front door and Dominic couldn't help but pick up on an air of unease about the house and the man stood in front of him.

"Well don't leave the man standing by the door." The voice came from Dominic's left and he turned to see a woman smiling at him from a doorway. "Come through please," she signalled to Dominic who followed her into a large sitting room where tea and biscuits waited for them on a low coffee table.

Mrs Forthright signalled for Dominic to sit and started pouring tea as her husband paced the room. This wasn't feeling at all like a usual house visit to Dominic.

"Did you find the place ok?" she asked as she passed a cup and saucer across to him.

Putting his rucksack on the floor and gratefully accepting the tea, Dominic nodded. In these situations having something to do with your hands was always appreciated.

"No problem at all. Although I did nearly end up in an accident with a wheelchair." Unnoticed behind him, Mr Forthright stopped pacing and stared at the back of Dominic's head. Almost imperceptibly the expression froze on Mrs Forthright's face and her eyes flicked up to her husband then back to Dominic. Dunking his jammy dodger, Dominic had missed the interaction.

"He just pulled out in front of me as I turned into your drive. Maybe he's a possible buyer for you? He was looking up at the house."

Another look passed between the Forthrights and Wilbur quickly left the room. Having regained her composure, Mrs Forthright smiled again at Dominic.

"Well, necessity does require we make a quick sale so hopefully you're right." She paused while Dominic took another sip of tea and reached for another biscuit. The sugar was doing a sterling job of attacking the final residues of his hangover. After a few further moments of silence, Mrs Forthright softly cleared her throat.

"I don't mean to rush you Mr…?"

"Morgan. Dominic Morgan, please just call me Dominic," he replied, suddenly embarrassed.

"Well Dominic, unfortunately certain circumstances have arisen within our family that require Wilbur and I to pack up this house very quickly. With that in mind, what is the process for today?" Again she smiled reassuringly, easing Dominic's embarrassment instantly.

"Of course. Well, if either you or your husband could walk me round the house and show me exactly what it is you need us to pack and move then I can get a feel for the scale of the job. Then we just need to know the size and location of the property you are moving to and we can go from there."

"Seeing as my husband has disappeared I think I should give you the grand tour."

They both stood and Dominic pulled out his quotation pad from his bag and signalled he was ready to start.

"We'll start upstairs at the back." Mrs Forthright led Dominic out of the sitting room and towards the main staircase. "We're moving abroad so all of our possessions here will need to be stored. Is that something you can help with as well?"

Dominic explained that Swift & Smooth owned their own secure storage facility so that wouldn't be a problem.

As his wife and the removal guy disappeared upstairs, Wilbur tentatively peaked round the doorframe from his office, which faced the lounge from across the hallway.

The paranoia was back, but with what their visitor had said—what was his name again? Darren? Dwayne? Dominic, that was it. With what Dominic had said about the wheelchair, Wilbur now knew that SSoH were watching him. It had to be Derek keeping tabs on him after the awards fiasco, and if that was the case then he would easily put two and two together; the cat was already out of the bag. It wouldn't take more than a handful of seconds to answer the question: what possible reason could Wilbur have for being visited by a removal firm?

Following that day's morning constitutional, Wilbur had outlined the situation to his wife. It had been very difficult to begin with as she had no idea of the severity of the situation they now found themselves in. It had taken some time to persuade Mabel of the danger his indiscretion had put them in and what he feared would be the response of the SSoH. However, with her pragmatic mind allowing her to see things as they were, she finally understood and agreed to Wilbur's plan.

It wasn't anything fancy, they just needed to run—run fast and far. If they could get the house sorted in a matter of days, the actual sale could be managed from wherever they found themselves. The important thing was to be gone and be gone quickly.

Returning to his desk, Wilbur sat, took a clean piece of Basildon Bond writing paper and uncapped his fountain pen. He needed to convey the urgency of the situation without instilling abject fear:

Dear Sir,

You are in immediate and considerable danger…

Wilbur screwed the piece of paper up and threw it in the bin. Great way not to scare the lad off. He tried again.

Dear Swift and Smooth chap,

It is imperative that from this moment fore, you trust no one!

Again, a fantastic way to break the lad in gently. Wilbur prepared another piece of paper and this time thought for a few moments before beginning to write. Within a couple of minutes he had composed what he hoped would be sufficient to grab and hold the boy's attention, without having him dismiss the words as a mad man's ramblings. Gently folding the paper he slipped it into the cover of his diary.

As Wilbur crossed the reception hall he looked out of the dappled glass in the front door. Outside sat Dominic's Fiesta, emblazoned across the back half of the car was a huge Swift & Smooth Removals logo and phone number. Typical that the very thing that had helped formulate his plan was also the thing that would alert SSoH to it. Without the brightly painted car prompting Wilbur's actions, he may not have acted so speedily. However the same car had now undoubtedly alerted Derek as to their plans and there was only one place that information was going to end up: Jeff. Fleetingly, Wilbur wished Dominic's near miss hadn't been so much of a miss.

Wilbur quietly slipped into the lounge clutching the small leather-bound A5 notebook tightly in his hand, his knuckles white. He could hear his wife's muffled voice taking Dominic through their home, pointing out the valuables, those things with high sentimental value, how she wanted things done. She really was an amazing woman. Even once he had explained to her the danger he now believed them to be in, she had not fallen apart. She had been practical about it. There was a problem and it needed a solution. When he had proffered his take on the answer, she had thought about it and then agreed. No quibble, simple as that.

Wilbur looked at the book in his hand. He hadn't known how dangerous to him and his wife this book would become when he started it all those years ago following the meeting at Jeff's pub. He realised soon enough however, as events started escalating and people started getting hurt. And now, after the dinner and his loose lips, this small leather notebook had become the most dangerous thing he possessed.

He needed to find some way of transforming it into an asset rather than a hindrance. The moment of clarity had come, not from a lunchtime clearing of the pipes, as many of his clear thoughts did, but from watching a man put his bag down in order to accept some tea and a biscuit filled with rubbery jam. It wasn't the most earth-shattering plan in existence, but he had watched enough television and read enough books to know that the best way to protect oneself from knowing too much was by use of a dead man's switch. By ensuring there was a copy of the information held remotely by an unknown person or persons, Wilbur could hopefully ensure that the fear of it being released if anything happened to him would be greater than the desire to eliminate him. In return for his safety, he and his wife would disappear.

That was the plan anyway. Wilbur had no idea whether it would work or whether this Dominic fellow would help, but right now he didn't have a choice. He crossed to the sofa and reached down to where Dominic had left his bag. Unzipping it, he looked inside. There was nothing unusual in there, only a bottle of water and a screwed up rain jacket. Wilbur looked outside at the clear blue skies and offered a short prayer that the day's weather would remain clear and warm. He needed Dominic not to discover the book at least until he was back at his own home. The key was to get the diary out of the house, ideally without anyone knowing. Wilbur pulled out the jacket and carefully wrapped it around the notebook. Slipping it back into the bag, he zipped it shut. With a sigh he slumped onto the sofa.

The voices from upstairs were getting louder as Mabel took Dominic into the rooms at the front of the house. Wilbur chewed on a bourbon biscuit distractedly. What else could he do? What would he do if he were Jeff? He thought about this for a while before deciding that if he were Jeff, he would want to get eyes on whatever Wilbur was doing. Therefore, he had to prepare himself for a visit. He looked again at the bag. He wanted his diary and Dominic out of his home as soon as possible. If Jeff did come round and saw Dominic pick up a previously unattended bag it wouldn't take a genius to link the two together, even speculatively. He had to think quickly as he had no idea if or when Jeff would make an appearance.

Getting up from the sofa, Wilbur picked up Dominic's bag and headed off to find his wife and the bag's owner. He bumped into them coming out of his study. Offering the bag to Dominic he tried to cover his unease.

"Sorry Dominic, you don't mind if you keep this with you do you?"

Dominic shook his head and reached out for the bag.

"You know," Wilbur continued in response to his wife's questioning expression, "we have a few guests coming round later and I just want to tidy up and make the place look presentable."

"That's quite alright," Dominic answered to what he felt was a perfectly reasonable request and swung the bag onto his shoulder; the additional weight slight enough to go unnoticed.

Once the main reception room had been done Dominic and Mrs Forthright had completed their tour of the house. Dominic had several pages of notes regarding the content, packing requirements and specific insurance requirements, of which there were many. The Forthrights had amassed a considerable amount of very nice things, to the point where the company would have to at least review the level of insurance they held.

Standing in the main reception hall, Dominic shook hands with the Forthrights.

"I'll get all the details written up and a quote generated and I would hope you would have that by tomorrow if that's ok?"

"Lovely, thank you dear," Mrs Forthright replied. "That will do fine." She slipped her arm through that of her husband who smiled tentatively. He had been a bit odd the whole time Dominic thought, but the wife was nice.

Dominic opened the front door and saw a black Range Rover coming up the driveway.

"It looks like your first guest has arrived," he commented as he unlocked the Fiesta's driver's door.

Behind him, Wilbur visibly stiffened as he looked out at the luxury off-roader pulling up next to Dominic's car.

As Dominic climbed into the driver's seat and lowered the window, the door of the Range Rover opened and out stepped a man of similar years to Mr Forthright. He was dressed in black from head to foot with the exception of a crimson eye patch over his left eye.

Dominic waved as he drove round the Range Rover on the turning circle and just caught the first words from the new arrival.

"Hello Wilbur, I think we had better go inside and have a chat don't you?"

Dominic drove past the Barton's house to see how the rest of The Premiums were getting on. Thankfully he found the lorry gone, off on its first trip across to the new home in Clapham. A quick call to Gareth confirmed they were at the Clapham address unloading the first lorry full and nothing else had gone wrong since Dominic had left them. Otter had, to all intents and purposes, expunged the evidence of cat excrement, although they had failed to sew up the tear and had resorted to The Fuzz's solution of covering it up and forgetting about it. It came down to whether the Bartons didn't notice it for a month or two. If so, then it would be as if the tear had never happened on their watch.

Having told Gareth he was heading to the office to complete the quote and would meet them either back in Caterham or Clapham for the final offload, he hung up. He wouldn't count his chickens just yet but a small tear and a smear of cat shit would count as a major result for The Premiums. It might even shut O'Connell up for a bit as well.

He could feel the nerves build as he pulled into the small car park at the front of Swift & Smooth's office. He had no idea how much of his disastrous weekend with Beth would be common knowledge by now. The fact she was off for the week gave him limited hope that the incident would remain a secret for a little while longer at least. The only positive he could take was the fact The Premiums and the other removal teams were kept out of the way round the back, so that any visiting clients didn't have to see the riffraff who would actually handle their possessions before they had committed their signatures to the contracts.

The removal teams always used the rear fire escape to get in and out of the building. Whichever of them got in to work first disabled the alarm and wedged the door open for the rest. Typically this would often be Dominic but they all knew the routine.

Dominic grabbed his bag and edged his way around the building to the fire escape. Sure enough, he could just make out the red of a fire extinguisher stopping the door from closing completely. Slipping into the corridor, Dominic quickly made his way to the crew room. As expected it was completely empty of the teams, all of whom were currently out on jobs.

The crew room was nothing special. With a kettle and small fridge, a sofa and a page 3-style calendar many decades out of date, there were sufficient facilities for the guys to sit down with a brew on the rare occasions they weren't out lugging furniture and crockery. The only other piece of equipment in the room, perched on a rickety table in the corner, was an ancient PC. It was slow and crappy but it was connected to the company networks so Dominic could draw up the quote and submit through the systems without having to go into the main offices. Hopefully he could be out without having to see any of the team in accounts and definitely without seeing O'Connell.

Forty-five minutes later Dominic was done. Far more of the inventory had been submitted through the field **HIGH VALUE ITEMS** than any job he had done before. He knew the insurances carried by the business would cover it, but the price charged to clients was influenced by the quality of their belongings.

He had a quick look around the room to make sure he could make a speedy getaway. As soon as he submitted the form, it would be sent through to his line manager for review, sign off and then processing to be sent to the customer. As soon as O'Connell received the notification he would know Dominic was on-site and may come looking for him.

Content that all was as it should be, Dominic took the Fiesta keys from his pocket, swung his bag on his shoulder and clicked **SUBMIT QUOTATION.**

By the time O'Connell's desktop chimed a notification that he had a new quote to review, Dominic was halfway to the emergency exit. By the time O'Connell had opened his email, Dominic was out of the building, and by the time O'Connell registered this was the Forthright quote and therefore from Dominic, his quarry was in the Fiesta about to gun it from the car park.

Dominic allowed himself a smile of success as he pulled out of the car park having managed to complete the quote without having to see or speak to anyone and headed towards Clapham. He had spoken to Gareth again and they had decided there was no reason for him to head to Caterham as he would arrive just as they were leaving. He lowered the window, cranked up the stereo and reached for his bag.

Rummaging through it his hand felt the hard edges of something at the bottom. The uniform shape went unrecognised by his hand as he continued searching. Eventually his hand came to rest on the bottle of water. He pulled it out, took a long drink and headed off towards Clapham Old Town.

Chapter 10

O'Connell sat at his desk, quietly seething. Not only had that little prick Morgan taken him at his word regarding the urgency of the Forthright quote and gone there immediately, but he had also not waited until he was in the office the following day to file the quote as O'Connell had expected. Alfie had hoped that for one reason or another, Dominic would have been caught up in the Barton's removal and been unable to make the appointment today giving him a reason to start disciplinary proceedings. Not only had Dominic been to the appointment but he had managed to sneak back into the building to file it and get out again without O'Connell getting a chance to speak with him.

He sat looking out of his window at the industrial estate Swift & Smooth were based on. A sprawling mass of warehouse units spread as far as he could see. Oh this is the life, he thought to himself sarcastically. Even with the sun shining and the sky clear and azure blue, this particular industrial estate managed to make him feel like he was in an ex-Soviet bloc gulag: nothing around him except grey buildings mirrored by sullen looking grey people.

As soon as the Forthright quote notification had hit his inbox, O'Connell had known Dominic had to be on-site. He had raced out of his office, knocking a pile of files off his secretary's desk, and sprinted through the building. Down the flight of stairs, through the main reception and down the long corridor that led to the pokey and shabby room the crews used between jobs. As he flung the door open he was greeted with nothing more than the ancient PC in the corner telling him it was installing updates prior to shutting down and should not be turned off in the meantime.

As he had returned to the corridor and slammed the door in frustration, he had seen the fire escape wedged open with an extinguisher. A smile briefly touched his lips. As he made his way back through the facility to his office he made two phone calls. The first was to the Head of IT requesting the ancient PC in the crew room be removed immediately. Being as old and out of date as it was, it clearly posed a threat to their jealously guarded ISO 27001 status. Secondly, he called the Head of Policy Compliance and asked for all policies regarding employee responsibilities for protecting company information, assets and premises to be emailed across to him and all compliance sign-off sheets as signed by one Dominic Morgan. In the relatively short time he had had that day to consider the Dominic-Beth issue, he had decided the long game simply wouldn't do and he had to find a way of eliminating the competition as soon as possible. Dominic's flagrant disregard for the security policies of the business was as good a place to start as any.

He turned back from the window and looked at the policy documentation and the sheet Dominic had countersigned as proof he had read and understood his responsibilities as an employee:

"All employees will at all times ensure the security and integrity of Swift & Smooth premises."

It wasn't an earth-shattering sentence but it did give O'Connell all the authority he needed in starting Dominic down the path to dismissal. He smiled to himself as a tiger shark might at the sight of a floundering swimmer. There were hoops through which he would have to jump to ensure he didn't fall foul of the HR brigade, but he would make sure Dominic's life was miserable while the process ran its course.

Sliding the policy document away from him, he clicked the link in the Forthright email which took him to the company's secure servers and brought up the quote Dominic had filed. A brief scan had O'Connell whistling through his teeth. While he despised Dominic, he fully appreciated that he had the experience and knowledge to properly and accurately formulate quotes.

Well he should do, O'Connell thought to himself, he has been here eight years and made it all the way to the heady heights of Crew Supervisor. Given the dearth of talent in that part of the business, O'Connell felt he could employ a monkey that would rise faster than Morgan had.

That was one of the reasons O'Connell despised Dominic so much. He clearly wasn't stupid. He had gained a good degree in English from a good university and then had proceeded to do bugger all with it, joining S&S as a box slinger only a year after graduating. Over the next seven years he had been earmarked for promotion no fewer than eleven times and turned them all down until the last one, six months previously. For someone as keen to progress and driven as O'Connell, Dominic's lack of ambition astonished and infuriated him.

What further added fuel to his flames of hatred was the fact no-one in the business seemed to judge Dominic negatively as a result. Everyone seemed to like him and overlook the fact that he was clearly treading water but as yet hadn't waded out far enough to even get his balls wet.

As he waited for the secondary, more detailed page to load, O'Connell leant back in his chair and sipped his coffee. He remembered the day he started at the firm four years ago. He had joined as a Senior Project Planner ensuring all the logistical requirements for a job were in place: resources, insurances, contracts, international travel if necessary, accommodation, port visas— everything that was needed to ensure the jobs ran as smoothly as possible.

On his first day he had sat opposite the chair he was now reclining in for a brief chat with the man he ultimately replaced, and received the "welcome to the firm" speech. Utter drivel as he remembered it, with the old man telling him that removals wasn't their business but that people were. Treat your people well and the rest takes care of itself, he had said. And then he had leant forward conspiratorially and singled Dominic bloody Morgan out as a man to watch, and in a good way rather than as a potential larcenist or peeping Tom.

O'Connell had left the old man's office that day and read Dominic's employment file. Instantly the torch of judgement had ignited the coals of hatred, smouldering initially but with every day gaining fuel. Over the next four years, O'Connell had risen through the business to now occupy the chair of second in command, Operations Director and COO. He smiled to himself, smug in his achievement. In that same period, Dominic had risen exactly one rung on the corporate ladder, and then only because they had gone through a particularly high staff turnover period and the firm had needed him to be Crew Supervisor. O'Connell had simply made the announcement and told Dominic if he didn't like it he could find alternative employment. Dominic's lack of ambition and security in his current job meant there was no way he would risk leaving the comfortable nest.

O'Connell firmly believed the ambition to be better, to push yourself, to earn more and have more, to never be satisfied, to always be on the lookout for the next opportunity, to be willing to put yourself first at the expense of others was what separated people like himself from people like Morgan.

Finally, the second page loaded and O'Connell sat forward in surprise, nearly spilling his coffee across the table. The contents of the Forthrights house were unbelievable. From vintage jewellery to centuries-old antiques, their whole home was a museum piece and Dominic had itemised every gem and every stick of furniture.

O'Connell breathed in deeply.

"Come to papa," he said quietly as he scrolled through the long list of items.

What O'Connell took for ambition, most other people would see as greed; what he saw as focus, others saw as self-centeredness; what others saw as the fruits of a lifetime of hard work and success, O'Connell saw as the unfair distribution of wealth—unfair because it meant distribution of wealth away from himself. But all was not lost. His job had afforded him a profitable sideline.

He reviewed the complete quote again, clapping his hands and laughing to himself. This was perfect: a job with a very short completion date, the owners requiring the contents to be stored rather than moved to another location, an open-ended requirement for that storage as the owners were travelling abroad, and a removals team with a reputation for destruction. It wouldn't take much for that reputation to grow to include theft. He smiled again. This really was too perfect; an opportunity to increase his own wealth and who knew, perhaps a further opportunity to drop Morgan into the mire.

Of course he couldn't possibly get involved himself, with his ever-growing paunch he wasn't in any kind of shape for this particular type of nighttime activity and he had a reputation to uphold. However, he knew a man who didn't have such considerations to worry about.

He removed a key from the pocket of his waistcoat and slipped it gently into the lock of the bottom drawer of his desk. Turning it he pulled it open. The drawer was empty except for a slim oblong device.

Retrieving it, he pushed the red power button and waited for the phone to turn on. Once it was on and he had a signal, he clicked on the email programme and quickly typed **From A-B** into the subject line. He then clicked on the only email address the phone held and pressed send.

Chapter 11

It never rained, it poured. Hank, sat next to a warming fire in his local pub enjoying a bottle of beer, glanced down at the table where his phone was vibrating again.

The thing had practically had a life of its own that day with contacts from clients coming in one after the other. Most required no immediate action but a request from Help Wanted always caught his eye. The discussion had been brief—far briefer than usual anyway—but then the request was more straightforward than normal, no exotic sourcing missions this time. No, all that was required was a simple breaking and entering, followed by a little bit of theft. Nothing like the usual type of request from these guys, Hank had thought as the client explained where and when the break-in should happen. It was only once the client had explained what exactly he wanted stolen, that some semblance of understanding dawned on Hank. Any diary held by one of this group must hold some explosively powerful revelations considering their activities over the previous forty years. The client had left no ambiguity as to the contents of the diary and by doing so had ensured that Hank wanted the item recovered as much as the SSoH. If there was a diary and it contained information of the group's activities, it was a practical certainty that it would make reference to Hank himself, and the services he provided. The importance of Wilbur Forthright's diary had increased dramatically during the conversation and as Hank hung up, the course of action he needed to follow was laid out. The job was important enough that he would have done it for free, for his own protection, but payment had been offered, and like any good capitalist had duly been accepted.

He had spent the majority of the day researching the location of the Forthrights' home, the architecture of the building, the drawings and architect's blueprints, the planning applications that had been submitted and passed over the years—everything necessary for Hank to have as full a picture as possible of the environment he was entering that night. He wasn't overly concerned for his wellbeing bearing in mind the age of the targets. He felt comfortable he could resist an enraged septuagenarian, but experience had taught him that to assume a favourable outcome was to invite disaster. They may be old, he told himself, but old people could still fire guns and a bullet's trajectory was indifferent to the age of the firer.

He checked his watch again, 5.30pm. He would head home and put the final preparations to his kit then make his way over to Caterham to start the surveillance on the house. As he got up his phone buzzed. Checking his emails he saw the subject **From A-B**. With everything else going on at the moment it hardly constituted a priority. The guy was an idiot. He was, however, an idiot whose plans had never previously offered any danger in their execution and always realised sufficient profit to make them worthwhile. He clicked into the address book, scrolled down to **From A-B** and dialled the number.

Ten minutes later, Hank's already interesting life had just got a lot more interesting. **From A-B** had just informed him of a large haul of valuable antiques in a house his firm had been asked to clear and store. He had also mentioned that he didn't want the job to go ahead until the items were safely in his company's facility, but wanted to let Hank know the job would be on at some point over the next couple of weeks, assuming the removal went ahead in the next few days as planned. That in itself wasn't unusual for this client, but during the conversation he had innocently mentioned the location of the target's house as being Caterham. Hank didn't believe in coincidences and although the likelihood of there being a crossover in jobs was remote, it was important to ensure he had as complete a picture as possible. He had asked what the address was, a not unreasonable question in the circumstances, and his client had seen no reason not to tell him.

Hank's face was inscrutable as he hung up and continued his measured walk home. The situation was unprecedented for him. Never before had two clients' requests converged at the same point. He started running scenarios through his head. Was **From A-B** trying to tell him that he knew about the activities he conducted for **Help Wanted**? That he knew of the existence of the diary and its contents and was making a soft approach that would result in blackmail? He certainly wouldn't put it past **From A-B**.

Hank always referred to his clients by their elected subject line moniker and to himself by his professional pseudonym, Hank not being his real name. In so doing he afforded each of them the illusion of security; after all, if neither of the parties knew the specific details of the other then there was little risk in the event of one of them being arrested. An illusion of security was all it was however as Hank never went into business with anyone without fully understanding who they were and what he was letting himself in for. The widely held belief that what you didn't know couldn't hurt you, protected him far more than his clients. The background work he had done on O'Connell had returned exactly what he expected it to. A middle-class man who was unhappy with his lot and thought he had discovered a way to enhance his lifestyle with minimum risk. The month Hank had spent investigating him had turned up some interesting information regarding his fidelity, his relationship with the taxman and a small—but not insignificant—relationship with class A narcotics. Photographs had been taken and filed for potential future use. If O'Connell was planning on blackmailing him then Hank's first approach would be a polite conversation suggesting a different path might be more sustainable.

That said, it was even more important to get into the Forthrights house and get hold of the diary. O'Connell may well be waiting for the removal to steal it himself, if he knew of its existence, in which case Hank would have to beat him to it and then possibly with it.

It would however, be a little amateurish to tell the person you intended to blackmail that you were planning on acquiring material with which to do so, and then tell them where and when you intended to acquire it, and nothing Hank had seen of O'Connell had led him to believe he was that stupid. Hank slid the key into the lock on his front door and pushed it open. O'Connell was an amateur, he thought, that's why he needs me, but could he really see him as a potential blackmailer? Realistically no, he thought. There was little chance O'Connell was looking to up the ante on him but he needed to be sure. If it became necessary to remove **From A-B** from his revenue streams, Hank was perfectly comfortable in doing so. Of course the knock-on effect for O'Connell would be less comfortable.

Half an hour later, Hank had completed the final check on his kit and swung a small rucksack onto his shoulder. The last thing he did before leaving was log on to a secure remote server and set his bespoke security system. Any activity in his flat would instantly activate cameras and send the images to Hank's phone. Clicking the screen off, Hank headed out of the flat and disappeared into the busy streets of London, heading for Caterham.

A couple of hours later, Hank was crouched behind a hedge just inside the grounds of the Forthrights home. The drive into Surrey had been slow but simple and uneventful, heading out through Brixton and Streatham, continuing to Croydon and Whyteleafe, where he had left the car, before continuing the final couple of miles on foot. Jeff had told him that given the current situation, it was unlikely the Forthrights would venture out in the evening so he would have to deal with their presence in the house when he entered. He had gone on to say that with Wilbur experiencing the wave of guilt that was threatening the foundations of SSoH's success, he couldn't see him putting up much of a fight in the eventuality that Hank was discovered. All very reassuring, Hank thought as he flexed his shoulders, forcing the rucksack to twist and the bulk of the crowbar to dig momentarily into his ribs. Guilt-induced passivity was one thing, but a bloody great lump of metal offered a more reliable method of control.

Forty minutes had passed since Hank had started his surveillance and what he had seen had required him to rethink his strategy. Initially he had planned on waiting until the early hours and then do what he did best: break in and rummage around the house until he found the diary, subduing the occupants if it became necessary. However, since Hank had been in place, he had periodically observed nervous twitches of the curtains from each of the four windows he could see. The occupants were clearly very agitated. Maybe not expecting a specific threat but clearly understanding there was a very clear and present danger to their wellbeing. Whatever hope Hank had fostered that he would discover an old couple, defences low, blissfully unaware they were being targeted, proved to be very far from the truth.

Having circled the property a couple of times since his arrival, Hank had also noted the security technology in place. Each window had a stand-alone frame detection system with backup redundant circuit connectors, ensuring that even if he bypassed one of the circuits and forced the window open, he would have no idea how many redundant contact points there were, all waiting to set off the alarm. The doors were heavy-duty affairs as well, which at a glance Hank knew were the real deal. It was even possible there were pressure sensors outside on the approach to the building that activated if sufficient weight rested on them once the system was live. Clearly he was dealing with a man interested in self-preservation.

Eventually Hank had decided the bold approach was the most likely to succeed. As he had cut through the side and back streets of Caterham he had noticed a pizza shop, its rear door open to the evening. Leaving his backpack secreted in the hedge, Hank headed back into town.

Half an hour later he was back and pulling on the uniform shirt he had stolen from the pizza shop. A little short in the sleeve, he thought as he stretched his arms away from him, but that didn't matter. The subterfuge didn't have to last for long, it was just those first few seconds he needed to get the door opened and be dismissed as no threat. Hank pulled the matching hat onto his head and swung the backpack over his shoulders. Grabbing the pizza box he had also lifted, Hank took a deep breath and stepped out from the hedge into the centre of the Forthrights driveway and walked confidently towards the house.

He waited at the door as the bell rang and heard whispered conversation beyond. Eventually, from the window to the right of the front door, the room which Hank knew from the plans was the study, an old man's face appeared, the skin stretched taut with stress, the eyes rheumy but alive to any possible dangers. Hank watched as the old man's features softened as he took in the box, shirt and hat and shook his head.

"I'm sorry, there seems to have been a mix-up. We didn't order any pizza," he quite audibly heard Wilbur say through the glass. Oh well, Hank thought. It had been a long shot to think Forthright would automatically open the door, even to an innocent-looking pizza delivery, especially when they hadn't placed the order.

Hank exaggeratedly leant forward and mouthed "What?" Inside, Wilbur repeated his insistence the order was not for them with Hank responding with another mouthed "What? I can't hear you!" After the third aborted attempt, the curtain twitched back into place and Wilbur was gone. Hank started counting in his head the ten seconds he thought it would take for Wilbur to get from the window in the study to the front door. He got to nine before he heard the security chain being attached and a couple of dead locks being released. Hank smiled to himself. Eventually the door snicked open an inch and a voice pierced the burgeoning gloom.

"I'm sorry there seems to have been a mistake. You see we didn't order any pizza."

"That's a relief," replied Hank, "because this box is empty." With that he took half a step back before lunging forward, the sole of his right foot connecting with the door at the point where the chain was attached, before being driven through it. Hank felt a moment of resistance before the force of his weight passing through the two small screws holding the chain in place gave way, splintering the edge of the door before hitting Wilbur full in the face and knocking him backwards into the hallway.

Quickly, Hank entered the house before gently pushing the door closed behind him and dropping the latch. As he had expected, none of the expensive alarm system he had observed had been activated and what greeted him as he turned back to the occupants was Wilbur sprawled on the floor, a gash on his forehead beginning to ooze blood and the sight of his worried wife rushing down the stairs to aid her stricken husband. Your second mistake, thought Hank. Firstly, having all this expensive alarm equipment but relying on an eighth of an inch chain to protect you and now, not hitting the panic button, wherever it might be, before checking on the husband. Hank slowly took in the reception area and then looked at Wilbur and Mabel. Wilbur was clearly seeing stars from where the door had caught him and Mabel was cradling his head, tears rolling down her cheeks, but an undeniable look of hatred aimed directly at Hank. He would have to watch her; unlike her husband she hadn't yet realised this was a no-win situation.

"I have been reliably informed that you will, in all likelihood, know why I'm here and who has asked me to pay you both a visit." Hank reached behind him to his pack and unzipped a compartment at the bottom of the bag as he slowly advanced on them. Withdrawing the crowbar, he stopped a metre in front of them and let the tip of the crowbar drop to the floor where it embedded itself a few centimetres into the parquet. He noticed the look on Mabel's face change as realisation dawned this was no ordinary burglary. Wilbur sighed deeply, visibly deflating, then nothing. Eventually Hank broke the silence.

"I need the diary and I need it now."

Wilbur looked up, sadness etched across his face.

"And what if I can't give it to you?" he managed; no trace of bravado, simply a question.

"So you admit there is a diary?" Hank crouched down on his haunches so Wilbur could more easily look into his eyes and understand there was no compassion there.

"I destroyed it when we got back from the awards dinner."

Hank stared at Wilbur, the old man's face already coming up in a swollen lump tinged with brown and purple. He saw fear and concern but not for himself, and above all resignation. What he didn't see was any trace that Wilbur was lying.

"Is that true?" Hank asked, looking to Mabel for confirmation.

"Absolutely," she blurted. "As soon as we got back from the awards, Wilbur burnt it in the fireplace in his study. Nothing was left of it."

Hank dropped his head in disappointment—too much information. After a few moments he looked at Wilbur again.

"Your wife appears to be a very capable woman. It's just a shame her life's work hasn't required her to lie as convincingly as yours has." Hank stood up and turned away from the couple.

Wilbur raised his eyes to his wife's. In all of their time together there had never been an occasion for which Mabel had needed to apologise to her husband. Through nearly fifty years of life's trials and tribulations Wilbur had had cause to apologise innumerable times, but his wife had never done anything in his eyes that warranted an apology. As Wilbur heard the intruder moving towards the front door and the locks drop into place he silently prayed that the look of desperate sorrow on his wife's face, pleading for his forgiveness, was not the last look she would ever give him.

Chapter 12

"Aaaahhhhhh. That's bleddy bootiful thadis."

The Premiums watched as Gareth sank his pint in two large gulps and swapped the empty glass for a full one. After taking a much smaller sip, he considered the glass in his hand.

"The main difference you see, once you geddover the additional quality, taste an' care tha's gone into its creation compared to yours," he waved dismissively at the barely-started pints of lager his workmates were cradling, "is ale has considerably less gas in it, which means I dun't practically explode after a couple a mouthfuls." He smiled at the group.

It was always the same after a hard day's graft shifting other people's stuff. Finish the job, collect the tip if one was forthcoming, which more often than not it wasn't, and then head straight to their local pub for a relaxing evening of getting drunk. It didn't even really matter whether the removal had gone well or badly, the one thing they all wanted once the last box had been dropped was a pint.

Dominic raised his glass.

"Here's to a relatively successful day with almost no major fuck-ups." The rest of The Premiums raised their pints to the centre of the table and chinked.

"Apart from the cat shit," The Fuzz reminded everyone.

"And the torn sofa," added Weasel helpfully.

"Not to mention that undisclosed crash from the back as we pulled up outside the new house," said Gravy. "You know, that really big one that sounded like crockery smashing?"

"And that wall I accidentally demolished," contributed Gareth, reflecting on the three-foot-high wall he had managed to back into and then through, while doing a three-point turn outside a school in Clapham. Thankfully it hadn't been playtime and none of the kids had been struck by falling masonry, or the back of the van.

Dominic considered the litany of errors from throughout the day.

"Well I did say relatively successful," he said after taking a moment to reflect. "And it's the best we've managed in recent memory. As long as we don't get hauled in front of O'Connell tomorrow morning I think we're scot-free."

The Premiums all took another large swallow from their beers in agreement, taking pleasure, for them, in a job well done—or at least as well done as they could manage.

"So whason for tonight then?" Gareth asked, looking around the group with mischief writ large on his face. "Oo's up for a bidof dwarf tossing? I saw a sign furit outside the Green Dragon on the high street. And," he added looking at the slight frame of Weasel, "the evening comes fully catered as far as little people are concerned." He smirked at the respondent raised middle finger from Weasel at the inference.

"I have to be honest, they freak me out," Gravy said in his cultured tone. The rest of The Premiums stared at Gravy as if a slice of alternate bigoted reality had just slid into place, leaving Gravy completely on his own and visibly riling The Fuzz. "It's all that green hair and Donald Trump tan. And what is it with their incessant singing?" Gravy looked up from the rollie he had been making to a sea of eyes looking at him incredulously. Dominic broke the silence.

"Gravy, those aren't dwarves you're thinking of. They're Oompa-Loompas!"

"I know what an Oompa-Loompa is," Gravy responded indignantly. "That doesn't stop them freaking me out though," he said, placing the roll-up in the corner of his mouth, as if this was his evidentiary proof. The rest of the group looked at each other as Gravy started on another rollie, before once again leaving it to Dominic to point out the hole in Gravy's argument.

"You know that not all dwarves are Oompa-Loompas right? And that Oompa-Loompas aren't real?"

"But all Oompa-Loompas are dwarves are they not?" Gravy asked smugly, "Ergo…"

The silence this time was longer still, only punctuated by the five members of The Premiums not deluded on the subject of dwarves, downing the remainder of their beers and signalling to the barmaid for a fresh round. Eventually The Fuzz succinctly summed up what the others had all been thinking.

"You're a dick," he said before taking the proffered roll-up from Gravy and the pair heading out to join the rest of the smokers on the pavement.

"That was fairly odd," observed Weasel, getting up. "Even for a toff, that was fairly odd." With that he picked up his full pint and crossed the pub to the fruit machine, Otter trailing after him.

"I never know whether he is genuinely very weird or just deliberately taking the piss out of us."

"My vote goes for 'im being both," replied Gareth. "That aside, whaddaya reckon? You've 'ad a face like a slapped arse most of the day and a little light entertainment might be just what you need."

Dominic sighed as he took another sip of his beer.

"I don't know mate. What with everything that's happened over the last couple of days and the whole Beth thing, I think I may just head home and get my mind straight. I think I really need to sort my life out." Dominic looked across the table at Gareth hoping that this heartfelt declaration amongst the obvious madness of a conversation with Gravy would move his friend to be lenient with him.

"Alright mate, I understand that," Gareth said, patting Dominic's hand across the table. "Yer life's a fuckin' mess. You live at 'ome wi' yer mum in yer sister's bedroom surrounded by *The Incredibles* and you've just turned thirty. You work a dead-end job with a variety of misfits and yer boss hates yer fuckin' guts. You've finally found a woman you like but her mum beat the crap out of you because you couldn't keep yer 'orny 'ands off 'er tits. If anybody in this world needs to sort their life out, it's you."

Hearing it all laid out so succinctly, Dominic felt even less inclined to go out.

"I didn't know it was her mother. I thought it was Beth and I don't have horny hands," he managed eventually, finding the only spurious element of Gareth's 'This is Your Life' précis of his situation. There was a gleam in Gareth's eye.

"Did you press your erection between 'er bum cheeks?" Gareth's grin was so wide it nearly split his head in two. The deep flush of colour rising up Dominic's face was all Gareth needed and he roared with laughter. "You did, di'n't yer? You dirty bugger. Thas her mum tha' is."

"You don't understand. From behind in the dark they look really similar. And my night vision had gone because of the light in the bathroom."

If anything, Gareth's laugh got even louder. Eventually he regained control of himself. "Bleddy 'ell mate, night vision? You're not a bleddy sniper." He took a swig of his beer as Dominic seethed quietly. "I can't believe you got your arse handed to yer by a woman in 'er fifties no less, Christ alive." he said provocatively, shaking his head sadly.

Dominic knew he was being wound up, knew he should rise above it but couldn't help himself.

"Like I've told you a hundred times, she caught me by surprise."

"She caught *you* by surprise? Well I think we can safely say you're not much of a sexual predator mate," Gareth replied.

"I'm not a sexual predator!" Dominic said a little too loudly. He smiled uneasily at the couple on the next table as they glanced furtively at him. "I'm not a sexual predator, I'm just saying that if I were, I would be better prepared for them to fight back. I'd be anticipating it right? And then be able to deflect and overpower." Dominic waved his hands in front of him in a poor imitation of kung fu. Gareth stared at his friend before roaring with laughter again.

"Bleddy 'ell mate, have you 'eard yourself? It sounds like you're developing a blueprint for becoming a predator. Was this a dry run? You know, work the kinks out yer plan?" He laughed again.

"Oh fuck off, Gareth. You know what I mean," Dominic replied, drawing pictures in the spilled beer on the table.

"Well, whether Beth looks fifty or 'er mum looks thirty, you'll hear no argument from me that you need to sort yer life out." Gareth shuffled round the table until he was next to Dominic, who was staring forlornly into his pint. "But just think," he said, as he put an arm around Dominic's shoulders, "every journey needs a first step, and what bedder first step could there be than watching a very small man being lobbed 'round a pub with carefree abandon? Huh? You know it makes sense."

Dominic could feel the weight of Gareth's personality, and a fair portion of his moobs, weighing down on him, forcing him to another's will. But the last few days had shone a light on his life that had raised some uncomfortable questions for Dominic. In the face of these questions, dwarf tossing was a new low Dominic wasn't willing to sink to.

"Absolutely not." Unexpected strength and conviction flowed through Dominic's words. "I've just told you how shit my life is and in no way do I consider tossing dwarves at an inflatable Velcro-covered wall improving that situation in any way. Is that even legal in this day and age? I thought 'The Wolf of Wall Street' had put an end to that?"

Gareth raised his hands in acknowledgement to the sincerity of his friend's outburst.

"In poor taste? Possibly. Illegal? I dun't think so. But alright, understood. No dwarf tossing." Dominic relaxed slightly. "But as your friend," Gareth continued, "it would be a dereliction of my duty to let you slink off 'ome and mope around 'bout 'ow shite you are."

"Hold on, I said my life was shit, not that I was shit," Dominic said defensively.

"Ah, potato, tomato. You know what I mean. There's only one thing furit." Gareth and Dominic looked up as the rest of The Premiums headed back to the table, Weasel walking like he was in a Western, his pockets chinking every step he took, as if he were wearing spurs, from his jackpot win. "Tonight, you're all experiencing Gareth's World Famous Crash Course in Real Ale."

Two hours and five pints later, Dominic, Weasel, The Fuzz and Gravy were drunk and discussing all the horrible things they would like to see inflicted on O'Connell as Gareth came back from the bar with another round.

"You know, I don't want him to die, as such," Weasel slurred, "just experience a period of intense pain."

"I'd like to see him licked to within an inch of his life by cats," Gravy offered, gripping the pint glass offered by Gareth. The rest of The Premiums stared at him.

"By cats?" Dominic asked, once again not sure how much was Gravy weirdness or Gravy piss taking. "What, lions and tigers and that?"

"No, domestic." Gravy took a sip of his new beer. "What's this one?" he asked Gareth.

"This is Dry Hump, a cheeky number from the Camel Valley down in my 'ome county," Gareth replied, a big smile on his face. Although the rest of the team were clearly well under the vespers of alcohol's influence, Gareth seemed as unaffected as he had when they arrived.

"What's the percentage?" asked The Fuzz as he tentatively sniffed the drink. "And is this cloudy or am I really pissed?"

"Both," replied Gareth. "An' it's 6.9%." To a man, The Premiums coughed into their Dry Hump. "Whaddaya think Dom?"

Dominic lowered his pint, screwed one eye shut and peered at it warily.

"I think the removal gods are going to make us pay for this tomorrow. More importantly," he turned to Gravy, "what the hell are you talking about, domestic cats?"

"You ever been licked by a domestic cat?" Gravy said, swaying slightly.

"Of course, it's a sign of affection," Dominic replied, inescapably drawn back to the 6.9% pint of cloudy, pending recriminations.

"Wrong," Gravy replied angrily. "They're checking to see how easy you would be to eat. All that licking is just tenderising you, you fool." He stumbled to his feet and leaned across the table, angrily pointing his finger directly into Dominic's face. Gently, but with the inevitability of continental drift, Otter reached up and placed one of his massive hands on Gravy's shoulder and pulled him back into his seat. The flash of anger passed and Gravy took a swig from his cloudy beer as the rest of The Premiums considered cats and flashes of anger. Completely calm again, Gravy continued, "I'm thinking stake O'Connell to the floor, let him dehydrate over a few hours and then release the cats. He'll be in agony in no time and have skin flaying off him shortly after. Perfect."

After a moment's consideration Weasel turned to The Fuzz.

"I don't think he likes cats."

"I think he's an idiot."

A commotion at the bar drew The Premiums' attention. Two doormen were manhandling two men towards the exit to loud proclamations of "It was only a joke" and "Fuck off you fascists!" As the two men were bundled past them, Dominic and Weasel looked back to the bar for the cause of the disturbance. Stood in a tight circle, equal measures of anger and embarrassment on their faces, was a group of dwarfs, seven of them.

"Well it is panto season," Weasel said, pushing his chair back and heading towards the group at the bar.

Dominic watched as Weasel introduced himself and after a few moments of the group shaking their heads and refusing whatever Weasel was offering, he turned around and headed back to their table, the group from the bar following him.

"Budge up everybody," Weasel said, shooing The Premiums down the benches they were sat on, opening up space for the new arrivals. "I'd like to introduce you to the Seven Dwarfs."

The Premiums' jaws dropped and their eyes bulged at Weasel's rudeness. Even Otter looked like he was going to jump down Weasel's throat. It was actually Gareth who voiced what they were all thinking.

"'Ere, bloody 'ell Weasel, wind yer neck in. Dun't be so bleddy rude." Weasel just smirked at him as Gareth turned to the group to apologise. As he did so, the young woman who had sat next to Gareth held her hands up, smiling.

"Don't worry, Casper's just winding you up. We are actually the Seven Dwarfs."

The Premiums paused for a moment taking this new information in.

"Er, couple of things," The Fuzz said, raising a finger, "isn't it a little anti-woke referring to yourselves as the Seven Dwarfs, even though I appreciate there are seven of you, but secondly and way more importantly, who the hell is Casper?"

The Premiums looked from Weasel to the young woman who had spoken. Even through their drunkenness an unmistakable glint had come to all their eyes, except Otter's who still looked shocked.

"Thanks Zoe, I owe you one," Weasel said sarcastically.

She laughed and turned to The Fuzz.

"We really are the Seven Dwarfs. We're in final rehearsals for the panto over the road." The rest of the new arrivals lifted their drinks in a silent toast.

"Oooohhhhh. Snow White and the..." Gareth said, meeting their glasses with his own. "That makes much more sense."

"And to the second point?" The Fuzz asked, exaggerating the motion of turning his head towards Weasel.

Zoe looked at Weasel, unsure what she had walked into. Sighing deeply before downing the last of his pint, Weasel finally looked at The Premiums' expectant faces.

"Zoe and I went to school together." There was a slight pause as they waited for him to elaborate. When it became apparent he wasn't going to, Gareth picked up.

"And at school she and all yer other pals knew you as Casper?" The Premiums looked at each other as if all their Christmases had come at once. "As in the friendly ghost, Casper? That is fuckin' priceless!"

The Premiums fell about laughing as Weasel, christened Casper, pushed his chair back and stood up.

"Screw you all. I'm going to the bar and I'm not buying drinks for any of you twats."

Dominic managed to compose himself as Weasel staggered off and reached his hand across the table towards Zoe.

"I'm sorry it's very rude of me not to introduce myself. I'm Dominic, it's lovely to meet you Zoe."

"Likewise Dominic." Zoe shook his hand. "And these are my friends and fellow cast members."

One by one The Premiums and The Seven Dwarfs introduced themselves. As well as Zoe, who played Yawny, there was Gary (Moody), Claire (Nervy), Peter (Growler), Mark (Jumpy), Stephen (Baldy) and Bryony (Snotty).

"What's with the names?" Dominic asked Peter. "I thought it was Doc, Bashful, Sneezy, that lot."

"Yeah, annoyingly they're Disney trademarks and Disney protects their trademarks litigiously," he replied, drinking from the bottle of beer

Weasel had just bought for him. True to his word he hadn't bought The Premiums a drink.

"Not that friendly a ghost, Casper," Gareth joked, ruffling Weasel's hair as he stood up and headed to the bar.

"And then I had to get the bus home," Dominic finished. They had been drinking together for another hour or so and once the introductions had been done with, the two groups naturally split into their own conversations and the shots had started. Gareth and Dominic had been chatting to Stephen and Bryony, although after the third shot Dominic had been monopolising the conversation somewhat.

"Wow!" exclaimed Stephen sympathetically. "That's a hell of a story." He looked at Bryony who nodded her head in agreement.

"I know. And Beth's been calling, probably to tell me how angry she is. And I really liked her. It's like fate has it in for me," Dominic slurred miserably, swigging from his beer.

"How many times has she called you?" Bryony asked.

"I dunno, seven or eight, plus a couple of texts here and there."

"Now that is terrible." Stephen replied.

"I know, it was clearly an accident, and they're holding it over me." Dominic swayed as he tried to focus on Bryony and Stephen at the same time.

"No, I think you misunderstand me." Stephen leant forward. "It's a terrible story because you're sitting here moping about it. It *was* clearly an accident, and more to the point, Beth has tried to call you multiple times. Those aren't the actions of someone who never wants to see you again, or hasn't seen this for what it is – clearly a mistake. And fabricating your worst-case scenario is just creating and perpetuating your own suffering."

Dominic looked at Gareth to see him nodding in agreement.

"But it's so embarrassing, and her mum broke my nose." Dominic pointed to the black eyes and broken nose just in case they'd forgotten about them. His three companions rolled their eyes.

"Really?" Bryony asked. "Embarrassing? I thought you said you really liked this woman. And you're going to run the risk of losing her just because you're embarrassed and her mum broke your nose? It sounds like you need to get a grip, Dominic, otherwise Beth is definitely going to kick you to the curb," she added, drunkenly sliding a new shot across the table to Dominic. He paused for a second before slamming it.

It was funny the things in life that finally resonate. For years, Dominic's mum had been pestering him about his future. When would he move out, when would he get a proper job, when would he settle down with someone. And then there was his sister, the go-getter. She just took the piss the whole time, pressing his buttons just to wind him up. Even his uni mates saw it for what it was. Every one of them had gone on to at least try to forge a grown-up life for themselves, and although they didn't say it, he knew they thought of him as the screw-up of their year. All of this Dominic knew and had known for years, but it had taken the words of Baldy and Snotty, two of a cadre of non-Disney dwarfs to finally break through the walls of self-denial he had carefully constructed over the years. Still, some trace of the denial remained.

"Yeah well, it's not that easy," he managed. Even he thought it sounded weak.

Stephen and Bryony turned towards him, their eyebrows raised.

"Are you seriously playing the 'life's not easy' card to us? In case you missed it, Bryony was effectively assaulted earlier by those two fucking dickheads, picked up and passed between them like some sort of trophy." Stephen slammed his bottle down on the table in his anger. Bryony rested a hand on his arm in a gesture of placation.

"Each of us has to deal with a huge amount of prejudice and disrespect every single day by idiots who, because we're shorter than average, think we fundamentally don't have the same rights as everyone else," Bryony added. Holding his hands up in surrender, Dominic leant back in his seat.

"I don't mean anything by that. Our situations are very different and mine has a little more complexity to it than I have let you know so far," Dominic slurred. "It's not that I don't appreciate your advice," he added, reaching for Bryony's beer, before its owner slid it gently further away from him. "I know I need to sort things out, and I need to make it ok with Beth, but right now I'm very drunk and I need to go home." Dominic struggled his way to his feet leaning against Gareth and Stephen in the process and unsteadily slung his backpack over his shoulder. "It's been a pleasure to meet you all." He gestured to their new friends who each raised their beer bottles. "And you, I will see tomorrow," he pointed at Gareth, spun on his heels and staggered for the exit.

Chapter 13

Dominic lay in bed, his hands behind his head, looking up at the luminous stars his sister had covered the ceiling with two decades earlier, and which he hadn't as yet been bothered to remove. The happy buzz Gareth's real ale tour had given him had worn off once he walked back into the house.

His cheeks bulged exaggeratedly before a focussed stream of air escaped his lips as he exhaled deeply, an underlying feeling of anxiety growing and still a thousand miles from sleep. He tried to remember the last time walking into the house hadn't produced that feeling. Eventually he settled on coming home at the end of his penultimate term at university. Back then things had been a lot simpler. His lack of a plan and direction hadn't been a problem then as no one he knew had a plan. Not only that but it had still felt like a long time before they would need one. University was all about enjoying yourself under the guise of advancing your education.

Looking back, Dominic found it difficult to comprehend that had been nearly ten years ago. So much and so little had happened in the intervening years that he felt it had flown by yet dragged at the same time. All the decisions he had made during the last ten years had brought him to where he was now: lying in his sister's bed looking up at her stars, unable to sleep.

He didn't have any particular problem with his sister; in fact he was enormously proud of what Lisa had achieved in such a short period of time. But what was that skulking behind the sense of pride? Anger? Jealousy? Resentment? As much as he hated to admit it, even in the confines of his own head, Dominic knew all those feelings were real and although he could honestly stand up and state his pride in his sister, those other emotions had a voice too. Pride in another's achievements is a positive emotion: being happy for someone else is freeing in a way that striving for personal happiness never is. Because it is felt for someone else, it doesn't matter if the resonance of the feeling dims periodically as personal events take precedence. It is of no personal detriment in the way a loss of self-pride would be. But the voices of jealousy and resentment, they have a resonance that cuts through the white noise of life, the constant mental burble that accompanies us all. Jealousy and resentment, like tumours, start small but left unchecked become all-consuming monsters, clouding and shaping thoughts and judgements.

Dominic's legs twitched beneath the duvet—restless legs to match a restless brain. He kicked his heels into the mattress repeatedly, tensing every muscle while he did so in an attempt to discharge the jittery energy.

Of course, once he had identified these feelings it was inevitable that another should come gambolling up to join the party. Shame. He didn't want to feel that way about his sister and it wasn't really her fault, but the way everyone treated him made him believe everyone had completely forgotten the reason he moved home in the first place. Had he not then perhaps she would have had to. And that was why he felt shame. He knew that his sister would have dropped everything had it been necessary but she had only just started at university and he had just finished. It was obviously the right thing for him to do it.

Rolling onto his side brought a photo of his graduation day into his eyeline: him in his mortar board and gown, his mother dressed in pearls and twin set and his father looking pale and drawn. Seeing the picture, Dominic now found it dumbfounding to believe they hadn't noticed at the time, especially as he would go months without seeing his dad so the contrast should have been even more dramatic. Too caught up in the drama of his own life he supposed. When they finally told him, he remembered feeling breathless, shocked to the point of inaction. He couldn't believe it.

That seemed to be a regular occurrence for Dominic—not believing. Not believing it had been ten years, not believing he hadn't changed the wallpaper or the bed covers, not believing he had messed up the best date he had had in years, not believing he was still working in the same job, not believing he hadn't recognised his father's cancer until it had been too late.

It had never been an option that he wouldn't move home. By the time his parents told him, his father was in the final stages of bone cancer and wasn't predicted to last the summer. In the end he held out until just before Christmas. His mum fell to pieces and he had been there to make sure she got through it.

Fast-forward five years and Patricia had come to terms with the loss and had successfully rebuilt her life. Unfortunately, fast-forward five years more and for one reason and another, Dominic still had not. The move home had been so sudden and his father's death come so quickly that Dominic hadn't had the chance to think of where he wanted his life to go. It had become increasingly easy just to let things drift along. A year had flown by, then two and three. Eventually ten years had passed and he was still no nearer to making a success of himself.

Dominic had quickly slipped into the routine of life after his father died. He certainly wouldn't ever admit it out loud, but he had also accepted it as an excuse not to have to be ambitious. His lack of career progression was excusable as a by-product of the difficult circumstances he found himself in. How many times had he said "But what about Mum, who's going to look after her?" That's where the shame came in. Whether consciously or not, he had taken his family's grief and co-opted it as an excuse for mediocrity, as permission to be entirely average. Not that there was anything wrong with average—by definition most people were—but in his sister Dominic had a constant reminder of his wasted potential.

During the same time period, Lisa had channelled her grief into drive. Now she ran her own advertising agency based in Central London. She had just branched out to New York and was being lauded as an innovator in her industry. All that and she was barely twenty-eight.

Now, in the darkness of this prepubescent girl's bedroom, the gentle green glow from the ceiling glinting off Mr Incredible's cheeks, Dominic took stock. Maybe it was the comments from Gareth earlier, perhaps it was the unusual situation between him and Beth, or maybe it was the sagacity of a short-statured stranger in a pub. For any future retellings of the story, Dominic hoped it was the short-statured stranger, they added a certain nuance that the other elements failed to. Whatever it was, Dominic finally understood he needed to make some changes.

Struggling out from under his duvet, his head spinning slightly as he sat up, he peered around the room. He needed to act, needed to take some specific action now the final vestiges of his protective cocoon had been exposed for what it was: a fool's excuse. The only problem, he reflected as his eyes stopped on the digital read out of his alarm clock, was assertive action was limited when you were still half-cut and it was 1 o'clock in the morning. He continued the search of his room, the light from the red digital numbers just enough to make out the room's contents. As he searched, a new feeling became evident to him, swelling and churning inside him, displacing the other emotions like so much flotsam on the face of a tidal wave. He suddenly had the feeling that if he didn't manage to do something positive right now then the opportunity his realisation had offered would pass him by and tomorrow morning he would wake to a long and slow decline to death. The fear rapidly turned to panic as he forced himself to his feet and lurched for the light switch. He had to do something.

With the panic threatening to overwhelm him, his eyes caught sight of a small rectangle of paper on his desk. On it his mother had scrawled a few items she had wanted him to pick up on the way back from work that day and which he had completely forgotten and a note reminding him she was away for the week, but Dominic ignored the note. What he needed was a list.

In the circumstances he found himself in, it was perfectly reasonable to not actually achieve anything—it was 1 in the morning for God's sake—but everyone knew that the next best thing to actually doing something was making a list covering the things it was you wanted to do. His brain reeled as he searched for some blank paper and a pen. *Get a proper job, fix things with Beth (somehow), buy a new bed, change the wallpaper, remove the stars from the ceiling, move out, commit to something.* He was on a roll. If only he could find a pen and blank bloody piece of paper he would be flying and well on his way to happiness. He started sweeping the detritus from his desk onto the floor in the hunt for a humble Bic. Bollocks, he thought, as none was forthcoming. He felt the icy fingers of resignation pierce the lining of his gut. He felt them flex, trying to get a better purchase, eager to claw their way through him, to pull him away from any positive action, to trap him forever in his slow decline. His panic was real and wild as he spun round. All this for a pen, a pencil would do, hell a fucking crayon would be a start. The freezing feeling of failure reached his chest and dropped Dominic to his knees in desperation. He couldn't believe his own weakness, or that this moment, for some reason, resonated with such importance for his future self and happiness. The brief window of self-realisation and critique was closing. He could almost sense the sweet smell of change and possibility receding, the monolith of conformity and mediocrity rising to overshadow his hope. The weight of his own failure pinning him down, squeezing the hope he had momentarily felt from him. He'd failed. His fear and inertia had won out.

Dominic's head slumped to the carpet, utterly defeated. And then, as he turned his head to avoid the suspicious stain, salvation. Slung inconsequentially under his bed he saw his backpack, complete he remembered, with quotation pad and branded Swift & Smooth ball point pen. He could have cried with relief as a renewed hope blossomed and the monolith shrank slightly. He hadn't turned his life around yet, but here was a start. Pulling the bag out he yanked at the zip and forced his arm inside.

"Yes," he stage whispered as he pulled out the quotation pad, threw it on the bed and returned his hand to the bag in search of a pen. He was a little confused when he felt what to the touch seemed like another, smaller quotation pad. Pulling it out he saw immediately it wasn't a pad of anything, but a notebook. Along the top edge of the book, a small cream-coloured corner of paper protruded.

Dominic stared at the book for a while, all thoughts and urgency regarding changing his life momentarily forgotten. Slowly he lifted the cover of the book and watched as the folded cream piece of writing paper slowly slid into his lap. Placing the book gently on the bed next to the quotation pad, Dominic unfolded the piece of paper and started to read. He re-read the letter five times before incredulously turning back to what he now knew to be an old man's diary. Unsure what to make of the letter, Dominic shuffled back onto his bed until his back touched the wall and started to read.

Chapter 14

The initial feedback regarding the attempted recovery of the diary had been disappointing to say the least, Jeff reflected as he sat in his den, enveloped by his adapted leather wingback. He had always looked down his nose at the American style Lazy Boy, hating the vulgarity of the chair's look, feeling it too common, and therefore beneath him. He did however, like to recline. To solve the problem he had purchased an ornate green leather wingback chair and had a reclining mechanism fitted. He now lay forty-five degrees from horizontal, a glass of scotch gripped tightly in his hand, the sound of the ice clinking against the glass as he slowly rolled the liquid, rhythmically marking time as he brooded.

Wilbur had refused, or been unable to deliver the diary, even under the significant persuasive talents of the man Jeff knew as Hank. He had however confirmed there was a diary, which to Jeff's mind was the worst-case scenario. Deep down he had known, right from the moment he had overheard the bimbo at the dinner a few nights previous, that the diary must exist. The confirmation had however provided vindication for Jeff's approach, to the rest of the members of SSoH. Spying on one of their friends had grated badly with his colleagues, especially as the decision had been made on the basis of an overheard conversation. Now they were in possession of the facts, his colleagues had had no choice but to agree with Jeff.

The diary did still need to be recovered however. Hank had been firm and confident that he would be able to retrieve it and already had a lead to follow up on.

Jeff swirled the glass again and surveyed the broken glass in the corner of the room that had once been a fully equipped drinks trolley. The poker lying on top of its shattered remains testament to the surge of rage which had engulfed Jeff following his brief conversation with Hank. The destructive transference of force from his soul to the bottles and glasses had been the only way Jeff could vent his feelings without returning to Wilbur's house and snapping his neck.

He peered around his den at the carnage surrounding him, his one good eye now an empty pit of emotionless reason, his bad eye hidden behind the patch just an empty pit. Damn, he thought as the extent of the damage swam into focus now the red mist had been burned away. In hindsight he should have smashed up Wilbur's house and belongings. This clearly didn't hurt anybody but him. Bloody uncontrolled rage. He corrected himself; bloody partially-controlled rage, he had after all not snapped Wilbur's neck.

He hadn't expected Wilbur to crumble and admit everything, but having been caught red-handed he had expected a little more respect. The barefaced lies he had been told that afternoon showed that, even after all this time, Wilbur clearly had none for him. The insistence that the Forthrights were merely looking to "de-clutter" by having a few things placed in storage when asked what Swift & Smooth were doing there, had lit the fire. Wilbur's refusal then to admit there was a written record of the SSoH's activities over the previous four decades, kindling to the fire. His blatant inability to explain his comment to that dim-witted, big-titted bitch at the awards dinner the accelerant transforming Jeff's smouldering anger into a conflagration large enough to consume all in its path.

Jeff looked at the whiskey glass as the roll of his wrist failed to elicit the expected clink. He had been sat there reviewing his thoughts so long the ice had melted without him having taken a single sip. Reaching for the button that would raise his chair to the vertical, Jeff wondered what had changed for Wilbur to cause this betrayal of his brothers. They had all known what they were getting themselves into all those years ago and all had become richer than they could have ever hoped for. Yes, there had been a price to pay but on the balance of things a price worth paying. With the chair having inched its way to vertical, Jeff stood up on legs made jelly-like with adrenaline, and stumbled to the liquor trolley. Pouring from the only bottle to survive, he gave himself an additional three fingers of whiskey and two more ice cubes, then left the den.

The reassuring clink of the ice returned as he walked through the ground floor corridor of his stately home, his moleskin-soled slippers adding only a slight whisper as he moved. He passed through the main reception hall of the house, silent as a ghost. The first room to the right of the staircases was the library. A magnificent room packed corner to corner with floor-to-ceiling bookcases, the requisite rolling ladder attached to a rail high above him. Jeff paused for a moment in the centre of the room. There was no denying he was a traditionalist in almost every way. Except that is in his approach to his profession. He prided himself on his blue-sky thinking (and his adoption of management speak) when it came to brewing but in all other matters he was straight down the line.

The room was a testament to Jeff's avid research and determination to create a library worthy of a nineteenth-century viscount. Around the large room, small tables were scattered, each with an ornate green glass shaded light stand. Deep carpets covered the floor, adding to the sound absorbing effect of the books themselves. Low leather chairs provided ample space for perusing whatever tome a visitor fancied and of those there were thousands. Jeff allowed himself a small smile. Tradition, essential in understanding who one was, he thought, and how to achieve what one wanted. He ran his hand along the spines of the books on the closest shelf. Half way along the shelf he stopped, his hand on a book that looked very much like all the others. Jeff's index finger tapped the leather bound spine affectionately and looked at the title, 'The London and Country Brewer' (1736), an early English book containing information and processes to anyone who could read, with the sole aim of eliminating bad beer. Jeff had amassed a large collection of original first-edition manuscripts surrounding the brewing profession from as far back as the mid-fifteen hundreds, but it was this one that matched his own raison d'etre so simply that it had become his favourite.

Gently running his finger up the spine he hooked the first joint over the top. He paused long enough to take his first large swallow from the tumbler of amber liquid and pulled his finger back.

The book slid easily toward him a few centimetres before it became apparent the base was stuck. Jeff pulled the top further out, eventually feeling resistance. With a modicum more effort, there was a satisfying click and the book stopped completely. Five metres along the wall another click was followed by the well-oiled sound of cogs engaging and turning. As Jeff drank deeply, a complete section of bookshelves receded from the formal line set by the rest of the room, and withdrew some eighteen inches. Once fully retracted, a second set of gears quietly engaged and the bookshelf smoothly shifted left, finally coming to rest behind its neighbouring shelves.

Jeff smiled to himself again as one by one, low-level lights flickered into life, gradually illuminating a half-helical staircase dropping away down a stone stairwell, the tightness of the stairs preventing anyone seeing what lay beyond. Tradition, he thought. You couldn't have a library like this without a secret compartment activated by a specific book of personal importance, especially when you were the founding member of a secret society. It was tradition. Jeff grabbed the handrail and started the long descent.

At the bottom of the stairs the space opened up into a large red-brick room with cavernous arched ceilings. It had originally been part of the old sewers that ran through the area but Jeff had had it adapted. Now it provided a completely private place for Jeff and the other members of SSoH to work. The main area of the room was taken up with vast barrels and fermenting chambers and vats for the cooking of hops. Convoluted pipework connected one chamber with another, allowing evaporated liquid to condense before being heated again, its journey continuing through yet more pipes, each time leaving ever smaller particles and impurities behind, eventually arriving in a final chamber for the fermentation. An elevated walkway ran around the room above the vats and pipes allowing access to the top of the equipment.

In the far corner of the room was an antique-looking lift. It would slowly crank its way up the shaft, arriving at ground level in a shed at the back of Jeff's property, allowing for the easy delivery of ingredients, both traditional and more "exotic".

Hopmen Breweries owned a production site in South London, which produced their high-volume beers. Millions of pints of high-quality real ale for clients and punters the world over were brewed and delivered every year. Each founding member of the SSoH and brewery had a standard named after them: One-Eyed Jeff, Silent Clap, Stuck in the Mud, Chopstick Grip, Shout Louder and Hopalong—each of them hugely successful in their own right. So successful were they that their competitors were always trying to steal their secrets by infiltrating the brewery with spies. Copies of their six standards could be found everywhere, but it wasn't the standards that made Hopmen Brewery famous, and the founding members rich beyond the dreams of avarice. It was the Specials that made the headlines; it was the Specials that their competitors wanted so badly, and it was the Specials that required Jeff's unique approach.

Far beneath the cellar of Jeff's mansion, housed in the cathedral-like, high-arched grandeur of the converted Victorian sewers were the only incubators that would know the secrets and deliver the Specials. They were only ever made here, in limited volumes and only ever by the six members of SSoH. No other soul, not even Jeff's wife, God rest her soul, or house keeper had ever entered SSoH's inner sanctum. Never had one of their beers failed to win an award. As a result, the large drinks companies were desperate to emulate them, churning out beer after beer in an attempt to capture the magic, and sales, of the Hopmen Brewery Specials. But they had all failed to match the sublime taste and smoothness of the speciality ales. They all had something missing.

But, as well as the fantastic taste, it was Jeff's marketing and the SSoH's decision to keep each Special to a limited run that ensured their success. They had followed Ferrari's approach to its cars. Ferrari had reasoned that if they thought they could sell 500 of a particular car then they would only make 499, thus always ensuring there was an unfulfilled demand. Jeff had therefore insisted on only brewing in limited volumes and once the beer was gone there would be no more. It had worked fantastically well with the public taking to each of their beers like crack addicts desperate for the next limited edition run. Each Special sold out within hours of being announced, the very fact the public knew the run would be limited and never repeated, guaranteeing the products sold regardless of the price. And the next one, scheduled for a little under a month's time, had already sold out before the first hop had been steeped.

The vats were empty at present, no alchemical-like percolation taking raw ingredients and turning them into a refined finished product as yet. The burners were cold and the presses sat open like baby birds waiting to be fed. The barrels sat waiting expectantly for Jeff's next foolproof guaranteed idea. Next to the vats was a small bottling station where the first 60 test pints would be prepared before being sent to the other members of SSoH for quality testing. Above the bench was an ever-growing line of labels, one each for every batch that was passed fit for distribution.

Jeff ran his eye along the line: Lurcher's Last Stand, Grouchy Goat, Posturing Pig, Cat's Curiosity, Penguin's Prerogative, Nun's Chuff, Bambi's Nightmare, Badger's Attitude, Lion's Mange, Soused Stoat, Betrothed Bat, Melodious Mink, Chimp's Cabaret, Budgie Smugglers, Lounge Lizard. Every one had been an unbridled success.

Jeff looked around at his subterranean domain. This was what his life was about; this was the source of his success and place in society. Many had tried to learn his secrets over the years and all had failed. It was only now, coming towards the end of his career that he and the rest of SSoH were exposed—and by one of their own members no less.

This was what Jeff had needed. After his rage had burned out he had felt empty. Unsure for the first time in his life what he should do, incapable of making the decisive decisions necessary to protect himself. In short, he had felt old and impotent in a way that not even one of Wilbur's blue pills could help. But now, having come down here, having revisited the centre of creation for his whole world, he had seen the light. Looking at the proud history of the brewery, those names still mentioned by punters across the country and around the world, longingly wishing for another taste, he knew what he had to do. He had to fight and, unfortunately for the diary's author, that meant Wilbur had to be dealt with. In the short term he needed the diary and in the long term he needed Wilbur and his conscience to no longer pose a threat, however that had to be attained.

Jeff rested a hand on one of the presses, a plan now assembling itself, as he stood amongst the tools of his success. Now he had made the decision to act, he was happy again, the destruction that awaited him upstairs all but forgotten. As he climbed the staircase back to the library he couldn't help his thoughts expanding. Wilbur posed a specific threat and had to be dealt with but he wasn't the only one who knew the intricacies of the SSoH. There were four other members of the organisation who could cause Jeff just as much damage as Wilbur. In the beginning he had felt he needed them, but now they had created such momentum that all that was needed were the new ideas and their reputation would take care of the rest. Jeff was the ideas man; Jeff was SSoH.

As he waited for the bookcase to slide back into place behind him, he reached into his pocket for his phone. He clicked on the email icon. The diary first, he thought as he typed **Help Wanted** into the subject bar. Hank had said he had a lead and Jeff was keen to ensure no time was lost. He didn't think Hank would hang around as the diary would almost certainly contain information about him, but Jeff wanted to be sure. He would deal with Wilbur himself. Once the immediate threat had been dealt with, he would make a decision regarding the other four. Dealing with Wilbur and the book, before they went into production of the next limited edition batch, was critical. As Jeff hit send he stared out of the library window, his one good eye darker than the pre-dawn night.

Chapter 15

There was something indescribably pathetic about a grown man tied to a chair wearing nothing but his Y-fronts, tears pouring from his eyes as he tried not to choke on his own socks.

It was the sort of situation O'Connell would have found amusing, assuming of course, it was someone else in the chair. He no doubt would have postulated on the relative weakness, the lack of awareness demonstrated by the individual, in finding himself in such a compromising position. He would most certainly never have been caught out so easily as he had a sixth sense for things and would undoubtedly have noticed an atmospheric change that would alert him to any pending danger. All of these things and more would have fallen from his lips in an attempt to impress whoever was unfortunate to be near him. Danger, he would have added, had a smell and feel all to itself, which anybody as au fait with it as he was, living his life as he did—on the edge—couldn't fail to notice and take the necessary action to avoid.

Of course, that all seemed rather redundant now, as he peered through his tears, trying to make out where he was, who had brought him here and what they wanted.

The previous hour had perfectly illustrated to O'Connell that while he spent some of his time outside the confines of legality, he was in no way prepared or cut out for the darker side of a criminal's lifestyle. Before this evening he had thought himself a player: swaggering around as if he owned everything, exuding contempt for everyone. As a big guy he found it easy to intimidate those people he worked and played golf with and assumed he was therefore "well 'ard". What he had failed to understand, and had received an explicit lesson in earlier, was that the people he intimidated were all law-abiding citizens who through social conditioning shied away from confrontation and the threat of violence. The men who had brought him here, via a good kicking in the back of a van, exhibited neither of those characteristics.

Now, tied to an uncomfortable metal chair by his ankles and wrists, blood dripping from his nose and his lips swelling, O'Connell tried to blink the tears away and assess what the hell was happening to him. He could make out two powerful halogen lamps on stands and, from the two shadows cast diagonally to the left and right in front of him, deduced there must be two more lamps behind him, holding him in the middle of a square. Above him he could just make out black metal rails, criss-crossing the ceiling and just outside the circle of light provided by the lamps he thought he could see white tiled walls. His main concern, and the thing demanding his attention the most, was the large drain set into the floor just in front of him and the three deep channels that led to it.

His heart was pounding as he heard muffled voices outside of what he now thought of as his protective circle of light; protective because while he was in it on his own he was ok. His terrified mind skipping over the myriad possibilities available to someone who wanted to hurt him from the darkness. A gun for instance, or a long pole with something sharp attached to it.

He picked up the sound of rattling as the tears began to flow again and looked up at the track above him. A dull glint flashed at him as the huge meat hook rattled to a stop just in front of him. Oh fuck, he thought, this is an abattoir.

"Good evening Mr O'Connell."

The voice behind him grabbed his attention, but he was unable to turn and see who it belonged to.

"I would say I hope you're feeling comfortable but I think we both know your comfort is the last thing I'm interested in."

O'Connell became aware of a figure slowly moving round, through his peripheral vision, eventually stopping directly in front of him, from his waist down illuminated in the light from the lamps, his upper body still shrouded in darkness.

"What I am interested in," the voice continued, "is your knowledge of a certain property in Caterham and its owners, a Mr and Mrs Forthright."

The voice had remained behind him, which meant there were at least two of them. The figure in front of him let something slip through his hand and O'Connell watched as another large steel meat hook hit the ground with a clunk. He struggled against his bonds, desperately trying to loosen the knots, so he could free his hands at least, with absolutely no idea what he would do if he managed it. After a few moments of futile effort, the voice was back accompanied by an unpleasant snigger from the man in front of him.

"Calm down Alfie. You don't mind if I call you Alfie do you? Seeing as we're going to become such good friends." The voice was moving around the circle of light, its owner eventually coming to stand next to the first man. On an unnoticed cue both men stepped forward into the light for the first time and O'Connell got his first glimpse of his abductors. On first inspection there was little to differentiate them from each other. Both were dressed head to toe in black from their black trainers and jeans, to their black jumpers with matching gloves and balaclavas. It was only after a few moments, as the shock began to wear off, that he could make out differences at all. The one with the meat hook was fractionally taller and his eyes were odd: one blue and one milky white. The other man, the one who had so far done all the talking, walked closer to O'Connell and crouched so he could look directly into his face. All he saw was a pair of emotionless eyes staring at him.

"Now, this is going to go one of two ways. Either it's going to go easy, you're going to answer all our questions to our satisfaction quickly and honestly, in which case you'll leave here basically in the same state you're in now, give or take. Or," he signalled to his accomplice who stepped forward and placed the sharp hook under O'Connell's left nipple. "Don't look at that. Look right here." The masked man indicated to his own eyes as O'Connell involuntarily kept returning to stare at the hook. "Or my colleague is going to show you what it's like to be a heifer in this plant and then we'll hose your remains away before we leave. Do you understand me?"

O'Connell's eyes were out on stalks and he could feel his heart thumping away in his chest, practically see the tip of the hook waver with each beat as his chest thundered at one hundred and seventy beats a minute. O'Connell managed to nod his head.

"So you understand me. That's good. Do you believe me?" O'Connell's head nodded desperately. "Because I can arrange a demonstration if you're unsure." He turned to his colleague who imperceptibly moved the tip of the hook against O'Connell's chest. O'Connell screamed as the razor sharp tip pierced his flesh, the socks in his mouth muffling his cries, his two captors staring at him.

"I'll take that as a yes," Hank replied. He didn't particularly enjoy this part of the job. Not like Razor, who loved any opportunity to inflict pain on another living thing. Hank thought of himself as more creative than that. But he also knew that there came a time in his walk of life when you had to crack a few skulls and he had ensured he had a capable partner to do so. He waited until the cries from O'Connell subsided. "Are you done?" A feeble nod was all his captive could manage. "Ok. Time for some answers." With that, he pulled the socks from O'Connell's mouth.

O'Connell gasped, like a fish out of water, desperately trying to get enough oxygen into his lungs. As he panted the tears came again, blood and snot mingling as they dribbled over his split lips.

"Question one, do you know who I am?"

O'Connell shook his head vigorously and muttered "No, no, no, no."

Hank considered this for a moment. "You mean to tell me that you have so many dealings with bad people that the list is too exhaustive for you to make a guess at who we are? Wow, maybe I underestimated you." Hank nodded his head slightly and Razor twisted the hook still piercing O'Connell's chest.

His scream bounced around the room, echoing from corner to corner as the blood flowed from his chest, down his torso and started pooling around his feet. He was desperate for his screams to be heard by someone outside, for them to raise the alarm and the police come and rescue him. But he knew there was no chance of that; this clearly wasn't the first time these two men had done this.

"Ok, I'll help you with that one. You sent me a job earlier today. Do you remember that? A house in Caterham, owned by a Mr Forthright. Ringing any bells?"

A seed of understanding sprouted in O'Connell's terrified mind. Of course, this was **From A-B**, or at least the man at the other end of the email. Who else could it have been? He didn't make a habit of knocking around with gangsters, regardless of what he let people think. It wasn't

From A-B who had underestimated O'Connell, it was the other way round. He had never considered he would be in any danger other than possibly from the police. Now he realised he was completely out of his depth. O'Connell saw his questioner turn to his crazy-eyed accomplice, that small gesture sufficient to galvanise him to action.

"No, no, no, wait, wait, wait. I remember, I do." He was babbling but at least the meat hook had not pierced further into his chest.

"And?" Hank asked.

"It was a job we quoted for, um, earlier today. There was a short timeframe on it. They wanted to know how quickly we could do the job for them." O'Connell looked pleadingly into Hank's eyes.

"Anything else?"

O'Connell didn't know what to say. He'd never been tortured for information before but was very keen to please Hank.

"Nothing unusual. I saw they had a lot of things that we can sell on and make a few quid. You know, just like we normally do." He looked from one balaclava to the other, desperate for some indication he was pleasing them.

"The problem I have Alfie, is that your email wasn't the first one I had today about that very same house." Hank watched O'Connell's reactions carefully. He had always been good at reading people, the moment earlier in the evening when Wilbur Forthright had deceived him a rarity. Currently all he was getting from O'Connell was blank incomprehension and fear. "Two jobs, from two separate clients, focussing on the same house. Now that makes me a little suspicious, especially considering the importance I have now attached to the first job." He paused a moment, weighing up the situation. O'Connell watched him, keen to please, if only his captor would ask something he knew the answer to.

"What do you know about a diary?" Again, Hank watched O'Connell carefully, but once again there was no sign of concealment as he denied any knowledge of the diary, only excrement, his captive having voided his bowels at some point. That was two for two from Razor in the last thirty-six hours. If he ever chose to retire from the life he could hire himself out as an alternative to laxatives.

"Ok, let's try a different tack. What did you make of the Forthrights?"

"What?" O'Connell responded, lack of understanding writ large across his swollen face.

"The Forthrights, how did they seem to you? Were they agitated or seem nervous? Or were they relaxed? Did you think they were hiding something? Anything at all."

A look of relief flashed across O'Connell's face as he realised he could finally answer a question, and in a way that he hoped wouldn't incriminate him. "I don't know, I didn't go, I sent one of the guys from one of my teams over there. They were doing a job in Caterham already, so it made sense. Had I known it was as important as it is I would have gone myself."

Hank thought this through. O'Connell hadn't done the job himself. That made sense, what with O'Connell being COO, you would have minions to do the grunt work.

"Ok. Who did, and more importantly, where do they live?"

Another question O'Connell could answer, and this one he was happy to provide all the details he could think of. Like a drowning man thrown a lifeline, O'Connell grabbed the opportunity with both hands. The faintest glimmer of light appeared; perhaps he would get out of this, mostly in one piece, and if he could direct these psychopaths towards Dominic, all the better. He told Hank all about The Premiums, highlighting each of the team's faults and weaknesses in painstaking detail, paying particular attention to his character assassination of Dominic.

Hank listened carefully, taking everything in. He had seen the effect fear could have on people and O'Connell's reaction to a question he finally knew the answer to confirmed his lack of knowledge to Hank's previous questions. It also confirmed O'Connell was a survivor, and a ruthless one at that. Hank couldn't help wondering whether there was more to his dislike of his employees, and this Dominic guy in particular, than he was letting on. He was obviously aware of what the outcome of this conversation was likely to be for his employee and clearly couldn't care less. Hank had to stop himself telling him to shut up at one point as the inconsequential drivel continued; you never knew when a nugget of gold would get washed ashore through the tidal wave of shit. It was at the mention of Beth that Hank congratulated himself on his patience. He now had some leverage should the conversation he was shortly to be having with Dominic not prove as fruitful as he required. Now he just needed to decide what to do with O'Connell. After a few moments he turned back to the bound man.

"Thank you Alfie, you've actually been very helpful. Now this is going to hurt you considerably more than it will me. Razor."

Chapter 16

The clock on the wall of the crew room showed 8.50, the world momentarily passing through one of the timepiece's twice daily instances of accuracy. The four other teams had long departed for their Concourse la Pit du Merde or Boulevard Magnifiques, leaving half of The Premiums slouched on the grubby and torn chairs, reading very old copies of Nuts magazine. Weasel was trying to coax some life from the old and battered kettle as Gravy and The Fuzz poured over the featured and scantily-clad soap star.

"Well that's knackered," Weasel finally concluded, clicking the button on and off repeatedly. Restless, he looked around the room for something to distract himself with. Ordinarily they would have booted up the decrepit PC and played solitaire but the ancient machine had disappeared, to be replaced with a note stating that *"All quotes and company specific correspondence must now be processed via one of the Scheduling Department's terminals."* Beneath the two lines of text was a signature of sorts, *"by order of Alfred O'Connell, COO."*

This wasn't the only change to the crew team's basement realm. Printed large and attached prominently on the rear fire escape was another notice, also by order of the COO, stating that any disconnection of the alarm or use of the fire escape, except during an actual building evacuation, would henceforth be considered a sackable offence.

Weasel looked around the crew room, ignoring the request to provide a score for the buxom women puckering her lips at him from the proffered centrefold, and sighed. This place had always been a craphole but now the company were really taking the piss. No internet—no matter how slow—and no bloody tea. They were removal men for God's sake. Without a constant supply of tea they were like diabetics without insulin, twitchy and useless. To assuage his ever-increasing feeling of hopelessness he turned to the wall of happiness and the solace of Linda Lusardi and Sam Fox. A blank wall stared back at him, an oblong patch of paintwork, slightly less faded than the rest of the wall the only evidence to the 80's Page 3 calendar that had survived more than three decades, but was now no more. Weasel could feel the tide inside him turn. This was too much. O'Connell, already considered to be a massive tool, had gone too far this time. It was one thing to take their internet connection away. It was further, almost suicidal provocation to leave them without adequate access to PG Tips. But to throw away the embodiment of 80's big-boobed, glam-rock soft porn was tantamount to sloshing a can of petrol around the room and lighting a match: nothing good could come of it.

"Bastards," Weasel shouted, finally dragging The Fuzz and Gravy's attention away from the out of date magazine, pointing to the scene of the crime.

"Where's Linda?" The Fuzz asked, finally understanding Weasel's outburst and jumping to his feet.

"Bloody gone, that's where," Weasel replied indignantly. "I tell you, they can only push us so far."

"Who can only push us so far and why din't one of you buggers open the back door? I 'ad to come in through the main entrance. Everyone was staring at me like they ent never seen a Cornishman before," Gareth asked as he momentarily filled the doorway before crashing down on the seat vacated by The Fuzz.

"Bloody O'Connell, that's what happened," The Fuzz replied pointing to the blank wall to illustrate how far he had been pushed. "And he's made using the fire escape a sackable offence."

"Alright, calm down. Stick the kettle on will yer?" he asked, rubbing his face.

"It doesn't bloody work," Weasel shouted, the annoyance at no one else getting so worked up at what he saw as an erosion of their workers' rights finally becoming too much.

"He's been banging on about one thing or another for over an hour now," Gravy said, completely indifferent to Weasel's mutterings.

Gareth looked about the room, slight confusion furrowing his brow at the lack of boobs and tea. Eventually formulating what was really bothering him he asked,

"Why 'aven't we been sent on a job yet and where's Dominic?"

The three members of The Premiums present all looked at each other and shrugged.

"Dunno. We thought once all the other teams had left that we must be in for a bollocking from O'Connell but so far we haven't heard anything," The Fuzz said. "We haven't seen Dominic yet this morning, we thought he would be with you. Anyway, why are you late and where's Otter?"

A mischievous grin split Gareth's bearded face and the glint returned to his eyes.

"Otter's just followin' me in." He indicated to the corridor outside where the big Pole could be heard making his way towards them. "Otter an' I got chatting to a couple of lovely ladies in the pub last night after you all left. Flatmates it turned out, and man, could they put it away." Gareth leant forward in his seat and raised an eyebrow at The Fuzz. "And I ain't just talking 'bout beer either."

Before The Fuzz could react, Otter came into the room to find himself the focus of attention. A naturally shy man, he tried to make himself as small as possible—not an easy feat if your starting point was six and a half feet with a frame that could rival The Rock's.

"O'Connell's not in either. His car's not in the car park and 'is office is empty," Gareth continued. "It's not like Dominic to be late though. Has anyone tried calling 'im?" The Premiums looked at each other and shook their heads, the wonders of modern technology seeming to evade their simple minds. "Maybe I'll try that then," Gareth said, giving Otter a conspiratorial wink. The embarrassment flushing Otter's face momentarily lifted and was replaced with a shy smile, he and Gareth now inextricably linked via the previous evening's shenanigans.

Pulling out his phone, Gareth scrolled through his recent call list. Selecting Dominic's number he turned to Gravy while he waited for the call to connect.

"Do me a favour and get upstairs and see if the planning team 'ave a job for us. We can get Dominic to meet us there."

Gravy headed out of the crew room and Gareth waited patiently for Dominic to pick up. He had been in quite a bad way the previous evening, what with the beer and the admonishing assessment of his life by two complete strangers, and Gareth was becoming a little concerned as the phone rang and rang.

Why the hell did people set their phones to ring more than ten times before diverting to voicemail? Surely if someone was going to answer the bloody thing, a maximum of ten rings was sufficient, and if they weren't then ten rings was too many. As Gareth passed the twenty ring point he made a mental note to discuss mobile phone etiquette with his friend: a short number of rings subsequently diverting to a personalised voicemail message. That way you could phone a number of times—the greater the number of missed calls, the greater the urgency for contact. Simple. At this rate Gareth could probably walk to Dominic's house before this bloody thing diverted. Eventually, after nearly thirty unanswered rings, he was welcomed to an answerphone service for the number he had dialled and would he like to leave a message after the tone.

"Dominic, it's Gareth 'ere mate. Gimme a call soon as you can. We're all just stood 'ere waiting for you to get in. Um, O'Connell's not around either so you're ok from that point. Anyway, gi' us a shout. Cheers."

Gareth disconnected the call just as Gravy came back into the crew room.

"Good news boys. Looks like we've got the day off. Nothing on the books for us today."

Everyone else in the room muttered their annoyance. No work meant no pay, Gravy being the only one unaffected by it. Sensing rather than understanding the annoyance, he continued.

"There is more good news. Firstly, procurement have agreed to provide us with a new kettle. Apparently, as the rest of the building can make tea and coffee so too should we be able to. Unfortunately there's bad news as well. Apparently the calendar was in direct contravention of the company's Equal Opportunities policy or Political Correctness policy, or something, and cannot be returned or replaced. The crew room is now a boob-free zone, except possibly Gareth, and those are more moobs really."

Gareth threw a cushion across the room and hit Gravy in the face, his moobs wobbling slightly at the effort.

"But that's not all," he continued. "Apparently O'Connell's gone missing." At this, The Premiums all looked up, alert and truly interested for the first time. "Apparently there is a big board meeting this morning with some would-be investors and O'Connell is nowhere to be found. He hasn't rung in, won't answer his phone, isn't responding to emails, nothing."

"How do you know that?" asked The Fuzz.

"Well some of us have learnt how to talk to people The Fuzz, without making them feel scared for their wellbeing or personal possessions. Some of us can even talk to girls. I bumped into O'Connell's secretary Nancy rushing around and she told me."

The Premiums sat in silence contemplating what might have happened to their nemesis.

"Maybe he's had an accident, or a heart attack," suggested Weasel, failing to keep the sound of hope from his voice.

"Or maybe he's been kidnapped and beaten," added The Fuzz. "Or," his eyes wide as a lightning bolt of an idea struck him. "Or, maybe he's kidnapped Dominic. We all know he hates him. I wouldn't put it past him."

It was a measure of their opinion of O'Connell that none of them felt this idea should be immediately dismissed. Gareth sat stroking his beard thoughtfully. In the absence of their official team leader, the remaining Premiums deferred the decision making to Gareth, watching and waiting as he turned things over. Eventually he got to his feet and headed to the door.

"Well, there's nothin' for us to do 'ere. I reckon we 'ead over to Dominic's and make sure he's ok." With that he made straight for the fire exit, launching the doors open to the sound of the ear-splitting alarm, and headed for his car. Behind, The Premiums scrambled to collect their things and followed him outside before anyone could arrive and sack them.

Chapter 17

The swirling blue lights had long been extinguished and the frantic battle to beat the flames lost. Very rapidly the fire crews had understood this would have to be a containment job. The fire had been too strong, had too great a grip on the building by the time they arrived, devouring the structure in huge bites. Softening the support beams in one room, rushing through the resultant void once they inevitably lost the fight and crashed to the floor, desperately seeking more fuel to sate its rapacious appetite.

Ten hours the crews battled the fire. All the time protecting the cordon surrounding the property, gaining ground on it as its life source was consumed, leaving less and less fuel to sustain it, its eventual demise hastened by its fierce growth. Now the tenders were retreating to their stations, their firefighters exhausted. Leaving behind nothing but the shattered and charred remains of what had once been Wilbur and Mabel Forthright's home.

The ambulance was next to leave. None of the urgency and hastened activity that was usually required; their cargo in no danger of becoming any more dead if the paramedics lingered over a conversation for another minute or two. Two bodies, one body bag, fused together in the intense heat as they clung to each other in a final eternal embrace.

Once the ambulance had pulled away, all that was left was the Fire Investigation Team to comb through the remains of the ruins, to piece together the events of the previous night and discern how the tragedy had occurred: a careless cigarette, faulty electrics, a cooking accident or worse, foul play. It wouldn't be easy as the fire had been truly ferocious and destroyed nearly all in its path.

As the investigation team commenced their work, careful not to trigger any further collapses of the remaining structure, the crowd of onlookers who had gathered through the night began to disband, returning to the homes they had been evacuated from or merely continuing about their days, saddened by the loss of life yet thankful they had survived unscathed.

With a final glance in the rear-view mirror, the brake lights of the black Range Rover glowed. A brief flash of the white reversing lights before the red glow faded and the vehicle slowly rolled forward, picking up speed before cresting the brow of the small hill and disappearing from view.

Wilbur's dead man's switch had failed.

Chapter 18

How many Premiums can you fit in a Fiat Uno? Five, but only just, especially when one of them is Gareth and one of them is the man mountain, Otter. The lack of space, combined with the morning-after effects of the team's post-work relaxation method, and the forty minute drive from Swift & Smooth's head office to Dominic's house, had become an Endurance-style test of stamina. The scream accompanying the onset of cramp necessitated a large breath, filling the lungs with the fetid flatulence-laced air. And like the 80's Japanese television show that so popularised sadism, the car journey would really have only been fun for anyone not actually involved.

During the dash across the car park, Weasel had called 'shotgun', irrespective of the logical approach being to have the two largest men, Gareth and Otter in the front. Gareth, as driver, obviously warranted one of the seats but Weasel was adamant on his claim for the second. Additionally, The Fuzz refused to sit next to Gravy, who had wound him up by saying he ran like a girl, leaving the only solution, as Weasel still refused to relinquish his claim on a front seat, being to have the tallest and widest Premium sat in the middle, squashing the two smaller men against the sides of the car and completely obstructing the view out the back. Gareth couldn't remember the last time he had had to use first gear so much once the Uno had actually started moving, but the weight in the back forced the thimble-sized engine to struggle heroically against the inertia. With the mechanisms for lowering the windows having seized up, and the heater stuck on full blast, The Premiums turned into Dominic's road not a moment too soon and in a very sorry state. More worrying still was the fact that Dominic was still incommunicado.

As Gareth pulled up outside the house Dominic shared with his mother, there was a mad panic from the three rear passengers and Weasel, who had spent the whole of the journey with boney knees imbedded firmly in his lower back, barely made it out with his head still on his shoulders, as The Fuzz was seemingly catapulted out of the car the second the front seat was pulled forward. He lay on the grass verge outside Dominic's house panting heavily between retches.

"Bloody hell," he managed between coughs, the tears streaming down his cheeks. "What do they put in beer that makes it taste so good on the way down but becomes so evil on the way out?"

Gravy and Weasel had joined him, both taking deep lungfuls of the comparatively clean air. Otter on the other hand, being less easily disposed to histrionics, was merely stood next to the car wrinkling his nose as if trying to dislodge some particularly persistent smell.

"Yeah, seriously Gareth, what the hell is in that stuff you drink?" Weasel managed.

"Shuddup you bunch of pansies. Can we all remember why we're 'ere? Come on."

The whole road was silent as Gareth led the team through the small gate and up the path to Dominic's front door. From the outside the building looked deserted. Carefully stepping over the flower bed, Gareth peered through the front window into the lounge. No half-drunk cups of tea, or plates of toast, or bowls of cereal evidence of someone having been there that morning. One by one, The Premiums peered into the house and came to the same conclusion.

"There doesn't seem to be any sign of a struggle," The Fuzz offered, trying to make his words sound hopeful. After a moment to reflect he continued. "Then again the rest of the house could be a disaster zone for all we know."

Gareth smacked him on the shoulder and scowled. He ignored the muttered apology and stepped backwards across the lawn, looking up to the two front-facing windows searching for any signs of life. None were in evidence. As much as Dominic barely cared for his job he was always punctual and none of them could remember the last time he had missed a shift. It just didn't feel right.

Tentatively Gareth approached the front door, his index finger hovering momentarily over the doorbell before giving it a forceful push. The bell sounded loudly inside the house and they waited for a response. After a couple of minutes Gareth pushed the bell again, this time holding it for five seconds. As the echoes of the bell died away they were once again plunged into silence.

"Jesus Christ," whispered Gravy, "this street must have been built on some kind of cursed burial ground, or maybe it was the scene of some heinous crime that left such strong negative energy that wildlife don't venture within its boundaries." The Premiums all stared at him, each of them desperate for some kind of familiar noise: a bird, a car, a human voice, anything to break the tension that had been growing since they arrived. The loud bang of an exhaust backfiring at that very moment sent them into palpitations, Gravy and The Fuzz actually holding onto each other in their momentary state of terror before pushing each other away once they realised the compromising position they were in.

"What are you talking about, everyone's at bloody work you idiot," The Fuzz said regaining his composure. "For God's sake somebody ring him again. This isn't bloody Blair Witch."

Gareth pulled out his phone and hit redial. After a few moments he signalled it was ringing and the group strained to hear whether any noise was coming from the house. With his phone away from his ear, Gareth cocked his head towards the door and pointed. Was that the sound of a phone ringing? He moved his head even closer to the door and listened. He wasn't certain but he thought he could hear something. He briefly thought it wasn't such a bad thing that Dominic's unanswered phone would ring thirty times given the current situation. Still unsure, he crouched by the letter box and forced his fingers into the flap. Now he could make out the persistent traditional ringtone playing somewhere in the house. At the very least Dominic's phone was inside.

"'is phone's definitely in there," he said, getting to his feet and trying the door handle. It was locked.

"So what do we do now?" Weasel asked. The fact Dominic and his phone seemed to be separated was having a greater effect on the group than all the spooky silences had previously. Dominic was thirty years old and no one any of them knew went anywhere without their phone, even the toilet. How else could they Tweet, TikTok and Snapchat? Otter made a gesture readily understood to be asking whether they wanted him to put his shoulder through the door. Gareth waved the suggestion away, at least for the time being. Contrary to his claim to Dominic the previous morning, Gareth was not as good at gaining entry as he suggested. He was only half as good as he had made out: ladies' thighs he could manage, locked doors were a mystery to him. He did however know someone who might be a little more familiar with them. He hoped so at least.

"'Ere, The Fuzz, you're dodgy. Can you open this?" he asked pointing to the lock.

"What's that supposed to mean?" The Fuzz asked indignantly. "I have a couple of misunderstandings with the Rozzers and you knobs tarnish me for the rest of my life." Gareth didn't have time for placating The Fuzz's hurt feelings, and besides, he didn't believe a single word he'd just heard.

"Look, Dominic could be lyin' face down in a pile of 'is own vomit. He might 'ave been stabbed or he could've 'ad an 'eart attack. But we aren't gonna know that unless we can get inside. Now can you open the door or no?" he shouted, Gravy, Weasel and Otter all standing by Gareth's side reinforcing their support.

"Yes I can do it," replied The Fuzz, after a brief pause unable to hide his annoyance that his 'I'm innocent' bit hadn't fooled anyone. "All of you stand round me and keep a look out," he muttered as he approached the door, staring at the lock. The Premiums gathered round him, their backs to The Fuzz, failing to consider how suspicious and conspicuous four men crowded around a door might look to any passers-by. Within moments there was a click and The Fuzz stood up, pulling something from the bottom of the keyhole and dropping it into his pocket.

"It's open," he said quietly, suddenly aware of the stillness in the house. "But I want you all to remember the only reason I did it was because of all the vomit and stabbing and heart attack stuff you were talking about." He stood aside as they each exchanged a glance before Gareth gently pushed the door open and took his first tentative step inside.

He had been in Dominic's house hundreds of times but had never felt an atmosphere loaded with such anticipation before. He took a few more steps down the corridor as the rest of The Premiums crowded in behind him. With a final look up and down the street, The Fuzz pulled the door shut behind them.

For the rest of The Premiums this was the first time they had even been outside of Dominic's house let alone inside. They watched as Gareth made his way down the corridor towards the back of the house, a barely audible call of "Dominic" accompanying every other step. With no idea what the etiquette was in this instance and with no specific guidance, they adopted the 'stand nervously where you are and try not break anything' approach and watched as Gareth disappeared into a room.

The hallway was a fairly standard reception area to this type of house. There was a small table with a small bowl containing house and car keys. At any other time that would have guaranteed at least one of them making a gag about suburban swingers but their nervousness and concern short-circuited that part of their brains. A mirror hung above the table and a row of coat hooks were mounted on the wall next to it. Dominic's coat hung from the furthest hook.

Gareth had returned from inspecting the back of the house and shook his head, holding up Dominic's phone, fifteen missed calls showing on the screen. Otter pointed to the coat and they nodded in unison. The coat meant Dominic obviously hadn't gone out, or if he had, it wasn't of his own volition, or if it was then he hadn't had time to grab his coat, so serious and urgent was the reason for his leaving. Either that or he hadn't thought that it would rain. Basically the coat told them nothing but somehow it felt vaguely portentous.

Gareth signalled up the stairs, tiptoeing as gently as possible, placing his feet at the edges of each step just in case they creaked. Behind him each of The Premiums followed exactly in his steps. The stairs might have been land mined for all the care they were taking.

As they climbed they passed four large photo portraits: two young women and two young men, each in graduation gowns and mortar boards. The pictures of the first man and woman seemed to have been taken a number of years ago, maybe in the 80's. Then they passed Dominic's picture, nearly ten years old itself, with their missing comrade smiling out at them. Finally, the most recent picture featured a good-looking young woman who each of them assumed to be Dominic's sister.

At the top of the stairs they were faced with five doors: five Premiums, five doors. It would undoubtedly have been quicker for them each to take a door but the tension had been steadily growing and none of them wanted to be on their own; their imaginations conjuring horrendous images of what they might find. Room by room they made their way around the top floor. The main bedroom came up empty. The study was clear. The little girl's room was empty as was the seemingly unlived-in spare bedroom. That left one door—the bathroom.

Gently Gareth turned the handle, the softest creak accompanying the action as the internal spring was stretched. With a slight click, the latch cleared the doorframe and the door opened a fraction. Taking a deep breath, their hearts hammering, the sound of blood coursing through their ears, Gareth silently counted them down: three, two, one. He eased the door open and looked inside. One by one the rest of The Premiums peered round the door like disembodied heads. What greeted them was their worst nightmare. There, slumped on the toilet, his pyjamas round his ankles and a book in his lap was Dominic.

Time froze as they took in the scene, too shocked to say anything, barely holding it together enough to keep their breakfasts down. First to regain any kind of self-possession was Gareth, and he sidled across the bathroom. He slowly reached his hand out and pressed it against Dominic's neck.

"Aaaaaaaggggghhhhhhh!" Dominic shouted, jerking awake and away from the strange sensation on his neck. Waking up to five pairs of eyes staring at you intently was something Dominic never wanted to experience again, especially while on the bog.

"Fuuuuuuuuuuuuck," screamed Gareth staggering backwards across the bathroom, sprawling on the floor and banging into the half-open door, forcing it back against its frame.

Various screams and shouts emitted from Otter, Weasel, Gravy and The Fuzz as their heads and throats were squeezed and crushed in the doorframe.

Suddenly very awake and aware of his, to all intents and purposes, complete nakedness, Dominic tried to pull his pyjamas up. Unfortunately he had been asleep on the toilet for some time, and the pressure from the seat against his thighs had cut off the circulation to his legs, rendering them jelly-like stilts on which he tottered and teetered before crashing to the floor on top of Gareth.

"What the bloody hell are you doing here?" he managed to shout as he fumbled for his trouser bottoms.

"We thought you were dead!" a flustered Gareth replied. "We phoned you and rang the bell and called yer name. You should bleddy well answer when people do that," he shouted back, desperately trying to disentangle himself from his naked friend, all the while trying to do so without touching him.

After a short but energetic scrabble on the floor Gareth and Dominic stared at each other from opposite ends of the bathroom panting and unable to speak. From outside on the landing, the mounting wave of tension had finally broken and all the two friends could hear was hysterical laughter.

As their pulses slowly returned to normal eventually Gareth broke the silence.

"Fuckin' 'ell. That were intense."

Twenty minutes later they were all sat in the lounge drinking tea. The Premiums had taken it in turns, except Otter who just nodded and shook his head in the appropriate places, to bring Dominic up to speed as to the sequence of events that had brought them to his bathroom door. In turn Dominic was now in the process of explaining his absence and their subsequent discovery of him on the throne.

"I don't know why, but for some reason when I got home last night I freaked out and was scrabbling around my room for a pen and paper." The silent questioning look that passed between Gravy and Weasel hadn't gone unnoticed. "It's a long story," Dominic said, the conviction in his voice letting everyone know that story was not for now.

"Anyway, while I was searching my bag for a quotation pad I found this." He lifted the thick leather diary. "Which also contained this." He showed them the cream-coloured piece of writing paper. "I think the guy whose quote I did yesterday afternoon must have put it in my bag for some reason." He passed the letter to Gareth. "Anyway, I ended up staying up all night reading the diary and then before I knew it, it was time to head to work. I went into the bathroom and must have fallen asleep on the loo. The next thing I know you idiots are staring at me."

Gareth looked unconvinced. "Just read it, please," Dominic said. Still unconvinced, Gareth dramatically shook out the folds in the letter and began to read.

"Dear Sir,

Firstly, please accept my apologies for imposing on you in this way. It was never my intention to expose anyone else to the evil to which I have been a party, but alas, my carelessness has brought my situation to a premature head and me to this moment of contrition.

I hope one day to be able to shake your hand once your custodianship of this tome is complete, but I cannot guarantee that will happen. Contained in the pages of this diary are secrets behind a fortune made and morality ignored. So explosive and damning are its contents that should those mentioned within its pages discover its whereabouts they will stop at nothing to obtain and destroy it.

My intention, hidden from myself until recently, had been to expose those concerned, including myself, and force us all to face justice for what we have done. Alas, I feel the wrath I have awoken may be too intense to sidestep and the justice I face may be at another's hand. Regardless, this story must be told. We, the perpetrators of the acts here described, must be held accountable.

Be careful, stay safe and godspeed.

Regretfully,

Wilbur Forthright"

Gareth paused and looked at Dominic.

"Bit dramatic innit?"

Dominic held the diary up again. "If you think that's dramatic, wait until you read what's in here."

Chapter 19

Hank sat in the Bedford Rascal (replete with new courier logo and number plates) thinking through what his next move should now be. The initial plan had been to go to Dominic Morgan's home and lift him in a similar way he had O'Connell. Time was of the essence. He had lots of other things he needed to be doing, not least for **Help Wanted**, and the sooner he had the diary in his possession the sooner he could refocus his efforts. His arrival at the house to find five men huddled together outside meant he would now have to factor in further delays.

He tried to rub the tiredness from his face as he watched one of the men crouch at the door and the remaining four form a tight semicircle around him, blocking him from view. As he had driven round the corner, he had noticed the group and pulled the Rascal swiftly to the curb, the exhaust registering its objection with a loud backfire just as they stopped. The five men had instantly turned in their direction and anxiously scanned the road. Very jumpy, Hank had thought—far too jumpy for a normal Tuesday morning. Something had brought them to Morgan's house at the exact same time as him. The crappy Fiat Uno was too small for all six of them, so a lift-share seemed unlikely. And the fact he had just witnessed them picking the lock of the house he had intended to break into meant that something was wrong. That said there were varying degrees of "wrong" in the world. These were five guys who shifted wardrobes and boxes for a living. It was unlikely that something being wrong in their world carried the same implications as in his.

Razor had been keen to follow them inside, kick the crap out of all of them then take whatever or whoever they needed. Not entirely without its charm, Hank thought. Then he remembered the two big guys. The hairy one looked out of shape but big guys were always strong, and the massive, lean, muscular guy was clearly an accident waiting to happen if he and Razor went off half-cocked without a plan or any intel on the property or its occupants. His desire to obtain Morgan and the diary tempered by his professionalism, they would wait and see how things developed.

It wasn't easy biding time in a small enclosed space with Razor, especially once his blood lust had been awakened. The previous night's work with O'Connell had been frustrating but had at least moved things forward, always assuming that Morgan would be able to help them. Their informant's willingness to implicate Dominic in the affair was too quick and insistent to merely be as a result of it being the only sign of hope for a man desperate to escape from the situation he found himself in. There was clearly some personal vendetta between O'Connell and his employee, one that O'Connell was ruthlessly gaining ground in by setting Hank and Razor in motion. O'Connell hadn't got away scot-free though. The initial flesh wounds caused by the meat hook had been necessary to soften him up. Hank had rarely seen people withstand being within five feet of Razor before spilling their life stories, but there was something about O'Connell: a self-awareness that whilst brash and arrogant, understood its place in a pecking order. In his normal life he was the big man and behaved accordingly. Dragged from his home in the middle of the night, stripped and beaten and bound to a chair, he became submissive. But that cunningness, the duplicity of thought and behaviour, rang alarm bells for Hank. People like O'Connell, deep down, believed they were superior to everybody else regardless of the situation they were in. Even naked, bound to a chair on the killing floor of an abattoir, in the middle of the night with a couple of men in balaclavas. His innate confidence and self-belief, his ingrained superciliousness meant he still believed himself the superior intellect and therefore only had to *seem* to comply with his captor's requests. The very fact violence had been used against him somehow confirming his superiority over two men who couldn't outthink him, whose only advantage over him was a physical one.

Hank knew people like that had to be broken twice. Once so they could show they were broken, and once so they could know they were broken.

Hank glanced across the Rascal's cab at his rabid-looking accomplice. Razor had been staring at the house since they had first arrived with his usual intensity, as if trying to deconstruct the building with his mind alone. Hank knew full well that had he not stopped Razor, he would have followed the five men into the house and taken them all on, beating them into submission or falling himself in the attempt. Hank's call for patience had brought that intense stare to bear on himself and for a brief moment he had thought Razor would ignore him. But whatever it was that made Razor defer to Hank's leadership kicked in, and he slowly returned his gaze to the house.

The air in the cab was stale. Their exertions from the night before, their sweat, the blood and excrement on the floor of the van, the bleach used to clean the mess, all mingled together to form a unique and unpleasant odour they had been sat in for the best part of an hour. Cracking the window an inch, Hank's thoughts returned to the previous night.

Razor was a double-edged sword. His insanity and willingness to resort to violence was a very useful tool in what was a very dangerous world that Hank inhabited. In so many situations, might was right and having someone like Razor on your side meant that you could cut it with the big boys regardless of how insane things got. That ability to do what someone else would not gave them an edge. It wasn't one Hank exploited very often but it allowed them to go about their business without the undue interference of others who similarly lived on the wrong side of the law.

That insanity however, could also be a huge liability. Just look at his actions when they were taking the DB12 two days ago. He had very nearly killed the car's owner with that piece of wood. Hank hadn't heard anything further on the man or any police hunt since hearing on the radio the man had been found and was in a critical condition. And it had almost gone the same way with O'Connell.

The initial beatings and humiliation had allowed O'Connell to get to the stage where he could show them he was broken. The meat hook and Razor's willingness to use it was to let him know he had been broken. The problem had been Razor's inability to see that point in time when O'Connell had finally understood. Go too far past that point and the fact you have broken them becomes meaningless, they become too far gone to be of any use.

Hank involuntarily rubbed his right pectoral muscle at the thought of what Razor had done to O'Connell—the vision of the blood and sound of his scream as the hook scored its way through the muscle vivid in his mind.

O'Connell had broken more quickly than Hank had expected, which was a blessing. The jolt of pain caused as the hook broke the skin for the first time enough to convince O'Connell there was to be no easy solution to his particular problem. He had spoken willingly and freely about Swift & Smooth, his family, the Forthrights, Morgan, everything. Even the girl he was convinced was in love with him but had dated Morgan to make him jealous. That was the point when Hank had known they would have to take O'Connell further. He was clearly deluded and deluded people hid things from themselves as well as from everybody else.

O'Connell had given them nothing more useful however and Hank had been unable to restrain Razor's blood lust once it was up. Hank wasn't naïve and if his time in prison had taught him anything, it was that he was not going back. Whatever dangers he faced in the real world were infinitely more preferable and solvable than those inside. That line in the sand meant there was always the possibility a situation would arise in which it was Hank or somebody else, and he was under no illusion that if that required the ultimate sacrifice, he was willing to assist another in making it so he wouldn't have to.

There was a big gap though between that philosophy and Razor's. There was no measured approach to what Razor did and if you looked in his eyes during one of his frenzies there was no acknowledgeable mental activity whatsoever. Razor was driven by impulse and fury, and Hank was too smart to get in the way of it. O'Connell would survive, probably, but Hank was being exposed to ever greater risk as a result.

The difference from a court's perspective between murder and the kind of grievous bodily harm Razor had inflicted when it came to sentencing was non-existent, but Hank didn't want to be racking up bodies for the sake of it. He had finally managed to pull Razor from O'Connell's limp body, before he killed him, but only just. Leaving O'Connell somewhere he would be found quickly but they wouldn't be observed leaving him had taken a while and Hank still wasn't certain they had succeeded. This job was getting more and more dangerous and the sooner it was finished the better.

He glanced to his right and saw the lace curtains of the house they were parked outside twitch back into place, concealing the occupant. He looked at his watch. They had been here over an hour and two men sat in a battered van for that long in a nice residential estate was bound to draw attention eventually. A sign on a lamppost next to the van proclaimed this to be a neighbourhood watch area and if the curtain twitchers were getting worried, it wouldn't be long before a police Astra provided a drive past and there was no way this van would pass even rudimentary investigation.

The five guys who had entered the house had still not come out and no one else had arrived. He had no way of knowing how long they had before the police turned up but he did know they were extremely conspicuous and this was the last job this particular van would be used for.

Hank turned the key in the ignition and revved the engine to life. Razor looked across quizzically.

"We need to make a move. We've got some twitchers paying too much attention." He signalled over his right shoulder. "Anyway, we have other options."

He pulled away from the curb and slowly drove past Morgan's house. He had hoped he wouldn't have to do this, but needs must when the devil drives. O'Connell had provided them with two addresses during the night. Morgan's had proved to be a no go, but the other might bear more fruit. As the curtains on Dominic's road came to rest, Hank and Razor headed towards Beth's.

Chapter 20

"Any word from the groper yet?" Beth's mum peered over the rim of her mug of tea, a mischievous glint in her eye.

"What did I say about calling him that? It was clearly a mistake. He thought you were me and this is getting boring."

"Oh, so you have spoken to him and that was his explanation was it?" Pamela's face had an overtly innocent look on it.

Beth sighed deeply.

"You know I haven't spoken to him yet, *Mother*." She emphasised the last word to her mum's obvious annoyance.

"I've told you before not to call me Mother because it makes me sound old. And Gropey Groperson can attest to the opposite being true." The innocent look was replaced with a broad smile and a wink.

"I'll stop calling you Mother if you stop calling him anything remotely associated with groping. His name is Dominic and I'm sure he's mortally embarrassed about what happened."

"Fine," her mother replied, raising her hands in a gesture of placation. "I'll cut him some slack if you stop moping about."

"I'm not moping," Beth said indignantly.

"Well you've barely taken your eyes off your phone for the last two days. I thought those things had an audible tone that sounds when you get a message."

Beth was silent.

"Well? Is your phone one of those special ones that wants to keep it a secret if anyone gets in touch?"

"No." Beth dragged the word out petulantly. Parents being right about anything beyond one's 12th birthday was always annoying.

"OK. You've sent him a number of texts and left him a voicemail. You send him any more and you're going to look like a stalker. The ball's in his court now," Pamela said, her tone softening as she reached across the table and took Beth's hand.

"Why are boys so dumb?" Beth looked up from her tea and into her mother's eyes. "And why do you have to be a smoking-hot fifty-five-year-old? If you were some kind of harridan we wouldn't be in this situation."

"Hey, you should be grateful. I'm you in twenty-five years." Beth rolled her eyes. "And it would appear my milkshake can still bring all the boys to the yard."

"Mother!"

Before they could get into a further squabble they heard a key in the front door followed a few seconds later by a cheery, "Hello?"

"In the kitchen, Naomi," Beth shouted.

A few seconds later, Beth's flatmate Naomi walked in.

"Hey," she said to Beth before moving round the table and giving Pamela a big hug.

"Hello my love," Pamela replied. "How's the show going?"

"Yeah, rehearsals are going well thanks Pam." She indicated to Beth and Pamela's mugs as she filled up the kettle. They both waved the offer aside. "We're into the final week before opening night now, so everything's pretty much there, just ironing out the crinkles."

She went to the fridge and took out a lemon and a large piece of ginger root before chopping a quarter of the lemon and a couple of inches of the ginger as well as a good squeeze of honey into her mug before topping it up with boiling water. She joined Beth and Pamela at the table. Pamela looked questioningly at Naomi's mug.

"You losing your voice?" she asked.

Naomi's hand went to her throat which was tightly wrapped in a cashmere scarf.

"Not yet, touch wood." She tapped the table top. "I always get a bit paranoid that I will just before we open and I read somewhere that keeping your neck warm, along with regular ginger, lemon and honey drinks is a great way to keep any bugs at bay." She took a sip of the scalding liquid and winced slightly. "You two are going to come to the show right?"

"Of course," Beth answered, "just let us know when you want us there."

"I think it will be great from the start but you know, a couple of weeks in, everyone's on their game so I reckon end of November, early December."

"Lovely. I do enjoy panto," Pamela said. "All that 'he's behind you'. It always makes me laugh. What about you Beth?" Pamela looked at her daughter barely making an effort to look innocent.

Beth glared back.

"Ooooooh, heavy on the subtext." Naomi said, intrigued. "Something I should know?"

"It's not my place to say," Pamela said, although the subtext was clear that if Beth didn't fill her friend in then that is exactly what she would do. Naomi looked at Beth questioningly.

"Wait. Is this about Dominic? How did the date go? Was it everything you wanted?"

Beth sighed a little dramatically.

"It was a little more than I wanted to be honest," she said, a very wry smile touching her lips. She filled Naomi in on the events of Saturday night and early Sunday morning, excluding the more intimate details, right up to the point Dominic had mistaken her mother for her.

"Oh my God!" Naomi's jaw dropped. "What did you do?" She looked at Pamela.

"She punched him in the face, kneed him in the balls and dropped him to the floor is what she did," Beth said, still not entirely sure how she felt about it. On the one hand she was very proud that her mother had fought off what she thought was a sexual predator. On the other hand, she'd actually assaulted a guy Beth quite liked and with whom she had hoped something would develop.

"Oh my God!" Naomi said even louder, her hand covering her mouth. "Are you OK Pam? That must have been a hell of a shock."

"It was a shock, Naomi. It really was," Pamela replied with exaggerated sincerity. "But my training kicked in and you know, actually, he was very gentle for a sexual predator. If he's that gentle with my daughter then I think I'm ok with it."

Beth choked on her tea before slamming the mug down and pointing a finger severely at her mother.

"Don't make me use the M word," Beth threatened.

"What, MILF?" Pamela replied, smiling broadly. Naomi laughed.

"Mother!" Beth almost shouted, genuine shock in her voice

"What? I've been reading about it in Cosmo. Apparently it's where there's an older woman who is a parent and a younger fellow would like to…"

"I know exactly what it means," Beth interrupted.

"Well, I don't know anything about Dominic, other than he has soft hands and a glass jaw. Perhaps he has some older woman thing going on?" Pamela continued, clearly enjoying the discomfort she was causing her daughter. Naomi laughed even harder. Beth just scowled.

"How is he?" Naomi finally managed to ask.

"She broke his nose and that ring took a huge gouge out of his cheek. And I dread to think about the state of his family jewels."

"Hardly a glowing endorsement of his performance," Pamela commented.

"Mother. Stop trying to wind me up," Beth snapped, used to her mother's sense of humour but genuine irritation creeping into her voice for the first time.

"How is he, really?" Naomi asked, attempting to steer the conversation on to more serious ground.

Beth glared at her mother for a few seconds daring her to make a smart quip but it appeared the irritation in Beth's voice had halted the jokes.

"I don't know," Beth replied eventually. "I haven't seen him since we dropped him at A&E Sunday morning. He hasn't responded to my texts or voicemail yet."

"In all seriousness, darling, you were right earlier" Pamela said, adopting a placating tone, "this is getting boring. He's almost certainly just licking his wounds. It's not every day you accidentally grope your potential future mother-in-law."

"Steady on. It's a bit early for that," Beth replied.

"And it's definitely not every day you get your arse handed to you by said same potential future mother-in-law," Pamela continued, unable to repress the smile on her face.

After a few seconds, Beth begrudgingly smiled as well.

"I think Pam's right, Beth. He just needs a bit of time to get over the shock, and himself," Naomi added.

"I guess so. I just wish he was being a bit more mature about it and seeing it for what it was, an unfortunate and embarrassing misunderstanding."

"Well he is a man, darling. Maturity is something men develop much later in life than us women, if they develop it at all. I'm sure given a few days he'll come to his senses and realise my daughter is far too good a catch to miss out on purely as a result of his bruised pride," she paused. "And testicles, obviously."

The three women laughed. Draining her mug, Beth stood.

"Right, I've now officially spent far too long thinking and talking about Dominic. I have four more days off and unencumbered access to my mother's credit card." She turned to her mother. "Pamela, in recompense for punching my date you are taking me shopping again and then for another expensive lunch. Naomi, would you like to join us?" She looked at Naomi, giving her mother no chance to interject or object.

"Thank you but I'm a bit paranoid about winter bugs. We've got a day off rehearsals so I'm just going to stay in and watch boxsets."

"OK, if you're sure." Beth said, swinging her coat over her shoulders and shooing her mother towards the front door. "Can we bring you back anything?"

"Chocolate please," Naomi shouted from the lounge as they heard the TV being turned on.

"No problem. See you later." With that Beth and her mother slammed the door and headed off to shop and lunch.

Chapter 21

This is the diary of Wilbur Bartholomew Forthright and is intended as a chronicle accompanying the rise and successes of the Secret Society of Hopmen. Knowing what I now know, what do I hope to achieve from this diary? Nothing more than a record of events starting today and finishing who knows where and when. I have made the decision to document these events and so I shall:

August 17th 1984

It has been a day of mixed emotion and I find myself at a crossroads, the destination of each fork a mystery. On the one hand the normal vagaries of life: the challenges, successes and failures it throws up. On the other, an adventure, the outcome unknowable.

Jeff contacted me a week ago and said he was arranging for each of the 6 publicans in Little Bithrall (Steve from the Oarsman's Rollocks, Terry from the Coq in Cider, Derek from the Turn and Slip Inn, Martin from the Crusty Pie and myself as owner and publican of the Pikeman's Helmet) to meet at Jeff's pub, The Cockswell Inn.

Jeff greeted us in the snug, a beautifully intimate area of his pub that until recently still precluded women from entering. We all knew he had been playing around with the new fad of small in-house brewed ales and he greeted us with pints of beer from his most recent batch. Experience told me that Jeff's beers would be thin on flavour and low on aroma. Jeff possessed a strong desire but seemingly insufficient skill. You can imagine then the surprise we had, once the first drops past our lips and enveloped our taste buds. This was more than just a beer. Yes, the traditional tastes were there: hops, biscuits, fruitiness, bitterness, sweetness, the whole gamut of flavours associated with real ale—literally every one of them. In no single barrel of beer should all of those flavours have been able to coexist, they should clash and overpower each other, spoiling the entire batch. Yet here we were, experiencing exactly that and the result was nothing short of nirvana. "It tastes like God's tears," was all Derek could manage, his own tears welling up at the joy we were all feeling.

Congratulations were offered and backs slapped heartily—Jeff had done it, he had finally brewed a masterpiece. This then was the reason he had mustered us all to his pub, in effect to show off. Well yes and no.

The pints of Lurcher's Last Stand, named in fitting memory to Jeff's recently deceased canine companion of the last fifteen years, lasted but a moment in the hands and mouths of six healthy landlords and more was duly called for. What we got was insipid and crude, flavours clashed in our mouths, insulting the very memory still singing in our brains and on our tongues of the extraordinary pint of Lurcher's. Jeff proudly told us we were drinking a pint of Trendle's Old Spot, the most popular ale in the country and one that each of our own pubs served. We were gobsmacked to a man. Having been in and around the publican lifestyle all of our lives and considering ourselves experts when it came to ale, not one of us had been able to identify the beer that occupied a place in all of our top three favourites. Not only that, but the contrast between the sublime Lurcher's and our previous favourite, had rendered Old Spot no more desirable or palatable than sewer water.

This was truly astounding and I made a point of speaking to Jeff about securing a steady supply of the elixir he had created, something each of us quite naturally was keen to do, fearing we would never again enjoy a beer unless it was Lurcher's.

Jeff however was quick to calm us. The sensation we were experiencing was transitory. Once our bodies had flushed the remnants of Lurcher's from our systems, our typical response to other ales would return, a fact we all had mixed feelings about. It was good to know that should Lurcher's be unavailable we could still enjoy a beer but why would we ever want to drink anything below the standard of Jeff's incredible creation again?

Replacing the now undrinkable Old Spot with more pints of Lurcher's, we enthused over the magnificence of Jeff's achievement. The effect the beer had on us was quite remarkable and almost certainly responsible for what happened next.

I write this now with clarity of thought, the first clear thinking I have been able to do since that first sip, sufficient hours having passed so my body and thoughts are once more returned to my control. It transpired that presenting his newest beer to us was only half the reason he had asked us to attend, and without us understanding how, we suddenly found ourselves in a dark room lit only with candles, thunder and rain reverberating around the chamber and a fragrant smoke pluming up to the ceiling. Each of us was dressed in long, ceremonial cassocks with hoods to mask our faces, sat around Jeff's circular solid oak dining table. Like Arthurian knights we waited for whatever it was Jeff had brought us together for. Unfortunately for Jeff, some sinus problems and poor hearing meant the elaborate lengths he had gone to in order to invite us to become founder members of his secret society were wasted and the decision to retire to the beer garden with more pints of Lurcher's won out over ceremony. Jeff was none too happy about that so I hung back to reassure him I liked the ceremony and the idea of a secret society was excellent. I would have said anything at that point to secure my own supply of his beer.

Outside we were surprised to find Jeff had closed the pub for the duration of our meeting, signalling this event being much more important than we had at first thought. Once we had all had our tankards refilled, Jeff outlined the reason for our meeting and his plan.

We were under attack, he began. Under attack from a new wave of competition that cared nothing for tradition or standards, caring only about the bottom line—how much money they could make. They brewed high volumes with low quality and punted it out cheaply, insulting the drinker who more and more seemed only interested in getting drunk rather than enjoying a sophisticated pint.

We were all of us independent Free House landlords, able to purchase and sell whatever drinks and products we liked to our customers, but times were changing. We had all seen great chunks of business stolen away by the ever-growing beer conglomerates as they opened their 'chain' and 'theme' pubs, offering cut-price beers and la-di-da eight bottle wine lists for the ladies, who they were freely encouraging into their establishments. No longer was a choice of red or white sufficient; now you needed to know the grape variety as well and how many sons the vintner had.

Jeff had us all spellbound. We knew what he was saying was true, but being six independents what could we do? The big breweries controlled too many pubs and regulated prices too strictly for us to cause them even a moment of concern. As little as we wanted to admit it we all knew we were at the start of what would be a steady decline into obscurity. The independent English pub, you remember, they used to be so quaint.

But Jeff had other ideas. We six would form The Secret Society of Hopmen, whose sole aim would be not to crush the large breweries, but outperform them. We would deal in excellence where they purveyed mediocrity. We would highlight the difference between the mass industrialised process of beer making against the hands-on love and attention of the small brewer. We would elevate our products far beyond mere after-work tipples. We would make them talking points—the reason people visited pubs. And we would do so with the secret behind Lurcher's.

At that point, had Jeff asked us to charge the headquarters of our now despised enemy, we would to a man have done so with no thought to our own safety or the outcome of our crusade. It was truly a Churchillian moment and where Churchill would fight on the beaches, the landing grounds, fields, streets and hills, Jeff and the newly formed Secret Society of Hopmen would fight them in the breweries.

More Lurcher's was poured and one by one we each vowed our allegiance to The Society, the cause and The Crown, long live the Queen. To be honest I wasn't entirely sure what I was agreeing to should I ever find myself unable to stand by my vow, such was the euphoria in the group. But Jeff had been clear, only those who had taken the vow could know the secret.

With the six of us all now newly sworn-in members of a secret society, Jeff led us through the pub to his cellars and a large, heavy, wrought iron door set into the rear wall. With great ceremony, Jeff unlocked the huge door and pushed it open. One by one we filed in. What lay beyond was typical of small brewing ventures across the land: vats and distillation chambers, burners and copper tubing, condensing tanks and oak cask barrels. The only unusual piece of equipment being a large hopper over which were two large, studded, interlocking rollers. We all looked around, eager to discover the secret to Jeff's success, what alchemical process he had pioneered to render—in a heartbeat—all other beers obsolete.

Gareth's lips moved silently as he read on, Dominic waiting for the bombshell moment he had himself experienced a few hours previously. After a few moments it came. Gareth's head snapped up from the diary and he stared at Dominic.

"What? You've gotta be fuckin' kiddin' me!"

Chapter 22

Oscar. He had been the start, Jeff ruminated as he descended the concealed staircase into his subterranean domain, a large glass of whiskey once again accompanying his thoughts. Beer was all well and good, better than well and good to be honest, but sometimes it just didn't cut it. Now was one of those times.

From Oscar, through a journey of forty years to the unfortunate but necessary death of Wilbur and his wife, the symbolism was not lost on Jeff. Their adventure had begun with a death and so this phase of their journey would end with one. They still needed the diary, but Jeff was confident their contact would acquire it soon enough, and now the weak link had been removed, the chain was once again strong. Jeff took a large swallow of his whiskey, wincing as the fiery liquid burned its way down his throat before blooming in a pulse of warmth in his stomach, helping to hold back the demons, at least for the time being.

He gently ran his fingers along the bottling bench, then onto one of the distillation tanks, coming to rest on the ignition switch for the burner. Ordinarily he revelled in these moments, the time just before the creation of a new batch, the burners still cold, the vats empty and his underground brewery void of the sounds of bubbling liquid and the mechanical grind of gears as the rollers pulped. In the next few days he would collect the ingredients and the process would begin. Eight weeks later, the latest limited edition Hopmen Breweries ale would be ready to be distributed to each corner of the world, every drop already accounted and paid for.

He thought back to the eventful day and laughed bitterly. In theory it made no sense, would never have got past the brainstorming phase had it been conceived in a corporate environment. Scratch that he thought, any environment would have dismissed it as lunacy had anybody been unhinged enough to suggest it. Fate, it seemed, had other ways of bringing its workings to light. Who would have assumed that mould could fight infection? Ridiculous in principle, yet for thousands of years this knowledge had existed. Penicillin as a medicine specifically had been around for nearly a hundred years. Microwave technology for cooking, artificial sweeteners for flavouring, vulcanized rubber, the pacemaker, all had one thing in common: they were discovered or invented by accident. The cosmos had decided these things needed to exist and a chain reaction of events had started that resulted in these now everyday items. And the food and drinks industries were full of similar accidents: coke — accident, potato chips — accident, popsicle — accident, brandy — accident, champagne — accident. The real genius was not in deciding to create something, but recognising when something unexpected happened and not dismissing the results as a failure.

Jeff sat in the battered old armchair next to the vats and sighed heavily. His very own accident had survived for two reasons: money and an irrational emotional bond with a pet. He had made the decision to strike out from the big breweries and make a name for himself, so Jeff had invested every penny he had into the equipment required to brew his own beer. After multiple attempts, creating nothing but generic or insipid ales he had one last chance. With the money almost gone he had enough for one last roll of the dice. And he had gambled on that last roll making a much larger batch than he had of any of his failures. He had no choice; he had to be successful or he and his business were finished.

And it seemed the universe agreed. But there was always a price to be paid.

He enjoyed the process. The malting where the barley grain is prepared; mashing, where the resultant starch released from the malting is turned into a sugar-rich liquid or wort. The mixture is then moved to a copper kettle and heated with hops and any other flavouring required. Once this is complete the liquid is rapidly cooled and yeast added, which transforms the sugars into alcohol. The beer is then conditioned in a separate tank to age and smooth out the flavours before a final filtration, carbonation if required and bottling.

Jeff and Oscar had spent hours and hours in the large barn he had hired for the purpose, painstakingly following the process, determined to get it right. Periodically, Oscar would run through the barley grain or the hops as they dried, licking a few before spitting them back out. Never mind, thought Jeff, it all adds flavour, and besides he couldn't afford to start again. All had gone smoothly, man and beast increasing their bond over the age-old desire to make inebriating drink, until the process required Jeff to move the now sugar-rich wort into the copper kettle for heating and the addition of hops.

The barn they were using still contained some of the farmer's equipment and Jeff had set up his vats and stills beneath a hay loft, amidst random heavy farming machinery. He had just opened the Mash Tun, where his barley had been releasing its sugary goodness, when Oscar raced into the barn and started excitedly leaping around the machinery. A quick look reassured Jeff that Oscar was far enough away from the vats not to interfere and he pressed on with the transfer. The sudden sound of gears engaging and massive rollers turning distracted him. He looked up to see Oscar looking at him from the control panel of one of the machines, wagging his tail excitedly. Above him, two massive rollers turned, their purpose unknowable. Oscar leapt from the panel and sprinted up the ladder to the hay loft as Jeff carefully decanted the wort into the copper vat directly beneath the rollers. Time stood still as he heard a crack and he looked up to see Oscar, his companion of fifteen years, fall through a hole in the hay loft, legs running in mid-air in an attempt to escape his fall, tongue lolling out of his mouth, plunge into the rotating teeth of the rollers. The funnel beneath the rollers had channelled Oscar's pulped and liquefied remains directly into the kettle on top of the wort.

Traumatic events affect people in varying ways. Some collapse and break down in a wail of screams and tears, unable to function normally. Some withdraw into themselves and shut down, no longer able to interact with the world around them. For others, the trauma is so great and inconceivable that they behave as if it never happened, to acknowledge it would make it a reality that required a response.

Jeff fell into the last category. He stood motionless for an hour, just staring at the funnel dripping with blood, unable to process what had just happened. Eventually his brain moved past the initial shock, started providing inputs to the rest of his body, moving him forward, putting distance and action between himself and the now unmentionable accident. So focussed had Jeff been on the processes required to make his beer, that his brain picked up where those processes had been interrupted. Acting with no conscious input at all, Jeff gathered together the remaining hops and added them to the kettle. Absent-mindedly he wiped the blood spatters, fur and bone chips from the kettle's edge, before replacing the top and sealing it. He knelt and turned the valve on the gas canister and then lit a match lighting the burner beneath the wort, hops, Oscar mixture and stood back. In the corner of the barn was a battered old armchair, which Jeff slowly sank into. The springs had gone a long time before and dropped lower than expected, his backside only a few inches from the floor, but he didn't notice, so focussed was he on the blue flames beneath the copper kettle.

Jeff snapped back from the memory and sighed wearily. These were the only times when uncertainty visited him—when Oscar invaded his thoughts and dreams. These were the only times when the sounds that accompanied his work returned to haunt him.

He had come to terms many years ago with what had made him continue with the process of that special batch so long ago. Yes he would have been bankrupt had he stopped the process but that wasn't it. In the light of his best friend and companion's untimely demise, what was bankruptcy? He had continued because he couldn't bear the thought of going on without Oscar. He had nothing to bury (the rollers had seen to that); he needed something tangible, and so he had continued. He had finished the process. After the heating, he had let the liquid settle in the whirlpool, which allowed for the removal of the more solid particles. Jeff couldn't remember performing this task, his brain once again circumventing his conscious mind in order to prevent the horror of what he was doing registering. His memories kicked in again for the cooling process and addition of the yeast and the transfer to the fermentation chamber. Once this process was complete, he transferred the fermented beer into the conditioning tanks and left it for four weeks.

He had no expectations or even understanding of what he was doing when he arrived that Monday morning four weeks later. He hadn't even decided he was going to taste it but once again his brain removed what free will he thought he had and before he knew it, he had poured himself a tankard of his last chance home-brewed ale. Tentatively, hands shaking and tears pouring down his cheeks, he took his first sip. The result was remarkable. Who knew that adding squashed dog to beer made it taste better than anything that had passed Jeff's lips in his life?

The tears kept flowing, but now they were of joy. Somehow, a chemical miracle had occurred and transformed what otherwise would clearly have been a complete disaster, into the nectar of gods. Jeff had whooped and shouted in happiness, dancing around the barn, unable to stem the feelings of joy he felt. Eventually, exhausted, he collapsed into the battered old chair. He couldn't believe the effect one pint of beer had had on him. This was something even more miraculous. He had no idea what had happened but he knew it represented a fundamental shift in what in the world as he knew it. As the initial wave of euphoria that had crashed on top of him receded, his brain kicked in. He had been right to continue when others would have given up. He had been right to honour his fallen companion who had given his life for something extraordinary. Jeff would ensure Oscar achieved immortality as the perfect name for his magical brew came to him: Lurcher's Last Stand. Oscar had given him the secret for fighting back against those behemoths that would see him beaten and destroyed. His brain was free-wheeling now, a hundred ideas a minute crashing into each other in their race for recognition. With the effects of the beer so unexpected—possibly the biggest understatement in the history of the world—Jeff was already thinking about marketing, distribution and sale price. He was going to take over the world. He pulled himself from the chair and poured another pint of Lurcher's Last Stand. Half way down it he paused, suddenly aware of the limited stock he had in his possession. He gently placed the tankard down on the workbench. He had to know whether this was a fluke, some unrepeatable miracle that would leave him chasing this perfection for the rest of his life. He had to try again.

Roused from his memories, Jeff looked up at the beer pump badges they had created for each of their 'Specials'. The first two, testament to one man's determination, or insanity depending on which side of the fence you stood. If the fact Lurcher's had been so good was unlikely, then the outcome of Grouchy Goat was a miracle: different animal, same effect. The taste of the beer was different to Lurcher's but just as incredible on the palate. Jeff was ecstatic and his logic, now completely twisted by the run of events his life had taken, made the obvious leap: if this worked for dogs and goats, clearly there was no animal it wouldn't work for. Jeff had his business plan. He had been right too. Everything he and the subsequent members of the SSoH had tried had resulted in the same, if slightly nuanced, phenomenal beers. Except pigeons for some reason, Jeff reflected. But pigeons were crap in the first place so maybe that explained it, you couldn't after all polish a turd.

Jeff had approached the other publicans in their small village, and once they had tasted Lurcher's, the incredible reality of its conception seemed to wash over them, immaterial given the vast opportunity that stood before them. The six of them united that day and forever more: Jeff, Steve, Terry, Martin, Derek and Wilbur. Six brothers-in-arms. Now though, only five remained.

The faint smell of smoke from standing outside the burning house, as the firemen had fought to save the occupants, was still evident on his clothes. It had been unfortunate to have to take such direct action against Wilbur, but he had brought it on himself. They had agreed all those years ago, on pain of death, to take their secret with them to the grave. Jeff's black eye was unfocussed as he tipped his glass to his lips, rewarded with nothing but air. He stood and crossed to the bottom of the stairs. He looked back at the empty vats and chambers as he clicked the lights off one by one. Soon they would be fired up again, for SSoH's latest Special and this one would be dedicated to Wilbur. As the last switch was flicked and the cavernous space plunged into darkness, Jeff climbed the stairs guided by the step-level lighting. He would have to watch the other members of SSoH; Wilbur had been the obvious one likely to break but none of them were getting any younger and facing one's final judgement could do funny things to a man's conscience.

He also needed to make sure everything was on track for his shipment. Without it there would be no new Special. While he was at it he would get an update regarding the diary. His contact had mentioned he had a lead and Jeff was eager to see how useful that had proven. As the bookcase slid back into place, Jeff headed for his office. In the face of adversity, everything was coming back into line.

Chapter 23

"You mean there's actual fuckin' budgies in my beer?" Gareth demanded.

As there was only one copy of the diary and Gareth had taken it on himself to see what all the fuss Dominic was making was all about, the others had turned to the TV and started watching *This Morning*. Gareth's outburst had proven more interesting than the bland presenters though. They looked from Gareth to Dominic.

"Um…yeah. Well, actually, according to that," Dominic pointed to the diary, "it's only the Budgie Smugglers that has budgies in it. You haven't got that far yet but your other favourite, Soused Stoat, does appear to have actual stoats as a prime ingredient."

"Bollocks. It's a joke, 'as to be. You can't ave actual bits of animal in beer, even real ale. It's godda be a gimmick," Gareth stated, returning his gaze to the diary. "Some old codger's busy makin' stuff up cos he's bored an' lonely. And you, you muppet, in your freaked out state last night, believed it." He was shaking his head, the disappointment at his friend's gullibility much easier to deal with than the possibility there was actual body to his favourite tipples.

Gravy, The Fuzz, Weasel and Otter stared at their colleagues.

"Wait a minute. Are you trying to tell us that in all these weirdly named beers, they're pretending to actually put whatever it's named after into the drink?" Weasel asked, his eyes narrowed, clearly unconvinced.

"I'm not saying anything," Dominic replied, his hands held up in the universally understood 'not guilty' pose. "The diary is saying that. And it isn't pretending to put whatever the beer is named after in it, it claims that the name follows the inclusion of a specific animal into the mix. And it's not like they're publicising it."

They looked at each other, weighing up what Dominic had said.

"Bollocks," they chorused.

"I agree it sounds a bit far-fetched, but you guys haven't read the whole thing." Dominic reached across the table and grabbed the diary from Gareth, who was still shaking his head, and started flicking through the pages. "I was as sceptical as you when I first read it. There's no way they'd let a product like that be sold. But, ignoring the tone of the letter, as you go through this it seems to make more and more…" he struggled trying to find the right word. "Not sense, exactly. Clearly it doesn't make sense, but after a while it does seem to be perfectly possible if not probable that they're doing exactly what they say they're doing."

The Premiums, all bar Otter, sat back in their chairs, distancing themselves from Dominic, crossing their arms as barriers against his ridiculous claims, their body language broadcasting their scepticism. Dominic ploughed on undaunted.

"So the first beer was Lurcher's Last Stand, and as the first entry in the diary would have us believe, there is actual dog in it. The second beer they produced was called Grouchy Goat and was an experiment to see whether the first one had been a fluke. Apparently it wasn't. Third beer down they called Posturing Pig, and guess what? The diary claims the key ingredient is indeed pig."

"That isn't proof though," Gravy interrupted. "I could claim anything, it doesn't make it true. For instance I could claim that The Fuzz is a useful member of society, which clearly isn't true." He sat back, smiling.

The Fuzz swung a fist towards Gravy but Otter raised his palm and effortlessly caught his hand midway. A slight exhalation of air from The Fuzz combined with a quiet "Ow", proof that Otter's hands were as hard as iron.

"Absolutely, I agree," Dominic replied. "So far these are just crazy stories in a diary with nothing to prove or contradict them. They're just the ramblings of a man who has seemingly lost his mind, or is looking for a job as a writer of fiction, possibly both." He flicked through the diary as he spoke. Finally he found the page he was looking for. "This though, begins to cast it in a different light."

He turned the diary round so the others could see it better. The left hand page was covered in the neat hand writing of the author. On the right hand page, an article from a newspaper had been cut out and stuck to the diary. The article had been folded in half to fit within the smaller confines of the diary and as Gareth unfolded the paper, the rest of The Premiums leant forward, their curiosity overriding their scepticism.

"That article is taken from a local paper that covers the area in and around Little Bithrall, which is a small town in Surrey. It covers the story of what was considered a heinous crime at the time. There is a cat rescue centre in Little Bithrall, or at least there was. One night, people unknown broke into the centre and made off with all of the cats that had been there. Twenty-five moggies went missing that night with no trace of them ever being found. It was a complete mystery as to who committed the crime and what the fate of the twenty-five cats was."

The Premiums looked out from under their brows, knowing where Dominic was taking them but waiting for him to say the words.

"Anyone care to hazard a guess at what the name of the fourth beer these guys brewed was? No? Cat's Curiosity." Dominic sat back, his case made.

There was a pause as The Premiums mulled this over.

"Nope, that's still not proof," Gravy said having weighed both sides of the argument, the rest of the group agreeing with him, although Gareth was a little less vociferous than he had been earlier. "For all we know the diary could have been written after the article. Just because it's dated earlier doesn't mean it had to be written then. The article could have been the influence for the whole thing. Let's face it, it makes a pretty good story."

Dominic looked from face to face, seeing the same thing in each: a mix of mild embarrassment for him at having believed the diary and the unmistakable glint that said he would not be allowed to forget it.

"I take your point that this doesn't constitute actual proof, but if you read the whole thing, there is an air of authenticity about it. You know, these are the guys behind Hopmen Breweries. Why would you write this bearing in mind how successful they are? If it ever got out it would be horrendous publicity, even if it is all made up." Dominic was annoyed. Annoyed at his inability to convince his colleagues but more annoyed at the fact their scepticism was rubbing off on him. Gravy made a perfectly lucid and logical argument. Nothing he had read in the diary could in any way be considered more than anecdotal evidence at best, and as each minute passed under the scrutiny of his friends, it appeared more likely the diary was just a story—an old man's ramblings.

"Well, I still think there's something weird about it," Dominic muttered, closing the diary and sitting back in his seat. He felt deflated and a little foolish. The harsh light of day and Gravy's analysis moving him further and further away from his conviction the diary was true.

"You know, come to think of it, I think there may be something to this after all," Weasel said, breaking the contemplative silence which had filled the room. Dominic looked up cautiously; this was just as likely to be a massive piss-take in the making, as any actual take-up of his point of view. Weasel continued, keeping his cards close to his chest. If a punchline was coming they wouldn't be waiting long.

"It actually makes perfect sense. What's in an orange juice or an apple juice?" The beginning of a smile touched the edges of his mouth as he spoke. "Of course I may never drink a Bloody Mary again."

Weasel started laughing expecting the others to join in.

"That's disgusting," Gravy replied, as Otter turned away from the crudest of their number. He may have been massive but there was a sensitivity to Otter that surprised them all from time to time.

"So these are the blokes be'ind Hopmen Brewery right?" Gareth asked, glaring at Weasel.

"Yes," Dominic replied, resigned to the piss-taking.

"Hopmen Brewery is renowned for its Specials, tha's how it made its fortune right?" Dominic looked across at the hairy Cornishman. He didn't look like he was setting up for a joke of his own.

"Ok, so?"

"They also 'ave six standard beers that they make all the time. And to be fair they're pretty good, but not really any bedder than everybody else's," Gareth continued.

"What's your point?" Dominic asked, all The Premiums now interested in where Gareth was taking them.

"Why the vast difference in quality 'tween the standards an' the Specials? If you can make beer as good as the Specials, why not make that all the time? Nobody would ever drink anythin' else." Gareth looked round the group, an anxious look on his face—almost desperation—as he waited for someone to explain any possible reason for the approach the brewery had taken. He turned to Gravy. "Come on Gravy, explain it to me, cos it's beginnin' to freak me out a bit." Gravy stared back clearly trying to find a logical explanation for the conundrum Gareth had posed. After a moment he shook his head, forehead furrowed. He had nothing.

"They're probably just keeping demand high. You know, drip-feeding their customers," The Fuzz offered, but it sounded thin even to him.

"Have you ever 'ad one of their Specials?" Gareth asked. They all shook their heads. "They are phenomenal. You 'ave a session on one of those beers and you're depressed for a week. Not from the 'angover but from the fact you ent drinking it anymore. If you could, you'd drink it like water. From a business perspective why wouldn't you make that available all the time?"

"Because it's too risky. Of course!" Dominic's eureka moment suddenly allowed him to make sense of it. The rest of the group looked blankly, not getting there as fast.

"If you're going to make a beer called Cat's Curiosity and the key ingredient is actually cat, you're going to need a hell of a lot of them to keep making it for twelve or thirteen years. People are going to notice when that many cats go missing. They're going to start asking questions."

"Right." Gareth was now on the same page. "Keep the run limited an' therefore the need for any key ingredient to a minimum. Even if somebody does notice that a lot of cats are going missing, you've made yer batch and moved on to the next thing; cats stop goin' missing, people get over it and put it down to some unexplained phenomenon. It's genius. Evil genius I grant you, but genius all the same."

Dominic was convinced again and now so too was Gareth. As they looked around the rest of their team they saw, one by one, they too were coming to the realisation that Dominic had stumbled across something huge. First Gravy, unable to find the flaw in the logic, then Otter, whose usually indecipherable expression was now fluctuating between shock and sadness. The Fuzz was even persuaded and becoming distressed; he liked cats and the idea of them being pulped for someone's gain was proving hard to take. That just left Weasel. The Premiums all stared at him, not sure what his agreement would mean or crazy adventure they would end up embarking on. He sat there, eyes narrowed in thought looking around the group. Eventually he came to a conclusion and shook his head.

"I'm sorry, are you all mental? You expect me to believe that somewhere there is a group of old men liquidising cats to add to beer in order to improve the taste?" He articulated each point slowly and clearly, to ensure there could be no misunderstanding. "And that sounds plausible to you all does it?" He genuinely couldn't believe what he was hearing. "Christ, I know university educations aren't what they used to be but really."

The Premiums looked sheepish. Sometimes it took breaking an idea down to its component parts to see it for what it was. Gareth and Dominic looked at each other, a grin of embarrassment touching their lips.

"Well, when you put it like that, it does seem a little unlikely," Dominic said.

"Unlikely? And what about the Food Standards Agency? I'm fairly sure there are rules that would mean you had to declare it if ground-up goat was in your beer. Now can we please treat this with the contempt it deserves? We have an unexpected day off and I for one want to go to the pub, see how many animals I can drink."

Dominic started laughing. Whatever had caused his panic attack the previous night had well and truly done a number on him. Clearly it had put him in an overly suggestive state and when he started reading the diary he wasn't able to apply his usual logic and scepticism to its contents. Now that Weasel had burst the bubble, he could see it for the ridiculousness it was. The rest of The Premiums joined in, a weight and tension that had been evident since first thing that morning finally released.

As The Premiums got to their feet, Dominic collected the mugs and took them through to the kitchen. Yet another reason to sort his life out: gullibility brought on through lack of life goals. Right, he thought, today the pub but tomorrow a plan, and then the world. As he followed the rest of the team towards the front door he grabbed his bag and quickly ducked back into the lounge to retrieve the diary.

He pulled the front door shut and deadlocked it before catching up with the guys as they made their way to the nearest pub.

"You know, it's just as well this is all made up," he said as he fell into step with Gareth. "Because there are some really nasty people in here, and if it were true, I can't imagine they would be too happy at this diary being in our hands."

Chapter 24

Gulls wheeled above the dock as the last of the containers was manhandled from the enormous container ship Valkyrie Dawn, the weight of each container unnoticed by the mighty cranes standing 40 stories high, wheeling backwards and forwards in an almost perpetual dance to keep the supply of goods and produce flowing into and across Europe. Sirens wailed through the night as vehicles moved around the hustle and bustle of the port. Forklifts moved cargo from here to there; cranes rumbled along fixed rails from one ship to another; articulated lorries backed into loading bays, their own warning sirens drowned out by the louder horns from the ships themselves.

In the area of the terminal given over to the loading of lorries, Bill Humble waited for the paperwork to be completed so he could collect his container and then get loaded on the ferry that would take him to Hull. He had been waiting for six hours now due to some delay in getting the particular container he was collecting cleared through customs. That in itself wasn't unusual—with the increased security in and out of airports, ferry terminals had naturally come under increased focus from criminal gangs from around the world. The same heightened security that was preventing terrorists hijacking planes hadn't quite filtered down to the ports and as such provided a much easier method of transporting all manner of illegal cargo, from drugs to counterfeit designer labels, to people. What greater security checks had been brought in had really only acted to slow the whole process down. If a country started opening cargo ports as tourist attractions then the security situation would improve but as it was, he wasn't holding his breath.

An hour later a customs official came to the counter in the drivers' lounge and called him up for a few final signatures to legalise the paperwork that would allow him to take his lorry into the container area and get loaded up before boarding the ferry. Once onboard he had a 12 hour sailing before arriving back in England and a drive to the container's final destination, wherever that may be. He would receive the location when the GPS tracker on the container reached Hull. With his paperwork stating that his cargo of washing machines had been cleared by Dutch customs officials, Bill climbed into his cab, started the engine, and drove into the port to collect his container.

The joy of driving had been with him ever since he was seventeen and had passed his driving test twenty years ago. He had got his HGV licence ten years later, having been made redundant from the plastics factory where he had spent the previous ten years doing night shifts, cutting small plastic mouldings from central sprees and putting them into boxes. Twelve hours a night he had performed essentially the same task for ten years and solely down to his own lethargy and laziness had never had the impetus to change things. When the letter arrived notifying him of the redundancy, he had taken the news with the same lethargic complacency. The only reason he was now an HGV licence holder was because his previous employer felt a responsibility to its employees and enrolled him onto a programme of retraining. Bill had been lucky enough to be taken on by a haulier and develop a skill that came naturally to him. It was the first time in his life he had actually gained any kind of pleasure from his job. There was nothing else that gave him the simple pleasure and enjoyment he gained from driving his lorry across Europe. As much as he loved the driving though it was barely enough to keep him in the game anymore. Thank God for the 'special' runs he thought.

He smiled to himself—easy money on an easy run. He had been told when he first agreed to do these runs that they needed his English licence and clean record to help move a few 'items' into the country. He didn't have to worry about customs as that would be taken care of and all he had to do was deliver the container to an address he would be given as he arrived in the UK. Simple. Each time he and his special cargo got to the port of Hull, a GPS tracking device activated and he received final delivery instructions. After that it was a case of turning up, unhooking the trailer unit and going about his business. He had absolutely no idea what was in the back of the containers, or even cared. To him, each journey meant £15,000 tax-free. Add those fifteen grands to the wages his employer paid him and he was on a comfortable little earner.

An hour later he pulled his lorry onto the haulage deck of the ferry. With one final once over to ensure the cargo was secure he made his way to one of the many bars and ordered himself a pint of flat beer. He wouldn't drink much, his clean licence was non-negotiable if he wanted to continue with these trips, but a couple of pints wouldn't hurt.

As Bill settled into the brief crossing, a green light on the GPS tracking device on the container blinked silently in the cargo hold. It had been blinking constantly since the container had been sealed, updating a terminal many hundreds of miles away as to its precise location, thirteen orbiting satellites pinpointing it to within a few feet every mile of its long journey.

Chapter 25

There were times in life when you really had to sit down and examine why you continued to do things a certain way. For Hank, that moment came with a vibration from his pocket, and focussed on why he ever let Razor do anything of significance or that may require subtlety.

Of course he knew the answer: he needed Razor in situations that called for more aggression than he himself brought to the party. Razor in fact was more politically correct than Hank could ever be; he had an equal opportunities attitude to violence—he'd batter anyone. But that was the problem. That fire, ready, aim approach shut down options rather than opening them up.

The task had, he thought, been very simple. Once the chance to grab Dominic Morgan had been missed, their focus had turned to the other avenue O'Connell had provided them: Dominic's girlfriend, Beth. So, they would head to the address O'Connell had given them and invite Beth in for a chat. They would then call Dominic and offer to exchange the diary for Beth. Foolproof, he thought.

And so it had proved to be. He had pulled up outside the address they had for Beth and checked the street for anyone obviously taking an interest in them. The neighbourhood watch from earlier still on his mind. This street seemed less vigilant or community-spirited because there were no signs on the lampposts and no curtains twitched as they waited.

As they had been about to make their way to Beth's front door, Hank's phone had started buzzing. Ordinarily he was very strict about compartmentalising jobs. While actively pursuing one objective he didn't think about the other jobs he had, let alone engage with messages. To do so interrupted your concentration and disrupted your focus, preventing you from effectively completing the job in hand. A lesson that was being reinforced for him as he sedately drove through leafy Surrey with a woman bound and gagged in the back of the van.

Distracted by events and the buzzing he had made a snap decision. He decided that abducting a young woman was something Razor could handle on his own, so sent Razor off and checked his messages.

Any concern he had felt was shortly dispelled as Razor came running down the path with a struggling young woman in his arms. Hank had leapt into the back of the van and opened the side door just as Razor had thrown the body in. Hank slammed the door closed after Razor climbed in and then jumped into the driver's seat to make good their escape.

The woman in the back had hardly made a sound as Razor duct taped her hands and feet together and covered her head in a black bag. While binding them, Razor discovered a phone in her hands which he passed to Hank who slid it into his pocket. The whole kidnapping had taken less than a minute and the likelihood of anyone having seen them was slim at best. Hank had been pleased as they pulled away; with a fair wind he would have the diary before dinner time and could then focus all his attention on the latest delivery of ingredients.

Having pulled the phone from his pocket now he wasn't so sure.

The picture of a pretty blond had appeared on the screen. Below the picture was one word: **Beth**. Not impossible that someone called Beth could have a friend also called Beth, but Hank didn't like it. The happy place he had been inhabiting since the abduction was shrinking around him.

"Razor, just out of interest, you're sure we got the right woman?" He indicated over his shoulder at the prone figure in the back.

Razor nodded his head.

"Did you ask?" he said, keeping his tone neutral. The blank expression that met him told him all he needed to know.

Another dilemma: should he answer the phone? The answer to that was quite clearly yes, however bearing in mind the illegality of using a phone whilst driving and the fact they had a bound and gagged woman in the back of the van, Hank decided to wait until they reached their warehouse. Being pulled over by a plod was one thing, but trying to explain that it had been necessary for him to take the call in order for him to ascertain whether they had kidnapped the right woman didn't seem like the kind of excuse that would see him sent on his way with wrapped knuckles. It was more likely to see him wrapped round the head with a baton and conveyed, unconscious, to prison.

Ten minutes later they arrived at the warehouse he sometimes used as a holding area for whatever he was involved with. Razor dragged the woman out of the van and dropped her onto a rotten-looking sofa in the corner. She whimpered slightly as she thumped down and a broken spring stuck in her side. Pulling his balaclava on, Hank turned to their prisoner and removed the black bag from her head.

She started screaming as they stood over her, the sound muffled by the gag.

"Calm down," Hank ordered. No hint of compassion was evident and the woman fought to control herself, eventually managing to contain the screams that her wide eyes indicated were still rattling around her brain.

"Very good. Now I am going to remove the gag and ask you a question. If you scream again my friend here will be very unhappy. Do you understand?" The captive's eyes flicked across to Razor then snapped back immediately to the lesser of two evils. She nodded tentatively. Hank removed the gag and waited for the screams to start again. Reassured that the woman did have control he dropped down onto his haunches and stared directly into her eyes.

"Is your name Beth?"

She shook her head insistently. Fuck, thought Hank.

"Are you sure? Because you don't know whether that is a good or a bad thing to us at the moment." That probably wouldn't help her decision making but Hank was annoyed that Razor, and by extension himself, had fucked up again. She shook her head even harder, still too scared to utter a sound.

Hank stood up and stared down at her.

"Then who are you and what were you doing at Beth's flat?"

"Naomi," she finally managed after three attempts to speak. "I'm Beth's flatmate."

Fuck, he thought, we've kidnapped the wrong bloody flatmate. This was the problem with any plan. What was the military saying? No plan survives the first engagement. Well that had been proven. The error Hank had made was to act on the desperate words of O'Connell who it appeared had only known half the facts, without the time to verify them.

He turned from the woman and walked across the warehouse to an office in the opposite corner. He needed to salvage the situation and fast. An idea struck him and he stuck his head out of the office and shouted across the warehouse.

"Do you like each other?" The woman nodded. Ok, not a complete loss. Taking her phone from his pocket he walked back and held it up to her face to unlock it. A moment later he was taken to Naomi's home screen. Tapping the phone icon at the bottom of the screen brought up a list of recent calls. Top of the list was an entry named *Beth*. Hank touched the entry and the phone started to connect. After a few seconds he heard the ringing tone and before it could ring for a third time it was answered.

"Hi Naomi, how're you doing?"

"Is this Beth?" Hank asked, ignoring her question.

"Yes, who's this? Is that Joel? Why do you have Naomi's phone?"

"Beth who works for Swift & Smooth?" he continued. This time he was determined to intimidate the correct person.

"What? Yeah, who is this?"

"Do you also know a Dominic Morgan?"

"What? Who is this?"

"Do you know Morgan?" he shouted. There was a brief pause on the other end of the line.

"If you don't tell me who you are this conversation is over," Beth said.

"I don't think you want to do that. Not when Naomi's life is in the balance." This time the pause from the other end of the line was longer and deeper. "Do you know Dominic Morgan?" Hank asked again. When Beth finally spoke, the anger in her voice was palpable.

"Not funny, Joel." With that she disconnected the call.

Hank stormed out of the office and marched across to Razor and the captive woman. She recoiled as far into the filthy green sofa as she could, the terror writ large on her face, expecting to see her captor's fist driving towards her. Instead, Hank flicked through the apps and selected the camera. Holding the phone out towards Naomi, he took a picture and then stormed back to the small office.

He flicked through the phone until he found the text message app and then opened a new one. Call me, he wrote, then attached the picture he had just taken and pressed send. After a minute the screen lit up and the picture of the pretty blond appeared again. He let it ring for a while before answering, aware of the tension the person on the other end of the call would be feeling.

"Do you know Dominic Morgan?" he said without preamble. In kidnap situations there was little call for small talk.

"Yes, I know Dominic. What is this?" Beth finally managed, the realisation that this was real adding a tremor to her voice.

"Dominic has something that I want returned to me. You are going to get him to do so or I am going to start cutting bits off your friend. Do you understand?"

There was a slight pause as the true horror of what was happening sank in before Beth replied in a whisper, "Yes".

Chapter 26

December 12th 1984

This evening's meeting of the SSoH has resulted in the unanimous decision being taken to proceed along the path discovered by Jeff. More than one dissenting voice was raised (including my own) against the idea, once the effects of the Lurcher's had worn off, but a single further sip of this remarkable drink has left us all in a state of agreement where to not proceed would seem like the greater crime.

It has also been agreed that to formalise our arrangement, and indeed create a pact of joint culpability, the next experiment, or at least the procurement of the necessary produce, will be conducted by all of us. My belief, when my head is clear of Lurcher's, is that what we are embarking on is clearly wrong and could have untold consequences for us all. I know this to be true yet it is an absurd after-effect of the beer that once imbibed, this most rational of thoughts seems voided of logic, the very idea not to try again an affront.

Following my most vocal dissent, Jeff has decided two things: One – the name of the new batch will be Posturing Pig and Two – that I will be the one to provide the produce. I am filled with dread at the thought of what the next few days and weeks will bring. What is clear is that if we are successful, then we will have confirmed the greatest discovery of all time and almost certainly consigned our souls to eternal damnation.

"Bleddy 'ell," said Gareth as he put the diary on the table and raised his pint. "He really is melodramatic in 'is storytelling isn't he?"

Dominic, sat opposite, raised his own glass and clinked it against Gareth's. He had taken more stick when they got to the pub for ordering a lime and soda, but he just wasn't ready to embrace beer just yet.

"He does have a certain tone about him doesn't he?" he agreed. "I quite like it though. It's sort of stately and having met the bloke it suits him."

"What you gonna do with it? Once I've finished it, that is."

Dominic hadn't really thought about it. He himself hadn't finished the whole thing yet, his narcolepsy on the toilet that morning robbing him of the time to complete the read.

"I guess I'll return it to Mr Forthright when we do the removal. I didn't get the feeling they were shopping around for quotes so I imagine in the next week he'll get it back. I might have to ask him why he gave it to me in the first place though. It's all a bit weird."

"Well, I think it 'as 'Bestseller' written all over it." Gareth picked up the diary again and continued to read.

December 15th 1984

There's no time like the present according to Jeff. Operation Posturing Pig is scheduled for the early hours of tomorrow morning. Mabel knows nothing of what we are doing, as is the case for the other wives also. We have therefore arranged a fake fishing trip to cover our absences. By this time tomorrow I will be fully immersed in the actions of the SSoH.

January 26th 1985

An omen if ever there was want for one. I write this entry from my bed still convalescing from the events of six weeks ago. The doctors and surgeons who have attended me are confident that I will make a full recovery. Full except of course for my left leg, amputated below the knee.

It was nothing more or less than a freak accident. At least that is how Jeff is describing it. The mere unfortunate confluence of myriad options that all went awry at the same time leaving me short on blood and low on limbs.

It had started as we had planned. Derek collected me in his Ford Capri Ghia mid-afternoon and I bade farewell to Mabel. So preoccupied with the forthcoming evening's events was I that I completely forgot my tackle box. A note of suspicion was evident in Mabel's face as she ran out to us before we drove off. She knew there was something I wasn't telling her but trusted me there was good reason for keeping it from her. I feel I have betrayed that trust. I hope one day she can forgive me.

Derek drove us to Jeff's pub where Martin, Steve and Terry were waiting. Steve had managed to acquire what looked like a miniature horse box, which we hooked up to the back of Derek's pride and joy. Jeff knew of a small farm approximately twenty miles away that kept pigs. The animals were effectively allowed to roam freely through a copse on the edge of the farmer's land and as such were suitably secluded from view, bearing in mind what we had planned. After a few rounds of Lurcher's, we set off with our hopes and ambitions suitably raised, the unmistakable air of invulnerability about us.

We approached the farm on a small B road and pulled up in the entrance to a field, directly adjacent to the copse. As our watches told us it was midnight, myself, Martin and Derek climbed the five bar gate and made our way round the field hugging the hedgerow as we went. We paused at the edge of the copse and listened; from within the darkness came the sound of snuffling as if something was rooting through the foliage on the ground. We had found our pigs. I braced myself and forced my way into the wooded area and started my search.

I had no way of knowing what the best way to attract pigs was, so had settled on the element of surprise. I moved slowly and quietly through the trees, stopping often to recalibrate from where the sounds were coming, then moving off towards them. The plan was that once I had discovered a pig, I would drive it or usher it towards Martin and Derek. They would then usher it towards the mini horse box that Jeff and Terry were positioning close by. Steve would then lure the beast into the box and close the door behind it. It sounded easy.

The plan started to veer off course as I was carefully stepping through a particularly thick bit of gorse. I was well protected in my tweed jacket and trousers but nevertheless I became hitched on the thorns. This threw my weight off and I stumbled, my left foot coming down in a hollow full of recent rainwater which caused me to land on all fours. As I knelt there trying to extricate myself from the intractable gorse and the roots and hollows where my foot had become trapped, I came face to face with the pig I had been tracking. What became apparent was that what Jeff had confidently identified as a pig turned out to be a wild boar and not a well-natured beast either. Threatened by my sudden appearance and with thick gorse and tree roots blocking its preferred option of escape, it attacked me. It lowered its head and charged right at me. I managed to get to my feet but one of its tusks penetrated my tweeds and gouged a deep tear in my left calf. In a panic I tore my foot free and fled.

You would have thought with its escape route clear the ghastly thing would have resumed its search for acorns or whatnot, but no, this boar had revenge on its mind. As I ran, it ran after me, biting at my trailing left leg, worsening the damage with every swing of its head and bite of its powerful jaws. It seemed as if the boar had developed a taste for Wilbur as even when I burst clear of the copse out into the moonlit field, the boar kept coming. The other members of the SSoH had backed the travel box into position and were standing in a tight semi-circle to help crowd the expected pig into it. But the animal was not cowed by fear. If anything it seemed to redouble its efforts, possibly already aware the end would not be good but hell bent on tasking me with it. I sprinted towards the travel box as best I could and managed to throw myself on top of it just as the animal closed its jaws around my calf again. It was swinging in and out of the box with each arc of my leg, all the time desperately trying to tear my muscle from my leg. Thankfully, Jeff stepped forward with a large stick and struck the animal on the head. At last I felt the relief as its jaws loosened from around my leg and it slumped to the floor of the box unconscious.

We wrapped my leg as best we could and returned to Jeff's pub where unsurprisingly we discovered that Lurcher's also made boar attacks seem better. Even so I couldn't help feeling that this venture may have started off on the wrong foot, if you will forgive the terrible pun.

My greater mistake was to assume that the injury would heal of its own accord. It was a week later, once the infection had truly taken hold, that Mabel commented on the foul smell following me around everywhere and demanded to know why I was limping so badly. She was far from impressed when I rolled the leg of my trouser up and showed her the damage. No arguing this time, it was straight to the doctor who confirmed the worst. I had waited too long and the bloody thing would have to come off. So here I am, sat up in bed, waiting for the wound to heal sufficiently for me to be fitted with a prosthetic, feeling very sorry for myself. The only positive is that after such a debacle, the beer-making experiments have ceased.

Mabel has just told me that we have guests. The SSoH have come to visit…

…They have just left and I have reviewed what I wrote before their arrival and I must say it seems to me a most depressing recounting of that night. Of course it didn't go as well as we hoped but to say it was a debacle is clearly wide of the mark. What a difference a few friendly faces makes when you're down and feeling blue. It also turns out that my assumption that the beer making had ceased was a little premature also. The name remains, even if the produce

changed slightly. Posturing Pig is another winner. It seems Jeff was right, it isn't just dogs that make this stuff good. I can't wait for the next one.

"This old boy's got some imagination, I'll give 'im that." Gareth was shaking his head. "I assume there's a story behind 'ow each of 'em get their particular disability?"

"Absolutely. Jeff losing his eye for Penguin's Prerogative is quite funny and Derek having his back broken by an enraged chimp makes for a good read as well. I haven't got to the end yet but there is some pretty weird stuff in there."

Gareth picked up his fresh pint, one that Dominic had bought while Gareth was buried in the diary, and took a large mouthful.

"Where are the others?" he asked, already eyeing the diary again as if keen for his next fix. It was like the beer within its pages, Dominic thought: conceptually questionable but always leaving you wanting more.

"They buggered off about half an hour ago. Otter got a call from a mysterious friend and Gravy was saying he's just had a pool table delivered so they went to his place."

They sat in silence for a while, each lost in their own thoughts, Gareth periodically taking another deep gulp from his pint then burping, while Dominic stared out of the window and thought about the diary.

"What you thinking?" Gareth asked, a tell-tale glint in his eye.

"What? Nothing," Dominic replied too defensively.

"Clearly not. After all, thinking of nothing tends to put a large frown on my face an' all." Dominic gave a shrug of resignation.

"It's the diary. I can't get over how real it felt last night, even with what everyone was saying earlier it just seemed real. And there are a couple of guys in there," he tapped the diary by way of emphasis, "who are properly dangerous. One of them's called Hank who has a psychotic sidekick." Dominic sighed heavily. "I don't know. It's all just feeling a bit odd at the moment."

Gareth looked genuinely surprised.

"Really? I woulda put money on you bein' all caught up with what yer gonna do 'bout Beth." That was what the glint was for Dominic thought. "It's obvious you really like 'er and I 'ave to say, from what little I know about 'er, I can't imagine she thinks what 'appened was anything but a misunderstandin'. And 'er mother clearly came out on top so definitely can't 'old a grudge. I mean look at what she did to yer face."

Dominic sat back in his chair and put his face in his hands. In all the excitement he had felt surrounding the diary, he had actually managed to forget about Beth and her mother. Not that he wanted to, he had merely been sidetracked.

"You really think she'll forgive me for, you know, getting intimate with her mum?" the faintest twinge of optimism evident in his voice.

"Who knows mate, but I dun't think she's the kind of girl who invites you back to 'er flat if she di'n't actually like you. I think if you can get over 'er mother breaking yer nose, she should be able to get over you fondlin' said mother's tits." Gareth laughed at the pained expression that crossed Dominic's face.

"That's not funny man," he managed as his phone started vibrating on the table. With a speed his large frame belied, Gareth snatched the phone from in front of Dominic and smiled.

"Well 'ere's yer chance to find out," he said as he slowly turned the phone round to face Dominic.

Dominic wasn't creepy enough to have a picture of Beth in his phone so all that flashed on the screen was **Beth**. He glanced at Gareth. Now was as good a time as any to see how the land lay so he took the phone and climbed out from behind the table and headed towards the exit. Gareth had enough time to hear Dominic say a very sheepish 'hello' then after a few moments a more urgent 'calm down, calm down,' and for Beth to 'start from the beginning' before he made it outside and beyond the range of Gareth's hearing. He thought for a minute then downed his beer, grabbed their stuff, and followed Dominic out into the sunshine.

Chapter 27

"This feels wrong. He should be here." Steve was pacing the room like a caged animal, the tension rising every time he turned on his heels and made a return pass. "If he's having doubts then shouldn't we be trying to help him through them? Doesn't that make more sense than ostracising him?" He was merely voicing what most of the other members of SSoH had been thinking since the awards dinner. The fact they had been ordered (for that is what it had been) to ignore Wilbur, had required each of them to resist their normal reaction to a friend having difficulties, which would have been to discuss it. Or to reach out and let Wilbur know he wasn't the only one who felt such doubts—that he wasn't the only one who felt weighed down by their deeds. But Jeff was a hard man to say no to.

Terry fidgeted in the large, ostentatious leather armchair. The fact he was missing the whole of his right arm and shoulder creating the sense he was a much smaller man than he was.

"Agreed," he said. "But what do you want to do about it? Speak to Wilbur and then try to keep that a secret from Jeff? Good luck. He may only have one eye but he sees far more than the rest of us." His left hand rubbed the area where his shoulder and arm should have been—a nervous tick that presented during times of high stress.

"Jeff has really got himself worked up over this," Derek added from his wheelchair positioned close to the window. "And not just with the spying he made me do, but with his attitude generally. He's been in this barely-controlled rage for the last few days. I'll be honest, it scares me."

"You're all talking as if he's acting completely irrationally. Let's not forget what Wilbur did. We all saw how drunk he was. He had no idea what he was saying or who he was saying it to. And the fact that he kept a diary in the first place exposes us to an unacceptable level of risk." Martin poured himself a large brandy as the others considered what he had said. "I don't want to think the worst of Wilbur either but it seems Jeff is the only one of us looking out for our best interests. If we get caught we're going to jail and everything we've worked for disappears." He returned to his position next to the fireplace, his elbow perched on the mantelpiece. Without plan or orchestration the four men had arranged themselves as if in an Agatha Christie whodunnit, waiting for an incompetent policeman and a genius private detective to explain how the terrible crime had been committed. The room fell silent as each man considered their own personal ramifications if the truth came out: the impact on their families, children and grandchildren, as well as the idea of spending the rest of their lives in prison.

They had been summoned to Jeff's grand country pile by their leader earlier that morning with no explanation as to the purpose. On arrival they had been ushered into the study and left there for what was now approaching an hour, while Jeff dealt with 'some important business'. They still had no clue to what end they had been summoned but Jeff had clearly been preoccupied when they arrived.

Their Agatha Christie tableau was interrupted a few minutes later when Jeff burst through the door whistling. The four men looked up, surprised at the dramatic change in Jeff. None of them had ever heard him whistle before, and although he clearly wasn't practiced at the art, they could each discern Queen's *Another One Bites The Dust*, as he strolled happily into the study.

"Sorry, sorry. Sorry for the delay. I just had a few things I needed to take care of." He looked around at his friends and noticed the pensive and sombre atmosphere that had developed. "It's a bit tense in here isn't it? Come on, who wants a drink? Martin, I see you have one, good man. Derek, Campari and Orange?" Bewildered by the turn of events, Derek nodded. "Excellent. What about you Terry? G&T or something stronger?" Jeff's positivity had taken them all by surprise, and like Derek, Terry nodded his head before looking questioningly at the others. Jeff busied himself making the drinks then turned to Steve. "Last but by no means least, what can I get Big Steve?"

This really was too much. Never had any of them ever referred to Steve as 'Big Steve'. Large as he was, affectionate nicknames had never featured in their relationships before, and forty years in seemed an odd time for it to start.

"Are you alright Jeff?" Steve asked as Jeff bounced around the room delivering drinks to their recipients. "You seem a bit…" Steve paused searching for the right word, "hyper." Jeff turned to him, surprised.

"Hey, what's wrong with a little happiness? Being a bit upbeat? Come on, it's been a tough week, but things are eventually coming round to our way of thinking. I'll fill you all in but first, a drink." He pointed at Steve, motionless as he waited for the response. Eventually, embarrassed by the focus being solely on him, Steve asked for a whiskey over ice. Jeff clapped once and turned back to the drinks trolley, dropped ice into two tumblers and covered them with amber liquid. He passed one to Steve and raised the other into the air.

"To problems solved and challenges overcome." He peered from one man to the next, beaming, until all had their glasses raised. "Cheers."

"Cheers," they chorused in return.

Jeff dropped into a spare seat and sighed contentedly, but offered no explanation as to the change in his mood. Eventually, unable to cope with the peculiarity of the situation, Steve piped up again.

"And?"

"And what?" replied Jeff.

"You were going to explain about the upbeatness, and cheerfulness, and the whistling?" Steve reiterated, becoming more and more concerned that Jeff might actually be on drugs, so unusual was his behaviour.

"Oh that, of course." Jeff got to his feet, seamlessly fitting into the unplanned crime fiction cliché they were recreating, as he took over from Steve in pacing the room. It appeared Jeff's role was to be the narrator, bringing them all up to speed before the big revelation. "Well as you know a few days ago, at what was supposed to be the crowning moment of our careers, our good friend, confidant and co-conspirator Wilbur, dropped a bombshell. Now I don't need to tell you how potentially dangerous that bombshell could be if it was proved that he had in fact kept a diary charting the history of the Secret Society of Hopmen." He paused purely for effect, slowly turning to each man before continuing. "I don't know about all of you, but I remember taking an oath all those years ago that what we were embarking on would remain the sole knowledge of the SSoH. The sad news is that with the help of Derek and some other resources at my disposal, I have confirmed the existence of the diary and have been engaged in its recovery. One of the reasons I had to leave you was to take a call from one of the resources I have been using in its retrieval. Whilst it isn't currently in his possession, he has guaranteed me that it will be by dinner time today. I think we can all agree, that in itself is worth a celebratory toast." He smiled broadly, expecting the others to join him, but was faced with more confusion.

"I don't understand. What about Wilbur?" Terry asked.

"What about Wilbur? We have the diary, or soon will have. All is good," Jeff said, a trace of annoyance evident in his tone.

"Yes but I think Terry's point is the diary is one thing; excellent that we're getting that back. But the diary had an author, and I think we understand now that said author has a confession to make unless we help him. Where is he? Why isn't he here?" Steve said. Terry nodded, pleased he wasn't the only one to see the gaping flaw in what Jeff seemed to see as the solution to their collective problem.

"Wilbur isn't an issue. He's fine. I spoke to him the other day, talked it all out and he's promised not to discuss the matter further. He has however ended his connection with the Society." Jeff's pacing around the room had increased from leisurely to purposeful as his colleagues asked more and more questions.

"What, just like that, after forty years he leaves the organisation without a word to any of us?" Derek asked.

"Yes Derek." Jeff spun to face him, his one good eye boring into him as if challenging him to ask another question. "He felt it best that having betrayed our brotherhood, he removed himself from our lives with as little fuss as possible. Do you have a problem with that?"

"Well yes, actually, I do," replied Derek, his incomprehension and annoyance finally overpowering the fear he felt from Jeff's aggressive tone. "I've known Wilbur nearly fifty years, been in business with him for more than forty and you're telling me he decided to just slink away?" The look from the three other men was just as incredulous as Derek's. They had all been friends for too long, knew each other too well for what Jeff had said to make any sense. Of all of them, Wilbur had always been the nicest—plain and simple. He had been the mediator when relationships between the others had faltered, the most considerate and probably the most caring. It had been no real surprise to any of them when it was Wilbur who seemed to be having the most difficulty living with what they had done, but none of them believed for a second that Wilbur would walk away from half a century of friendship without so much as a goodbye.

Jeff eyed the other men in the room. He was aware he had worked with them for more than four decades but at this moment, he barely recognised any of them, so far had they seemed to fall from the goal they had agreed all those years before. As his anger boiled within him, fighting to gain control and thus an outlet, Jeff realised he was completely alone. He was the only one willing to defend what they had built, to protect their secret and keep them safe. He could feel the rage building. When he had lost control previously in his life it had been as a result of this power within, this hatred and anger overpowering him, but this time he would consciously give in to it. Just as he was about to unleash the fury there was a knock on the study door.

He struggled momentarily to reassert his conscious control over the broiling demon raging inside, then slowly walked to the door and opened it a few inches. On the other side was his house keeper. Ordinarily she would never have interrupted one of her employers meetings but she had no choice this time.

"Sorry to interrupt Jeff, but there are a couple of policemen here to see you. They said it's about Wilbur."

Chapter 28

There had been a steady stream of builder's strength tea since Dominic and Gareth had arrived back at his house. Having followed his friend from the pub, Gareth had expected to find him slowly pacing around the car park, as he and Beth worked through whatever it was they needed to work through after the events of a few nights ago.

Gareth himself had known many walks that would typically fall into the category 'of shame'. Some of them would even be considered more embarrassing than Dominic's. The key difference for him was he had got to the point where that *was* the point. A sexual encounter, to Gareth, might as well not have happened unless it gave him another amusing story to add to his already considerable canon of work. Had Dominic and Beth's encounter happened to him, he would have worn the black eyes with pride; the idea of blaming them on an unsteady pissed person, unthinkable.

The situation for Dominic however, was very different. For a start he had already been half way down the road. Gareth had needed to run to catch him up and when he had he'd seen that Dominic was white as a ghost and trying very hard to calm Beth down, with what sounded like little success.

The two of them were now sat in Dominic's front room, Dominic with his head in his hands and Gareth with his head in the diary, waiting for Beth. At the slightest sound, Dominic bolted from his chair and lunged towards the window, flicking the net curtains and peering out into the street, desperately searching for either Beth or the psychopaths he now knew were after him. Once again there was nothing there and he returned to his chair and ignored his third cup of tea.

Sounds of incredulity emitted from Gareth periodically as he read another unbelievable entry in Wilbur Forthright's diary. The latest groan drew Dominic's attention; this one had a definite 'we may be fucked' tone to it.

"What?" he demanded.

Gareth looked up and sighed heavily. Since Dominic had brought him up to speed regarding Naomi's kidnapping and the reasons behind it, his scepticism had evaporated almost as quickly as his stomach had jettisoned his beer. Once they had got back to Dominic's house, he had busied himself with trying to get as much detail from the diary as possible.

"You were right." He turned his eyes back to the diary. "These guys oo 'ave Naomi are proper fuckers. I mean we're in deep shit 'ere. I think we should just take this diary and give it to the police."

"We can't, I told you that," Dominic said, standing and pacing to the window again. "They told Beth that if she or anybody else contacted the police they'd kill Naomi. No ifs or buts, no maybes, they would slit her throat and then they'd kill the rest of us." He was barely holding on to his sanity. Little more than twelve hours ago he had thought he knew what freaking out felt like, but now he realised that was just the realisation he was wasting his life. Now the world was a very different place. It didn't seem to matter so much that he had a wanker of a boss, or that he had turned down promotions, or even that he was working in a job he didn't like much, still living at home with his mum. The whole Beth thing—the catalyst to his mini freak-out the night before—had even been rendered inconsequential. What mattered now was that some 'proper fuckers' were threatening to kill his would-be girlfriend's flatmate because of a stupid book an old man had slipped into his backpack. If Dominic and his friends got out of this alive, he was going straight round to Forthright's house and was going to punch him in his wispy eyebrowed face, the bastard.

"I know that mate, but seriously, listen to this." Gareth cleared his throat and started reading from the diary.

March 17th 2009

Another St Patrick's day, our 25th since we entered into our pact and set the tongues in the beverage world lolling in desire and wagging with rumour, everybody desperate to know how we do it. In celebration of our ever-growing success (we received a request for a couple of cases of Penguin's Prerogative to be sent to the White House last week) I bought Mabel a vintage Cartier watch.

It was ridiculously overpriced, but that term has conceded its meaning to me now so much money do our beers make. Suffice to say she loved it; its beauty distracting her sufficiently so she missed the bitterness I felt at the means with which I had afforded her it. Oh well. She has suffered as each of the founder members has suffered. She deserves it and much more, so I shall think no more about it.

"Is there a point to any of this?" Dominic interrupted, the strain and frustration evident on his voice.

"Absolutely. Bear wi' me. This is the important bit now." He cleared his throat again and continued.

...so I shall think no more about it.

We had a meeting today where Jeff introduced us to a couple of gentlemen, though I fear they are far from qualifying for that moniker, who will be assisting us in the procurement of certain key ingredients. I looked around the room at the announcement and couldn't help thinking, better late than never. The other chaps were similarly buoyed by the idea. I did however notice that Jeff had laid on plenty of Betrothed Bat to oil the proceedings. We were introduced to Hank and Razor (I doubt they are their real names) who proceeded to offer some of the highlights from their resumes. I can't help thinking that had we been drinking one of the standards, we might all have revolted at their presence.

Hank appears to be the man in charge, their Jeff if you will, with this Razor character providing, as far as I can tell, the intimidation factor, crazy-eyed and pointy-toothed as he is. Hank mentioned he had been briefed by Jeff regarding the type of work they would be carrying out for us and he wanted us to rest assured he would fulfil his end of the agreement as long as we fulfilled ours. For us, money has almost become trivial so this will not be hard to do.

"Gareth seriously. Are you going to get to the point?"

"Right now."

He then proceeded to confirm his felonious credentials: robbery, burglary, extortion, theft, kidnapping if necessary. Although he didn't say he could arrange for people to disappear he certainly left us under no misapprehension that such was so. All the while his tone was calm, matter-of-fact. There was no bravado or arrogance, merely the calm and confident assuredness of a professional.

The off-handed way he mentioned the more violent side of his profession, as much a warning to us I believe as intended to breed confidence in them. As he spoke, his colleague with the unnatural eyes and teeth merely stood there staring at each of us in turn, as if indelibly burning our likenesses into his brain. He wasn't foaming at the mouth, but he may as well have been. Had they not been drinking the Bat as well I can't help thinking they may have been more cautious with their tale. Regardless, I can't help thinking Jeff has made our already repugnant situation considerably worse. Now we must fear these villains as well as the authorities. I pray I never come to incur their wrath.

Gareth looked up at Dominic, the terror in his eyes obvious.

"This is fuckin' mental Dom. We 'ave to go to the police. We're fuckin' removal men for God's sake, and shit ones at that. We aren't equipped to deal wi'this," pleading flashed across his face.

"You don't have to tell me we're out of our depths. I know." The pitch and tone of Dominic's voice rose with each word. "But they are going to kill Naomi if we do. Let's just wait until Beth gets here and we can decide what the fuck we're going to do." Dominic genuinely didn't know whether Gareth would go along with his 'I don't have a plan' plan until the big Cornishman slumped slightly and nodded.

Dominic breathed heavily, attempting to get his heart rate back under control. His heart had been hammering since Beth's phone call, adrenalin flooding his system. He didn't know how to fight and he currently had nowhere to run, so for the time being at least, it was uselessly pumping round his system, constantly ticking the meter over—a bill that would have to be paid at some point by a very long sleep. For now though he was wide awake and right on the edge.

Chapter 29

The remaining members of the SSoH sat in silence, the weight of the news that Wilbur and Mabel had perished in a fire at their home almost too much to bear. Two policemen, Kostatis and Grieg, had spent approximately twenty minutes informing them of what had happened and asking them questions. At first the shock robbed them of their abilities to compute what they were being told.

A fire last night.

Raged uncontrollably.

House completely destroyed.

Two bodies removed this morning.

Waiting for positive identification.

Too early to say where the fire started.

Too early to say *how* the fire started.

The last comment forced its way through their incomprehension, dispelling the mists of confusion and disbelief, reverberating around their heads. They each snapped their heads up; what did they mean, 'too early to say *how* the fire started'? Steve shot Jeff a momentary look, almost too fast to notice.

Too fast that is unless you were someone trained to notice things, especially at times when it was too soon to say *how* the fire had started. DCI Kostatis watched the group as his colleague talked them through what they knew so far. His eyes followed Steve's to rest on Jeff. Merely a coincidence? Perhaps. But it didn't take long for police officers to become cynical, and Kostatis had been a copper for nearly twenty years. He noticed the brevity of the glance, the renewed focus with which the man now stared at Grieg. That their shock seemed genuine had given Kostatis pause. The men were scattered around the room, assaying them all at once rendered impossible. He had swept his glance across the group backwards and forwards; all as he would expect: shock, disbelief, uncertainty, confusion. But then that glance. He wasn't able to look from Jeff to the man who had been introduced as Steve, without moving his head. Had he caught something in Jeff's face just as Kostatis turned towards him? That fraction of a second it took to refocus from Steve to Jeff would have been enough for the mask of surprise, if that is what it was, to fall and register something else; the movement of Kostatis' head sufficient warning for someone practiced in deception to reinstall the expected expression. Interesting, thought Kostatis.

Grieg was well used to his superior's preferred approach to these interviews. Kostatis would sit back, allowing him to take the lead—in this case breaking the bad news to the five men, that their colleague of forty-odd years was dead. In his mid-fifties, a fraction under six feet tall with thinning light brown hair, Grieg had been in the force for twenty-five years and CID for almost twenty. He had long since gotten over the frustration of his career stalling at the rank of DS and was known for going about his business calmly and dispassionately. The monotone voice he affected for these purposes wasn't to everyone's liking but it served its uses. A highly expressive tone made the giving of bad news somehow worse, if that was possible. Grieg's tone had none of those problems. It did, though, help in the approach he and his boss had developed. If someone was receiving shocking information for the first time, i.e. their long-time colleague and his wife were dead, burnt to a crisp in what was, by any fireman's account, a suspicious-looking burn site, then the tone was irrelevant. The power in the meaning of the words kept the listener riveted until the disbelief kicked in. If, however, the power of the words were diminished by the receiver's foresight, then the tone becomes much more noticeable. And like any monotonous tone, bored of quickly. The combination of Grieg's grey voice and the seriousness of the news he was delivering provided ample opportunity for Kostatis to notice if any of the group weren't quite as ignorant as their expressions would have them believe.

"I truly am sorry for your loss. We do have a couple of quick questions though if that's ok?" Grieg asked, keeping his face as expressionless as his voice. The men around him were still dazed, reeling from the death of their friend, but one by one they nodded. Grieg removed a notebook and pencil from the inside pocket of his jacket. Turning to a fresh page he touched the tip of his pencil to his tongue then looked each man in the eyes before proceeding. He didn't need the pencil to write darker, which was the primary reason for licking the lead, it was just one of those things he had done forever and it helped to focus the minds of those he was questioning, underlining the significance of his note taking, reminding them that a permanent record would be kept of what they said next. Sobering for someone with deception on their mind.

"When did you last see Mr and/or Mrs Forthright?"

Steve, Terry and Martin all gave the same reply: a few days ago at the gala dinner in their honour.

"And you two gentlemen?" Grieg turned to Derek and Jeff. "When did you last see them?" All eyes were now on the two men. Derek fidgeted in his chair as if wrestling with something. Eventually he came to a decision.

"I bumped into them yesterday morning. I was just passing and they were heading out for a walk on the heath. We just said a brief hello and that was it."

Kostatis stared at the man in the wheelchair. He had been surprised when he first walked into the room. Jeff's eye patch had been unusual enough to cause him to pause and stare momentarily, but when he saw the other men and their various physical states his jaw nearly dropped. Had they been a generation older or younger he might have assumed they were veterans from the Second World War or the more recent Iraq and Afghanistan conflicts, but their ages didn't marry with that. Regardless of what Grieg's questioning did or didn't uncover, Kostatis was going to take a much deeper look at this peculiar group.

Grieg carried on as if the moment of indecision had never occurred.

"And you sir?" he asked Jeff.

"Oh, I saw them more recently, yesterday afternoon actually," he answered without so much as a moment's reflection or pause. "I popped round their house to catch up after the gala."

Grieg made his notes, keeping the men waiting as he painstakingly dotted his I's and crossed his T's.

"Were you all present at the gala dinner you mentioned?"

"Yes, we were all there. We were being honoured for services to the brewing industry," Jeff replied for all of them.

Grieg looked up questioningly, half way through writing the word 'brewing'. Jeff took the cue and explained.

"We run a small brewery making speciality ales that we export all around the world. It's become quite successful." Despite the gravity of the situation, Jeff couldn't help the note of pride that entered his voice and the slight smile that touched his lips.

Grieg made a note. Very interesting, thought Kostatis.

"And how did he seem at this gala dinner?"

Now the pause and discomfort seemed to spread through the men, Jeff once again taking the lead.

"To be honest officers, Wilbur had been a little distracted of late, and..." Jeff paused as if wrestling with something, unclear as to whether to continue or not. All eyes were on him. Eventually he came to a decision. "It's difficult to talk about, you see Wilbur was our friend for such a long time, but I think we can all say his behaviour had become more and more erratic over the last, well twelve months probably. We're none of us getting any younger and unfortunately poor Wilbur was beginning to show signs of dementia."

Kostatis watched the group as Jeff spoke. There were none of the usual responses to such a confession. Typically he would expect some of them to drop their heads, embarrassed at having to talk about their friend in such a way. The fact it was a posthumous confession as well should have added to the discomfort, but all eyes remained on Jeff.

"On the night of the gala I think we were all shocked at how badly he had deteriorated. He wasn't making much sense about anything really." Jeff dropped his head as if reflecting on the past twelve months. He looked up and spoke directly to Kostatis. "On top of that he was very drunk, which in itself was unusual. I know we work in the drinks industry but Wilbur wasn't much for partaking. Again, it was something that had changed and increased over the last year."

Grieg made no sign that he was interpreting what was being said, merely making notes.

"And how was he when you last saw him more recently—" he scanned back over his notes, "yesterday afternoon?"

Kostatis watched the other men. He was beginning to get a feel for this odd group and their obvious leader. Their stares remained fixed on Jeff.

"Yesterday he was having a bad day unfortunately. He hardly recognised me when I went round to see if I could do anything for him and Mabel. It's so very difficult for her, what with having no family of their own. We are effectively it after all these years." He smiled and signalled to the other men in the room; each man in turn jolting to a smile and small nod of the head as they realised one of the policeman's attention was on them. Kostatis spoke for the first time since being introduced.

"And presumably you take it in turn to visit and make sure all is well?"

"Absolutely," Jeff replied. "You don't work with someone as long as we have without building a bond stronger than most." He smiled at Kostatis who paused before looking at Terry, Steve and Martin.

"But you hadn't seen him for a few days?" He let the question hang in the air for a moment, almost allowing enough time for Jeff to respond before cutting him off as the words formed on his tongue. "And, without meaning to be indelicate, the level of assistance you must be able to give is surely limited?" He looked at Derek, then slowly round the group, his stare eventually coming to rest on Jeff. Each man's face in turn had flashed the same look. Shame. All that is except Jeff. His face had shown something else entirely. The leader of this peculiar group of men wasn't exhibiting shame or sadness. Jeff was quite clearly very annoyed. At what Kostatis wasn't yet sure but things were getting ever more interesting.

"I had taken it on myself to see them over the last few days and help where I could. I hadn't even gotten round to telling my friends here how bad it had become. I was actually in the process of doing so when you arrived." He had managed to get his reactions under control.

"So, just to make sure I have it right in my own mind. You three gentlemen haven't seen your deteriorating and unwell friend of forty years in the last three days?" Kostatis looked at Terry, Steve and Martin who nodded uncomfortably. "You," he continued, pointing at Derek, "saw them yesterday as they went for their walk, and you, Jeff, have been in and out over the last few days?"

A firmness had edged into Jeff's speech as he replied.

"That's right." His focus switched from Grieg to Kostatis trying to gain a deeper understanding of what else was going on between the two police officers.

Kostatis was silent for a moment, as if working through what had been said and seeing if it all added up. His brow furrowed as if wrestling with a difficult point, unable to balance the two sides of an equation. After a moment he shrugged his shoulders and slowly shook his head.

"Oh well, I guess sometimes there are just unanswerable questions." He stood up and stretched his hand out to Jeff. "Many thanks for your help today and we really are terribly sorry for your loss. We'll keep in touch." He walked around the room shaking each of the men by the hand. Grieg had flipped his notebook shut and followed his superior around the room.

Jeff was in two minds. On the one hand it was good they were leaving but on the other he never liked to be kept in the dark, and the DCI's shrug and comment about unanswered questions was gnawing away at him. Eventually it got the better of him.

"Just out of interest, what did you mean when you said there were unanswered questions? If there is anything we can do to help, you know we will."

Kostatis stopped at the door, one hand on the door handle.

"It's nothing really sir. The difficulties of being a policeman I think and the reliability, or rather the lack of reliability in eyewitnesses."

Now it was Jeff's turn for his eyebrow to furrow. Kostatis took a step back into the room towards Jeff.

"It's just that we have four or five eyewitnesses who swear blind they saw your Range Rover outside Mr Forthright's house this morning sir. Whereas you said you last saw them yesterday afternoon." Kostatis paused, watching the man in front of him. Nothing flashed across his face this time; it was as expressionless as stone. After a few seconds Kostatis shrugged again. "I guess they must just be confused. You've been over there so often over the last few days they obviously can't remember which morning it was. We'll be in touch." With that he turned on his heels and left.

Outside on the drive Grieg and Kostatis climbed into the unmarked BMW and looked at each other.

"What do you make of that?" Kostatis asked.

Grieg fumbled with his seatbelt momentarily then started the engine. "Well, on the balance of things, I'd say they're guilty. Did you see his look when you mentioned the witnesses placed his motor in Caterham this morning?" He put the car into first gear and pulled past the black Range Rover.

"Yeah." Kostatis looked at the imposing house as they circled the fountain back towards the exit of the driveway. Or lack of a look, he thought. "Definitely guilty. We just need to figure out what of."

"So what now?"

Kostatis was scrolling through his phone. He had just received an email from one of his officers back at the station. He read in silence for a few minutes.

"We pay a visit to one Swift & Smooth removal and ask them why they have provided the Forthrights with a quote for removal and storage of their entire house." He showed his colleague the screen briefly. "What with the house burning down the postie had nowhere to drop the letters so we are getting them. Top of the pile this morning was a brand new quote from said removal company. That doesn't seem entirely consistent with what our friends have just told us, does it?"

Grieg accelerated down the road to see what light Swift & Smooth Removals could shed on what was now looking more and more like a possible double murder.

Chapter 30

The sound of tapping at the window directly behind him nearly had Dominic diving behind the sofa. His breathing shallow and rapid, he finally mustered the courage to pull the curtain aside. Outside, hugging her coat to her body, looking pale and gaunt, was Beth. Dominic ran to the front door as Gareth ran to the kitchen shouting, "I'll make tea." Dominic nervously ushered her in, pausing only to scan the road outside, before slamming the door, throwing all the deadlocks and wedging the hall chair back under the handle.

He followed her into the lounge where she was anxiously twisting her coat in her hands. For a split second Dominic's chaotic mind stilled. As tense and frayed as Beth now looked, he couldn't help but think how beautiful she was. He was dragged from his thoughts by the disconcerted look on Beth's face.

"Sorry, please sit down," he mumbled, the pent-up wave of nerves and embarrassment choosing that precise moment to crash over him. He knew it was stupid but he couldn't help himself. "Sorry I didn't call, I've been…busy," he said weakly. "How've you been? You look great."

For a moment it seemed as if Beth hadn't heard him, then, just as Dominic was about to speak again she looked up forcing a small smile.

"I'm fine." She replied. For a second, engrained conditioning prompted her to ask him how he was. She could see Dominic was shaken and even as recently as a couple of hours ago she had wanted to make him feel better about her mother breaking his nose. But the world had done what it inevitably does—move on with alarming speed—and massaging Dominic's wounded ego was not her concern. "My flatmate however is in all sorts of shit and somehow it's because of you."

Dominic took a step back, surprised as much by the steel and anger that flashed across Beth's face as he was by the accusation he was somehow to blame.

"Um, what? What do you mean? How's this my fault?"

"What's your fault?" Gareth asked as he came into the room, three steaming cups of tea in his hand.

"The fact that Naomi's been kidnapped and is being threatened by a fucking psychopath, that's what's Dominic's fault." Beth replied, her anger almost bubbling over.

Dominic stepped back bumping into the sofa and collapsing into it in complete shock.

"Woah, 'ere wait a minute. What're you talkin' about?" Gareth asked as he handed each of them their tea. "I'm sure Dominic's to blame for many things but how the 'ell can *this* be 'is fault?"

"I don't know," Beth conceded, unable to hide her frustration and annoyance, "But this psycho started with two questions, one, was I Beth and two, did I know you." She pointed accusingly at Dominic who simply stared back blankly.

"Alright, let's back it up a bit. We all need to take a breath." Gareth said, looking from Beth to Dom and back. He took an exaggerated breath and let it go. "Come on." He indicated to them both to join him, "Breathe with me." He inhaled again and nodded reassuringly to Beth.

After another couple of deep breaths from the Cornishman she shook her head slightly, placed her tea on the floor and joined him. "Tha's good." He said, "And you Dom. Dom. Dominic."

Gareth's raised voice finally brought Dominic back from wherever his mind had taken him. He looked as his friend mimed breathing in and out and after a little encouragement joined Gareth and Beth as they took five deep breaths.

"Right," Gareth looked from Dominic to Beth, an air of calm surrounding him. "Are we feelin' a bit calmer?"

The intense shock Dominic had been feeling had passed and Beth's anger had abated. They both nodded at Gareth.

"Good." He replied. "Now Beth, please tell us what the fuck is goin' on."

Taking a few moments to marshall her thoughts Beth took one last deep breath, held it then let it go.

"Ok, how far back do I need to go?" Her tone was rhetorical but Gareth answered anyway.

"I know that Dominic groped yer mum and she broke his nose and that 'e's been moping around for the last couple a days worried that you won't forgive 'im for havin' groped yer mum. I think tha's the last bit we all know. 's'at right Dom?" Gareth looked at his friend, his face a mask of innocence.

Dominic burned with embarrassment. Despite everything Beth managed a small chuckle.

"A little over-simplified, Gareth, but ok, I'll pick it up from there." She looked across at Dominic who had screwed his eyes shut as if willing the ground to open up and swallow him.

"Ok, so, after Mum and I dropped Dominic off at hospital…"

"Tha's the mum you groped Dom." Gareth said, pointing a finger at his friend, the slightest trace of a smile causing the edges of his lips to rise slightly.

"Thanks Gareth, I think we all know which mum Beth's talking about," Dominic replied, the look on his face switching from wanting the ground to swallow him to wanting it to swallow Gareth instead.

"Anyway," Beth interjected. "By Monday I'd given up on trying to make you feel better or you texting me back." She looked pointedly at Dominic who shifted uncomfortably in his seat. "So Mum and I went out for lunch. Naomi, my flatmate, had decided she was going to stay in. Mum and I have lunch, we do a bit of shopping and then I go home."

Dominic and Gareth were both leaning forward, hanging on Beth's every word. "When I got in, I noticed a few small things out of place. You know, the rug seemed to have been kicked about, a couple of pictures on the walls were askew, but that was it and hardly anything to ring alarm bells. There was no sign of Naomi but she's an adult, she can come and go as she wants. I thought she'd headed back to her boyfriend's." She took a sip of her tea before continuing. "She had said she was just going to watch a bit of telly though so I thought I'd call just to check everything was ok. She didn't answer my call. A bit later she called back. Before I could say anything a man asked me whether I was Beth and then whether I knew you." She looked at Dominic, the reason for her earlier accusation of him becoming clearer. Dominic held her stare for a moment before looking at Gareth.

"What did you say?" Gareth asked.

"I threatened to hang up and he told me I shouldn't if I cared for Naomi's life." She took another sip of her tea, craving the burning sensation as it scored its way down her throat—something normal and known, even if uncomfortable, in a completely alien situation.

"Wha'did you say to that?" Gareth asked, transfixed by her story.

"I called him an arsehole and hung up." Had it just been an arsehole making a prank call that would have been fine. As it was, they all understood the implications.

"What happened then?" Dominic asked, eventually finding his voice. Beth felt in her pocket and pulled out her phone. She keyed the screen a few times then turned it to Dominic and Gareth.

"He sent me this." The phone's screen was filled with a picture of a very scared woman. Her hands and feet were bound and a dirty rag had been forced into her mouth. Tears were visible streaming down her cheeks, which were obviously bruising. Her eyes, dark and shadowed, projected nothing but terror. The vague silhouette of the cameraman was cast over the prone figure. In the top right corner they could also make out another arm and the side of someone's torso. Dominic and Gareth looked up and stared at each other.

"Hank and Razor," Gareth muttered.

Dominic sat back and stared at the ceiling, running his hands through his hair. "Fuuuuck."

"Who the hell are Hank and Razor and what have you done to piss them off so much?" Beth asked, fear for her friend evident in her voice.

"I haven't done anything," Dominic replied, defensively.

With Gareth's help, Dominic filled Beth in on all that had happened since he had last seen her. He told her about the Barton job and being told by O'Connell that he had to provide a quote elsewhere in Caterham. He described the Forthrights and their house, recalling the strangeness of his visit. He then told her about meeting The Premiums in Clapham and going to the pub. Gareth chimed in with an explanation of his real ale tour.

"I don't care about your drinking," Beth interrupted, her frustration at what seemed like a pointlessly rambling story finally getting the better of her. "Get to the point."

"We're getting there I promise," Dominic replied, holding his hands up in a placatory gesture.

Sheepishly they continued. Dominic explained a little about his freaking out in the middle of the night which had led to the discovery of the diary. Gareth picked up the story in the crew room and the disappearance of O'Connell and their rushing to Dominic's house worried that their boss might have had their team leader killed. Even with it being extraneous detail, he took extra time to describe how The Premiums had discovered Dominic with his pants round his ankles asleep on the toilet that morning. As Dominic's embarrassment and Beth's annoyance flared again, Gareth quickly moved on.

They told her about the conversations they had had regarding the validity of the diary, explaining they had all decided it was bollocks, right up to the call Dominic had received from Beth and their mad dash from the pub to where they now sat.

The room was silent as Beth digested what the pair of them had told her.

"So you're telling me that beer has budgies in it?" Even considering the situation it was a fair question to ask.

"Not all beer, just the one beer called Budgie Smugglers." It was now Dominic's turn to want to get the conversation back on track. "Oddly that isn't important right now. What did this Hank guy say to you?"

"He said he wanted the diary and that you were to bring it to him. I was to call Naomi's number again once we'd spoken and he would tell me where and when."

Dominic's insides froze.

"This is so bad," he said.

"I still think we need to go to the police," Gareth said. "I get that Naomi is in a shit load of trouble, but I don't see 'ow marchin' Dominic out as a sacrificial lamb is gonna help."

Dominic would never admit it but he could have hugged Gareth at that point. It had felt somehow cowardly to say so himself but the idea of wandering up to these guys on his own and trusting they wouldn't hurt him and Naomi anyway was the last thing he felt inclined to do.

"I mean they're gonna want you to deliver it somewhere quiet. So what's to stop these bastards takin' the diary and then killin' Dominic and Naomi anyway?"

He was met with silence as they each considered the trustworthiness of kidnappers. Dominic's gratitude was short-lived as visions of himself getting stabbed and shot paraded through his mind.

"We can't go to the police." Desperation was obvious in Beth's voice. "They said they would start cutting bits off her if they even suspected we had called them." The tears that had been threatening eventually spilled over and ran down Beth's face, her chin trembling as she tried to control them.

"This is so fucked," Dominic said, rubbing his face. "Ok, we have to think of something." He pushed himself out of his chair and started bouncing on the balls of his feet trying to shake an idea loose. "We can't call the police because they'll kill Naomi."

"And you can't go out there cos if you do they'll kill you," Gareth contributed.

"Good point," Dominic pointed to Gareth. "But we have to do something."

"What about a compromise?" Beth asked.

"Hey, I don't want to get killed so I'm all ears."

"What about, we agree to meet them but we make it a really public place," Beth said, looking from Dominic to Gareth who in turn looked at each other.

"That might work actually," Gareth muttered searching for the flaw.

"How will we know that Naomi's ok though?" Beth asked, acting as challenger to her own idea.

"Another good point," Dominic said. "What if we insist that they bring her with them and we do a hostage exchange?"

"I'm not sure we're in much of a position to insist on anything are we?" Beth asked. "We're not going to the police and the facts confirm what you've told me about Hank and Razor being genuinely dangerous people."

The silence was stretching away when Gareth had an idea.

"What if we take a load o' copies o' the diary and 'ave 'em as an insurance policy or summat?"

"In principle it sounds like something we should do," Dominic replied. "But in practice we want these psychos to leave us alone. I think having evidence of their criminality keeps us squarely on their radar."

"So what the 'ell are we gonna do then?"

"Look, we have something they want and they have something we want," Beth said. "I think we can insist on a public place. We also try to get them to bring Naomi with them." She shrugged. "Ultimately though I don't think we have a whole lot of choices available to us."

It wasn't a perfect plan but it was all they could come up with.

"Alright, let's do it," Dominic said, a surge of bravery washing over him. "Let's go and find a public place we're happy with and then call them to set it up. Ok?"

Beth nodded almost imperceptibly.

"Ok, let's go." Dominic marched out to the front door, pulled the chair away and undid all the locks. Finally he slid the chain from its rail and opened the door.

Immediately in front of him on the doorstep, hand raised and hovering over the bell, was a man in a suit. Immediately behind him was another man in a suit. Dominic froze, terror turning his blood to ice in his veins. Could this be Hank and Razor bored of waiting and come to take the diary and their lives?

"Mr Morgan? Mr Dominic Morgan?" The man slipped his hand inside his jacket.

This is it thought Dominic, he's going to shoot me.

The man slowly withdrew a small leather wallet and flipped it open revealing a shiny EIIR emblem on one side and a piece of paper on the other.

"DCI Kostatis and this is DS Grieg. Can we ask you a few questions?"

Chapter 31

Kidnapping was a stressful business, regardless of how compliant the kidnapped individual was. There was a lot to consider, from the initial kidnapping, to the transportation and the holding. The first few hours after a kidnapping were often the most stressful. It was in that time that any witnesses to the crime would most likely come forward and provide the most useful information to the police. Hank knew that eyewitnesses weren't reliable and that having one come forward might actually help him evade capture. They might not know the difference between a Bedford Rascal and Ford Transit. They could get the colour wrong. They could get what they thought was a partial of the registration but in fact it could be a million miles away. All of these snippets would need to be run down by the police and ruled out. It could literally take days to filter through it all. Hank didn't need days; as long as Beth and Morgan played by the rules, he and Razor would be leaving this warehouse in a few hours, never to return.

Those few hours however would almost certainly be tortuous. The slightest lapse in concentration could see a well-honed plan unravel faster than a cartoon jumper. And it was the compliant ones you had to watch the hardest. Both Hank and Razor had experience of all manner of people being on both ends of a kidnapping. The ones who fought the situation were often the easiest to deal with. If there was even the slightest chance that someone's aggression could cause them problems, then a swift dose of unconsciousness was administered via Razor's brass knuckles and they were bound and gagged and periodically thumped around the head to maintain the status quo.

The problem with the quiet ones, those who acquiesced in the first instance, was they didn't elicit the strong-arm tactics that the aggressive captive did. They avoided the punch in the face with a brass knuckle; they avoided the torsion-inducing kick in the balls or the bone shattering strike on the shin. They showed their compliance and desire to survive as unscathed as possible and thus assessed their kidnappers in a false frame. Clearly violence was an option; you'd be a very unsuccessful kidnapper if you relied solely on the good sportsmanship of your target to get them into the boot of a car, but the violence was usually tempered and blurred somewhat by the shock of the initial event itself.

As the kidnapping goes on, the initial shock and fear recedes a bit and the victim is able to think. Not clearly—it's jumbled and distorted and still impeded by some fear—but think nonetheless. It is then down to the victim to decide how they continue. They either accept their fate, and make no attempt to impede their kidnappers, trusting to those of whom the ransom has been demanded, or they try to get creative, attempt an escape even. Hank was perfectly aware that you could head off any belligerence with serious violence, but as strange as it sounds considering he was a professional criminal, he really preferred not to have to kick seven shades of shit out of people. He wasn't an animal, he had Razor for that.

The problem he had now was that the initial fear Naomi had shown was beginning to recede. He was confident she wasn't at the 'try to escape' phase yet, but with everything else going on he might have to preempt it.

He was sat in the office again, waiting for the call from Beth letting him know Morgan was going to hand over the diary, and he could hear her trying to talk to Razor. He had initially done his usual and growled back forcing her into silence again, but as the minutes ticked by, Razor's psychotic appearance seemed to be having less and less of an effect on her. She was now even confident enough to ask if she could go to the bathroom. This request elicited an even bigger growl from Razor, his way of telling Hank that something needed his attention. He looked at his watch—time was marching on. He was expecting notification of the arrival in the UK of the special consignment he had procured for the SSoH and this diary bullshit was in serious danger of fucking with his schedule.

He had to admit that the last time he had felt this exposed was when he had been nicked for burglary. Since then he had worked tirelessly to protect himself from detection by the authorities, or reprisals from clients or those affected by his actions. It had been his number one focus when setting up. This was a business and as such he had exit strategies for everything.

He thought back over the years he had been working for the group run by Jeff. Could he claim ignorance of what they were doing? To anyone who asked such a pointed question, of course he could, and would, loudly and repeatedly should the need arise. But if he was being honest with himself, and for a man in his line of work it was vital to be so, he had to admit he had stopped thinking about it once he had put two and two together and found it impossible not to make four. He remembered it was the third shipment he had acquired for them that finally persuaded him that ignorance was bliss. Although there is a school of thought that says coincidences don't exist, Hank was more than happy to put the first job they did together down to just that. He had procured two lions, at great financial cost but little personal danger—either of being mauled or arrested—and delivered them to Jeff. A short while later, Jeff and his colleagues launched a beer called Lion's Mange. Of what became of the lions Hank had no idea, but he was more than happy counting the money they had paid and more than happy to put it down to coincidence.

The second order had been for a pair of chimpanzees. Hank had acquired them from a contact he had in the pharmaceutical testing industry. As he had delivered them, he had thought the chimps' life would be infinitely better in the private zoo he allowed himself to assume Jeff was building, compared to the cages at the testing facility. The release of Chimps Cabaret a little while later caused a raised eyebrow but nothing more. It was only when Penguin's Prerogative was launched, after a fishy-smelling delivery, that Hank attempted to discover more about what was actually happening. Information is power after all, especially in his line of business. After weeks of investigation he had to conclude there was no zoo. The conundrum he faced then was what to do with his new found partial knowledge. Should he continue and get to the bottom of it or just ignore it and keep counting the money, which was increasing significantly with each job? And that had been the deciding factor: money almost always talks. He could honestly say he didn't *know* what they were doing with the shipments he got for them, but if he thought about it for too long it never led anywhere he wanted to go.

He had done what innumerable people before him had done and innumerable more would do after him: he took the money and left it at that. He was a crook after all and felt under no moral duty to understand what he was involved with. He just took the money and negotiated a deal through one of his many contacts. It was easy work. There was always someone willing to help in return for a suitable slice of the pie and all the while Hank's nest egg grew. His association with SSoH had brought his retirement plans forward at least ten years and up until the last few days, he was happy with the situation.

The last few days however had seen him break into an old couple's house, threaten and physically assault them. Later that same night he had been forced to kidnap one of his own clients and threaten and physically assault him also. He had then fully intended to kidnap somebody else, and in all fairness probably have to assault them to get what he wanted, his intentions only being frustrated by a group of amateurs breaking into the house he himself had intended to break into. To top it off he had now kidnapped a woman—the wrong one—who he had threatened but so far not assaulted, instead using her abject terror to threaten yet another woman, who he should have kidnapped in the first place. He was currently sat in a dingy office in a disused warehouse on a derelict trading estate, waiting for a phone call to arrange a meet with people he knew next to nothing about, all for the sake of one man's fucking diary. The possibilities for being arrested in the last seventy-two hours and for the foreseeable future were astronomical. He thought of the money he had been paid. Up to now it had definitely been worth it but as of the moment he found out Razor had kidnapped the wrong woman, the balance had tipped. If he were caught then the police would freeze all his assets. They even had teams of forensic accountants who could worm their way through someone's records and discover the most secret of hiding places. All that work would be for nothing. The risks had become too great. As soon as he retrieved the diary and delivered the final shipment his working relationship with Jeff and his merry band of psychopaths was over. Even without the events of the last three days, the content of this latest shipment was enough for Hank to want no further part of the relationship.

His thoughts were dragged back to the present by another loud growl from Razor. He glanced at his watch again. It had been nearly an hour and he hadn't heard anything. He would give her ten minutes then he would have to make good on his threat from earlier. He swung his legs from the desk and walked through to the main warehouse. Razor was still stood over the girl, not speaking, just growling, in what Hank considered to be a menacing fashion. Their guest however seemed to have got over her fear completely and was now berating Razor on his lack of manners.

"Oh here comes the other one. Well I hope you're a little more talkative than him." She nodded towards Razor. "I really need to go to the loo, but your friend won't even acknowledge me, he just growls. What's that about anyway?"

Hank looked at the woman sat on the sofa. He didn't have the patience for this right now.

"Don't tell me you're the strong silent type as well."

Where the hell was she getting this confidence from? It didn't make sense. Then he got it. Suddenly he understood. She didn't think this was real. That was the other problem with not beating the crap out of them. If you did them no obviously illegal harm they held on to the hope it was all a joke.

"Come on, this is boring now. It was scary to begin with but now it's a waste of time." She smiled at Hank, showing him that she was in on the joke, happy to collude up to a point but now she felt the joke had run its course.

Hank sighed—the hard way then. He took two fast steps towards her and slapped her hard across the face with the back of his hand. His knuckles connected perfectly across her cheek bone and her head snapped to her left. As she lay on the sofa, shock and fear vying for supremacy, Hank leant down to her ear and spoke softly. As the tears spilled down her face, her world narrowed. She could sense nothing now except tiny pin pricks of light and the sounds of her kidnapper's voice, itself almost drowned out by the ringing she now had in her head.

"If you need to go to the toilet, go to the toilet. But if you so much as move an inch from where you are now I am going to ask my colleague to beat you unconscious. Do you understand?"

To Naomi the words were barely whispers but the meaning struck home. This was real. She nodded, her head instantly exploding in pain.

Hank stood up, content that he had at least sorted one problem out. He massaged the back of his right hand as he walked back to the office. "If she even thinks about moving, cut one of her fingers off. We're going to need it anyway unless her mate hurries up," he said over his shoulder. The growl that emitted from Razor now had the desired effect. Naomi lay where she was trembling and praying. *Please Beth, help me,* she thought.

As Hank sat back and swung his legs back onto the desk he felt a vibration in his pocket. At last, he thought. Maybe they wouldn't have to cut their guest up after all. He pulled out the woman's phone, briefly annoyed when it became apparent it hadn't received a message from Beth, before realising it was his own mobile vibrating.

He pulled it free and clicked into his emails. A new email was waiting for him. This one was not from any of his clients but from an automated programme that ran from his servers. It was designed to notify him when the GPS tracking module on one of his deliveries was within a certain range. On his authorisation the programme would then send general delivery directions to the driver, allowing him to get to the general area for the delivery, before the programme alerted Hank once again and he could authorise the specific delivery address. The email told him his shipment had just disembarked from a ferry at Hull.

Fuck, he thought, clicking the link with the email that acted as the authority for the programme to send the first set of delivery details. He now only had a few hours before he had to receive a freight container on behalf of SSoH. Hank thought quickly. Everything had to be wrapped up by the time he made the final hand over to Jeff later that night. He was just going to have to push Beth and Morgan a little harder. With a bit of luck and concerted effort, he would have retrieved the diary, received the last shipment, been fully paid and severed his links with SSoH, all before the sun came up the following day.

First he needed to push Beth. "Razor, come here," he shouted, and watched as the woman on the sofa visibly stiffened but remained where she was. He was about to tell Razor to cut the first knuckle of one of her little fingers when his phone buzzed again. He saw instantly that he had a message from **Help Wanted** but there was more. Unlike any of the emails he had received before, and contrary to the processes he insisted upon, following the basic two word client identifier they had agreed on, Jeff had added something.

Help Wanted: The police are snooping around

Shit, he thought. That was the last thing they needed at this juncture. He turned to Razor. "Keep watching her. I have to make a phone call."

Chapter 32

"I said, can we ask you some questions?" DS Grieg was once again leading proceedings as Dominic stood inside his front door, and tried his best not to show the panic that was ripping through his body.

As he stood, unable to muster any kind of response, Gareth and Beth hustled out of the lounge and stopped at the sight of the badge the man at the door was holding out. Dominic looked helplessly at Beth as her eyes bulged, already considering the consequences should her flatmate's captors have his house under surveillance. She recovered quickly though.

"Unfortunately we were just heading out. Sorry," she said, ushering Dominic out of the door in an attempt to push Grieg backwards. He held his ground though, forcing Dominic to grab both sides of the door frame to prevent Beth pushing him bodily into the policeman.

"It won't take long," he said, taking a step nearer and placing one of his size thirteens inside the door. Dominic stared down at the shoe unsure what to do. He had heard somewhere that if someone managed to get their foot inside your door they could take your telly. That might be bailiffs, he thought, but it was something like that. The second policeman stepped up behind his colleague and Dominic could feel the space between himself and the policemen shrink, as the two men loomed in front of him. Dominic lost the game of chicken. The moment before DS Grieg was about to chest bump him, he folded and turned to the side, effectively offering them access to his home.

"Thank you. Through here is it?" Grieg asked as he marched past Dominic, Beth and Gareth. Dominic nodded helplessly. Kostatis closed the door behind himself, motioning for Dominic and his friends to follow Grieg as he would bring up the rear.

The three friends sat nervously on the sofa. Every part of their beings silently screaming for the two policemen to leave. Didn't they understand what damage they could be doing?

"Where were you off to?" Grieg asked nonchalantly. Kostatis took up his role as observer. The fact the three of them were sitting next to each other, shoulders touching, was going to make this considerably easier than the last interview. He sat back and crossed his arms.

"Um, you know, we were just going out to meet some friends, that's all," Dominic replied nervously. Whatever happened they had to get rid of these guys as quickly as possible. "What can we do for you, how can we help?"

Grieg went through his usual routine of removing the notebook and flipping to a fresh page. "As I said, this shouldn't take long. Can I just take down your names please?" He licked his pencil. "Now you're Dominic Morgan, correct?" Dominic nodded. "And you two?"

"Gareth Rowe."

"Beth Cooper."

Grieg nodded as he made a note. "Right, can I just say you seemed very surprised to see us at the door. Any reason for that?"

Dominic searched for an excuse that wouldn't condemn Naomi to a digitally impaired future. "You know what it's like. You were just about to ring the bell and I opened the door to find you there. You know, you just made me jump." Dominic laughed nervously and looked at Beth and Gareth who joined in. Grieg and Kostatis were impassive.

"No, I meant when I showed my warrant card. You seemed surprised to see us, as in the police."

"Well, er, um, you know," Dominic fumbled before finally pulling it together. "No one expects to find the police at the door." Beth and Gareth nodded in agreement.

"You'd be surprised in our line of work." Grieg flicked through his pages of notes, as if refreshing his memory. "When did you last see or speak to Alfred O'Connell?"

"What?" they replied in unison, caught completely off-guard by the question.

"O'Connell, what's he got to do with this?" Dominic asked, not thinking or guarding what he said.

"And what 'this' might you be referring to Mr Morgan?" Grieg asked as if he were inquiring about what colour the paintwork in the bathroom was.

Dominic realised his mistake moments before he received elbows in the ribs from both sides. Scrambling, he tried to recover.

"No, I was just wondering what that had to do with anything. That's all."

Grieg looked up from his pad and stared at Dominic. He could almost see the sweat about to break through his forehead, and knew the fact would not have gone unnoticed by his boss. "We'll get to that. Now, when did you last see or speak to Mr O'Connell?"

"I saw him last Friday at work," Beth replied, easily the most composed of the three of them."

"Last Friday," Grieg made the note. "Not since then?"

"No. I've been off this week." Beth could tell she sounded evasive despite telling the truth but couldn't do anything about it.

Grieg nodded his head. "And you?" He turned to Gareth.

"Well we did a job yesterday mornin' and he was texting Dominic. Dom's the team leader, see. But I 'aven't seen or spoken with O'Connell since Wednesday last week I think."

"Hmm." He took more notes, aware the whole time of the tension in the room. "So you got some texts from him yesterday is that right?" he smiled at Dominic reassuringly.

"Er yeah, we were doing a job in Caterham."

"How did you get the black eyes and broken nose?" Kostatis interrupted. He had noticed the evasive tone in Beth's voice and seen an almost imperceptible flinch from Dominic as well.

"What?" Dominic stuttered. His hands went up to either side of his nose. "Oh that was just an accident."

There was that flinch again, from both Beth and Dominic.

"What kind of an accident?" he pressed.

Dominic had nothing. There was no way the 'man in a pub' story was going to work on the policemen. For a terrifying moment he actually considered telling them the truth. Thankfully though, Gareth came to the rescue.

"It were an accident at work. Dom and I was shifting this dresser and it slipped out me 'ands. Dominic broke its fall with 'is face. Bit embarrassin' for both of us really. I think tha's probably why Dominic didn't say that straight away. Innit Dom?"

"Yeah absolutely. That's it, I was just embarrassed." Dominic and Gareth petered out to silence under the combined stare of Kostatis and Grieg. There was a slight nod from Kostatis to his colleague as he sat back in his chair.

"Go on," Grieg prompted. Dominic was stumped. He had absolutely no idea what the question had been or what kind of hell was unfolding that meant he was actively engaging in lying to the police. "When you last spoke with or saw Mr O'Connell," Grieg prompted patiently.

"Oh right yeah. Um. Well, it would be as Gareth said. We were doing a couple of jobs yesterday and he was texting details through to us. I would have spoken to him on the phone on Friday but I haven't seen him since last Wednesday as well."

"Do you know how long he's been in hospital?" Kostatis interrupted again.

The shock on each of their faces was undoubtedly genuine.

"Oh my God, is he alright?" Beth asked, irrespective of her personal feelings towards the man.

"Is that why he weren't in the office this morning?" Gareth asked.

Kostatis sat there taking in their reactions. As far as he could tell the fact their boss was in hospital was news to them. He hadn't thought they could have been involved but it paid to ask the question you thought you knew the answer to, just in case.

"It appears that Mr O'Connell was attacked and badly beaten sometime last night. He is currently critical but stable in St George's," Grieg told them.

There was a perceptible change in the atmosphere in the room. With nearly fifty years experience between them, Grieg and Kostatis didn't acknowledge it, but something had just changed, they just needed to find out what.

Dominic, Beth and Gareth felt as if they had been thrown a lifeline. This wasn't about Naomi or the men who had taken her. Nor was it about the diary and SSoH. O'Connell had pissed off the wrong person or merely been walking in the wrong place and got himself beaten up for it.

Well, as long as he lived it couldn't have happened to a nicer guy, Dominic and Gareth secretly thought. Now they just needed to get rid of the policemen and contact Naomi's kidnapper, hand over the stupid diary and get Beth's flatmate back. They were dragged from their thoughts by Grieg's next question, with a crash.

"When did you last see Mr Wilbur Forthright?"

Dominic's head snapped up and Gareth unconsciously gripped his backpack containing the diary closer to his chest.

"Mr Forthright?" Dominic asked, confused. "I saw him and his wife yesterday afternoon. They contacted the office to get a quote and we were the closest crew to them. It was an urgent job apparently and O'Connell sent me. That was one of the texts he sent. Why are you asking about the Forthrights?"

Grieg was busy taking notes and ignored his question. "And how did they seem?"

"What do you mean how did they seem?" The security the three of them had momentarily been experiencing was ripped from them as unceremoniously as Dominic's duvet the previous morning.

"Exactly that, how did they seem? Were they agitated or confused? Nervous or perfectly relaxed?"

"I guess they seemed a little on edge maybe." By now Dominic was very confused and getting more so by the minute. He was also getting scared.

"And what exactly were you there for?"

"They wanted a quote for the removal and storage of all their possessions. They mentioned they were going abroad at short notice and understood there was a premium involved. That's it, why?" Dominic had a very bad feeling about this.

"Unfortunately Mr and Mrs Forthright died in a house fire last night."

Dominic's mouth dropped open as he stared at Grieg. Suddenly, the memory of the silliness he had felt earlier that day when his friends hadn't believed that the diary was real came flooding back. It was followed by an ever growing feeling of terror. He remembered the words Gareth had read from the diary earlier regarding Hank and Razor:

"He then proceeded to confirm his felonious credentials: robbery, burglary, extortion, theft, kidnapping if necessary. Although he didn't say he could arrange for people to disappear he certainly left us under no misapprehension that such was so."

Things had been serious beforehand, what with Naomi being kidnapped, but it now looked like the two psychopaths had killed the author of the diary. Dominic looked across at Gareth. It was clear from his eyes he was thinking exactly the same thing Dominic was: what the fuck had they got themselves involved with?

Surely this changed everything. They couldn't be expected to deal with this on their own. This was a matter for the police, anybody could see that, and here they had two perfectly good policemen to confide in. They could just tell them the whole story and wash their hands of it. The police would most likely find Naomi in time, wouldn't they? Dominic wanted to believe that so badly but deep down he didn't think so, and with the knowledge that people were prepared to kill to protect the diary he was under no illusion that Naomi was as good as dead if they said a single word. Dominic wanted off this ride, but he wasn't ready to sentence someone else to suffer in his place.

As they sat there, coming to terms with what had just been said, a shrill tone pierced the room causing the three of them to jump. The two policemen sat calmly watching. Beth scrabbled for her phone, Dominic and Gareth watching every move she made. As she turned the phone over to look at the screen, the colour visibly drained from her face. A picture of her flatmate was flashing on the screen. The kidnapper was trying to get in touch.

Beth stammered over her excuses, said she had to take the call and almost tripped as she hastily tried to leave the room. Kostatis watched everything but maintained his own council.

With Beth out of the room, Grieg turned his attention back to Dominic.

"Is there anything else you can tell us about yesterday? Anything at all, even the smallest thing might be of help."

Dominic racked his brains. Rattled by the news of the Forthrights' murder, for that is what he believed it to be regardless of what the police had or had not said, he could barely think. Finally he dragged something from the depths of his mind.

"They were expecting guests and one of them arrived just as I was leaving. Another old guy. He pulled up in a black Range Rover. They clearly knew him even though he didn't sound overly friendly when they let him in."

Grieg made a note. All the time his and Kostatis' brains were fizzing with ideas and connections. Nothing Dominic had said moved them on really but it did confirm that Jeff had been there the previous day.

"Oh, and I nearly ran over a man in a wheelchair when I arrived."

"And what time was this?" Grieg asked innocently as if he was just covering all the bases. Kostatis stood as Dominic was about to answer.

"Just need the loo, upstairs is it?" he asked.

"Yeah, first door on the left," Dominic replied distractedly. Once Kostatis had left the room Grieg prompted Dominic for his answer.

"Um, I think it was early afternoon but I can't remember exactly."

"It doesn't have to be exact, but you're sure it was the afternoon?" he asked, his flat tone really beginning to grate with Dominic.

"Yes, definitely the afternoon."

"Thank you very much," Grieg said underlining his last note. "You've been very helpful." He slipped his hand inside his jacket and pulled out a business card. "If you think of anything else just drop me a line."

Beth walked back into the room visibly shaking, Kostatis right behind her. Dominic wondered whether he had needed the toilet at all or just wanted an excuse to snoop around and eavesdrop on Beth's conversation. Either way whatever she had discussed was obviously not good.

"Is that us good then DS Grieg?" Kostatis asked.

"It is indeed sir. Mr Morgan and his friends have been very helpful. I've left my number just in case anything occurs to them."

"Excellent. Thanks for your time. Now you can get off and meet your friends." Kostatis and Grieg walked out of the lounge, Dominic following as if he were the visitor. Grieg was halfway down the path as Kostatis stopped just outside the front door and turned back to Dominic.

"By the way, would you say Mr Forthright was showing signs of dementia? Something more than the agitation you mentioned earlier."

"Nothing I can think of. As I said he seemed a little tense maybe but nothing more than that."

Kostatis nodded. "Very well. If you think of anything, anything at all, you let us know. We'll be speaking to you soon."

Dominic nodded and shut the door.

"I guess that counts as two for two as far as odd interviews go," Grieg said as they pulled away from Dominic's house.

"I know. It must be the day for it. What do you make of it all?"

"Well, he confirmed that the two brewery guys, Jeff and Derek, had been there, but he said the afternoon for Derek as opposed to the morning. There's no way a dresser broke his nose and whatever the call the girl received was about, it scared them all."

"Agreed. And they were specifically scared and surprised to see us up to the point we mentioned O'Connell, when they all seemed to relax a bit."

"You don't think they had anything to do with that do you?" Grieg asked as he flashed the headlights to allow a bus through.

"No. But they tightened up again when you mentioned Forthright. I've no idea how but somehow they're involved." Kostatis stared out the window. It had been a confusing and enlightening day all at once. What was certain was they had a lot to follow up on, not least to contact Forthright's doctor and confirm whether there had been any signs of dementia. He silently berated himself for waiting as long as he had before following the girl. She was just finishing the call as he came into the kitchen but it was clear it had not gone well.

His phone buzzed in his pocket.

"Kostatis," he said into the battered handset. He listened for several minutes taking notes. He hung up without a word to the person on the other end of the line and turned to Grieg.

"The initial reports are in from the fire brigade: definite evidence of accelerants present and no sign of accidental ignition." Kostatis sighed wearily; a double murder and two separate groups of witnesses, both lying to him. A wry smile touched his lips. He couldn't do anything for the Forthrights now except catch their killer, which was exactly what he was going to do. If five old men and three young adults got caught up in it along the way, then so be it.

"Was that all?" Kostatis had been on the phone longer than it would take to pass on the preliminary findings of a fire brigade report.

"No." Kostatis pulled his stare away from the rapidly passing hedgerows. "You remember that trader bloke who managed to get himself beaten half to death and his car stolen? The one where we received an anonymous tip off."

Grieg nodded, "Todd Masters I think. What, has he died?"

"No, he's just woken up and given a partial description of one of his attackers who by the sound of it, assuming he has form, will be very easy to pick out of a book of mugshots."

Chapter 33

Jeff had a lot of explaining to do once the police officers had left. Steve immediately demanded to know what the hell was going on and did Jeff know about the fire and the likely deaths of Wilbur and Mabel. Then they had wanted to know what Jeff had been trying to pull with the dementia stuff.

Jeff was amazed and deeply saddened that he alone was able to comprehend what danger they were in, but also craft a viable means by which they might make it through the turmoil intact. He had painstakingly pointed out that, since they now knew Wilbur and Mabel to be dead, all that mattered was their own survival. The dementia story provided them with a handy explanation regarding Wilbur's drunken declarations at the gala dinner regarding a diary, something—in case they had forgotten—that Jeff was the only one doing anything about recovering.

The toughest moment for Jeff had come once he had managed to calm them all down. They had been sat around in sullen silence thinking about Wilbur and Mabel, Jeff presumed, when Terry asked a question that put into stark contrast the difference between Jeff and the other members of SSoH. In that moment, Jeff realised he had wasted the incredible discovery, shared the unimaginable riches that followed with a group of men as different from himself as it was possible to get.

Not one of them had the creative or entrepreneurial spirit that he possessed. None of them had the determination and drive to succeed that he had. Had it been one of their dogs which had fallen through a macerator and blended with a new batch of beer, he was absolutely certain none of them would have had the foresight to actually drink it, let alone the balls to try again and again. They had all grown fat, rich and lazy off the sweat of his brow and now, when things were difficult for the first time, they demanded answers as to what he had done, how he had brought them to this place, as if he were the only one culpable.

But when Terry had asked him whether he had set the fire which had murdered Wilbur and Mabel, he could take no more. Him, a murderer? How dare they? Was a farmer a murderer for killing the fox that threatened his livestock? Was a vet a murderer for putting down an injured racehorse? Was a soldier a murderer for engaging his enemy on the battlefield?

None of them could see his point of view. None of them could see the parallel between each of his examples and their current situation. The farmer was merely protecting his livelihood; that was all Jeff was doing for all their sakes. The vet could not be condemned for putting the horse out of its misery; as neither could he, for doing the same for Wilbur. The others couldn't grasp that fact at all. Even after repeated explanations. It was simple for Jeff: what they had created was incredible, borne from unusual beginnings, granted, but incredible nonetheless. He had passed bottles of Lounge Lizard around the room and forced the men to drink, the effects of their most recent creation in line with all that had gone before. But even with the clarity of thought provided by the Lounge Lizard, Jeff couldn't get them to see the truth in what he was saying. They couldn't seem to grasp the fact that for the past forty years, they had been walking this path of enlightenment, all facing the same way, preaching the same sermon. Now that one of them had fallen from the path it didn't mean that the path itself was wrong, just that the fallen had lacked the strength to maintain it.

He had changed tack, come at it from a different angle. What about when Wilbur had been gored by the wild boar? His leg had developed gangrene, an infection that if untreated would have killed him. Is that what the doctors had decided to do? Sacrifice the whole because one part was rotten? No, they had excised the rotten element so the remainder of the whole could continue. That was what the current Wilbur situation was. His thinking had become infected, was threatening to poison the rest of the whole and might ultimately lead to all of their demises if left unchecked.

At that point he thought he had cleared Martin's thinking. He could see a slight nod of his head as Jeff continued to speak. He thought he was winning the room over; Steve was next to nod his head in understanding. Of course none of us like it. Did Wilbur like it when he lost his leg? No, of course not, but he got over it and even ended up with a better leg. And so too would they recover. He thought he had Derek at that point, the incessant squeaking of his tyres as he nervously adjusted the chair's position stopped as the Lounge Lizard and Jeff's reasoning did their jobs. Now it was just Terry, and it was here Jeff had made his mistake.

He could see and feel the change in the room owing to SSoH's most recent pint of golden frothy wonderfulness and he struck what he hoped would be the decisive blow to their concerns, and win Terry over once and for all.

He mentioned the next beer on the slate, the one for which the ingredients had been procured and they were waiting for delivery. The one the vats and condensers and the macerator were waiting for below, pristinely clean and hungry to get to work making another sensational beer.

He knew he had made a mistake the moment he finished his speech. The latest beer about to go into production had been the hardest sell of them all, including the original Lurcher's. In truth Jeff had realised it was all over, at least for his colleagues, at that moment, with their reaction to his latest creation. They were going too far, was the cry. They couldn't possibly see this one through, it was barbaric. And Terry, after Wilbur, had been the most vociferous in his objection. On mention of the newest beer, the spell Jeff had been weaving broke. Terry was rabid in his fervour and anger against Jeff and any other member of SSoH who couldn't see that what they were doing was wrong. He was no friend to anyone who continued on this path. They needed to retire immediately, dismantle the vats and fermenting chambers and spend their ill-gotten gains and the remainder of their worthless lives trying to find redemption. He had moved round the room, grabbing each man by his shirt front, shaking him violently. Jeff had given a sigh of disappointment, after all you couldn't let one bad apple spoil the barrel—or even a second gangrenous leg—and stepped forward, a fire iron in his hand.

Fate though, it seemed, had other ideas. The kind of idea that fuelled the fervour of zealots like Jeff, that reinforced the perfection of their behaviour, also ratified their thinking. As Terry grabbed Steve, shouting and spitting into his face, the 'big man' had pushed him away defensively. Terry's feet had caught in the rug and, rigid as a tree, he had toppled towards Jeff, who sidestepped lithely, presenting the marble corner of the fireplace surround for Terry's temple to connect with.

There was panic in the room. Steve was shouting, "Oh my God! Oh my God!" over and over while pacing the length of the room. The squeal of rubber on parquet was back as Derek veered around the room to who knew what end. And Martin just sat there, staring at the still body. The only person who was calm and together was Jeff.

He knelt by the side of his fallen comrade and felt for a pulse. The faintest beat of pressure could be felt as Terry's brain and organs desperately hung to life.

"He's dead," Jeff had said.

Jeff was now reflecting on the day from the comparative comfort of the battered armchair in his underground brewery. It had been an absolute catastrophe to be honest, made a thousand times worse by the arrival of the police. He berated himself. For some reason he hadn't foreseen their interest in what he hoped they would consider an accident. Their involvement and interest, in him particularly judging by their questions earlier, was going to be inconvenient. Not unmanageable, he was confident of that, but inconvenient. Jeff would have to speak to Hank and see what he suggested could be done about it.

There were also the matters of the ingredients delivery, and the bloody diary, which still hadn't been recovered. Hank had called immediately upon receiving Jeff's email. Jeff had been certain Hank wouldn't mind a departure from protocol given the circumstances, and he had been correct. Once Jeff had brought Hank up to speed with regard to the Forthrights, the police and Terry, Hank had given his own update as to the diary and the expected delivery. The delivery was on time and would be ready for collection later that night as arranged. As for the diary, he was currently negotiating its return and was confident of doing so that day at the latest.

Jeff had pointed out that he had been saying the same thing for two days now and seemed no closer to actually succeeding. It was the first time Jeff had ever heard Hank lose his temper. Suffice to say Jeff was placated that Hank was as motivated as any of them in securing the return of the diary.

He had then sent the ever-dwindling members of the SSoH home with a promise that he would sort everything out and they just needed to stick together. He wasn't confident that Steve, Derek and Martin could keep it together indefinitely but all he needed was for the diary and delivery to be completed, then he could sort things out with the other three.

He sipped from the large whiskey that had become something of a permanent fixture with him and sighed. Perspective was all you needed. Perspective released pressure, which freed thought, which in turn allowed clarity of vision. Simple. He smiled.

He drove his heels down into the rest he was using for his feet, trying to kick it into some semblance of comfort. Terry, bound and gagged, groaned under the bony onslaught, and stared at Jeff through terrified eyes.

Chapter 34

Through the grimy window of the small office, Hank watched Razor pacing menacingly in front of their captive, and considered his options. His feet crossed on the small desk, he tapped the girl's phone against his teeth. What had become abundantly clear was that his golden rule, set in stone from the very first day following his eureka moment in the Post Office all those years ago, had not just been broken but smashed. It was evident he was no longer in control of his own situation. And that meant he was no longer in control of his own safety. The walk of life he had chosen was fraught with dangers, but Hank's approach to his work was based on there being no personal link between the crimes he committed and himself. That distance meant he was separated from the sphere of police interest once a particular job had been completed. What he felt now was an unsettling feeling of being drawn closer to the centre of things rather than orbiting far from the focus of events.

The email from Jeff and his secret society had contravened the safety protocols Hank had insisted upon, on pain of extreme harm to anyone breaking the covenant. The fact the circumstances ultimately warranted it was no panacea to Hank. By breaking the rules, Jeff had provided Hank with yet another reason to end their working relationship. Money was one thing, but he had learnt during his time in prison that it wasn't worth serving time for. If he was caught, everything he had been working for over the last fifteen years would be for nothing and there was no way he was going to lose it all on account of someone else.

So the police were interested in Jeff and his cronies, that much was obvious and once Jeff had mentioned the fire at the Forthrights' house he knew exactly what had happened. Even at that first meeting, all those years ago, there had been something about Jeff that distinguished him from his co-conspirators. Razor had dismissed them all as soft middle-aged men whose ambition had outstripped their abilities and so needed to blur the lines between what was acceptable and what was not. He had even laughed at their requests initially, Razor's mind barely seeing the illegality of providing an aviary full of budgerigars or a couple of lions to a bunch of publicans. In his eyes if you didn't have to batter something over the head with a bat it barely counted as illegal. He thought them harmless, far beneath him and Hank, holding them in contempt for their straddling the line between the legal and illegal worlds. Dismissing them because they refused to fully embrace their darkest desires.

It was a good job then that Hank was the brains of the organisation. Hank had recognised something in the group that Razor had missed. The ambition Razor had attributed to the whole group was in fact possessed solely by Jeff. His eyes shone with excitement born from being the progenitor of an idea. Whatever purpose the group had for using Hank's services, it was Jeff who was behind the decision. He was in control. The others were just along for the ride. Hank had wondered at the time whether the other five members of the group were aware of that fact—that they were there in the room and part of Jeff's broader plan solely at his discretion.

More importantly he had also recognised the sparkle of zeal in the man's eyes. Zeal was an interesting trait. In the right person, held in the right idea, it was a power that could drive the seemingly unattainable to fruition. Held by the wrong person in the wrong idea, it could destroy everything within its gravitational pull. It was that pull, the heavy gravity caused by the zealous pursuance of an idea, that had caught hold of Hank and was pulling him towards the centre.

He was amazed at how quickly things had escalated: years quietly procuring peculiar and often protected animals without so much as a whisper to disrupt them. And then in the space of two days they had accelerated through the intimidation and assault of the Forthrights and O'Connell, to kidnapping and now murder. Hank had no doubt that Jeff had set the fire which had taken the lives of the Forthrights. His reaction to Hank's update following his visit to the property had been explosive. Even from the other end of the phone, it was apparent that Jeff had other plans when it came to his supposed friend that didn't require any more of Hank's help.

That had been the second golden rule Jeff had broken. Under no circumstances was unilateral action to be taken by anyone except Hank. This rule was reiterated during the courtship phase of his client relationships. If they showed any signs this might be difficult to adhere to he simply refused to work with them. It was difficult for some people to abdicate responsibility for their own plan to another, but Hank was always adamant. The reason for it was simple: if Hank controlled all aspects of the job, he could mitigate any risks that arose, ultimately walking away should that prove impossible. If the client was allowed to run around in the background doing their own thing it could have untold implications on the job, and ultimately Hank's safety or freedom.

Now that Jeff had murdered Wilbur and Mabel, the interest in them would increase. The fact that Hank was currently in the process of getting hold of a diary that almost certainly implicated him in whatever atrocities Jeff and his minions had been committing, at exactly the same time the new and most illegal shipment he had procured for them so far was due for delivery, meant that increased attention by the police could prove catastrophic. Ultimately he cared little whether Jeff was arrested and rotted in jail for the rest of his life. His only interest now was ensuring they didn't share a cell. If the police had an interest in Jeff for murder, then how the hell was Hank supposed to deliver the container that was currently wending its way towards him?

Hank swung his legs off the desk and pushed himself from the chair. He needed to think and the sound of Razor growling through the glass was seriously hampering that process.

"I'll be back in a bit ok? Keep an eye on her." He passed Razor and disappeared into the shadows. A brief flare of light tried vainly to pierce the gloom as he opened the door, before being beaten back as he slammed it after him.

Outside, his head snapped round as the sudden and ear-splitting shrill of a police siren came around the corner. He froze as the riot van squealed its tires then relaxed as it sped past him taking a right hand turn and nearly knocking a woman and her pushchair over. He forced himself to breathe deeply, exhaling the growing tension and frustration, and crossed the road. He knew a café a few minutes walk away that had remained the same since it opened nearly fifty years ago. The soporific atmosphere of the elderly eating their soft vegetables and drinking strong tea had a calming effect on him, and right now he needed to be calm, otherwise he might do something stupid, like kill Jeff.

Three minutes later he was safely ensconced at his corner table at the back of the café, a steaming mug of tea in front of him. The walls of the café had that sickly yellow tinge that came from decades of enclosed smoking—the fact the smoking ban had been in place for nearly 20 years was too inconsequential an amount of time to flush the atmosphere clear.

Hank took a large mouthful of tea, closed his eyes and cleared his mind. For the briefest moment there was just him, a mouthful of tea and the pungent aroma of stale smoke. A clatter in front of him brought him back to the present as a bacon sandwich was thrown down in front of him. The sullen uninterested waitress bringing a small smile to Hank's lips as she sauntered past with a large plate of pie and mash to be slung at another patron.

He took a bite from the sandwich and turned his mind to the problem at hand: to what level was he exposed directly?

1. There was a diary which probably contained content about him. Medium to low risk.
2. He had kidnapped a woman (as leverage to exchange for the diary) who was currently in a warehouse under guard from Razor. Very high risk.
3. He had a very illegal shipment on its way to him. Very high risk.
4. The end recipient of the shipment had murdered two people and the police were now interested in him making the final delivery complicated. Very high risk.

He took another gulp of his tea. In hindsight, he now had to admit, escalating to kidnapping just to retrieve a book that *might* contain information about him but that ultimately would be fairly useless in actually catching him, could have been a mistake. He had allowed himself to get caught up in the situation, assuming that it would be a quick solution to a trifling matter. Had he severed the relationship at the point Jeff had told him of the diary he would already be enjoying a well-earned rest somewhere hot, working on his tan while supping from drinks with umbrellas in them. Now he was considerably more exposed than if he had just ignored the request from Jeff and let the diary fall into the hands of the police. But again he had been swayed by money, allowing it to blur the ever-increasing risk until he arrived at his current predicament.

In truth, the diary was now the least of his worries. It only became a problem for him if he was discovered with the shipment or Jeff. That said, he was intrigued as to what was in the diary and although he was confident there would be nothing to actually tie him to the deeds he had committed, there was always the possibility it might.

Another bite of the sandwich was lubricated with tea and he tapped the table as he ate. What was the worst-case scenario if he walked away now, left Razor and the girl in the warehouse, went straight to his flat, packed it all up and bolted? Fuck Jeff and his group. Fuck Razor, fuck Morgan and Beth, and fuck the diary. He could just walk away. The police weren't looking for him and it was always better to leave before that status quo changed.

The more he thought it through, the more he felt this was actually the best possible approach. Once he had packed up and left, he could drop Razor a line telling him to do the same, that they had been burned by Jeff and his colleagues and he should implement his exit strategy. He knew full well that Razor wouldn't have an exit strategy despite Hank having told him to formulate one dozens of times during their professional engagements. But that wasn't his concern; he wasn't the man's nanny for God's sake. Razor was a professional criminal and he had to accept the inherent dangers that came with it.

Decision made. Hank was going to disappear. He stood from the cracked formica table, the perma-stains of spilled tea and coffee looping across the surface, and threw a note down. He took a final deep inhalation of the smells in the café: the grease from the fryers, the sweat of the customers and the stale cigarette smell seeping from the walls. He wouldn't return here again, not for many years anyway, so his recharged olfactory memory would have to suffice.

As he let the door swing closed behind him and headed off towards his flat he felt a vibration from his pocket and the muffled sound of a sonar ping. He had set up specific alerts from his home security system and this particular notification was telling him that someone had just pressed his doorbell. He pulled the phone from his pocket and clicked open the message the system had sent him. He clicked the link and waited for the system to verify his phone. A few seconds later all his plans had changed. There, in glorious high definition, via the camera in his front door through the ether to his smartphone, was the unmistakable image of two police officers stood outside his flat.

He stopped mid-stride and stared at the phone. Fuck, what were they doing at his flat? His mind spun. Morgan and Beth, they had contacted the police. He looked around him, searching for the hidden riot team, waiting to take him down. Fighting the urge to panic he slowly stepped backwards into a doorway and tried to think. He shook his head. There was no way that Morgan and Beth had caused this. The fear he had detected in Beth's voice when he had called her earlier had been genuine. There was no way she would have put her friend's life in danger. Even if they had gone to the police they didn't know who Hank was and certainly didn't know where he lived.

His immediate thought to run was no longer viable and he was now logically running through the potential reasons for the police to be at his door. Jeff and his group—could they have led the police to his door so quickly? No. Regardless of what may or may not be in the diary there was no way it could lead anyone to him so fast.

That left the shipment, the girl or O'Connell. If the shipment had been intercepted anywhere and opened, the on-board sensors would have been triggered and a message would have been sent to his phone. That left the kidnapped girl or O'Connell. The girl was the easiest to check. If she and Razor were still safely holed up in the warehouse then it had to be O'Connell, which made him a dead man.

Hank took a final look up and down the street and calmly headed back to the warehouse. Any police presence would be obvious should they have been discovered, in which case he would disappear into the cover London provided and then on to his countryside retreat. As of right now however, the plan to walk away was on hold. He had acted in haste when getting involved with the diary and he was determined to think through this current problem and make sure that whatever his next move was it was the right one. One thing seemed certain though—it was unlikely all the players currently involved would make it out alive.

Chapter 35

The usually unnoticeable sweep of the second hand thundered its way around the face of the clock mounted on the kitchen wall. Each increment of time threatening to shatter the windows, such was the intense contrast between the beat and its offbeat partner. None of them had said a word since the two policemen had left, each consumed by their own thoughts.

Beth imagining the unspeakable acts her friend was being put through. Her thoughts so vivid they nearly rendered the imagined screams audible.

Dominic reeling from the news that the people who wanted him had—in all likelihood—just murdered two innocent people. Innocent as long as you ignored the fact that Wilbur was involved in liquidising animals and adding them to beer. He could practically feel the pain Hank and Razor would inflict on him even if he did give up the diary.

Gareth, one step removed from the horrors compared to Dominic and Beth, was still concerned for his friend. As far as he could see there was no way Hank and Razor wouldn't want to silence Dominic and Beth, given what they now knew. As an extension of that, could he really let his friend walk into the waiting shitstorm on his own? In a vain effort to find an unexpected way out, his nose was once again buried in the diary.

The latest round of teas had cooled, thin layers of skin forming on the surfaces. Eventually Beth pushed her chair back and headed out of the kitchen.

"Where are you going?" Dominic had absolutely no idea as to what their next move should be and whatever Beth had in mind he was more than happy to follow. He pushed his own chair out and went to follow her. She stopped him just as he walked through to the hallway.

"Um, not really a two person job this Dominic." She signalled upstairs. Regardless of the lake of un-drunk tea that had been poured down the sink over the last few hours they had still consumed more than technically and biologically necessary. She gave him a gentle smile as the flush of embarrassment rose up his cheeks.

"Right, of course. You can probably manage that on your own. Good. See you in the kitchen in a bit." He fumbled his way back to the kitchen.

Back in his seat, Dominic thought over the preceding hours. Less than twenty-four hours ago the biggest problem he had seemed to be discerning between a mother and her daughter. Now his life as well as that of Beth's flatmate and probably Beth herself were in danger. It put an unintentional fondling in perspective, he thought. His eyes roamed the kitchen, searching for what he had no idea, but anything that would solve their problem would be awesome he silently beseeched the universe. His eyes fell on the note held to the fridge door by a comedy magnet shaped like a naked man in profile holding an oversized banana where his genitals would be. It was from his mother and reminded him that she was staying with her sister Mary and that she would be back in a few days. Dominic wondered whether she would come back to a knock on the door from a policeman informing her of his untimely demise or just letting her know what the visiting hours were as he recovered from a beating similar to O'Connell's.

He looked across the table at Gareth reading the diary. He thought he could understand why Wilbur had felt the need to get the diary away, to give it to someone who might know what to do with it. Why the hell he had chosen Dominic, he had no idea. Necessity he supposed. Had Gareth been told to do the quote this would be happening at Gareth's house now instead of his. For a fleeting, uncharitable moment that is exactly what Dominic wished had happened, or if not Gareth then Gravy or Weasel or anybody else in the entire world other than him. The momentary thought was followed immediately by a bout of shame. In all honesty he wouldn't wish this on anyone, not now they knew how serious it was.

He heard the toilet flush upstairs, the sink run and then the lock click open. He looked at the kitchen ceiling and imagined Beth crossing the short landing and making her way down the stairs. Instead of the creak of the stairs he heard the sound of another door opening upstairs. Irrespective of the danger they were all in and the completely ridiculously screwed up situation they were in the middle of, Beth was taking the opportunity to have a bit of a snoop. Dominic was stunned that at such a time she could think of anything else. He was just about to mention it to Gareth when he suddenly realised which room it was most likely she had entered. In the next second he understood how she could have other things on her mind. Gareth was momentarily disturbed by the clatter of Dominic's chair on the floor as his friend raced from the room, but his attention was immediately drawn back to the diary; if possible it was getting even more interesting. Wilbur had just started discussing the latest beer, the one that was about to go into production in a few days.

Dominic charged through the hallway and took the stairs two at a time. As he reached halfway there was a simultaneous urgent knock at the door and the continuous sound of the bell. His nerves were frayed to the point of disintegration as he spun on the stairs and nearly tripped, stumbling down them two then three at a time as he overbalanced. Above him was the unmistakable sound of someone trying to silently retrace their steps without being discovered.

Down in the hallway Dominic stumbled into the door catching his shins on the chair jammed beneath the handle. On the other side he could hear the agitated sounds of discussion and a shout from someone to keep pushing the bell. The incessant ring once again filled the hallway. His immediate panic allayed, he moved the chair and undid all the locks before finally pulling the door open and revealing the rest of The Premiums jostling on his doorstep.

"What's going on?" The Fuzz asked, peering over Dominic's shoulders and spotting Beth as she came down the stairs. A broad grin split his face as he waggled his eyebrows suggestively. "You sly old dog," he whispered, leaning forward.

"Shut up and come in, quickly." Dominic took a step back and ushered them into the house. Despite the obvious effects of alcohol, The Fuzz and the rest of The Premiums picked up on the urgency of Dominic's demand, pushed past him and followed Beth into the kitchen.

With the contagion of a crowd, the new arrivals stood looking at each other as Dominic returned the chair underneath the doorhandle and double checked all the locks again before joining them. The addition of four men, now also in the grip of a shared anxiety, with no knowledge of the recent developments, served to intensify the atmosphere even further.

"What's going on? We only left you a few hours ago." Weasel finally broke the silence, his brow furrowed questioningly.

"Yeah, what's happened? It's like someone's died." Gravy's sensitivity shone through no matter what the situation.

"A lot," Dominic replied as he deflated into his seat.

Weasel looked from Dominic to Gareth, whose face now wore a look of disturbing intensity, and on to Beth whose face held no colour as she sat with her arms wrapped tightly around her.

"Gravy? Get the kettle on. Now, tell us what the bloody hell has happened in the last couple of hours to take you from getting pissed in the pub to what feels like a wake in your kitchen," Weasel said, the happy buzz they had been feeling from the five pints and cheeky spliff driven back by the obvious discomfort and fear in the room.

There were insufficient chairs for them all to sit round the table so Otter perched on the counter top. With another big sigh, Dominic filled them in on what had happened in the intervening hours since they had left the pub.

To their credit The Premiums sat and listened, a brief shout from The Fuzz as he burnt his tongue on the tea and another shout from Weasel as Gareth readjusted his chair directly on top of his foot the only interruptions. Even the news that O'Connell was seriously hurt and in hospital had only drawn a subdued cheer and a muted chorus of 'tool' from them.

It took half an hour to bring them up to speed, Dominic providing most of the details with Beth pitching in where her knowledge exceeded his. For the most part Gareth remained quiet, still reading the diary. Once they had finished there was silence.

The Premiums normal reaction to something so outlandish would be a simple 'bollocks' but the intensity and seriousness with which Dominic and Beth had told the story precluded any frivolity. This was insane, it was real and it was happening to them.

"So what now?" Gravy asked.

"Well, unless your father happens to be a general or an admiral and can lend us a Special Forces unit, I'd say I'm pretty screwed," Dominic replied resignedly.

"And what about the kidnappers?" Weasel asked. "Surely if you just give them the diary this all goes away doesn't it?"

"Well that's part of the problem," Beth replied. "We think there's the very real possibility that even if we do give them the diary they may not let us walk away. I don't know that we have much of a choice though. He said he would call back in," she checked her watch, "about ten minutes from now with directions as to how the drop is going to go."

"So we have ten minutes to come up with the mother of all plans or into the valley of death walked the supervisor of The Premiums?" Weasel summed the general thoughts up quite succinctly.

Dominic looked around the group hopefully, desperate for a spark of inspiration to flare somewhere and a Baldric-style cunning plan to shuffle forth. The depressed looks on everyone's faces proved that it wasn't enough to just wish for something to happen. What you needed was MacGyver, but Richard Dean Anderson had put on a bit of weight, got comfortable with all his success and probably wasn't quite as creative as he had once been, necessity being the mother of invention and all that.

The minutes ticked by, everyone desperately trying to think of something. Just as the minute hand on the clock approached zero hour, Gravy chirped up.

"I've got it, why don't we go to the police?"

Everyone stared at him, incredulity evident on all their faces.

"Are you serious?" Dominic leant forward, wanting to grab him by the throat. "Didn't you hear all that stuff about Naomi and having bits chopped off her? We can't go to the police."

"Oh yeah, sorry." The effect of the spliff was evidently more long-lasting on Gravy than Weasel.

Beth's phone rang, the screen plainly showing the face of a smiling brunette. Nervously Beth picked it up.

"Hello."

The full complement of Premiums stared at her as she nodded and shook her head to whatever the person on the other end of the phone was saying.

"Yes we have it. Please don't hurt her!" She looked pleadingly at Dominic, tears pouring down her cheeks. They had all heard the scream through the phone.

"Ok, let me get a pen and paper." She motioned for one of them to get her something to write with. Dominic pointed to the drawer directly underneath where Otter was sitting. The big man fished around in it, eventually coming up with a stack of Post Its and a pencil.

"Ok, go ahead." Beth scribbled an address and some directions on the paper. The only one not completely transfixed by the phone call was Gareth.

"Hello? Hello?" The call had only lasted a matter of seconds. Beth almost shouted into the phone before looking at the screen on her phone. "He hung up." She was desperately trying to control the tears but there was something else as well.

Almost like a death row inmate waiting for the last-minute reprieve he knew would never come, Dominic cleared his throat.

"Well?"

"He wants us to head to the town centre and wait outside Argos. The diary has to be in a plain brown envelope. Once we are in place—backs to Argos facing Greggs—and he is confident you and I are alone and haven't notified the police he'll call and give us the final instructions." She stared at Dominic who was desperately trying to fight the optimism her words had provided.

"You mean he wants to meet in public in the middle of the afternoon, surrounded by other people, rather than in a remote lane somewhere in the middle of the night with a couple of ready-dug graves in a field?"

"That's what he said," she replied tentatively. "Although he did add that he knew all of your mates and if he saw any of them the exchange was off."

"This is a good thing," The Fuzz said. "He's hardly going to try and top you all outside a bloody Greggs, is he?"

"Unless he's a complete psychopath and he's planning to detonate a bomb when you're in place," Weasel added as a counter-balance, distractedly watching the thick skin move around his cup as he swirled it slowly. "I mean that would be some classic misdirection wouldn't it? Killing dozens just to get you two and the book. The police would have no idea that you two were actually the targets."

Beth and The Premiums stared at Weasel. The brief moment of hope Dominic had experienced earlier had evaporated, a pit of fear and despair left in its wake.

"Nice one Weasel, way-to-go makin' everybody feel bedder 'bout the situation." Having been buried in the diary, Gareth's contribution was his first for a long time.

Weasel looked up at the group and tried to backpedal from their horrified faces.

"I'm not saying he's definitely going to blow Dominic and Beth up, just that it's an option for him, that's all." He paused, realising his words were not having the soothing effect he was hoping for. "A pretty bloody extreme option if I'm being honest. And I think this guy has a little more self-control than to sacrifice dozens of shoppers just to get you two."

"Oh yeah, 'e's been the epitome of self-control so far, what with killin' that old man and kidnappin' Naomi. 'e seems the very exemplar of clear thinkin'," Gareth replied.

"Whose side are you on Gareth?" Dominic couldn't quite believe anyone would blow up a high street just for him, Beth and a diary but you never knew, maybe there was a core of animal-based beer religious fanatics, and everyone knew what religious fanaticism could make people do.

"I'm sorry mate. If it makes you feel bedder I dun't think 'e's going to blow up the high street. I genuinely think 'e wants to do a swap: the diary for Naomi, and then get the 'ell out. I think 'e's got bigger things to worry about."

"What makes you say that?" Dominic said.

"'cording to the diary, those wrinkly-bollocked old bastards are expecting the latest shipment o' ingredients for their next beer."

"So he's worrying about having to receive a load of llamas or peregrine falcons or something?" Beth asked. "I guess that might take up some of his time, especially as the police are interested in the Forthrights' murders."

"That might be part of it, but I think it's a liddle worse even than that for 'im," Gareth continued. They all stared at him. Slowly Gareth turned the diary round to face the rest of them and tapped the bottom of the page. "The next limited edition beer scheduled for production by the Secret Society of Hopmen."

Their eyes scanned across the page to where he was tapping. Their jaws dropped. There, in Wilbur Forthright's neat handwriting, was the name of the next beer.

"Mao's Marauding Midgets."

Chapter 36

Kostatis stared blankly at the monitor on his desk and wished he was somewhere else. Somewhere warmer, cleaner, somewhere less dangerous, less violent, with fewer people like 'Mad Dog' Sean 'Razor' Cunningham. He didn't know Cunningham personally, had never even heard his name before today, but there were certain things that eighteen years on the force equipped you with, and being able to immediately tell that anyone who had earned two nicknames was a guaranteed "wrong'un" was one of them. Mad Dog and Razor. It would be laughable but for the fact that that same level of experience which told him Cunningham was a wrong'un also told him nicknames like that were earned not given for comedy value.

He swivelled on his chair and turned his blank stare out of the window. Todd Masters had confirmed that Sean Cunningham had been the man who had assaulted him and stolen his car. The fact that his attacker had been wearing a balaclava would ordinarily have cast serious doubt over any identification. The victim's inability to see their attacker's face might be considered a hindrance to a positive identification, but once Kostatis had seen Cunningham's mugshot he was more than happy to proceed.

As he sat there staring out of the window, Kostatis sighed deeply and with his exhalation, like the uninvited revellers at a Facebook advertised party once the police turned up, went his fortitude, his drive and determination. He had heard a thousand different stories over the years of police officers whose focus and steadfastness to constantly keep battling against the shittier side of society had been worn away over the years. Until eventually there was one incident too many, and like that, in the time it took to snap their fingers, the last vestiges of that which had drawn them to the police service in the first place, died and they stopped caring. From that moment, each officer who confronted it had two choices: they could quit and find something else to do to pay the bills, something less emotionally taxing; or they could carry on, going through the motions, no longer really caring about what they did, or the victims they were supposed to protect. One way led to the loss of a good copper, the other led to the emergence of a bad copper. Kostatis had known a handful of truly bad coppers over the years and had always promised himself he would never allow the scale of the pain and suffering he encountered daily to kill off that part of him which could empathise with the victims and strengthen his resolve to help them find justice.

He also knew that it wasn't a single step that resulted in a bad copper. They didn't wake up one day to find they no longer gave a shit and immediately became that which they had previously worked against. No, the metamorphosis took longer than that; small steps, each one taking the traveller further from their starting point, inching ever closer to what they had formerly despised. Ignoring something here, bending something there, committing something you would only regret. Small steps but with each, retracting from them became harder and harder, the path of least resistance ahead rather than behind.

So far Kostatis had always managed to shrug the malaise off and refind his focus, but he couldn't deny the low points were coming more frequently. Crime had changed over the years. It used to be villains, crimes of passion/drunkenness and stupid people. That was it. Yes, there were always white collar crimes of embezzlement and fraud and the like, but those crimes were solved by cleverer coppers than him. For him it had always been villains, passion and stupidity. To be fair, as high-level definitions and criminal types, those three still stood but the subdivisions within each had evolved. His current caseload was a perfect reflection of the change. On one hand he had a very wealthy banker lying in hospital, lucky to be alive following a carjacking. So far they had turned up no suspicious activity or behaviour from the victim. Other than being a banker, and therefore intrinsically untrustworthy, there was no apparent reason for the crime other than to steal the car. Despite that, the thieves had beaten the man and left him for dead. The level of casual violence now displayed in society was both shocking and frightening. And it wasn't just professional criminals—it had taken only a few seconds looking at Cunningham's record to realise he was a 'professional', the emphasis very much on the lower case 'p'. Kids were stabbing each other to steal a mobile phone or as a result of a perceived slight. Women were beaten for their handbags where previously the thieves would just have stolen it and run away. Everything was accompanied by violence on a level that just kept escalating. It had reached the point where someone being robbed may as well resist and fight back because the chances of being seriously hurt were effectively the same, regardless of how much of a fight was put up. It used to be a trade-off: give me that and I won't smash your face in—the implied threat being that if you didn't acquiesce then you would be punished. Now, the threat was routinely ignored, the perpetrator immediately resorting to violence over bartering. Violence was everywhere and eventually it wore you down. You got to the point where you lost faith in the justice system and its ability to deliver punishments that would get through to these individuals. You started resenting the processes you were supposed to follow, the benefit of the doubt the law called for. You resented the smugness of someone who you knew had committed a crime but couldn't prove it, inconveniencing them for a few hours in a police cell as you tried to find the evidence to charge them, only having to release them knowing they would be back breaking the law the moment they were out of the station. As a result you started wanting to use tactics that they would understand, that were immediate. You started wanting to fight fire with fire. That was the line once crossed there was no retreat from; that was the precipice.

Then there was this group of septuagenarians in Surrey. Kostatis didn't yet understand what the hell was going on with that group of so-called friends, but the reactions he had witnessed when he and Grieg had visited them told him that something was definitely wrong. Whatever it was, a quick background check had shown that these were, on the face of it at least, very successful businessmen. So far they hadn't uncovered any obvious financial irregularities with their company. None of the men were in debt, which often led to the crimes of passion. The only problem was that crimes of passion tended to be immediate. The rage overtaking someone who then beat or stabbed or throttled their victim. A fire of the magnitude that destroyed the Forthrights and their home took accelerant and the Forthrights didn't seem the types of people to have petrol lying around the kitchen. That meant someone had been to get whatever the accelerant turned out to be, all the time thinking about what purpose they would put it to. They then had to travel back to the house, enter it, presumably incapacitate the Forthrights, douse the building then set the fire. All that meant premeditation. Of course, it was possible the murder had been an immediate crime of passion and the fire set to cover the tracks, but there was something about how Jeff had reacted, those minute reactions before he projected the expected response, that had Kostatis thinking. Murder wasn't unusual, more's the pity, but there was something about old men being involved that he found harder to take.

He closed his eyes as the sun broke through the cloud, filling his office with light and warmth. He knew he was teetering, and each time it happened he could feel he was edging closer to the point of no return, the point where he crossed the line, the point when the precipice seemed like the only option. Grieg coughed behind him. Not today though.

He swung his chair round to face his colleague. Grieg, ever constant in his stoicism, looked at Kostatis, a mug of something hot and brown in each hand and a sheaf of papers under his right arm. A flicker of something flashed across his face before the more recognisable impenetrability returned. What had it been? Sympathy? Whatever it was, it was sufficient to get Kostatis back where he needed to be. He was going to catch Cunningham and he was damn well going to find out what the hell was happening in Surrey.

"What have we got?"

Grieg gave a slight nod. "Nothing earth-shattering, but we're making progress." Grieg took the other chair in the room and started flicking through the sheets of paper he carried. "Cunningham seems a fairly safe place to start on the Masters case. There can't be too many people who look like that and have form, so we're taking it as read that he's the assaulter. What's proving a little harder to figure out is who his accomplice was." Grieg flicked through the pages searching for the specific paragraph. "Masters said in his statement that there were two of them. Cunningham pistol-whipped him and then drove the car to the small business estate between Esher and Thames Ditton, where we found Masters. He said that another man, also in a balaclava, turned up shortly after in a small van and seemed to take charge of the situation."

"That makes sense. Cunningham has no form for car theft and we're talking high-end here. My guess would be Cunningham is strictly the muscle and the accomplice is the brains. It's got to be theft to order on the car and Masters just happened to get in the way."

Grieg nodded. "My thoughts exactly. So we've been running Cunningham down. Looking up old acquaintances, checking addresses, employment history—of which there's none, people he's done time with, all the usual."

"And?"

"It's a long list." Grieg leant forward and slipped a piece of A4 paper across to Kostatis. The detail was split into two columns.

"Shit." Kostatis ran his eyes down the list of names filling the page. The columns were broken periodically with a heading: Prison, Arrests, Known Accomplices. Beneath each heading a list of names, the majority scored through. "Criteria for eliminating these?"

"Well, several reasons. The ones we've crossed out already are either dead, in prison, or have verified alibis."

Kostatis scanned the page again. Grieg's approach had so far eliminated fewer than a third of the names on the list. "It's a start but there's a lot of work to go."

"Exactly. So I started thinking let's try to be a bit more scientific about this." He paused, taking a sip from his mug. Kostatis did likewise, discovering the hot brown was actually tea. Suitably refreshed, Grieg removed three pieces of paper from the stack he held and passed them to Kostatis. "We know that cars aren't Cunningham's thing right? He's never been arrested or suspected of car crime in the whole of his very long career. So whoever his accomplice turns out to be, they have a very different approach to Cunningham. If you look at his record"—he indicated to the pages he had passed across—"we can immediately see a number of things. One, whenever he's served time there has always been a charge of assault, whatever the other charges are he can't stop himself from battering somebody."

Kostatis scanned the pages listing Cunningham's arrest record. It was true. Whether it had been burglary, robbery, shop lifting or anything else, it had always been accompanied by excessive violence. "Ok, what else?"

"Two, he can't stay out of prison. From his first stint at fifteen he does his time, gets released, re-offends almost immediately and in no more than three months he's back inside." Grieg paused to let what he had said sink in and give gravity to what was to come. "Except—"

"The last five years," Kostatis completed for him, flicking through the pages checking that this was a single anomaly rather than something they wanted to be significant but wasn't.

"Not in the last five years." Grieg nodded and took a long swallow of his tea. "For someone like Cunningham who's been unable to go straight, unable to contain his anger, five years is a very long time. Whoever he's working with now is somehow keeping this nutter out of trouble. Or if not out of trouble, he's keeping him from getting caught."

There was silence as Kostatis thought through what Grieg had said. This was the part of the job he loved. The processes were inescapable and absolutely necessary to secure the convictions, but the application of intelligence to help focus their attention was the exciting part. All the knowledge and experience they had gained over their years in the service enabled them to make informed leaps in thinking. Their years of sloshing around with the lowest members of society meant they knew things about human behaviours that others didn't. People could change, Kostatis was willing to concede that, but not people like Cunningham. He had two nicknames after all.

"Ok, I'll buy that," Kostatis said. He put the arrest record down and picked up the sheet with all Cunningham's known contacts again. "So how does that affect this list?"

Grieg's face broke into a smile. "Interestingly," the brief smile faded, "of the names on that list there are fewer than ten who are considered by the system to be above the average intelligence for the prison population. Half of them are already discounted on the grounds of being dead or back inside. That leaves us with the four highlighted."

"Bloody hell, Fraser Matthews is on this list." Surprisingly Kostatis had not registered the name on his initial pass of the list but now he had, his stomach felt cold as the blood rushed to his muscles in the classic fight or flight response. If two nicknames made you a wrong'un in Kostatis' eyes then Fraser Matthews had well and truly earned the multitude of nicknames he was known by.

"I know. But I don't like him for it. He's down on the Costa del Sol and he doesn't need liabilities like Cunningham in his outfit. Additionally, if you work for Matthews you don't moonlight and Matthews couldn't give a monkey's about one Aston Martin in Surrey. I know you may want to read more into it but I genuinely think it's a coincidence."

Kostatis unconsciously rubbed his back and felt the scar above his left kidney. He was silent for a while, lost in his own thoughts before snapping back to the present. When he did, it was with a slight shake of the head as if he were trying to clear a memory.

"Agreed. I can't see what use Matthews would have for a nutter like Cunningham. Let's cross him off for now. Who does that leave us with?" Grieg watched his boss for a moment before continuing.

"It leaves us with three, but one in particular I quite like." He leant across the desk and tapped one of the highlighted names on the list—Alex Pritchard.

"Who the hell is Alex Pritchard and why do you like him?"

"Alex Pritchard spent a grand total of three months with Cunningham as his cell-mate during a three year stretch for burglary in 1994. He served half his time, was released on good behaviour, completed his probation visits and stuck at his job until his sentence was served and then promptly disappeared only to resurface fleetingly to buy a flat in London four years later. After that he dropped off the radar again. Subsequently, Pritchard sells his flat to a Hank Foey three years after that. And then like Keyser Soze, he's gone."

"Pritchard's record notes he was very intelligent but lacked direction. He wasn't one of the muscle-bound or psychologically unhinged inmates and as a result Cunningham came to his rescue on more than one occasion. You've also got to wonder, how does an ex-convict with no direction or employment history buy himself a flat in London within four years of being released?"

Kostatis stared at the name Alex Pritchard and considered all that Grieg had told him. It felt like they were stretching.

"It's thin."

"I never said it was Stevie Wonder, we still have a lot to do to take this through signed and sealed before he's delivered and ours, but there's just something about him that piques my interest. Anyway, I sent a couple of uniforms over to the flat he sold to Hank Foey, just to poke around."

"And?"

"No-one in but we can pop back later. We've got guys running down the other leads and we'll see what shakes out of it. At the moment we don't have a lot else to go on."

"Fair enough. Let's hope our friend Alex makes an uncharacteristic cock-up." Kostatis finished his tea, tapped together the pages Grieg had given him and passed them back. "Where are we on the Forthrights now it's officially a murder enquiry?"

Grieg took a moment as if mentally filing the Cunningham case away and retrieving the Forthright case.

"Uniform are still running interviews with the locals who were there as the house burnt and we've requested information from Wilbur Forthright's doctor regarding the dementia comment from our friend Jeff. Haven't heard anything back yet. Unsurprisingly the number plate on the black Range Rover came back as a fake and should have been on a Nissan Micra owned by a retired school teacher in Pontypool."

Kostatis drummed his fingers on the desk. Old men doddering around killing each other seemed a bit far-fetched but you never knew—the world could be very weird indeed.

"That Jeff character is definitely lying to us. But then so are Beth and Dominic, and O'Connell's hiding something as well." He looked up at Grieg who had stood and was stretching his back. "You know, our job would be significantly easier if people weren't such lying bastards."

Grieg nodded. "But where would be the fun in that?"

Kostatis slammed his hands on the desk, coming to a decision.

"Let's go and pay a visit to Beth's flat." Grieg raised an eyebrow. "I know she was round at Dominic's but there's something very odd going on between those two and O'Connell, the Forthrights and Jeff and his merry band. Let's get over there and have a chat with the flatmate. See whether she can shed a little light on things."

Kostatis stood up, grabbed his coat from the back of the door and followed Grieg out of his office, the precipice he was teetering over earlier forgotten once again.

Chapter 37

Evolution: A gradual process in which something changes into a different and usually more complex or better form.

Whether you believed this applied to living organisms, with humans being the pinnacle of the evolutionary journey, depended on your religious beliefs. The principle however is not confined to living organisms or the rigidity of religious thought. Evolution is everywhere. The preservation of perishable foodstuffs: originally drying or salting, then freezing were the only options. Now, through the evolution of food processing, it is possible to prolong the life of food almost indefinitely given the right blend of additives. The dietary and nutritional value may suffer but it's possible. Technology: we all now walk around with more computing power in the smart-phones in our pockets than was available to the Apollo 11 team that put Neil Armstrong on the moon. Cars, bicycles, clothing, buildings, transportation, cities, people, expectations, human performance, scientific understanding—everywhere you look there is evidence of evolution. Processes and approaches are constantly evolving, moving through iterations, refining, improving, honing. Every idea is subject to someone somewhere asking, "Can I do this better?"

Jeff was undeniably an evolutionist. He had taken the millennia-old process of combining water, barley, yeast and hops and, in his own mind at least, moved it a quantum leap forward. He had single-handedly altered consumers' expectations over what 'great' was when it came to beer. Jeff knew though that to stand still in a world constantly evolving was in effect to go backwards.

He hadn't left his cathedral of subterranean brewing, except to make himself a sandwich, since he had dragged Terry down the low-lit staircase earlier. Now, with Terry slumped unconscious once again, he wandered amongst the equipment that had brought him riches and fame. He delicately brushed his fingers along the polished copper of the fermenting vats. The pads of his fingertips tingling as they traced the small dents in its surface, circling the rivets that kept it water tight. He allowed his hand to glide smoothly down to the burners, flinching slightly as he touched them. He couldn't help thinking that the balance necessary in the universe meant that their resting temperature was not ambient as one would expect, but they actually achieved a negative ambient temperature in contrast to the raging temperatures they would achieve whilst they warmed the barley and yeast in just a few days time.

Although a committed evolutionist, he didn't believe in change for the sake of change. He knew the big breweries had updated their technology decades ago, automating wherever possible in a drive to reduce cost and improve profitability, missing the key ingredient entirely—passion. Well, one of the key ingredients anyway. A smile touched his lips as the thought struck him but failed to reach his eye.

He thought back to the conventions he used to attend in the early days. SSoH had already made a name for themselves with Lurcher's and Grouchy Goat, a reputation that grew with Posturing Pig, Cat's Curiosity and Penguin's Prerogative. But even though he was hailed as an innovator, the large breweries still looked down their noses at him, his antiquated methods identifying him as a hangover from a bygone era. Once it would have bothered Jeff that even today the big boys didn't really see him as a threat. Oh, they wanted the secret to his success no doubt, but their thinking was on a different plain. Profitability was all they cared about, quality of their product coming some way down the list of priorities. They had long since conceded they couldn't match him on flavour and desirability but because he only produced his incredible beers in small volumes they genuinely didn't see him as a threat. Once, that too would have annoyed him but now he understood the difference between them. They believed innovation was finding different ways to do the same thing cheaper and quicker. He believed innovation was about changing the fundamentals.

He passed the vats and burners, his eyes moving from the stainless steel funnel above to the single most important piece of equipment he owned: the macerator. In the light of the converted sewer his eye passed lovingly across the cold metal, the dullness of the rotating blades giving way to their painstakingly sharpened edges, which gleamed brightly. Their sharpness could only be made more obvious if a 'ping' accompanied the light reflecting from their edges.

Reaching up he gently grasped one of the blades between thumb and forefinger and tenderly sent it spinning, mesmerised by the soft mechanical clanking that accompanied each revolution. He was happy.

A pained groan from behind him brought him back to the present and reality. He didn't know how long he had been stood there or indeed how long ago the momentum of the blade had petered out. All he knew was soon these elegantly simple devices would be working in unison to create something unique, something extraordinary, something new.

"You're worse than Wilbur you know."

He turned from the macerator and walked slowly back towards the chair and Terry lying on the floor blinking his eyes rapidly, trying to dispel the last vestiges of unconsciousness.

"At least Wilbur maintained belief." Jeff ran his hand along the row of beer pump labels, each one referring to a specific beer. "Not in the path we had all chosen and agreed was for the best. No, he had lost his way, capitulated to a fabricated idea of correctness that politicians, media and religion spout daily in order to control and contain." He passed the bottling plant, gripping an empty bottle and slowly sliding it down the gradual incline that took the bottles from the labelling machine the forty feet to the packing station. From the floor, Terry watched the label-less bottle pirouette down the ramp and come to a rest against the padded buffer.

"Wilbur lost his way, but he believed in his new path. He truly believed that through confession he would find comfort and redemption." Jeff laughed derisively at the thought and took his seat again, leaning forward to stare Terry in the eye. "He had belief. It was misplaced but he believed nonetheless." Leaning back he lashed his leg out, a resounding thud coming from Terry's chest and a groan from behind the gag.

"You though Terry, you disgust me in a way that Wilbur never did."

Terry stared up at Jeff, whatever understanding or relative calm that had overcome him chased away by what he now saw. He had long since come to believe Jeff wasn't in control of all his mental faculties but the cold disconnected insanity in Jeff's eye proved he had underestimated the situation.

"Passion and belief are important, Terry. They provide focus and drive. They give us something to embrace and draw joy and comfort from. Without passion and belief we meander through life, never fully committing to the opportunities we're presented with. Always holding back, never discovering quite how good we could be or how far we could go."

Jeff stood and aimed another kick at Terry. This time though, Terry was more aware and twisted out of the way, Jeff's shoe merely glancing his shoulder rather than connecting with his cheek.

The small victory was short-lived however as Jeff, incensed by Terry's resistance, rained kick after kick and blow after blow down on the prostrate figure, a deathly animalistic guttural scream accompanying every impact, his teeth bared in a snarl of hate, spittle frothing over his lips splattering Terry as he stole a glance at the madman above him.

As abruptly as the assault had started, the blows pounding into Terry ceased. The beaten figure on the floor heard the creak of the chair as Jeff sat down.

"Look at me." Terry was too frightened to do anything. "LOOK AT ME!"

Fearing another beating, Terry slowly turned his head back to Jeff. He was indeed once again sat in his chair, his face calm, the only signs of his previous rage were a slight flushing to his cheeks and a small lace of saliva hanging from his lips. A friendly smile spread across his face as he looked down.

"Here, clean yourself up." Jeff pulled a neatly ironed and folded handkerchief from his pocket and offered it to Terry whose hands, bound behind him, had offered small protection to his back in the onslaught. "My mistake," Jeff said cheerfully. "Allow me." He slowly knelt in front of Terry and delicately, almost lovingly, dabbed at the blood that was dribbling from his eyebrow and lips. Terry flinched at the touch and a flash of anger whipped across Jeff's face. "Now, now," he said. "Everything's fine."

Terry lay rigidly still as the psychopath who had once been his friend cleaned up the cuts he himself had inflicted.

"There, that's better isn't it?" Jeff stared at Terry as an entomologist might view a case of pinned butterflies. "Where were we?" he asked. "Ah yes, passion and belief. You lack both Terry. You see, you may have disagreed with my plans and the direction we have taken but you went along with it. And then, when Wilbur had the guts to stand up to me—an act I respect by the way, even if I disagreed with it—when he stood against me you lacked the guts to stand with him. I knew you didn't agree with me but when presented with another option, one I'm sure you did agree with, you left Wilbur to stand alone. What was it? Fear of prison? Fear of me perhaps? Either way, I knew then our relationship was over. What I don't understand is where this came from. What was it that made you waver in your belief? I'm genuinely interested." Jeff's tone was hard and commanding. It appeared as if Terry's silent cameo had come to an end and his input was required.

Gently probing the tears in his lips, Terry moistened them and attempted to speak. His mouth was full of saliva and blood and he noticed the disgusted look on Jeff's face as instead of words only blood-flecked bubbles emitted from his mouth. Coughing slightly he spat on the floor and tried again.

"You went too far," he finally managed.

"In what way?" Jeff's tone remained cold.

"In every way." Terry knew his life was now forfeit and with that knowledge, resistance grew. Jeff was right, he should have stood with Wilbur and he was right about the reasons he hadn't. He was too old for prison and he couldn't help thinking at the time, prophetically as it turned out, there was no way Jeff would let it get that far. But now, lying on the floor, bound and beaten, he would have his say before Jeff did whatever it was he was going to do.

"Please, expand."

"Alright. You're a psychopath. You chopped up animals and added them to beer. The fact the result tastes amazing is irrelevant. It's barbaric and inhumane. You're a lunatic and you've driven all of us along in this madness as well. There's no forgiveness for what we've done." Terry was straining his head from the floor. "And the latest idea, Jesus. I don't know what's happened to me over the years that I didn't go straight to the police."

"Greed. That's what stopped you going to the police. Greed and self-preservation. There's no mystery to it. You lack the moral fibre necessary to understand and commit, either to the plan or to blow the whistle. You're pathetically concerned with self-preservation."

"But you're proposing replacing the animal component with people. There's no word that sufficiently covers how completely and utterly insane that is."

Jeff stood again and drove his foot into Terry's face. Caught off guard, his head snapped back, the muscles in his neck barely managing to prevent his spine snapping.

"I am not insane," he enunciated clearly. "Insane would be trying to sell my beers without trying them first or putting them into production without a test batch. Is that what you think? That I would commit to Mao's Midget Marauders without any testing? If you think that then it's you who's completely insane my old friend." The words barely made it past Jeff's rigid jaw and tight lips.

Despite the ringing in his head, Terry couldn't help thinking he had missed an important point in the conversation but Jeff wasn't finished.

"None of you ungrateful and spineless cunts have ever understood the sacrifice required to provide you with the luxuries you've taken for granted." The dull shine of insanity was back in Jeff's eye and if he had been given the choice, Terry would have opted for the earth to swallow him there and then. "Firstly I had to watch as Oscar fell to his grisly death. I had to watch my best friend be sliced and minced, all so you could ultimately buy that fat bitch you call a wife a £10,000 necklace," Jeff screamed at Terry. "I understand that true innovation, genuine step change, always extracts its cost. So do you really think I would decide, just off the top of my head, to change from something we know works to something we have no fucking idea about?"

Five minutes previously, Terry would never have believed he could feel any less at ease than he had at that moment. Now though, as Jeff soliloquized like the madman he clearly was, Terry started to get a heavy cold feeling in his stomach that had nothing to do with the internal bleeding.

Jeff had stepped away from his chair and was standing in the middle of the chamber, his arms outstretched to the sides. Calm seemed to have befallen him; the insanity was still there but the accompanying rage had abated. It was with an almost reconciliatory tone that he continued.

"It's funny, by the time I die I will have been responsible for two fundamental discoveries within the brewing industry, whether they be widely known or not. Both of which were provided by those closest to me."

Terry didn't want to hear the rest, he had a terrible feeling where this was going. Jeff turned back to Terry and saw the understanding in his eyes and nodded.

"That's right, Oscar gave me my first breakthrough and Rose provided the second." He walked across to the bottling bench where an example of every specialist beer they had ever brewed stood. He scanned the line reaching for the one he wanted. Turning back to Terry, Jeff twisted the bottle and presented the label.

"Do you remember the wake?" Jeff asked, a distance coming to his monocular stare. Terry was deteriorating fast. A physical beating was one thing, but if someone could undermine your psychological foundations you disassembled very quickly. Snippets of memory were crashing in on Terry from Rose's wake five years previously. Bang: tears at the church. Bang: quiet control at the burial. Bang: finger food at the wake. Bang: Jeff handing out a commemorative beer. Bang: SSoH swigging 'Between Two Thorns'. Bang: the mood changing. Bang: everyone laughing. Bang: no pain anymore. Bang: the empty feeling the following day over a 'normal' pint. Bang: Terry back in the chamber, realisation over what Jeff had done. Bang: Terry remembering that Between Two Thorns was possibly the best beer he had ever tasted. He looked at Jeff disbelieving.

"You see?" Jeff said, nodding his head slightly, sorrow vying for supremacy in his one good eye. "If you haven't sacrificed, you can't judge." For a fleeting moment Terry thought he saw a broken man before him. Someone who had done terrible things and was now realising there was no forgiveness.

"Jeff, it's not too late. We can fix this." Terry watched as Jeff held his head in his hands. "Come on Jeff, untie me and we can fix this together. No-one else needs to get hurt."

Jeff sighed heavily and looked at Terry. Sorrow had lost.

Chapter 38

If Dominic had taken the time to consider how things had progressed over the last few days he would unequivocally have arrived at the opinion that he was completely out of his depth. That, had all this happened in a personal vacuum where the ramifications of the situation had absolutely no bearing on any of his friends or colleagues, he would probably still be sat at the kitchen table, staring at the latest rapidly cooling mug of tea, unable to make any sense of what was going on or discern any course of action, let alone the correct one.

As it was, his brain hadn't raised this point with him, whether through limited emotional intelligence and inability to perceive the truth, or through an evolutionary survival instinct protecting him from this debilitating knowledge, he was still to all intents and purposes functioning. Assuming he survived his current predicament, the resultant personal capability questions raised by his handling of events might well make for depressing consideration, but for the time being he was happy to abdicate responsibility to the competent adult sat next to him.

Beth indicated right and waited for the articulated lorry to blow past the interchange before glancing left and pulling across the traffic. She caught sight of Dominic, pale and expressionless, and gently reached a hand to his knee.

"It's going to be fine," she said, forcing herself to sound more confident than she felt. Beth did possess the emotional intelligence to see more than the bare facts of a situation, and in all honesty had no idea whether things would be all right or not. She had, following brief consideration, dismissed Weasel's suggestion that this Hank bloke would be willing to level a whole high street, causing untold casualties just to get rid of them and a poxy diary, irrespective of how incendiary it might be. Motives and actions like that were for fiction, not real life. She was less confident though, that all involved would walk away safely.

The location of the proposed meeting offered security she had argued, once the most recent wave of disbelief had dissipated following the disclosure of the SSoH's latest insane plan. The Premiums had seemed intent on focussing on the beer, whereas Beth wanted to focus on those elements they could affect in the short term. The fact the only thing they could actively influence was also the thing that would dictate their and her friend's safety instantly prioritised her actions. She was both annoyed and relieved that the mismatched group of men in Dominic's kitchen turned immediately to him for guidance. Ultimately not a bad thing she thought, as whether they recognised it or not, there was a hierarchy of decision-making going on, with The Premiums looking to Dominic for leadership and Dominic, whose eyes currently flashed 'We are experiencing a technical fault. Normal service will be resumed as soon as possible. We apologise for the inconvenience', looking to her. Thus a sensible decision was arrived at.

The first of which had been to comply with the kidnapper's first demand: they had to be there on their own. That meant no police and no Premiums, however well-meaning the latter's actions might be. She had proposed that the best way to ensure no problems arose was to go their separate ways until after the handover. The Premiums looked to Dominic, an incensed look on their faces at the suggestion they should leave the leader of their band of brothers to face his fate alone. Beth ignored the implied slight.

With everyone suddenly looking at him, Dominic's brain had defaulted to 'limp home' mode, allowing him access to just enough cerebral power to get out of the current conversation before needing serious attention.

"Beth's right," he had managed, a tiny amount of colour returning to his cheeks as he focussed on a single element of the crisis as opposed to trying to view its entirety. "He isn't going to blow up the high street and we want to make sure that one of you guys doesn't get seen accidently. This isn't like when I tell you all to be careful with crockery. We *really* can't afford any fuck-ups here all right?" The Premiums had seemed unconvinced until Dominic had proposed a compromise of sorts.

"Look guys, we know what they have planned for their next beer and we know where the handover is going to happen. If the naming convention of this one follows the pattern of the previous beers then, as crazy as it sounds, there's a lorry load of Chinese midgets on its way to Surrey, and if we don't do something about it, an unthinkable end. While Beth and I give this prick his diary back and get Naomi, you need to come up with an idea as to what we do about that."

Back in the car, Dominic sighed heavily as they approached Beth's flat. It was testament to the enormity of the situation that his mind didn't immediately return to the last time he had been there, the good and the bad. Beth parked the Renault Clio outside and the two of them walked to the front door, Dominic casting furtive glances up and down the road. Once inside, Beth led Dominic through to the kitchen. They had an hour before they were due on the high street.

"Tea?" she offered and was pleased to see a wry smile touch Dominic's lips as he nodded.

"Mint please. Look, I'm sorry I've been so…" Dominic searched for a phrase which mitigated his lack of input, but failed, "...utterly useless in all of this. It's all been a bit overwhelming really," he said, reinforcing his ability in understatement.

"For both of us." Beth placed his mug down in front of him and took the seat opposite. Silence filled the space between them. She watched Dominic sip his tea, his eyes never rising from the slowly swirling liquid.

"I'm sorry I got you involved in this." He finally looked at Beth, regret writ large on his face. Despite everything, all the danger she knew she was facing and the danger that her flatmate was currently experiencing, she also smiled wryly.

"It's not exactly your fault is it? It's not like I'm a Montague and you're a Capulet and we could predict this was going to happen."

"Well technically it would be the other way around but I get your point," he laughed.

"Check you out, correcting me on my Shakespeare," she said, mock offended. Dominic raised his hands in apology.

"Sorry. Slight pedantry runs in our family." He took another sip of tea and looked at Beth again. She was a little surprised at the intensity in his eyes.

"I'm also sorry about the other day and my radio silence." Beth was about to interject and steer the conversation to safer waters but Dominic wouldn't be deflected. "No wait. I know this isn't the most opportune time but given everything, I'm not sure when would be."

It was Beth's turn to raise her hands, deferring back to Dominic. Besides, there was part of her that really wanted to hear what he had to say.

"I'm not very good when I don't know what to do."

Beth raised her eyebrows as if to say really?

"All I mean by that," Dominic continued, "is that I had no frame of reference. I've never been in a situation where I've accidentally felt-up my..." he struggled to find the words, eventually shrugging. "I've never felt-up the mother of someone I really like before. All I could think of was how angry you both must be about it."

Beth's features softened slightly. "Dominic, anyone could tell it was clearly an accident. You aren't the first person to think I look like my mother. You are the first to confuse our breasts..."

Dominic writhed in his seat, his cheeks flushing red with embarrassment.

"I'm only joking," Beth said, reaching a hand out to reassure him. "The way I see it is that you came out of this far worse. She did break your nose after all."

Dominic unconsciously brought his hand up to his face. "It was a really good shot," he said, risking a look into Beth's eyes.

"I won't lie to you, she's very proud of herself." She took his hand in hers. "We're all fallible, Dominic. Accidents happen, mistakes happen, even really embarrassing ones. But to ignore the situation, to not talk about it or return any of my calls..." She paused as if deciding whether to continue or not. Eventually she did. "I'm not interested in someone who doesn't have the maturity to see this for what it is—simply an embarrassing mistake—and be willing to face that embarrassment because there's more to gain than protecting their wounded pride."

Dominic sat there feeling even worse than he had before. He desperately wanted to tell her that he was mature enough to face his embarrassment. That he really liked her and that the idea of their relationship fizzling out so soon and over something so stupid was unthinkable. He wanted to say so much but for some reason couldn't find the words. To his eternal gratitude, once again Beth stepped in to rescue the situation.

"Unless of course you're not interested."

"Oh my God, no," he said. "Of course I'm interested. That was the best date I've ever had, and you are by far the most incredible woman I've ever been out with. I'm so sorry that I let my pride get the better of me and didn't return your calls." He squeezed her hand and was rewarded with a small smile. "I was crushed with embarrassment." He felt Beth start to withdraw her hand. "Wait, imagine just for a second the situation was reversed. That you had accidentally gently caressed my dad's penis. How would you have felt?"

Beth relaxed her hand back into Dominic's and thought for a second.

"Ok, I take your point," she conceded. "But I would like to think that I would have at least returned a text."

"And I also would like to think that I would have done the same, but it turns out I didn't and for that I'm really sorry."

Beth nodded her head and sighed.

"Apology accepted."

"So, how would you feel if we put all of this behind us and never spoke of it again?" Dominic asked, almost managing to conceal the desperation he felt.

"I'm more than happy to. I can't speak for my mother though." Beth felt Dominic's arm tense. "Hey, that's just part of the deal. I'm afraid this is a storm you're going to have to weather, if that is you think it's worth it."

"Ah, very clever." Dominic managed a small chuckle at the glint in Beth's eye. "Of course it's worth it." Beth squeezed his hand and for the briefest moment both of them felt a sense of peace that one unpleasant element of their lives had been resolved.

All too soon though their main predicament loomed large in both their minds. With time still to wait until they were due at the rendezvous Beth considered their situation. Ultimately there wasn't anything more they could do about the handover of the diary until they met Hank at the specified time and place. And how that went would be entirely down to the kidnapper.

Silence stretched away in the kitchen as they each stared at their tea. Eventually Beth was the one to break it.

"What do you think The Premiums will come up with as a plan to foil the SSoH?"

"Oh, who knows? Experience tells me it will almost certainly be incredibly complex and completely unworkable."

Beth smiled and was pleased to see it reflected in Dominic's face.

"Do you think they'll consider phoning the police?"

"I shouldn't think so," Dominic said. "Not now that approach has been formally ruled out. You have to recognise that this is a group of guys with vast amounts of unearned confidence. Only ridiculous flights of fancy can save the world, and presumably those poor people from becoming Mao's Marauding Midgets. Anything else would be a wasted opportunity." Dominic nearly laughed at the mere thought of what his friends and colleagues were cooking up as they sat there waiting to deliver the diary which sat innocently between them on the table.

"We are just going to call the police though, right?" she asked, not entirely certain whether Dominic was a true Premium or not.

"Of course, as soon as we know that Naomi is ok, we're going to call the police and hope that they believe us." Dominic looked at the clock on the kitchen wall. "Right now though, we ought to get moving. Whatever happens, I think being late is a bad idea."

The pair of them jumped at the sudden and insistent sound of the doorbell, staring at each other with the universal questioning look of 'who can that be?' Beth got up from her chair and Dominic listened as she made her way to the front door. He heard her open it and then some muffled conversation and the door being closed again. Door to door salesman, or Jehovah's Witnesses he thought. Same thing actually, he joked to himself as he heard Beth come back into the kitchen.

"Who was it?" he asked distractedly.

"Mr Morgan, it's DS Grieg and this is my colleague DCI Kostatis, we met earlier."

Dominic jumped from his chair so quickly it would have clattered to the floor had Grieg not caught it on the way down.

"No need to get up on my account sir." He placed the chair back on its four legs and motioned for Dominic to sit. "There, that's better isn't it?"

"They want to speak to Naomi," Beth said, pushing past the two police officers. "Even though I told them she isn't in and I have no idea where she is or when she will be back, they insisted on barging in here."

"Don't you need a warrant or something like that?" Dominic asked, panic rising inside him at the appearance of the police officers. DS Grieg looked shocked.

"What on earth would we need a warrant for?" Grieg asked innocently. "You know the people who tend to say that are the very people who tend to have something to hide. Are you trying to hide something from us Mr Morgan?"

Dominic was in full panic mode now. The calm and relative clarity of thinking he had attained earlier had fled leaving the exit door banging in the wind. Thankfully, once again Beth was more in control.

"No, I think he's just pointing out that we don't live in a police state and that the actions of the police are governed by laws in the same way the actions of us as citizens are. You need a warrant to enter someone's property because that requires oversight from a judge, which in turn means that you have to have sufficient grounds to persuade a judge that a warrant is necessary, helping to eliminate the misuse of police powers."

Grieg looked at Kostatis who remained silently observing the situation as it played out. Grieg turned back to Beth and Dominic nodding.

"Well, that's all very interesting but as I said all we wanted to do was have a word with your flatmate. If she isn't in you should have just said."

"I did say," Beth said indignantly.

"Oh, my apologies, I must not have heard you." Grieg reached inside his jacket and removed three business cards. "I know I gave you both one of these earlier but just in case you've misplaced them, and there's one for your flatmate when she gets back. Very nice to see you again Mr Morgan." Grieg tipped an imaginary hat to Dominic and Beth. "Miss Cooper."

Beth followed the policemen out of the kitchen, herding them towards the front door, slamming it behind them once they had left. Back in the kitchen she found Dominic physically shaking and white as a ghost.

"Well that was interesting," Grieg said as they settled back into the BMW parked six spaces behind Beth's Clio. Kostatis grunted in agreement. Grieg looked back towards the house they had just left.

"What do you make of all that warrant and abuse of police powers nonsense? They don't strike me as the type of people who would normally pull that shit."

"Too much TV probably. What's confusing is that they're exactly the type of people who help police with their enquiries. For them to jump to warrants and the like means they're definitely hiding something from us."

"You don't think they're involved in the Forthright murders do you?" Grieg asked, knowing that wasn't his superior's theory but used to the need to draw Kostatis' thoughts from him at times.

"No. It doesn't feel right. There's no obvious motive and to the best of our knowledge Morgan didn't even know the Forthrights existed until the other day. Add to that the behaviour of Forthright's friends and I fancy one of them for it. We just need to decide which one, or ones."

"So what are these two hiding then?"

Kostatis stared out of the window thinking.

"I don't know," he said eventually. "But did you see the book on the table?" Grieg nodded that he had seen it but had failed to notice anything unusual about it. "It's the same book the fat Cornish lad was reading when we spoke to them at Morgan's house," Kostatis continued. "I thought at the time he seemed to have a Gollum-like possessiveness over it. He didn't stop reading the whole time we were there. Having the police turn up typically distracts people from whatever they're doing but not him. That book's important to him, so what are Morgan and Cooper doing with it? And there was nothing else on the table either, except a couple of mugs. But the book was right in the middle of the table, like a centre piece, almost like they feel some deference towards it. And Morgan kept flicking his eyes from the book to the clock and back again." Kostatis fell silent.

Grieg left him to his thoughts and looked out at the house they had just left. He didn't know about books or Gollums but he did know when people were lying to him and he didn't like it.

As he watched, the front door opened and a very pale and hesitant Dominic Morgan edged out, peering up and down the road as he did so.

"Sir," Grieg nudged Kostatis who looked on in interest.

Shortly after Morgan exited the building, Cooper followed him. While not as pale as Morgan, Grieg could tell that she was definitely agitated. Held tightly in Morgan's right hand was a small packet, just big enough to hold Cornish Gollum's precious.

"What do you want to do sir?" Grieg asked as they watched the couple walk away up the road.

"Have we heard back from Forthright's doctor yet?"

"Not as yet. Uniform is still trying to chase him down."

"Well in that case, in the absence of anything more concrete to go on, I think we should see what these two are up to, don't you?"

Grieg smiled and started the car.

Chapter 39

The walk to the high street was only ten minutes but as Dominic and Beth made their way it felt like a lifetime. Dominic had no idea what inmates on America's death row felt like but he imagined this was very much like walking that final mile, uncertainty about your immediate future a thing of the past.

The pair had walked in silence, each with their own thoughts, the tension ratcheting up with each step, their hearts beating ever faster until Dominic was certain it was about to explode from his chest like a baby alien.

Almost without thinking he reached for Beth's hand. Not a flirtatious action but one born from the need for solidarity and shared support. Beth's reciprocal iron-like grip showing him he wasn't the only one in need of reassurance. A walk into town had never held such fear for either of them. No conversation was needed. The kidnapper had been clear and precise about where they had to be: outside Argos facing Greggs.

The high street was full of shoppers going about their business, oblivious to the turmoil Beth and Dominic were going through. Beth felt Dominic's grip tighten further at the sound of a van backfiring and found she could barely speak as her heart hammered away in her chest and the lump grew in her throat.

Usually light on his feet in crowds, now Dominic just walked straight, focussed on his goal: the bench outside Argos facing the cavern of baked delights that was Greggs. He barely noticed as other people, too busy staring at their phones or talking to their friends to even consider avoiding a collision bounced off him, their insulted and self-centred indignation falling on deaf ears. Perhaps under different circumstances these collisions might have escalated but there is little better to dampen the fires of aggression than the sight of someone who has bigger things to worry about than a bruised ego.

Dominic felt Beth pull on his arm and focussed for the first time. One hundred metres ahead of them was Argos. Immediately outside its welcoming doors, in the middle of the high street, was the bench they had been told to wait on. Dominic checked his watch. They still had five minutes. Confused by Beth tugging his arm, he looked at her but all he got in return was a steely focus and a renewed effort to drag him forward. He was just about to ask what was wrong when he saw it: coming out of the Greggs opposite the bench was an elderly couple. The man had a plastic pipe running from his nose to a cylinder of oxygen he was dragging behind him on a small two-wheeled trolley. His wife clutched a variety of white paper bags in her withered and liver-spotted hands. They were clearly moving with one course of action in mind and that was a rest on the most convenient seat available—the empty bench outside Argos. Beth lengthened her stride, closing the distance at a far greater rate than the elderly couple could manage, but they were closer. The advantage was with Dominic and Beth until the old man took a brief look away from his wife and saw Beth focussed on the bench. With a rare burst of energy the old man doubled his efforts, increasing his pace from a slow motion shuffle, dragging his unsuspecting wife along.

Beth dropped Dominic's hand and launched into a full sprint to cross the final metres to the bench with Dominic close behind. Sliding across the bench just as the old man arrived out of breath, Beth stared at the elderly couple, daring them to say anything. There was a flicker on the woman's face as if she was weighing up whether it was worth it or not. After a few seconds she thought better of it and turned away, dragging her husband and his oxygen tank with her in search of a more easily claimed resting place.

Dominic caught his breath as he watched the couple shuffle off down the high street then turned to Beth. "You ok?" he asked.

Tight lipped Beth nodded and looked at her phone. "Three minutes," she said.

"So what now?" Dominic asked.

"We wait. He said to be here on the hour and we are here on the hour. It's up to him now."

Hank couldn't help but laugh. He had seen Cooper and Morgan break into a fast walk before he had seen the elderly couple. Once the old man had sensed the very real possibility of losing the bench he had put on a surprising turn of speed, relatively that is. Hank had wondered briefly whether British politeness would win out and was glad to see his captive's flatmate break into a run to clinch the prize—it meant they were focussed on what they were all there for, which was the safe return of the diary.

He took a large slurp from his diet coke and let his eyes wander the high street in front of him. The high street was an L-shape and he had watched Dominic and Beth make their way down the hill heading for the shops as instructed, almost to the point where it turned 90 degrees right and went back uphill. Cutting the corner of the L was a glass-fronted fast-food restaurant, a seat at the front of which offered views up both sections of the high street and a perfect vantage point for Hank to survey the area and make sure they had been compliant with all of his stipulations. He had been there for a little over half an hour and was grateful these places were advertising themselves as a destination rather than a place one visited for the ten minutes it took to inhale the reconstituted burger and fries. He had eaten a burger, which had left him feeling hungrier than before he ate it, and was now drinking a large diet coke. He would leave the two of them sitting on their bench for a while to see whether anyone else was with them.

It was a gamble, leaving Razor alone with the woman, but right now he had little choice. The arrival of the police at Hank Foey's flat had been an unwanted and unexpected inconvenience. Of course it was possible that they were just going door to door following some local crime, trying to drum up witness statements but he couldn't rely on that. It was more likely that Razor's antics with the Aston owner had come back to haunt him. He swirled the diet coke around the cup and stared at Morgan who was bouncing his legs nervously.

Even though it had been Razor who had nearly killed the Aston's owner, Hank couldn't really blame him for the situation as it now stood. Razor was a known quantity. He and violence were as synonymous as politicians and fraud or philandering, a fait accompli. Yet still Hank had kept him around for the last five years. Hank was under no illusions as to why that was. He told himself, and Razor for that matter, that he needed Razor's muscle, his ability to dominate a situation physically.

And to some extent that was true but the real reason was that Razor offered Hank a scapegoat. He had known all along that he wouldn't be able to conduct his little enterprise without one day coming to the attention of the police. The police would want the brains of the outfit, but the public optics would demand they prosecute someone. Razor was his sacrificial lamb.

Hank didn't possess Razor's fortitude. He had been to prison only once but it had stolen eighteen months of his life and he had sworn never to go back. Razor on the other hand had been wholly institutionalised by the time they met. Even now, Hank knew that Razor could go back inside for a ten stretch and it barely register as an inconvenience. He was built for it. Hank was not.

This would be the last job they did together. Once he had the diary back he would call Razor and tell him to let the girl go. He had never intended on really hurting her anyway. She was leverage—a necessary incentive to ensure Morgan's compliance. Once their business that afternoon was done she would be set free. Of course, she would go to the police and tell them of the horrible men who had kidnapped and threatened her, but importantly, she would only be able to remember one of them. Razor was so intimidating and psychotic looking that all her brain would be able to do was remember those eyes and teeth. Hank would blur into the background and soon enough would cease to exist in any meaningful way. The police would quickly track Razor down and with the dual charges of attempted murder and kidnapping he could look forward to a very long time behind bars.

The important thing was for the police to have someone to parade in front of the media and show they were doing their jobs and keeping the public safe, or at least catching the guilty party after they had failed to keep the public safe. That was Razor's role, his primary function since the very beginning. Razor would be arrested and Hank would disappear. Maybe he would try to cut a deal with the police. They would certainly try to get him to do so and who knew, maybe they would succeed. Hank doubted it though. Razor's only response if he managed to utter one was likely to be a big "get fucked". Even if he did tell them anything, Hank wasn't worried. All Razor knew was where the flat was, which had been a necessary risk to take in order to gain Razor's trust and buy in. If the film *Heat* had taught Hank anything, and it had, it was that you "don't let yourself get attached to anything you are not willing to walk out on in 30 seconds flat if you feel the heat around the corner."

All the London flat had ever been was a convenient place from which to do business. Ok, he had some expensive computer equipment there but computers could be replaced. Realistically he would lose the flat itself. Trying to sell it would be problematic at best, but he had come to terms with that as well. He had always thought of the value the flat represented as the actual amount of money he had paid for it rather than the hugely inflated worth the recent property market had given it. £600,000 market value was a lot of money to walk away from but he thought of the purchase price back in 2000 which had been around a quarter of that. Still not chicken feed but Hank would pay one hundred times that to avoid another stretch in prison. He would simply never go back. He'd get the diary, make the drop on the last shipment and collect his payment then disappear—easy. All that could wait. His plan was sequential and right now he had to focus on other things, namely the diary.

Dominic looked at his watch. They had been sitting there for nearly half an hour and both he and Beth were now far beyond worried. They had expected the kidnapper to call them on the stroke of the hour but as each minute passed, the possible implications sprang up like monsters in their thoughts. Every time they overcame the fear it was replaced by two more, a Hydra of imagination and terror.

"What time is it?" Beth asked for the twentieth time but before Dominic could reply, Beth's phone vibrated into life and Naomi's smiling face lit up the screen. Beth's terrified eyes rested briefly on Dominic's before answering.

"Hello?" Her voice was quiet and croaky, even that single word broken.

"I'm pleased to see you didn't succumb to British politeness."

"What?" Beth said, confusion spread across her face. Dominic, unable to hear the other side of the conversation, mouthed *what is it?* at her.

"The old couple in desperate need of a sit down. Especially the old man who was so frail he needed to drag his own supply of oxygen around with him. That last burst of effort he put in looked like it damn near killed him. Now wouldn't that be funny? In your haste to save your friend you might have inadvertently caused the death of an old man and probably his frail wife as a consequence." Beth heard Hank chuckle down the line. "Still, that's all circle of life stuff isn't it?"

"Where's Naomi?" Beth managed after a few seconds to regain control. She turned to Dominic and mouthed *he's watching us*.

"You want to dispense with the pleasantries do you? Cut straight to the chase? OK, fair enough, I can do that. Your friend is currently enjoying the company of my associate. Do you have the diary?"

Beth turned to Dominic, "He says he wants to know if we have the diary."

"Of course we've got the fucking diary, what does he think we're here for?" His fear and frustration finally bubbling over.

"Dominic says of course we've got the fucking diary, what do you think we're here for?"

"All right smart arse. Let's not forget who's got whose flatmate holed up with a psychopath. Show me the diary."

"He wants to see it Dominic."

Dominic looked around the street, desperate to get a glimpse of anyone paying them too much attention. Slowly he raised the small brown parcel into the air.

"How odd do you think it has to get before we go and have a chat?" Grieg asked Kostatis from their position a hundred or so metres further up the high street.

In the time they had been watching them they hadn't seen Beth or Dominic speak to anyone. Every minute or so Beth would say something to Dominic and he would check his watch. Now, Beth was on the phone looking very worried and Dominic was holding what Kostatis thought had to be the book above his head.

"I reckon we give them another couple of minutes and then wonder over, see if we can't be of assistance to two members of the public clearly in distress."

"That's good," Hank replied, the brown parcel clearly visible from his viewpoint. "Now, you need to convince me that you haven't been stupid and made any copies or told anyone else about the book's existence."

"Of course we haven't made any copies, and we definitely haven't told anyone else about it. You have to believe us. We just want Naomi back." Beth had to stop herself from shouting as she drew worried glances from some of the shoppers as they passed by.

"What about your boyfriend's idiot workmates?" Hank stared at Beth waiting to see what she did next.

Beth stared at Dominic, her eyes pleading for him to tell her how to handle this. Unable to hear the other end of the conversation Dominic had no idea what to say.

"Yes they know about it," she eventually muttered, "but that's only because Dominic told them before we knew what was in it."

"What about the police? Have you spoken with them?"

Beth didn't miss a beat. "Of course we haven't spoken with the police. We have the book and we just want to make the swap ok?" There was silence on the other end of the phone. "Hello? Are you still there? Did you hear me? We just want to make the swap. Hello?"

Hank stared hard at the couple on the bench. He hadn't seen anything untoward and from what he could tell he believed her. He pushed himself back on his stool and made his way down the stairs and out of the front entrance of the restaurant.

"I'm still here," he said. "This is what we're going to do. Your boyfriend is going to lower his hand so he doesn't look like such a fucking idiot and leave it hanging by his side over the side of the bench. The two of you are going to sit there, looking straight ahead as if deciding which tasty treat you are going to get once all this nastiness is over. Do you understand so far?" Hank slipped into the crowd and nonchalantly moved across the street so he could approach the bench from behind.

"Yes, I understand," Beth replied.

"Tell Morgan. We don't want any cock-ups at this stage do we?" Hank slipped into the entrance of Argos. From his new vantage point he could clearly see Beth telling Dominic what to do and his arm lower and hang by his side.

"Very good. Now I'm going to come up behind you and I'm going to take the diary. The pair of you are going to remain looking at the bakery. I am due to call my associate in exactly three minutes. If I don't he has instructions to kill your friend and then burn the building we're holding her in. Do you understand that?"

Beth was desperately trying to fight back tears but managed a feeble yes.

"Excellent." Hank gave the high street a final check. From his new position he couldn't see the other end of the road as it bore away at ninety degrees but he was fairly confident the girl had been up front with him. He was just about to step out from the doorway when to his left something caught his eye. Two men were walking down the street and looking directly at Beth and Dominic. As a seasoned professional in his field of work the way the two men walked was unmistakable.

"You told me you didn't call the police," Hank hissed down the phone.

"What are you talking about?" Beth's head was jerking from side to side trying to see what was going on.

"Your friend's a dead woman," Hank disconnected the call and retreated back into Argos and headed for the rear exit as the two policemen reached Dominic and Beth.

As Kostatis and Grieg approached Dominic and Beth it was clear there was a rapidly growing state of panic.

"Hello? Hello? Are you still there? Please?" Beth was shouting into her phone. Dominic was pale with shock as Grieg reached for Beth's arm and tried to calm her down.

"Calm down. Tell me what's wrong," he said, genuine concern at her distraught outburst showing on his face.

Beth held the phone away from her ear. She stared at Grieg.

"You killed her." She screamed at him. "You killed her."

Chapter 40

Gareth wasn't used to being in charge, or having to formulate a plan. That is unless suggesting a visit to the pub was considered a plan, in which case he was Supreme Commander, master of all he surveyed. To be honest he was sorely tempted to revert to type and head straight for the Duck in the Pond, down eight beers with chasers and wake up tomorrow and view whatever the aftermath looked like from the known discomfort of a splitting skull.

Of course, what he had read in the old man's diary suggested that he was likely to wake to a bloodbath. At least two people had lost their lives already and with the 'ingredients' drop looming, who knew how many more might be added to that figure. With Beth's flatmate being held captive as leverage, there was at least one more life under immediate threat, and if Dominic and Beth delivered the diary, theirs too could be in serious jeopardy. With Dominic and Beth heading off to make the drop it was down to him and The Premiums to come up with a way to save a lorry load of Chinese midgets. Not exactly your normal Tuesday afternoon.

It was an hour since Dominic and Beth had headed off and left the five of them to formulate a foolproof plan. It wasn't long before they ran up against their first hurdle: a complete absence of a grasp of reality and the resources available to them.

"What we need is some serious firepower and a group of highly trained individuals to wield it. We surround the handover location and then when the lorry turns up and these old bastards arrive to take delivery we give the signal, storm the area and disarm any bad guys that show up," Gravy suggested.

"Brilliant," The Fuzz replied sarcastically. "Just pass me the Yellow Pages there Otter," he signalled to his huge colleague, "and I can flick to H and give Hard Bastards a call, see if they're available."

"Hey, at least I'm trying," Gravy replied, annoyed.

"That's not trying, that's living in cloud fucking cuckoo land," The Fuzz added dismissively.

"Well you do better," Gravy retorted.

The Fuzz stared at his challenger, thinking. After a pause that felt like an eternity he started nodding, slowly at first but quickly gathering pace.

"Alright, I will." Everyone leaned closer. "What we need to do is get in touch with this Jeff character and change the collection point. That way we can arrange for a place where the police can be lying in wait. Get some armed police on the case, lorry turns up, bad guys arrive, good guys jump out waving their guns and jobs a good'un. The midgets are saved and the bad guys get their comeuppance." He looked around the group, a smug smile on his face. One by one The Premiums started nodding.

"That's actually not too bad," Gravy conceded. If it was possible, The Fuzz looked even smugger.

"Wait a minute," Gareth interjected before the congratulations became too effusive. "There are a couple of small problems with that plan. One, we 'ave no way of geddin' in touch with Jeff. Even if we did 'ave a means of geddin' in touch with 'em, we 'ave no idea how this fella Hank does it, and in order to change the location they would 'ave to believe that we were Hank, which it would take 'em approximately five seconds to realise we ain't. And B, 'ow the 'ell do we convince the police that there's a small group of pensioners 'ell bent on liquidising midgets, all in the name of good beer?" He looked around the group. "I for one dun't fancy the period of psychological assessment which inevitably follows that conversation."

The despondency amongst the group was palpable as they considered their position. Every now and then one of them would open their mouths, the others leaning forward, eager for any scrap of a plan, only to close it again and sigh as they dismissed their own idea even before it entered the crucible of interrogation.

The minutes ticked by, ratcheting up the pressure until each of them were predominantly looking at the clock, it's uninterested persistence stealing The Premiums focus from what they were trying to achieve.

With despondency giving way to desperation the silence was finally broken.

"I have idea."

The barrage of abuse that would ordinarily accompany any proposition of being able to help was conspicuous by its absence, the group momentarily disoriented by the origin of the words.

Eventually all eyes were on the speaker and Otter flushed deeply at the attention. Despite his obvious discomfort, he outlined his plan. Unlike the others there was no hint of arrogance or smugness in his idea and when he came to the end of his explanation he simply stopped talking and let his words sink into the muddled brains of his colleagues. It was testament to the limited options they had available that it wasn't immediately rejected and Otter pilloried. Eventually the plan required comment.

"It's pretty thin, man," Weasel offered, shaking his head.

"You got anythin' bedder?" asked Gareth.

After a further five minutes of discussion and deliberation The Premiums were in agreement, Otter's plan was the best and indeed only plan they had. As they headed for the front door, shaken from their inaction by the plan the largest of their number had provided, the atmosphere was sombre. It was very likely that some very serious shit was about to go down and they would all be in the middle of it.

"Given a guess as to which of the five of us would actually come up with the plan, I think it would have taken me six guesses to come up with Otter," Gravy mused as he held the door for The Fuzz.

"Yeah," The Fuzz agreed. "I didn't even know he could speak."

Chapter 41

The nose of the car dipped aggressively as Hank stamped on the breaks and came to a stop just short of the red light. He was barely hanging on to his anger, just about keeping control. The only apparent indication of his pent-up rage was the seesawing motion of his car as he alternated his lead foot between the accelerator and the break.

As he sat there seething, barely noticing the pedestrians as they streamed in front of him, all he could think of was the two policemen as they approached his quarry just as he was about to step forward and end the ridiculous situation he had become embroiled in.

He had been so close. He couldn't believe Beth had successfully lied to him about not contacting the police. Was he slipping? Was his judgement not as good as he needed it to be? What did that mean for the rest of his plan? Was it possibly just a coincidence? He thought of all the bizarre and almost comical cock-ups that had contributed to his current predicament. He could honestly say he had never even heard of such a confluence of events, let alone been involved in one.

The sound of a horn brought him back to the moment and the green light. He accelerated hard up to the speed limit, where his inherent discipline stayed his right foot, and exhaled deeply. Hank had always been a glass-half-full kind of person and regardless how bad things appeared, he could quickly envisage a far worse scenario and therefore see the silver lining.

Yes, he had missed the opportunity to grab Dominic at the beginning of these farcical last few days. Yes, he had then entrusted Razor to kidnap Beth and ended up with the wrong hostage. And yes, he had just missed his opportunity to extricate himself forever from the increasingly twisted actions of the SSoH. A litany of missed opportunities. But to focus only on the negative was to invite inertia. If all he could see was the darkness, then how could he find his way through it?

As his heart rate returned to normal he considered the positives. He had missed the opportunity to get his hands on the diary, but equally he had avoided being seen and probably arrested by the two policemen.

He had also avoided the visit from the uniform mob at his flat. As a result he was still in the game, he still had options, and as his acceleration and breaking became less aggressive his next move became more and more obvious to him. Ever since the Post Office all those years ago he had a single unbreakable rule: he was in control of his own destiny.

He indicated left and pulled up to the barrier of a multi-storey car park. He took the ticket and slowly the barrier rose in front of him. He eased between the pillars and headed up to the penultimate floor where he had a permanent parking space under a different name.

As he made his way up the car park he reviewed the last few days. He now realised he had allowed himself to think he was in control, that each decision had been his own and that at any given time he was the one with the most knowledge, and therefore directing his own future. He now realised that had been a fallacy. From the moment he had agreed to get the diary for Jeff he had been marching to the beat of another's drum. He only had to look at the things that had happened over the last few days to realise that.

There were very few things he wasn't willing to do in order to protect himself, but he now realised that kidnapping a young woman was not the action of someone in control of their situation—not this situation at any rate. Nothing was really off the table when talking about a means to an end, but any action had to be proportionate to the scenario being faced. A diary that almost certainly contained no information that could be directly linked to him personally, therefore posing him no real threat, did not warrant that level of response. As a result he had remained in the situation longer than necessary. And the longer he remained in the situation the more likelihood there was that something would happen that could result in him doing serious time. He had a young woman held captive in a warehouse across town for Christ's sake, and if that didn't land him in prison he would be very lucky indeed.

He pulled his nondescript VW Golf into a spare parking space, climbed out leaving the keys in the ignition and walked to the stairwell. Climbing the final flight of stairs to the season ticket holder's area his mood was lightened by the analysis of his recent actions. Understanding why you did things before doing them was preferable, but if that wasn't possible you absolutely had to conduct the analysis after the fact to ensure you didn't make the same mistakes again.

He had been motivated by greed, pure and simple. He had seen easy money with what he thought was no risk and had let that direct his actions. His usually thorough approach to risk analysis had been superficial and now things were considerably more dangerous for him. Ok, at first there had been limited risk, but as the scenario played out he had failed to reassess his exposure, and as a result things had escalated quickly. Not anymore though.

He pulled a set of car keys out of his pocket and pointed them towards the blue Audi R8. The indicators flashed once and the alarm chirped its welcome. Climbing behind the wheel Hank smiled to himself. He always felt better once a decision had been made and this one was a no brainer. He was leaving. Leaving the SSoH to solve their own problems, leaving his clients to settle their own scores and leaving Razor to manage his own escape. Once he had put sufficient distance between himself and the warehouse he would call Razor and let him know the situation was blown and that he should let the girl go and make a run for it. All things being equal, in about five hours he should be putting his feet up on the decking looking out over the Helford river in Cornwall, enjoying a very cold and well deserved beer. He owed himself a holiday at any rate and with things developing the way they were, now was a better time than ever.

Technically he was supposed to be at the drop off later that night with the SSoH but quite frankly, bollocks to that. Obviously he wouldn't be able to collect the balance of his payment, but what good was money when you were in a prison cell?

As London receded in his rear-view mirror and the M4 skittered away beneath the powerful Audi's wide tyres, Hank was happy. Action, inaction, decision, indecision. Certainty was an unrealistic goal. Things changed all the time and it was too easy to take credit for a decision which is made to look good after the fact. Like winning a poker hand on the river card—you still take the spoils but only a fool takes the credit. Equally, you can make all the right decisions based on the available information, and then something unforeseeable changes making your decision look poor. You shouldn't beat yourself up over that either. The one thing you *had* to do was make a decision. That might be a decision to do nothing, but a decision had to be made.

As Hank approached Reading he felt relaxed. Not only had he drawn a line under the whole diary debacle but he never had to speak or deal with that psychopath Jeff again. He thought back across the years and the correlation between the shipments he sourced for them and the name of their next beer. He hadn't ever concerned himself with what they actually did with the shipments; a few moments considering the options didn't leave you with many.

They did make good beer though. He could still remember the first 'special' he had tasted following that initial meeting with Jeff's colleagues. It had been just Jeff and Hank in the old man's study once everyone else had left. Jeff had offered him a drink to seal their new working partnership and Hank had happily accepted a Cat's Curiosity. He still couldn't quite believe how good it had been. The two of them had ended up chatting for hours about all sorts of things. It certainly hadn't been Hank's intention to stay there that long, and it was unusual for him to tell anyone anything about himself.

As Reading passed by, a small knot of uncertainty developed in the pit of Hank's stomach. He had stayed there a lot longer than he had intended and he had spoken considerably more than he would have normally but what had they spoken about? He wasn't sure. All he could really remember was how good the beer was.

The cold knot was growing as Hank searched his memory for the detail of their conversation. He vaguely remembered something about retirement plans and that Jeff never saw himself retiring. Hank's previously happy mood was evaporating quickly as he desperately tried to remember whether or not he had mentioned Cornwall and the Helford River property. The conversation had seemed innocuous at the time, but if he had told Jeff about his little retreat then that changed everything. It was one thing to walk away from a cash cow because it was too dangerous; it was something else entirely to walk away from his carefully planned retirement.

The sound of a lorry's air horn behind him dragged him from his thoughts to see he had let his speed drop to 50 mph. He buried his right foot and the powerful V10 pulled away from the lorry with ease. Hank pulled into the outside lane and continued accelerating. He couldn't be certain whether he had mentioned Cornwall or not, but the very fact that he couldn't be certain effectively made his decision for him.

His speed topped 125 mph as he saw the first indicator board for junction 13. Quickly checking his mirrors he pulled across the three lanes of traffic and flashed onto the exit slip. Plunging towards the roundabout beneath the M4 carriageway he briefly looked to his right and gambled. Piling on to the roundabout at 90 mph he narrowly missed the rear end of a Vauxhall Corsa and elicited numerous horn blasts as he cut his way across the flowing traffic, circling the roundabout and accelerating heavily up the return slip road to bring him back onto the M4 heading back towards London.

Surprisingly he was still calm as he built his speed in the outside lane, flashing his lights at those who dared to inhibit his progress, which meant anyone doing less than 130 mph. He thought quickly about the options open to him as a car pulled into his lane without looking. Hank swerved left across all three lanes and made for the hard shoulder, again barely missing the car inside his own. Blasting up the inside of the slower cars he pulled back out and after only a few seconds was back in the outside lane.

The diary was inconsequential. He had dismissed it earlier as unable to do him any real damage and the uncertainty around what he might or might not have told Jeff didn't change that. Jeff hadn't written the diary and Hank had the feeling that anything he may have told the old man would have remained private. The difficulty was the delivery of the shipment that evening. Now the police had the diary it was unfeasible to think they wouldn't arrange a sting for the delivery site and while Hank thought Jeff kept his own counsel while free to enjoy his freedom, he had no doubt that he would give up anyone he could think of in the event his liberty was threatened.

"Call Razor," Hank stated as the traffic got heavier. He dropped his speed to 100mph and flashed his lights again at the car in front. The dial tone gave way to the ringing tone and after five rings this gave way to silence.

"Razor, it's Hank," he received a grunt in reply. "There's been a change of plan. The diary is no longer a focus for us." Hank sped past the junction for the M25. "I'll be back in an hour and a half and will fill you in, but in short, I think we're going to have to kill the old man."

Hank thought he could detect a smile in Razor's grunt as he rang off and continued his way into Central London.

Chapter 42

"What do you make of that?" Kostatis asked, watching as a uniformed officer escorted Dominic and Beth to get a drink. Grieg shrugged slightly.

They had transported the hysterical Beth and shocked Dominic back to the station and once they had calmed them down, the whole story had tumbled out.

"What, the kidnapped flatmate, the mysterious Hank, or the fact the most famous brewers in the world appear to be grinding up pets to give body to their ales?" Grieg asked, slowly drumming his fingers on the cover of the diary they had taken from Dominic.

Kostatis watched their two witnesses being shown into an interview room then turned back to Grieg and extended his arm indicating for the diary to be passed across. Grieg handed the book over and Kostatis leant back in his chair.

"We did say they were hiding something," he replied, flicking through the diary. "How much of it do you believe?"

Again Grieg shrugged, too experienced to answer a question like that without further clarification. "Are you asking what I believe, or what I think those two kids believe?"

"Both."

"Well, the kids certainly believe that Beth's flatmate has been kidnapped, and judging by the picture on her phone I am inclined to agree with her. If we take that as a given we then need to understand how things got to that point." He crossed his legs and looked at Kostatis. "According to Dominic, the girl's been kidnapped in order to get hold of the diary. A diary incidentally, that our boy was unknowingly given by one Wilbur Forthright, whose suspicious death we are currently investigating. Forthright was a founder member of Hopmen Breweries, along with five other men, one of whom owns a black Range Rover similar to one reported as being present at the scene of the suspicious fire which killed him. The diary, written by Forthright, records the actions of a group of men who somehow discovered that adding animals to beer makes it taste incredible. He gets a dose of guilty conscience and ends up dead." He paused, as if reviewing whether he was actually going to say what he thought he was going to say. After a few moments he carried on. "I think, on the balance of probabilities, it isn't something we can dismiss."

Kostatis flicked to the page Dominic had shown them just before they had halted the interview, and tapped the page. "And what about this latest beer? You really believe they are smuggling midgets?" It was probably the oddest question he had ever asked.

All coppers got to the point in their careers where they thought they had seen it all, and Kostatis was no exception. Human trafficking wasn't as rare as it should be and was always incredibly sinister, but midgets from China smuggled with the intention of adding them to beer was even darker still.

Once again Grieg paused, framing his thoughts. "If you'd asked me yesterday whether it would have been one of the things I would need to look out for today, then no. But, if you're asking me today whether I think we can ignore it as a credible threat, then again, no, I don't think we can."

Kosatatis sighed deeply. What a world. There was something almost understandable about human trafficking normally. Abhorrent though it was, slaves and sex had been a constant throughout human history. A blight on human history absolutely, but certainly more understandable than what they were currently being presented with.

The two policemen sat in silence for a while, each with their thoughts: Kostatis deciding what they reported up the line to his superiors, Grieg grateful for his lack of progression past his current rank. As things stood he could offer advice if he was asked, which was something his current boss did frequently, but he didn't have to make the kind of potentially career-limiting decision Kostatis was faced with. The silence stretched away.

"Why Chinese midgets?" Grieg eventually broke the silence with a question that clearly illustrated the differences in the pressures of their respective ranks.

"What?" Kostatis asked, irritation evident in his voice.

"I'm just thinking, China is a very long way away, and moving a container full of midgets from there to here is thousands and thousands of miles. I'm sure that if you're determined to get your hands on some midgets there has to be somewhere a little closer to home."

"I have to say, with kidnappers, human traffickers and murderers roaming the countryside, I'm less concerned about the reasoning behind the particular nationality of the midgets in question, and more concerned with how we ensure the kidnapped girl is rescued and the midgets, if they exist and wherever they hail from, are prevented from becoming someone's morning after flatulence. If we can catch all the sickos behind this at the same time, even better." Kostatis pushed himself up from the desk and headed for the door. "Do me a favour and keep an eye on the kids will you? I have to speak to the Chief Inspector."

Grieg nodded and stood. "What are you going to tell him?"

Kostatis paused at the door. "Whatever it takes to get the support we need. Not sure we have an expert in this particular scenario, but we need CO19 for definite and a chunk of overtime to dish out." The two men left Kostatis' office and headed in different directions. Just as Kostatis was about to head through the door and climb the stairs to the Chief Inspector's office, Grieg called across the open-plan office.

"Don't forget to order an interpreter as well."

Kostatis managed a weak smile and pushed through the door.

Chapter 43

The grandfather clock ticked towards 10pm. Shadows stretched across the library, swaying as the light breeze outside played with the trees. As the minute hand reached vertical, the chimes from the clock commenced their hourly routine, followed by ten resonant bongs.

Finally drawn from his contemplations, Jeff only heard the final bong and momentarily panicked at the thought he had missed the delivery time. Double checking the clock he calmed himself; with an hour before he had to leave there was plenty of time.

He pushed himself stiffly from the wingback and grimaced slightly at the pain from his joints. I'm not getting any younger, he thought.

He had soon tired of his discussion with Terry. The man had no capacity to understand what Jeff had achieved and would continue achieving. He had given his old friend a final kick to the face and left the unconscious man slumped on the floor. He would check on him once the delivery had been completed, and the ingredients had been transferred to the holding facility next door to the library.

Moving towards the bookcase opposite the one which lead to his underground brewery, Jeff ran his fingers along the spines of his collection of first edition James Bond novels. Jeff wasn't a particular fan of James Bond but he did feel an affinity with some of the villains, especially those with lairs.

Sliding his finger over the top of 'Live And Let Die', he gently pulled. Just as with 'The London and Country Brewer', the base of the book remained in place while the top of the spine came towards him, accompanied by a faint click. This time the bookcase swung out revealing a short passage behind. Jeff walked through the doorway, and as he entered the passage, lights automatically flicked on illuminating the three metres to another door. Pushing through this door Jeff came into the most recently refurbished part of his house.

Beyond the second door was a beautifully appointed reception room. Comfortable chairs and sofas were dotted around the space and along the left wall was a long table, groaning under the weight of a vast spread of food and drink. Jeff smiled to himself. It was very important to him that his guests felt comfortable and safe when they arrived. They would clearly be hungry and dehydrated from their long journey, even though he had specified sufficient food and water should be made available to them on their voyage. He had a feeling that traffickers cared little for their cargo but he had included a bonus should every part of the cargo arrive alive.

The other certainty was that they would all be filthy—shipping containers were hardly renowned for their facilities after all. Through another door were ten shower cubicles, replete with Molton Brown toiletries. These were no ordinary showers though. For one thing they were soundproof. For another, they had unusual floors to each of the stalls.

Jeff reached into the first stall and pushed the button which started the flow of water from the rainforest shower head. The steaming water cascaded down and swirled around the plughole in the right hand corner furthest from him. An almost imperceptible seam ran the width of the shower tray splitting the unit in half. Jeff pressed the button once again and the water stopped. A second later there was a clunk and the shower tray split at the seam, the two halves falling away, hinged at their outside edge. There were no sharks below, but he could guarantee sharp teeth. Quickly checking the rest of the cubicles a dull glint flashed in Jeff's eye as a smile touched his lips. A neat solution to washing your ingredients before starting the process he thought.

Heading back through the reception room and into the library Jeff poured himself a whiskey—a single finger—as he needed to be sharp for the evening's activities, and ran a mental checklist of the preparations he had been putting in place over the last five years. He had remodelled areas of the house to allow for the somewhat bulkier nature of the ingredients for this batch. He had also solved the problem of having to deal with very irate little people following their transportation halfway around the world by getting them to pay for the privilege. He smirked at the thought. By offering asylum and accommodation while they set up their new lives to each of those coming, all at a very reasonable fee, he was confident each would accept his hospitality happily. Confident in his own abilities as he was, he was conscious of the fact he was a seventy-year-old, one-eyed pensioner and didn't much fancy his chances against a container-full of abducted and angry midgets. This way they did most of the work for him. His supplier had always come through for him in the past, and on this he had no reason to doubt Hank. The only real flies in the ointment then were both caused by Wilbur.

Pushing the bookcase back into place, a rumble in his stomach as the whiskey landed reminded Jeff that he couldn't remember when he had last eaten. Considering the speed with which things would progress later it was important to maintain good blood sugar levels and he headed through the grand house to his kitchen. In the fridge was a bowl of potato salad and a nice minute steak. Putting a heavy griddle pan on the heat he waited for it to reach the right temperature.

Wilbur: maybe killing him had been hasty. After all, he could do without the interest of the police at such a critical juncture. A few days and any obvious evidence of what was about to transpire would be long gone but these next forty-eight hours would be critical. If he hadn't written that bloody diary then none of this would be happening, he thought.

He held his hand above the bars on the griddle pan and felt the searing heat radiating out. Having seasoned and oiled his steak he placed it in the pan and listened to the sizzling as the bars etched their presence onto the meat.

His other concern was the time it was taking Hank to recover the diary from some half-wit of a delivery boy. If Jeff had taken it upon himself to get the book back he was certain he would have done so already. But then, he thought, he had more to lose than Hank did. As things stood, Jeff had absolutely no idea whether Hank was even mentioned in the diary. He however most certainly would be. Even if their procurer of ingredients was mentioned, there was no way Hank was actually his name, that much was obvious. And the distance he had kept from Jeff since that initial meeting made it clear he had wanted to protect himself with as much secrecy as possible.

Jeff lifted the perfectly cooked steak from the pan and left it on a board to rest while he compiled the rest of his plate. He pulled some fresh salad leaves from the fridge and dressed them lightly with some olive oil, lemon and salt and pepper and added them to the plate next to the potato salad. Finally he laid the steak on the plate and poured the resting juices over the meat.

He sat at his kitchen table with his whiskey and steak dinner and silently said grace, asking for God to watch over his evening's deeds. The support of his chosen deity assured, he tucked into his dinner and considered Hank.

He wondered how long professional pride in a seemingly simple endeavour would outweigh Hank's survival instinct. Once their criminal-for-hire had failed to retrieve the diary at the second time of asking, Jeff had genuinely wondered whether they would hear from him again, especially once the police had become involved. Money though was a powerful motivator, and Hank had remained in contact. Now though Jeff wondered if he hadn't had enough and decided to retreat to a safe distance while things played out.

Of course Cornwall could hardly be considered a safe distance when the man you were trying to avoid knew all about your bolthole on the Helford River. Jeff smiled, both at the taste of the steak and the power of his beers. All those years ago he had instantly recognised the slip Hank had made as he quaffed the sensational Cat's Curiosity. He had made no indication that he even recognised what he had said, but Jeff had filed the information away for a rainy day. He had even travelled to Cornwall and the Helford River to find the exact location. It had taken a while, the mere fact that the owner was away a lot of the time was hardly unusual in a county where city-based second-home owners had driven property prices skyward. There were, however, only a handful of properties with the view Hank had described, and eventually a helpful local had directed him to the right property. He had paid the local to keep an eye on the comings and goings at the house and when a text picture came through of the man Jeff knew as Hank getting out of a blue Audi, he knew he had his man.

The question was, would Hank remember that his safehouse had been blown? If not then it was perfectly probable that he was heading down there at this very moment, or might even have already arrived. The silence since what Jeff assumed to be another failed attempt at retrieving the diary that afternoon seemed to point towards the possibility. Whether

Hank made an appearance that evening or not didn't make any material difference now though.

Jeff got to his feet and carried his plate to the sink and stared into the dark beyond the window. With the light behind him he could clearly see himself reflected and smiled. If he didn't turn up though, Jeff would make him pay.

As he turned and left the kitchen he felt a buzzing in his pocket and pulled out the phone.

We're on, was all it said.

Jeff smiled again, he liked being in control.

Chapter 44

Hank had watched his flat for half an hour before deciding it was safe to go in. As far as he could tell there was no permanent police presence waiting for him and the unwelcome visit from earlier was probably linked to some unrelated inquiry in the area. Even if they had visited as a result of something he was involved with he knew they didn't have sufficient budget to leave a couple of uniforms waiting for him indefinitely.

Once inside he had taken the time to do some deep breathing exercises to calm the anger and stress which had been building. Having done so he had quickly packed the essential items he had identified during the drive back, changed his clothes and erased his hard drives. Then, he took a final circuit of the flat he would never return to, set the alarm and left. It wasn't a clean sweep of the property, that would have taken much longer and a well-paid cleaning crew but the presence of his DNA in the flat was of less importance if he managed to conclude his relationship with the SSoH that night as planned.

Arriving back at the warehouse he called Razor. As usual there was no audible response as the call had been answered.

"It's me. I'm coming in."

Hank hung up and pushed open the door. Inside things were very much as he had left them. Naomi was still bound and gagged on the sofa, and Razor was still pacing around just inside the circle of light, his balaclava providing an attempt at anonymity that his eyes and teeth rendered pointless.

As he crossed the warehouse floor, he signalled for Razor to follow him into the office. Razor made one exaggerated move towards the cowering figure of their hostage before turning back and heading towards Hank, a broad shark-like smile glinting out of the darkness.

"How's she been?" Hank asked, as he settled down in the chair behind the desk, and Razor pulled the mask from his face as he sat next to the door.

He shrugged as if it was a completely alien concept to inquire how the hostage was. Hank stared at Razor and realised there were times when he truly hated the man opposite him. However, for his plan later that night to work he would need him.

"We have a slight problem regarding that bloody diary," Hank said, uncertain whether Razor even remembered that all of this had been driven by the need to get it back. The wild but vacant look coming back at him told its own story. Hank then gave Razor a heavily edited version as to what had happened since he had left him several hours previously. The failure to retrieve the diary he put down to Dominic and Beth not turning up, rather than the interference from the police; he needed that to be a surprise later that evening. Other than a few growls and grumbles Razor listened.

"So," Hank concluded, "there are a couple of things we need to do. Firstly we need to get rid of her somehow." Both men looked at the broken form of their captive. Razor smiled menacingly. "Not like that. All I mean is we dump her somewhere as far east as we can, which still allows us to get to the rendezvous on time. That way, she's the wrong side of London even if she does get help. Regardless, she doesn't know where we're going so I feel pretty safe in letting her go. She hasn't seen either of our faces so won't be able to give a description to the police." Hank paused to see whether Razor had recognised his particular look might render a full description unnecessary, but his accomplice merely nodded and growled again.

"OK. Then we need to deal with these brewery pricks. I got a note from them earlier saying that because we haven't managed to get the diary back they're going to withhold the balance payment for the delivery tonight." Hank had no compunction when it came to lying to his partner. What he needed was for Razor to be angry and focussed on Jeff. The best way to do that was to play on the two things he cared about most: violence and money. Threatening him with violence wasn't a great idea since Hank was closest to Razor at that moment, and restraint was not one of his colleague's strong points, so money it was.

Razor practically bristled at the mention the old bastards were trying to stiff them on their payment, pushing himself up from his chair and baring his teeth.

"It's ok," Hank said, holding his hands in a placating gesture. "We're going to sort them out, ok? But we need to keep control of ourselves. The point of delivery is always the most dangerous time for us and before we do anything to these old fuckers we need to get paid."

Razor nodded and sat back down, his breathing gradually coming under control.

"Good. I need you to put a bag on her head then I need you to go and get the van." Hank stood and patted Razor on the shoulder and watched as he crossed to Naomi and forced a black bag over her head.

"Hey," Hank called across the warehouse as Razor was about to push the door open. "You need to take your balaclava off though. You might look a little bloody conspicuous otherwise."

Razor growled, pulled the balaclava from his head and left the warehouse.

Hank sank back in the chair and rubbed his face. The last few days had been insane now that he considered the risks he had run for the limited benefit he could gain. He felt he had been manipulated both by an old man and his own greed. As a result the next few hours would decide whether he could enjoy his retirement, or spend the next couple of decades in a cell.

He opened his bag and pulled out a pistol with a fat sound suppressor attached to the barrel. He pulled the slide back and chambered a round. One way or the other this was going to end tonight.

Chapter 45

The hallway echoed as the door slammed. Beth knew she had imagined it as it had never done so before, but the stress and tension she had been under over the last couple of days was playing tricks on her. Dominic followed her into the kitchen, a forlorn look on his face.

The police had finally finished interviewing them and at Dominic's insistence had begrudgingly agreed that they could go whenever they wanted. They had insisted on appointing a Police Liaison Officer, but Beth and Dominic had left before one could be contacted. They assumed that one would arrive later, but were indifferent to the idea.

Beth watched as Dominic moved around her kitchen like an automaton, blindly opening cupboards until he found mugs and then repeating the process to find teabags, his mind seemingly only able to register one thing at a time and missing them in the original sweep for mugs. He filled the kettle and flicked the switch to boil it. He added the water to the mugs and slowly swirled the water around, allowing the tea to infuse. He squeezed the bags against the side of the mugs and made to throw the teabags in the bin. Instead, pausing briefly to assess the distance, he flicked the spent tea bags across the kitchen and into the sink, one after the other. Beth was too exhausted to comment on the trail of tea drops between Dominic and the sink. He placed one of the mugs in front of Beth and sat opposite her.

They both took tentative sips.

"Now what?" Beth asked as she put her mug down. The drive and composure which had been fuelling her actions had deserted her at the point the police had turned up and Hank had said her friend would pay for their betrayal.

Dominic stared at her for a moment, his face unreassuringly blank. He was aware that when this was all over, however it ended, an objective performance report would not mark him kindly. He had shut down at the point when Beth needed someone to rely on, to offer a supportive arm and shoulder the burden, to offer productive input and help her through the horrors unfurling in front of them all. He had managed to be struck dumb, rendered impotent of ideas by the scale and magnitude of the events. His well practiced response of avoiding responsibility in all aspects of his life had failed to prepare him for the moment when he had to man up and be more than just a nice guy.

In the fleeting moments when his brain hadn't been free-wheeling, he had marvelled at how calm and resolute Beth had been. Her ability to compartmentalise the issues they were facing, allowing her to make decisions and take action had amazed him. While he panicked, she had been determined and focussed. The cock-up on the high street had robbed her of that focus and she needed someone to help her regain it.

"Well, sitting around here drinking tea doesn't seem like much of an option does it?" he said. Beth just stared at him, and he knew from his own shutdown earlier, all she would be thinking about was what might be happening to her friend as they sat there, drowning themselves with Yorkshire Gold. She needed another focus.

"I don't know whether you noticed earlier, but I'm not necessarily the person you want leading the charge on this type of thing. What we really need is that capable and decisive woman who was running things earlier. I don't know whether you saw her, but she was incredible and her input would be greatly appreciated about now." Dominic could see the tears beginning to form in Beth's eyes: the well of resolve was dry.

"But, I understand she might be dealing with some stuff at the moment," he paused and took a deep breath as a couple of tears ran down Beth's cheeks. "Which is absolutely fine. We're just going to have to make do without her for the time being." Dominic stood up and started pacing the kitchen.

"All we need to do is pretend that she was here and then act accordingly. First up, she would be worried about Naomi." At the sound of her friend's name, more tears spilled their way down Beth's face, threatening to overwhelm her. Dominic hurried to continue. "But she'd be practical and understand that we don't know where she is and can't know what's happening. The police are involved now and we have to trust that they *will* find her and she *will* be okay." He came around the table and gently took Beth's face in his hands, staring deep into her eyes, putting as much conviction into his words and his eyes as he could manage, trying to refill the well of resolve Beth had been drawing from all day, even if he doubted the reality. He noticed a slight change in Beth's eyes. Desperation was no longer all he could see.

"Once we rule out things we can't affect, what are we left with?" The question was as much to himself as it was to distract Beth. After a few moments it struck him. "We're left with The Premiums."

The last they had seen or heard of his colleagues was as they left Dominic's house and told them they had to come up with some way of foiling the SSoH's plan to acquire the Chinese dwarves for their latest beer. Several hours had passed since then and Dominic was well aware of the absolute carnage which could ensue in that sort of timeframe. He rifled through his pockets until he found his mobile. Flicking to the recent call list he scrolled to Gareth, touched the screen and waited. The line connected and rang. What if Hank had gone after The Premiums, Dominic thought? It rang again. What if The Premiums had gone after the SSoH? Another ring. What if they had gone to the police and were currently under psychological evaluation? The phone kept ringing.

"Answer the phone Gareth you idiot!" Dominic screamed into the handset.

"Alright? Dom, where the fuck 'ave you been? 'ow did it go? Did you meet Hank? Are you both OK? How's Beth? Guys, it's Dom," the Cornish baritone rumbled across the airways and Dominic could hear the rest of The Premiums firing questions at Gareth at the other end of the line, as well as an argument of some kind.

"Beth and I are both fine." Dominic looked at Beth and was pleased to see that the colour was returning to her cheeks. "But the diary drop was a complete cock-up. Kostatis and Grieg bloody well turned up and scared Hank off."

"Shittin' 'ell. So what are they gonna do?"

"No idea. They told us to leave it in their hands now and not to do anything stupid, which naturally made me think of you guys. How have things with you been?"

"Oh not too bad mate, Otter came up with a plan. An', well it's the best we've got, so we're puttin' the final touches to it now." The argument in the background seemed to be getting more heated. "Listen mate,

I 'a'nt really got time to explain, but get yer arse over 'ere and I'll fill you in." He quickly gave Dominic the address and hung up.

Dominic jotted it down and stared at his phone then looked at Beth, whose expression had gone from one of desperation to one of cautious interest.

"They have a plan apparently," Dominic said, looking up from his phone. "Otter came up with it. It's not much but it's all they've got, and they're here." He showed her the address.

"What, really?" Beth was incredulous. "They're at the pub? At a time like this those idiots are at the pub? Are you serious?" She pushed her chair back and stood up. "Right, let's go." She turned and headed back through her flat to the front door. Dominic could hear her muttering as she went. "We leave them alone for a few hours and all they do is head to the pub. I'll bloody kill them."

Despite himself, Dominic smiled as he followed her out of the flat. The well was never dry for long.

Chapter 46

Dominic prised his fingers from the dashboard of the Renault as Beth screeched to a halt in the car park of The Green Dragon. Without waiting for Dominic, she leapt out of the car and slammed the door. Dominic stumbled after her and burst into the gloom of the pub just in time to see the smile on Gareth's face freeze as he was confronted by Beth's glacial stare.

"What the fuck are you doing here? Have you any idea what the fuck is going on? My friend's life is in danger and you're all here getting pissed."

She had crossed the pub, her right arm raised ready to rain blows down on Gareth's head. Getting over his initial shock, the big Cornishman stood up quickly, his chair teetering behind him and caught Beth's wrist just as Dominic got to the table.

"Woah, wait a minute, we ain't getting drunk," Gareth said, looking from Beth to Dominic, pleading for help.

"Ok, let's all calm down," Dominic said, knowing the danger this kind of inflammatory comment might have, but keen to ascertain exactly what was going on, and whether it differed from what appeared to be going on.

Beth's eyes flashed at him, but she lowered her arm, and in a show of considered restraint pulled a chair out and very deliberately sat down. Laying her forearms on the table and clasping her fingers together, more to prevent her from punching someone than anything else, she looked at Gareth and the rest of The Premiums. She took a deep breath, and in a voice resonating with the increasing pressure her forced calmness was building asked, "Well?"

Dominic glanced at Beth, glad that having been with her he could in no way be held responsible for anything The Premiums had come up with. That said he was very aware that if they had wasted the intervening hours his cock would undoubtedly be on the block, by association if nothing else.

Gareth looked at Gravy, The Fuzz, Otter and Weasel and noted they all had the good grace to look terrified.

"Right, well after you left we all sat tryin' to think o' what to do," Gareth said.

"And you thought the best environment to do so was in a pub with a few pints, is that right?" Beth interrupted, indicating the empty pint glasses littering the table. Gareth was about to object when they were interrupted.

"Another round, guys," Zoe slid the tray of drinks onto the table and turned to Dominic and Beth. "You must be Beth. I'm Zoe, I'm friends with Casper, well you'd know him as Weasel for some reason." She smiled at Beth, who after a moment's hesitation, smiled back. "And this is my friend and fellow cast member, Gary." Zoe signalled to Gary, who due to sitting next to the vast bulk that was Otter had gone unnoticed. Gary raised a hand then took the proffered beer.

"It's a pleasure to meet you both. And please forgive me but there's a lot going on that you don't understand and my previous question still stands." She turned to Gareth. "You still need to tell me what the fuck is going on."

"Well actually we do know what's going on. That's why we're all here," Zoe said, pulling up a chair and sliding a pint across the table to Dominic, who reflexively reached for it before noticing Beth's look and sensibly declined the offer.

"Just le' me explain, alright?" Gareth said his hands raised in the universal sign of placation or surrender.

Over the next ten minutes Gareth, The Premiums and two of the cast of Snow White brought Beth and Dominic up to speed on their thinking, if you could call it that, over the last few hours. This had initially focussed around the need for a unit of heavily armed individuals to swoop in and secure the area and arrest the SSoH. Discounting this due to them having absolutely no access to such a unit, they had floundered for a long time before Otter, surprising everyone by speaking without direct instruction to do so, had mentioned the friends they had made a few nights previous and the assistance they may be able to offer.

Beth had raised an obvious question

"I certainly don't mean any disrespect by this," she said warily, conscious statements like that were almost always followed by some level of disrespect. "But why specifically would Zoe and Gary be of any particular assistance in this situation."

Weasel looked around the group to see if anyone else was going to point out the obvious. With no takers he pitched in.

"Er, because the next beer these old fucks are planning is called *Mao's Marauding Midgets*." He rolled his eyes and indicated to Zoe and Gary, as if he couldn't believe she had missed the point. Beth glared at him.

Beth looked from one Premium to the next and then to Zoe and Gary. All of them were looking back at her, their faces expressionless.

"Um, I don't mean to speak on behalf of anybody, Weasel, but I think the accepted term is dwarves," she said, deeply uncomfortable.

"What?" Weasel asked.

"They aren't midgets, they're dwarves."

"I know they're dwarves," he said, turning to Zoe and shaking his head as if the need to clarify was ridiculous. After a further uncomfortable pause, Beth spoke tentatively.

"OK, but I still don't really understand…" For a few seconds she looked like she was trying to find a way to finish that sentence and then decided it was fine as it was.

"Er, you don't think a group of dwarves who as far as we know have been transported from China, wouldn't feel a bit more comfortable on arrival being met by a couple of people like them?" Weasel asked.

Beth thought about it, her indignation and anger beginning to lower. It was a fair point, as long as you took out of the equation the criminals and the intent of the septuagenarian brewers, not to mention the language barriers.

"Ok," she conceded, "but height isn't the only consideration, surely?"

"I think I understand your point. We may be dwarves, but we aren't Chinese," Zoe said

"Exactly, thank you," Beth said, grasping the lifeline Zoe had provided. "The difference in language and culture is of significantly greater importance than a similarity in height. Now, unless you speak Mandarin, bearing in mind we don't know which part of China these people have been abducted from, then I still don't really understand 'the plan'," her tone sarcastic as she mimed the airquotes.

"What makes you think they have been abducted?" Zoe asked.

Beth paused. It was a good question. Her mind had jumped to abduction because no one would volunteer to be liquidised and added to beer, but now she thought about it, of course the SSoH would lie about their ultimate aim.

"Our first thought was abduction as well, but if what the guys have told us is true, then there are five men in their eighties who need to control an unknown number of people from the point they're delivered to the point they are murdered," Gary explained. "If that group of people is under duress then we don't see how five old men, one of whom is in a wheelchair, would have any chance of controlling them." Gary took a sip of his beer.

The Premiums were nodding their heads with every point being made, aware that in the hierarchy of credibility within the room, theirs ranked significantly below that of Zoe and Gary despite Beth having never met them before, and an explanation from either of them was likely to be far more convincing. Placing his pint glass down, Gary continued.

"But, if you have a group of people who have not been forced into the container, but have climbed in of their own free will, and are subsequently expecting assistance when they arrive in the UK, then there's no real problem to manage and five old geysers would be able to deal with the situation easily."

Shit, thought Beth. Her mind had understandably been so preoccupied with Naomi over the last few hours she hadn't given the implications of the revelation of the next beer much thought.

"We may not speak the same language, and we're clearly from different cultures, but you can't ignore the fact that we, like them, are dwarves," Zoe said. "We understand the persecution they'll have suffered. Understand the prejudice they face every day. If I was being transported halfway across the world to a new country, however much I wanted to go there, I for one would be happier if I was met by someone who looked a bit like me. By having two dwarves there we may be able to sow a little confusion and prevent these people from walking open armed to their would-be murderers."

"So we have to assume we're dealing with compliant people, and that Zoe and Gary may be able to offer some assistance. That makes sense," Dominic clarified, looking at Beth who nodded in agreement and smiled at Zoe and Gary, reserving a momentary scowl for Gareth. "But we do still need to deal with the SSoH."

"Not only them," Gareth said. "We also need to take into account Hank an' this Razor nutter. They're the real issue."

"And, have you managed to come up with anything while draining your beers?" Beth asked, watching as Gravy self-consciously swallowed the last of his beer and placed the glass down on the table and gently pushed it away.

"Well, not really. I'll admit we're relyin' quite heavily on the police takin' your story seriously and sendin' a busload o' armed coppers wi' itchy trigger fingers."

Beth opened her mouth, the look in her eyes leaving none of them in doubt as to the vitriol which was to follow. Gareth cut her off before she got into her flow, an edge of anger to his voice.

"Now wait a minute, before you go 'urlin' insults and accusin' us o' not takin' this 'ole thing serious." Gareth had his hand almost in Beth's face and it was testament to the rarity of the Cornishman's annoyance that she didn't immediately snap it off and shove it down his throat.

"We've read the diary," he continued, "an' that diary tells us that Hank and Razor are seriously dangerous professional criminals, who di'n't think twice before kidnappin' your flatmate to get leverage over Dom and the diary. And by all accounts this Razor guy is a proper nutter. In no version of this universe are six removal men with a track record of breakin' shit, in any way a match for these guys." He paused to let the truth of what he said sink in. "Nothin' would give me greater pleasure than to think that all the Arnie films I've ever watched 'ave somehow instilled a level of expertise in me wi' firearms and 'and to 'and combat that means I can take Razor. That some'ow, through osmosis, I know 'ow to field strip a weapon or render someone unconscious by tweakin' a pressure point. I would love to believe that, but I live in the real world, not some fantasy land where all this weird shit 'appens. The reality of it is the six of us are fuckups." He indicated to the rest of The Premiums.

A heavy silence descended on the table as each of The Premiums was forced to confront the truth of Gareth's outburst. Dominic stared at the pint in front of him and was reminded of the wave of panic which had overtaken him the night he found the diary. The realisation that he was exactly as Gareth had described, a fuck-up. There was no judgement in what his friend had said, just shame. Dominic glanced at his colleagues. All of them he realised, comfortably sat within the stereotypes that had been prescribed for them: Gravy, the out of touch rich kid with a trust fund; The Fuzz, the poor kid from a disadvantaged upbringing; Weasel, pigeon-holed for how he looked and comported himself; Otter, brawn instead of brains just because he was quiet; Gareth, the fat jolly beer swilling Cornishman; and himself, the middle class under-achiever, content to drift through life.

He remembered back to his school and university days, where he would continually be reminded that he had 'such potential' if he would only 'apply himself'. But with the assumption of potential came expectation, and the problem with expectation was you could only ever really be disappointed. If you achieved great things, well, that was just the realisation of all that potential people could congratulate themselves on having recognised. To fall short of that potential though, to fail in achieving your early promise, that was only ever the fault of one person. If he didn't exert himself he would never have to know what his limits were, never have to confront whether he was actually as good as his perceived potential and therefore never have to find out if he came up short. To combat it, Dominic had fashioned himself a protective coat of feigned indifference. A projected disposition of being too cool to care, that to be seen to try was to be seen to require other people's praise to feel good about yourself, which was the epitome of being needy. He had worn his comfort blanket for as long as he could remember, but here, in the Green Dragon surrounded by his friends and colleagues, two dwarves and the woman he was beginning to fall in love with, it provided him no comfort at all. He cleared his throat.

"I guess we can either get busy living or get busy dying." He looked around the group nodding as he caught each of their eyes.

"I'n't that a quote from Shawshank Redemption?" asked Gravy after a slight pause, his look of confusion mirrored on everyone else's faces.

"Yeah, yeah it is," Dominic replied, still nodding as if the reason for the quote was obvious.

"I ent quite sure what that means in this particular situation though," Gareth said.

Dominic looked around the group, noticing the confusion for the first time, the confidence he had felt at what he thought would strike a resounding philosophical note dissipating quickly. "It's just highlighting that this is our Shawshank moment, you know that we have the opportunity to put up or shut up, to shit or get off the pot, draw a line in the sand, carpe diem, nil desperandum and all that jazz." Dominic had got to his feet and was tightly holding his pint. "It means we don't have to be the fuck-ups everyone expects us to be." He raised the glass in a toast.

"You shoulda just said that," Gareth said, also getting to his feet, a smile touching his lips for the first time that evening. One by one The Premiums, Beth, Zoe and Gary all stood and smiled at Dominic. "So wha's the plan boss?"

"I have no idea," he replied with a glint in his eyes and a zeal he had never felt before.

Gareth raised his own glass.

"You're no Maximus Decimus Meridius, but I'll follow you into the shadow o' the valley of death." Each of them raised their glass.

"We need a battle cry," Dominic said.

"I've got one," Weasel said. "Let's go fuck up some old people."

Chapter 47

Dark clouds had been gathering over the last hour as Jeff had made his way to the rendezvous, the threat and smell of rain heavy in the air. He had parked his Range Rover between the trees on the edge of the clearing they had agreed as the meeting point. He watched as across the clearing Martin reversed the minibus into a gap between the trees, ready to transport their guests to Jeff's mansion.

He allowed himself a smile as the minibus door opened and a nervous-looking Martin stepped out and waved feebly across the clearing. He could see Brian and Steve's pale and drawn faces through the minibus' windscreen. And then there were four, he thought, for the time being at least.

He checked his phone to see whether Hank had contacted him. He didn't expect to see a note, in two minds as to whether he had been betrayed, but confident the delivery would go ahead as intended. He would deal with Hank later. Right now he had to stay focussed, after all it wasn't every day you took receipt of a group of illegal immigrant dwarves looking for a better life in the West.

There was a piece of A4 paper on the passenger seat beside him covered in the distinctive lines, ticks, flicks and squiggles of the Mandarin language. Jeff had thought long and hard about the obvious barrier his lack of spoken Mandarin presented between himself and his guests. He had toyed momentarily with the idea of a translator, but that would have required exposing their operation to a stranger. In the end he had plumped for an online translation website and the risk of the translation bearing no resemblance to what he had intended to say.

The basic message was, "Welcome to England. I know you must be tired and hungry following your long journey. There is a little food and water on the bus if you would like to have some and we will transport you to your accommodation where there is a hot meal and a hot shower waiting for you. We will also have a translator there as well to explain things. For now, please relax."

Not too much detail for them to get hung up on but hopefully enough to get them to his house without any distractions or complications. He didn't envisage any issues; they had voluntarily come to the country after all, but you shouldn't take things for granted. He glanced down and saw the dull glint of the tranquiliser gun. He had decided on a large dose, sufficient to fell a horse, in the event any of them made a run for it. The dosage was probably a little high and could well result in their death but he wasn't too concerned about that either. It would just be bringing their fate forward a little. His thoughts were interrupted by the small speaker lying next to the gun.

Brian: "I don't like this. How did we ever let it get this far?"

Steve: "I don't know, but we're all going to burn in hell for this."

Martin: "Well there isn't a great deal we can do at the moment. You saw what he was like with Terry. If we say anything he'll kill us."

Jeff had fitted a small audio transmitter to the mini-bus before Martin and the other surviving members of SSoH had collected it earlier, wirelessly linked to the speaker on his passenger seat. Sitting in the comfort of his luxury 4X4 he could feel his loathing for the other men grow with every word they uttered. Whenever he thought of it he was staggered at their lack of gratitude, their inability to grasp the scope of his vision.

Brian: "Look at him over there, staring at us. It's like he knows we're talking about him."

Steve: "I know. He terrifies me now." *Silence*. "Do you think he killed Wilbur and Mabel?"

A long silence.

Martin: "Yes, and I think he would kill every one of us if he felt threatened enough."

Jeff watched Martin from across the clearing turn to his old friends so he couldn't see his face.

Martin: "We're all just as deep into this as he is, but we absolutely can't let him kill these people. I would prefer to spend the rest of my days in prison than let that happen."

Jeff stared at the back of Martin's head and imagined a bullet entering it. Traitors, he thought. All great men were eventually betrayed by the jealousy of their serfs. These nobodies, whose lives would have left as much trace on history as a zephyr would on a hurricane, had finally turned against him.

Brian: "Ok, but what do we do?"

Martin: "I think we're going to have to kill him."

Now there was a surprise. Jeff would have thought Steve would have been the one with enough balls to propose the ultimate solution. But when would they strike he wondered.

Steve: "I agree, but not here. I think we get the Chinese folk into the bus and back to his house and we do it there, before he has a chance to kill them. He has that big vase in the den. Once we have successfully transferred them from the bus to the house I'll suggest toasting our success. While he's pouring the drinks, whoever's closest does the deed. Agreed?"

Jeff watched as Martin and Brian nodded before the three of them shook hands. I've just come up with the name of my next beer, he thought, *Hopmen's Honour*.

Chapter 48

"That went better than it might have." Grieg eased the BMW out of the police station carpark and accelerated down the road, two unmarked Volvo V90s following him.

"Yeah well I've still been earmarked as an absolute crackpot," Kostatis replied leaning forward and watching the two Volvos, containing a total of eight firearms officers, in the wing mirror.

"What do you think we're going to find?"

Kostatis thought about this for a moment before replying.

"The best result would be for Dominic and Beth to turn out to be massive piss-takers, because if that's the case we don't have a container of illegally-trafficked Chinese midgets somewhere in the Surrey countryside. Of course if that is the case, the Chief Constable left me in no doubt that I could expect any further development in my career to be a long time coming."

"That's not what I asked though."

"No, it wasn't."

Grieg was right. The conversation Kostatis had had with his Chief Constable had gone better than it might, but that wasn't because the explanation and argument he put forward was so compelling as to leave the Chief entirely convinced. In actual fact the opposite had been true.

His Chief Constable had listened when Kostatis had told him about a group of aged criminals perpetrating their horrendous crimes. He had continued to listen as Kostatis explained the activities of Hank and Razor. He had even remained interested at the suspicious death of Wilbur and Mabel Forthright. Then had come the tricky question: what's this all about? The truth had not so much set him free as freefalling. The idea that septuagenarians were liquidising animals in order to add them to beer proved a tough sell. The necessity of bringing the Chief's attention to the possibility there was a container full of Chinese dwarves on its way to be turned into Hopmen Brewery's latest beer almost saw him thrown out on his ear. It was only the presence of the diary and the corroborative evidence associated with the Forthrights' deaths and the pictures of

Beth's flatmate that ensured the Chief at least heard Kostatis' request for firearms support. The reason he was finally given two armed response cars was more to do with the force's recent string of bad publicity as a result of officers not taking reports from the public seriously enough, with murders, rapes, abductions and fraud being committed after the police had claimed there was no threat.

The Chief had let him know in no uncertain terms that he believed Kostatis to be the victim of an elaborate hoax, and that when that proved to be the case he could be certain of an embarrassing, long and painful accountability and rehabilitation process, which would probably involve a transfer to a different police service.

"In answer to your question, I think we're going to find a container full of Chinese midgets and a group of seventy-odd-year-olds intent on adding them to a beer. If we're really lucky we might even have a couple of professional criminals in attendance, at least one of whom is extremely violent, and who our friends behind can hopefully keep under control without actually having to kill anybody."

They sat in silence as they made their way to the location in the diary. The hedgerows flashing passed hypnotising, allowing Kostatis' mind to momentarily go blank. He was drawn back to the present by his phone ringing.

He listened intently to what the person on the other end of the line said, interrupting only a couple of times to clarify timing and location. When he hung up he looked at Grieg.

"Beth's flatmate has been found wandering the streets in the East End of London. She's confirmed everything Beth and Dominic told us. There were two abductors. Both wore balaclavas, but one had small razor sharp teeth, one blue eye and one milky-white eye. Even with a balaclava on she had no difficulty in identifying the mugshot of one 'Mad Dog' Sean 'Razor' Cunningham. Bearing in mind our conversation around the Todd Masters car theft and assault and the possibility he might be working with Alex Pritchard, how are we looking on running him down?"

"Nothing so far. Uniform have been round to the flat a couple of times but no one was in. One of the neighbours gave a description which has narrowed the search to all white men of average height. I don't think we're going to stumble across Pritchard. I think Cunningham is the weak link, and we need to nail him."

Kostatis nodded and checked the map he had on his lap. "Agreed. Once we wrap this up, all effort on finding Cunningham and hopefully Pritchard. Pull off the road at the next left. We'll leave the cars and then it's about half a mile through the woods to the clearing where this is all supposed to go down."

Grieg indicated left and saw the cars following do the same. The Volvos pulled up next to him and the officers got out. They reviewed the plan they had hastily pulled together back at the nick, such as it was, each of them aware that they knew precisely sweet FA about the situation they were walking into. No on-site intelligence, combined with unknown numbers of people, some criminals, some civilians, and an unknown number of guns potentially being waved around meant a high likelihood of things going extremely pear-shaped. As they headed into the woods, Grieg was once again comforted by the fact his career had already stalled.

Chapter 49

So far so good, Hank Foey, known to his mother and British penal system as Alex Pritchard, thought as he drove the Transit van through the lanes heading for the delivery location. They had finally got rid of the liability that was their hostage, dumping her down a dodgy back alley in the heart of the East End. They had blindfolded and gagged her before securely tying her hands. Hank thought they had a maximum of fifteen minutes before someone discovered her, and maybe a further hour before the police arrived, had a chance to take her story and escalate up the chain. That was plenty of time for them to be far away. They had swapped the Rascal for the Transit they were in at the moment in a multi-storey car park with faulty CCTV. In time the police would be able to track their original vehicle from where the girl was found to the multi-storey, but from there the trail would go cold. Hank had set a small fire in the back of the Bedford. By the time the police arrived it would be nothing but a shell. He had insisted Razor drive the Rascal while he sat in the back with the girl, far away from the unblinking prying eyes of the London CCTV network.

Since his moment of clarity on the M4 earlier he had been thinking about what might happen once the delivery was complete. He had absolutely no doubt that the police would be there. Having told Jeff he had recovered the diary there was also no doubt the SSoH would be there as well. The thought of Jeff being nicked, while he enjoyed a cold beer overlooking the Helford River had been a happy one until he remembered that Jeff knew of his bolthole. Now he found himself voluntarily going to a place where a large number of heavily armed police would be waiting. But for one slip of the tongue he wouldn't be within two hundred and fifty miles of this bloody clearing. He had made a slip of the tongue though, and as a result he had to silence Jeff.

In the back of the Transit were a Ducati Monster 1200s and a Kawasaki off road bike. He really only needed the Ducati as only he would be making an escape from this evening's festivities, but appearances were important and Razor liked the bright green dirt bike. A couple of grand was a small price to pay to keep things under control and allay any suspicions Razor would have had if there was only one bike.

He shifted in the seat and felt the stiffness of his shoulder holster beneath his jacket. He didn't really like guns but he thought it only fair if the police were carrying then so should he. He also needed to get rid of Jeff, and although he had a plan as to how to bring that about he didn't want to get to the point where it had failed and he had nothing to fall back on. In no way did he want to add murderer to his dubious CV, but he wanted to go to prison even less, and if shooting Jeff was the only way to ensure that didn't happen then so be it. That was a last resort though. For Plan A he had Razor.

Razor hadn't so much as growled since they had dropped the girl off and Hank was almost envious of the single-mindedness of the psycho sat next to him. He was a simple creature motivated by violence. His thinking wasn't cluttered with the ramifications of his actions, or even in the premeditation of actions to come. Even now, Hank was certain Razor wasn't actually thinking what he would do to Jeff when he saw him. He merely had the concept of Jeff in his mind and Hank had helped him associate that concept with action, and for Razor, action was violence.

Of course Razor's simplicity was the reason Hank was able to manipulate him in the first place. All those years ago back in prison he had needed a protector and once he had got over his own terror of Razor he realised he could have his own personal bodyguard just by playing on Razor's natural tendencies. Once they were released and Hank found himself in need of a little muscle, Razor was the obvious choice. There would never be any betrayal, ego or arrogance from him, just pure unfettered violence, as predictable as daybreak and mouldable as clay. The level of violence shocked him sometimes and he knew it could just as easily be turned on him, but it was a risk worth taking until it stopped being worth it. The shitstorm they had been in the middle of over the last few days had highlighted that time had come and if Razor left the clearing in a body bag it was one less thing for Hank to worry about.

Timing was going to be crucial when they arrived at the clearing. Hank knew that once Razor saw Jeff, the concept of Jeff in his mind would transmute into the action of violence and nothing would stop that except a volley of bullets, and even that wasn't certain. Hank had to ensure that Razor had clear access to the old bastard. There was no use in Razor charging in only to find Jeff safely secured in his bomb proof Range Rover. No, he had to be exposed, most likely at the point of the handover.

Hank pulled off the road through a gate and into a field where he parked the van against the side of the hedge. Climbing into the back he pulled the tarpaulin off the two bikes and signalled for Razor to open the rear doors and pull out the ramp. The recent cold weather had frozen the ground hard so although it was bumpy it was at least firm enough to ride the Ducati across to make his escape. He looked briefly at the clouds gathering and offered a prayer to a god he didn't believe in. He didn't bother to try to conceal the bright red bike and merely left it on its stand against the hedge behind the van. Razor did the same with the Kawasaki and the two of them made their way into the wood that would take them to the clearing.

Chapter 50

The sprung seat of Bill Humble's rig bounced up and down as his lorry bumped from one pothole to the next. He winced as he heard the trees and brambles lining the sides of the road scrape against the sides of his custom painted cab. The scrapes offered accompaniment to the rock tones of David Coverdale and his band Whitesnake as he approached the end of his epic journey and the epic paycheck which went with it.

He silently congratulated himself on negotiating such a good price for the latest job, choosing to forget that his contact had told him how much he would be paid. He had been far too excited by the £15,000 fee to even consider for a moment what that meant with regard to the scale or associated danger of the job.

He sang along loudly and out of tune to '80s glam rockers until he was interrupted by his satnav telling him to turn right and that in eight hundred yards he would arrive at his destination.

As he pulled into the clearing he saw headlights flash him from the treeline opposite. Manoeuvring the articulated lorry around the clearing, he reversed the trailer so it was facing the direction of the lights giving him a clear exit once the deal had been concluded. He killed the engine and saw a couple of figures come out of the tree line in his wing mirror. He opened the door and heaved his bulk down to the ground and walked to meet his contacts, groaning slightly at the stiffness of his hips and back.

"Do you have my merchandise?"

Bill was a little annoyed at the blatant arrogance of the old man stood in front of him. He was also trying hard not to laugh at the man's eye patch, even as the rubies glinted in the headlights from the treeline.

"Let's keep it civil shall we?" he replied, speaking loud and slow so the decrepit in front of him could understand. "Now I'm going to tell you how this is going to go down. I'm going to disconnect my cab from the trailer rig. You are then going to pay me at which point I will leave you to your business and drive away. I don't want to know what's in the trailer, so you'll wait until I've left the clearing to open it. Understood?"

Bill stared at Jeff unconvinced that the old man had grasped all the details, basic as they were.

Jeff struggled to control himself wanting nothing more than to beat this repugnant man to the ground and kick him unconscious. After a brief internal battle he regained his focus.

"Understood."

Bill paused for a moment, disconcerted by the dull enmity pouring from the old man's one good eye. The sooner he got unhooked and paid the sooner he could get the hell out of there and be on his way. He nodded finally and turned back to the cab. It took him a few minutes to winch the legs down on the front of the trailer to take the weight, and then disconnect the air lines for the brakes. Climbing down from the Lorry's catwalk he walked back to Jeff.

"Payment," he demanded.

Jeff's top lip twitched as he handed over a black briefcase. "Now leave."

Quickly checking the briefcase to make sure it did contain notes not bricks, Bill turned to make his way back to the cab to finalise the decoupling of the trailer. Behind him Jeff made immediately for the unusual digital lock keeping the container doors closed. With an audible click the locks disengaged and one of the doors popped open slightly.

Bill turned to admonish the old man for breaking one of the rules just in time to see one of the doors swing back flush against the side of the trailer and a Chinese face peer out into the gloom of the clearing.

A second later all hell broke loose.

Chapter 51

"Go, go, go, go, go," shouted Gareth as Dominic revved the Fiat Uno and piled into the clearing, headlights on full. Gravy, The Fuzz and Weasel were screaming their battle cry from the back seats as Dominic slammed on the brakes, narrowly avoiding crashing head on into Martin Humble's cab. Behind him Beth pulled into the clearing with a little less fanfare, smell of burning clutch and loose stones, Otter sat next to her with Zoe and Gary in the back.

On the drive down the two cars had discussed the plan via speakerphone with Beth reluctantly agreeing that a plan would present itself once they arrived. Now they were sat in the clearing, their headlights picking out one very fat and startled lorry driver and a more sinister old man with an eye patch and his hand inside his jacket, she was less convinced. From the Fiat next to her she could hear The Premiums shouting something about the old man and needing to fuck him up before Gareth and Dominic had thrown their doors open and the five of them had piled out into the clearing and were running towards the two illuminated men.

Without a moment's hesitation, Otter flung his door open and was charging after his colleagues and friends. This was The Premiums doing what they did best, charging around with absolutely no idea what they were doing.

"Beth, we should focus on the trailer. Those poor people will be in a really bad way," Zoe said from the back, pushing her own door open.

As she climbed out of the car she was assaulted by the sheer volume of noise The Premiums were generating. Indistinct snippets of their shouts and screams bounced back off the treeline, mixing together making it impossible to assign them to an individual.

"Fuck up the old guy."

"Hit the fat bastard."

"Grab a midget."

"They're dwarves."

"Grab a dwarf."

She watched as Zoe and Gary ran towards the back of the trailer. Just as they reached it, a second set of headlights flashed on from the treeline. A mini-bus with three terrified looking old men in it ploughed into the clearing heading for the exit, which Beth's car had almost entirely blocked.

"More old people."

"Fuck them up as well."

The rear doors of the trailer were now open and she could see Zoe gesticulating to the people inside, just as Gravy got within punching distance of the old man with the eye patch.

Jeff hadn't expected the handover to go completely smoothly, but it was fair to say he hadn't expected two carloads of idiots, a giant, and a couple of dwarves to come piling in ruining his deal. He flicked his head to the right and saw Steve, Martin and Brian trying to make a run for it. Cowards and idiots, he thought, as he gauged the gap left by the girl's car as too small for the bus to pass through, just as it crashed hard into the rear quarter, throwing the three occupants forward into the windscreen. He looked back in time to see a young man wearing burgundy trousers bearing down on him, his right fist pulled back threateningly.

Jeff side stepped as the young man threw his ineffective punch and watched as the effort and trajectory of the blow unbalanced him and pulled him forward off his feet, ending up in a crumpled heap at Jeff's feet.

Pulling the tranquiliser gun from his coat Jeff aimed at the body on the ground and fired a dart into Gravy's arse.

"Oww, fuck!" Gravy shouted, reaching behind him and pulling something from his right arse cheek. He peered, uncomprehendingly, at the dart with the brightly coloured flight. "Fuuuuuck."

"ARMED POLICE. Drop your weapon and lie face down on the ground."

From around the clearing eight police officers in full riot gear, helmets, goggles, balaclavas, body armour, side arms and heavy duty semi-automatic assault rifles were slowly closing in on the melee.

Kostatis and Grieg watched from the treeline.

"What the hell is going on?" Grieg asked. "Is that Dominic and those idiots from Swift and Smooth? Shit, they're going to get themselves killed." He turned to Kostatis who was staring across the treeline. Without warning he was suddenly sprinting out from cover and making a beeline for something or someone on the other side.

"Fuck the police," shouted The Fuzz.

Hank and Razor had taken up their position in time to see Jeff dodge a punch and then shoot the young man at his feet. It was time to set Plan A in motion.

"Did you see that Razor?" he asked, feigning incredulity. "That old bastard was going to kill us."

Razor let out a scream and charged into the clearing focussed only on Jeff, ignoring the armed police as they entered the clearing, hell bent on exacting revenge on the one-eyed old man.

Frighteningly simple, thought Hank, although he would have to hold his ground to make sure Razor did actually finish Jeff off. Just as he did so a weight crashed into him, knocking him to the floor.

"You're nicked sunshine," Kostatis shouted between his gulping for air. Staring down at Alex Pritchard, aka Hank Foey, he sneered. "Thought you were too smart to get caught didn't you? Well you weren't too smart for me and I'm going to make sure you rot behind bars."

Delight evident on his face, Kostatis got to his feet and watched his prisoner as he rolled onto his back. The excitement elicited by his sprint across the clearing and apprehension of Pritchard evaporated as he saw his prisoner pull a pistol from his coat.

"Not today," Alex said, cautiously getting up into a crouch. A second unarmed man in a suit was running across the clearing in his direction, the first policeman's partner he thought. "Don't do anything foolish now, I'm not worth dying over."

Grieg arrived, just as Pritchard got to his feet and took cover from the clearing behind a thick tree. Kostatis held his arm out to stop Grieg getting any closer. Having the dangerous end of a gun pointed at you gives you pause for thought and Grieg felt absolutely no desire to be a hero.

"Lie down, face in the dirt," Pritchard said as the clouds which had been threatening for hours finally broke and the rain fell. As Grieg and Kostatis got first to their knees and then their stomachs Alex stole a glance across the clearing at Razor bearing down on Jeff, a knife raised above his head. He watched and heard as the armed police shouted another warning for Razor to drop the weapon and lay on the ground; watched as his psychotic partner ignored them getting ever closer to Jeff. Time seemed to slow as Razor got within striking distance. Four muzzle flashes burned themselves into his retinas as Razor's body jerked under the impact of the four rounds. He slowed but did not stop. Eight more flashes illuminated the scene and this time Alex watched as his partner fell and lay still.

Alex watched as the armed police advanced on the now still body. As Razor had gone down he had taken Jeff with him and from his vantage point he could see the old man beneath the undoubtedly dead Razor. What was the likelihood that at least one of the bullets had passed through Razor and hit Jeff, he thought?

"Over here."

Alex spun round to see Kostatis waving his hand in the air, trying to get the attention of his armed colleagues.

"Shit," Alex aimed the gun at Kostatis for a second before bringing the handle of the weapon down on his face, nearly knocking him out and opening a large gash down the side of his left eye socket. Kostatis crumpled to the floor and Alex ran for it.

Chapter 52

There were ambulances and several police cars in the clearing, a police bus had also been organised to transport everyone to a local police station. The sound of a helicopter could be heard overhead, its powerful nightsun spotlight sweeping the countryside in an attempt to locate their lost suspect.

Kostatis was sat in the back of one of the ambulances having his head wound tended to and snapping at the paramedic.

"I wouldn't take any notice of him," Grieg said, leaning against the rear door. "He's just pissed that Pritchard bastard got away."

"I had him, I fucking had him and I let him get the jump on me."

"He had a gun and good as you are, you aren't bulletproof. There'll be time enough for Alex Pritchard, don't worry about that."

They watched as fifteen illegally trafficked Chinese dwarves were directed onto a bus. It had taken a while to track down an interpreter and the one they had found seemed a bit out of their depth. Understandable, Kostatis thought, the working environment they had asked the young woman to come into had crashed cars, exhausted trafficked people, injured OAPs and a dead body, not to mention a team of removal men, a couple of cast members from Snow White and some very hard-looking bastards with guns. Not your typical day at work.

Once the Chinese people had been given water and a quick medical check, they were followed onto the bus by the rabble that were Dominic and his crew from Swift and Smooth, with a supporting cast of Beth and the aforementioned actors. As they queued to get on the bus Grieg broke the silence.

"You don't see that every day." Kostatis nodded silently. "In fact, if pushed I would probably have to say this is the weirdest fucking day I've ever had on the job."

"Only on the job?" Kostatis asked.

Grieg just smiled at his boss, "You've not met Mrs Grieg have you?"

"Right, that's you good to go." The paramedic handed Kostatis his coat and patted him on the shoulder.

Kostatis mumbled a thanks and he and Grieg made their way towards a second ambulance as Dominic and his friends climbed on board the bus. Kostatis noticed that Dominic was holding Beth's hand.

"What do you think they were thinking when they came flying into the clearing?" Grieg asked.

Kostatis chuckled. "I'm not sure I really want to know."

They looked in the back of the second ambulance to see Jeff being tended to by two paramedics. He had been caught as Razor had fallen, pinned under the dead man's weight. It was only after they pulled the body off him that they noticed the knife Razor had been wielding had found its way into Jeff's chest, puncturing a lung.

"Will he live?" Kostatis asked. He might have let Pritchard get away, but he was going to flay these old bastards if it was the last thing he did.

"He's critical. We need to get him out of here now," one of the paramedics replied.

"Well get a move on then. If he dies I'm holding you personally responsible. He's got a lot of questions to answer."

The ambulance followed the bus out of the clearing and Grieg and Kostatis headed back to where they'd parked up earlier. All he really wanted was to get a hot shower, a hot meal and go to bed. That would have to wait though until he'd interviewed a handful of OAP brewers, fifteen Chinese dwarves and Dominic and his half-witted mates. What a joyful prospect he thought as he climbed into the passenger seat and Grieg pointed the car towards their home nick.

Chapter 53

Dominic looked questioningly at Gareth as the big Cornishman placed a bottle of red wine on the table and then slid a glass of it across the table in the Green Dragon. Gareth shrugged.

"What can I say? Turns out I've lost my taste for beer, thanks to the old bastards."

"Hey, sometimes change is good." Dominic raised his glass. "Here's to one hell of a couple of weeks."

"I'll drink to that." Gareth drained his glass in one before pouring himself another.

"Are the others coming down?" Dominic asked, sipping his.

"Surprisingly, The Fuzz is visiting Gravy. He's been 'ome a few days now but he's still claiming to feel out of it on account of the high dosage of horse tranquiliser he received in 'is arse."

"I'm sure he'll be fine. He did go to private school so it probably isn't even the first time it's happened to him. What about Otter and Weasel?"

"They've decided to 'it the town with Zoe and 'er mates to let off a bit of steam. How was Kostatis with you?"

Dominic took another sip of his wine and smiled. "Do you know, it was like he didn't have the energy to give me a hard time. It probably helped that we hadn't actually broken the law and he struggled a bit with the fact that what he saw from us was actually all the plan we had. But ultimately I got a half-hearted 'you're a very lucky boy', 'I should arrest you but I won't' you know, that kind of stuff. I know Naomi's bruises are healing and she's in a bad way mentally, but other than that no-one really got that badly hurt."

"Don't forget O'Connell."

"Well, nobody that counts," Dominic corrected himself. "I can't believe he was using Hank and Razor to steal from his own customers. What a dick."

A week had gone by since their misguided attempt at being heroes and the story was everywhere: in the papers, on the news, across the internet, everywhere. They had become minor celebrities in their own right and been interviewed numerous times. The fact that the world's most famous brewer had been uncovered as using blended animals as a key ingredient in their beers had not gone down well. The Food Standards Agency had come under severe attack for not having identified the issue themselves and politicians and journalists were demanding tighter legislation on all foodstuffs.

The final member of SSoH had been found in a cellar at the group leader's house. He had been dehydrated and had suffered a severe beating but would survive to stand trial for the group's crimes alongside his colleagues.

O'Connell had confessed to his crimes under police interview and been immediately dismissed by Swift and Smooth, much to everyone's relief. Over the last week Dominic and Gareth had hardly had a moment to themselves, the hoopla had been so great.

Gareth took another large swig of his wine. "Listen mate," he was unable to meet Dominic's eyes, "I'm sorry 'bout the 'fuck-ups' thing, I di'n't mean it."

"Yes you did. And more importantly you were right. We'd all of us just been drifting. For me, ever since Dad died I just didn't bother doing anything, didn't try at anything. But as they say, when the going gets tough the tough get going."

"You really are shit at quotes, you know that?" Gareth said, pleased that his friend didn't hold a grudge. "So what practical differences can we expect to see from Dominic Morgan now yer a go-getter?" he asked smiling.

"You may laugh but there have already been changes. Once O'Connell's innate skeevyness came to light Swift and Smooth found themselves in need of an Operations Manager and I will give you one guess as to who they gave it to."

"Congratulations mate, you deserve it." Gareth raised his glass to his friend.

"Thanks. And for my first act as Ops Manager I am promoting you to Senior Supervisor with a suitably meagre pay rise and the ongoing responsibility for The Premiums." Gareth laughed as they clinked glasses again.

"And 'ow's Beth?" Gareth asked, the old wicked glint back in his eye.

"Considering everything she's doing alright. She's spending a lot of time with Naomi as you'd expect. But in general she's really good."

"I see you're studiously omitting 'ow she feels 'bout you and 'ow you feel about 'er."

"Ha," Dominic laughed. "You know what? In a weird way I might actually owe those crazy brewery bastards a debt of gratitude. I think we can say with complete confidence that what's happened over the last couple of weeks has definitely put into perspective the fact that I, and I cannot emphasise this enough, *accidentally* fondled her mum."

"And all it took was for 'er flatmate to get kidnapped, us all to be dragged into an insane few days endin' up in a clearin' with a load of dwarves, some old buggers, a couple of seriously dangerous criminals and a bunch of police wi' guns."

"I did caveat that it was *in a weird way.*"

"And what about Beth's mum? 'ow's she been with you?" Again that distinct gleam flashed in Gareth's eyes.

"Well, I haven't seen her since 'the misunderstanding'," Dominic flexed his fingers to emphasise the official terminology with air quotes. "But apparently she's insisting on calling me 'The Groper', which is fun, but Beth says she's just testing how fragile I am and ultimately whether I'm worthy of her daughter. So I guess I've just got to suck it up." They clinked glasses again.

"And you know what they say 'bout daughters growin' up to be like their mothers. You already know what tha's gonna be like so no surprises down the line." Gareth winked.

"Thanks mate, I knew I could count on your support." Dominic took a sip of his wine. "I'm never going to live this down am I?"

"No chance, mate. It's far too good for that. I mean, you did grope 'er mum."

"As I said, there was no groping, it was a 'misunderstanding'," Dominic said with the practiced indifference that only comes with great effort.

"I'm only jokin' mate, I'm pleased for you I really am."

"Well, it's early days but thanks. And given our starting point I'm pretty happy with how things are going." Dominic checked his watch. "And on that note, I'm going to go home and make myself look pretty for Beth. Will you be ok on your own?"

"I'll be fine mate, and anyway oo said anythin' 'bout bein' on me own?" He pointed over Dominic's shoulder. Coming through the door were Gary and Zoe followed by The Premiums.

A cheer went up from around the pub as the odd looking group walked in. Gary and Zoe beamed at the attention while Otter visibly shrank back from it, although given his giant stature it was all relative and he still stood out. Gravy, now fully recovered, took a deep bow while The Fuzz shook his head. Dominic raised his hand as Weasel scanned the pub and the new arrivals headed across to their table.

"'Ow's your arse, Gravy?" Gareth asked.

"Ha ha, arse gravy," laughed The Fuzz. "Formal motion proposed to update Gravy's nickname to Arse Gravy."

The Premiums automatically turned to Dominic, their faces eager except Gravy's. Public school was brutal for long standing and derogatory nicknames and the prospect of this one did not sit well with him.

"Sadly gentlemen it is no longer my place to preside over such critical decisions," Dominic said, turning to Gareth. "Over to you boss."

Gareth looked uncomfortable for a second as the realisation he was now the leader of The Premiums finally dawned. After a second or two though he nodded slightly, shouldered the responsibility and looked around the group.

"Motion proposed to change Gravy's nickname from Gravy to Arse Gravy." The Fuzz already had his hand up. "But before I ask for your votes I would remind you all that precedents are dangerous things to set." He stared pointedly at The Fuzz before looking each of The Premiums in the eye.

"What's happening?" Zoe whispered into Dominic's ear.

"Democracy of sorts," he whispered back.

"They seem to be taking it very seriously."

"Well democracy is a very serious business."

"Now, with that in mind, motion proposed, 'ow do you vote? All in favour?" There was silence around the table, every one of The Premiums making a point to keep their palms flat on the table. Gareth nodded. "All opposed?"

One by one they each raised a hand into the air, Gareth waiting until four arms were raised before raising his own. "Motion defeated by a unanimous vote. Gravy remains Gravy."

Dominic and The Premiums let out a cheer, huge smiles across their faces.

"But you lost your vote," Gary said to The Fuzz, bewildered at his apparent happiness at the vote going against him.

"It's never about whether your motion is passed or not," The Fuzz said, putting his arm around Gary's shoulders. "It's the fact we all get a voice and make a collective decision. Trust the process Gary and the outcome takes care of itself. Trust the process."

"I'd like to propose a motion," Weasel said. All eyes turned to him. "Given everything we've all been through over the last couple of weeks I would like to propose that Zoe and Gary be made Honorary Premiums."

The sudden intake of breath from everyone who worked for Swift & Smooth indicated how big a deal this was. Oddly, given Zoe and Gary hadn't even known the group two weeks before, they both suddenly really wanted this motion to be passed.

"Right." Gareth sounded sombre as he looked around the group before fixing Zoe and Gary with his stare. "Motion proposed to make Zoe and Gary Honorary Premiums." He paused, raising the tension a couple of notches. "All in favour?"

Without a moment's hesitation all six of The Premium's arms shot up.

"Motion carried by a unanimous vote!" Gareth, The Premiums and now the Honorary Premiums cheered and clapped.

"These are on the house." The landlord and one of the barstaff had arrived at their table with two trays of drinks. The Premiums, Originals and Honorary, cheered again.

"And these are guaranteed animal free," the landlord smirked, winking at Gareth, as he placed the bottle of wine and seven pints of cider on the table.

"Now that is most definitely my cue to exit," Dominic said, getting to his feet. There were grumbles of disappointment as he shrugged on his jacket. "Hey, as fun as an evening with you bellends would undoubtedly be, I have other plans so I wish you a good evening."

A chorus of 'cheers mate' and 'see you laters' followed him towards the door before, just as he headed out into the cold evening air he heard Gareth ask, "Who wants to play a drinking game?" Before the door slammed shut behind him.

"What a perfect end to a perfect meal," Beth said as Dominic split the last spoonful of ice cream in two and gently pushed her half closer to her.

He paused with his spoon halfway to his lips and looked around. He scanned the restaurant making a point of checking the faces of the other diners and the staff.

"Hmmmmm," he said, his brow furrowed.

"What are you doing?"

"Well, I've just had a massive dose of déjà vu so I was checking to see what's changed."

It was Beth's turn for her brow to furrow as she looked at him questioningly.

"In the Matrix déjà vu is a sign that the machines have changed something," he said, smiling. "The restaurant is the same, I'm dining with the same beautiful woman, even the dessert is the same. So I'm just wondering what they've changed."

A smile crept across Beth's face as she slowly leant forward inviting Dominic to do the same. His eyes moved from hers to her neck as he leant in. He felt a slight shiver as her lips brushed his ear before whispering,

"I'll tell you one thing that's changed, Mum's gone home and Naomi is staying with her parents so I have the flat to myself tonight." She kissed his ear and sat back in her seat, twirling the stem of her wine glass.

Dominic sat transfixed, looking at the beautiful confident woman in front of him.

"God bless the machines," he said before raising his hand. "Can I get the bill please?"

Beth laughed.

Note From The Author

Beer Mats & Budgie Smugglers has had a long and tortuous road in finding its way into your hands and I sincerely hope you have enjoyed what is really a very silly story.

Having started writing it back in 2012 when I was in my mid to late thirties it has taken 13 years to get to be the copy you hold in your hands. And the truth is if the version of me I have become today, at 50 years old, had sat down to write a story with the same title it would have been very different for the simple reason I am a very different person from the version of me I was nearly a quarter of my life ago.

As you will now know…

(This isn't meant to be a spoiler so if for some peculiar reason you've skipped ahead to this section before reading the book, STOP RIGHT NOW because for you what follows will be a spoiler. Seriously stop reading you weirdo, just read the book like everyone else and you'll get to this point as a natural consequence of the way reading works – right I think they've gone and we're good to continue)...

One of if not the key plot point/device revolves around the shock I hope to generate when we discover the next beer to be made is called *Mao's Marauding Midgets.*

My hope is that you as the reader have been able to discern from the dialogue that I as the writer am bestowing my characters with varying levels of awareness about the experiences of different people and the appropriateness of language use. The Premiums have good intent but no sophistication or certainty as to what is appropriate or not. Grieg and Kostatis are products of their environment, not inherently prejudiced but also not surrounded by the daily challenge necessary to change behaviour. Jeff is simply a psychopath, completely indifferent as to how his behaviour impacts others and just enjoys the alliteration.

For my own part I vacillated for the best part of a decade over whether I should publish a story that seemed to rest so heavily on such a hackneyed and cliched plot device as dwarves, regardless of how they are referred to. I tried for years to re-engineer the story so that it contained the shock I wanted but did so in what felt like a safer way for me as the author. The 13 years it's taken to publish should let you know I failed miserably to find something that I felt fit the rest of the story.

So for a time *Beer Mats* was consigned to the scrapheap. But… it kept re-surfacing, nagging at me, and I kept ignoring it, worried about how I would be perceived as a result of the plot device.

Now though I want to free up the space this book has occupied in my brain for more than a decade and move on to other projects that are reflective of who I am now. I've also published it because I really like The Premiums and felt terrible for keeping them trapped in my laptop!

So, I have published Beer Mats & Budgie Smugglers almost as a time capsule of who I was all those years ago. I thought about rewriting whole sections of it but I think that to do so would be to attempt to erase who I once was, and if I feel the need to erase who I once was, what does that say about my relationship with every version of me that has got me to where I am now? The truth is I am who I am today in part because of who I once was and the things that version of me, lacking awareness though he did, found funny.

If you have found this book in any way tasteless or offensive then just know that was never my intention. And always remember this is a work of absolute fiction, no people, animals or girlfriend's mothers were harmed in any way during the writing or reading of this very silly story.

See you next time.

Acknowledgements

Many, many years ago, while I was at University myself and a few of my closest friends got jobs working for a removal company. Essentially the company employed students and a few people who had recently graduated. I'm not saying we didn't care for the stuff we moved. What I am saying though is that I am very picky about who I use when a removal company is necessary! I would however like to thank everyone I worked with at that time, as well as the wide spectrum of clients for planting the seed for The Premiums. The world is full of the weird, the wonderful, the disgusting and the beautiful. May that always be the case.

As always, I want to thank my wife, Louisa. Not only for all the support she gives me, which is unwavering, but also for specific ideas and inputs she provides. She's not one for constant feedback, (which is just as well because my "style" is not exactly at the top of her list of favourites!) nor is she always right BUT, whatever her feedback is it goes into the melting pot to be swirled around, reflected and cogitated on. What comes out the other side might bear zero resemblance to her comment but they are inextricably linked. Thank you for having my back and everything else.

I would also like to thank one of my longest standing friends, Jason. He and I have shared many an indelicate, puerile and sometimes just downright nasty conversations over the 30 years of our friendship. And without one of those conversations this story might never have been conceived, so thanks mate, here's to more of the same over the next 30 years.

I would also like to thank my sister, Megan, who read an early first draft. Back when I wrote the first draft of this book I was keen for feedback but really I wanted someone to tell me I was doing a brilliant job and not to change a word. Megan did not give me that feedback. She did however offer encouragement regarding The Premiums, everyone else needed work! I don't know whether I've hit the mark but this is a significantly better story now than it was back when she first read it. So, thank you Megan, muchos gracias.

Thanks also to my editor, Jon, for once again giving me a lesson in English grammar. Any inconsistencies or errors fall squarely at my feet because sometimes I just don't care what is technically correct. Where that jars, interrupts the flow and your enjoyment is on me and for which I'm sorry. I also owe him an apology for sending him what I thought was a finished draft only to find numerous erroneous snippets from previous drafts lurking later in the story. Suddenly being met by two Mexican dwarves, characters I had written out completely, as well as the aftermath of specific interactions I had completely changed made the last quarter somewhat confusing for him. But he persevered with good grace. Thank you for your keen eye and all the alternatives you have proposed throughout. Thanks also for fixing the timeline!

And lastly, thank you to you dear reader. If you've enjoyed this tale told in blood and beer, why not buy a copy and send it to someone who could do with a laugh? I'm sure they'd appreciate it. I know I would!

Printed in Dunstable, United Kingdom

73484003R00188